POST

POST

ARLEY McNENEY

thistledown press

Library and Archives Canada Cataloguing in Publication

McNeney, Arley, 1982-
Post / Arley McNeney.

ISBN 978-1-897235-28-7

I. Title.

PS8625.N45P67 2007 C813'.6 C2007-901271-X

Cover photograph©Elisa Lazo de Valdez/Corbis
Cover and book design by Jackie Forrie
Typeset by Thistledown Press
Printed and bound in Canada by Marquis Book Printing Inc.

Thistledown Press Ltd.
633 Main Street
Saskatoon, Saskatchewan, S7H 0J8
www.thistledownpress.com

Thistledown Press gratefully acknowledges the financial assistance of the Canada Council for the Arts, the Saskatchewan Arts Board, and the Government of Canada through the Book Publishing Industry Development Program for its publishing program.

Canada Council for the Arts Conseil des Arts du Canada

Canadian Heritage Patrimoine canadien

Acknowledgements

This book exists because of Lorna Jackson. I cannot imagine how I would have started *Post*, let alone finished and published it, without her guidance. Her insight and support were invaluable from the first line to the final edit and saved me from thousands of hours of frustration.

I am also grateful to Seán Virgo, who offered feedback on an early version of the book and later honed it into a manageable shape as my editor. His patience, acuity and compassion made *Post* better than I thought it could be. Thank you also to everyone at Thistledown.

Many people from both the University of Victoria's creative-writing program and the Canadian national team read and commented on rough drafts. Thank you especially to Shira Golden, who was present from the beginning and provided both a sharp eye and a valuable link to the wheelchair-basketball community.

Though *Post* is a work of fiction and I've taken care to not base any characters on real people, I am also grateful to everyone who helped me through my early years playing wheelchair basketball and those who continue to push me to improve. My first year on the national team was especially ameliorated by players in Vancouver, as well as my club team in Victoria (the first team I was ever on and the place where I was introduced to Cage Match).

Finally, I am grateful for the support of my family (mom, dad, Viki and Denver) and friends. A special thanks to Stephanie Clark, whose sense of humour is present in this book.

1

TWENTY-SEVEN HOURS LEFT AND I ATTEMPT a salve of hot and cold. A gel icepack and a pillow insulated with flax and lavender: gifts, both of them. One or the other, always a different decision to be made. Heat for the clenched muscles? Ice for the bone's inflammation? Once, when nothing else would work, I submerged myself in an ice-water bath as if arthritis was the same as a fever, a passing fit of the bloodstream. There are some cultures who believe that there are no colours but hot and cold, no medicine but hot and cold, that the body is governed by this dichotomy. This seems right. All the other prescriptions have been taken off the shelf: Vioxx, Celebrex, Bextra. The choice was easy: a sore hip or a damaged heart? Only one of those can be replaced with medical-grade cobalt chrome.

Twenty-seven hours and I use the routine to bring me to room temperature in this house. Ice right on the epicentres — hip and back — alternated with heat for the muscles. Twenty minutes each. Light stretching. In just over a day, someone will saw through my femur, scorching the bone with friction, and replace it with air-chilled metal.

Twenty-seven hours until the surgery, one hour of hot and cold, and I'm ready for cleaning. The doctor has recommended that I walk through the house to tape down loose cords and reduce the clutter. Think of your rooms with a post-op body in mind, he said. Still, I go too far. My arms are eager for tasks, anticipating weeks, (months, maybe years,) of inactivity. My housework policy up to this point has been laissez-faire but now, I want our fixtures to be white as bones, as if they'd never been exposed to light or human touch. The thought is wrong, though, because I can't think of my bones as clean, so close to the gore and glands of the rest of my body.

It's easier to think 'body' and see the word 'bawdy.' The surgeon gave me a manual to my new hip, outlining recovery right down to acceptable post-surgical sex positions. I imagine myself winking at Quinn, running my hand suggestively along my cane, maybe along the walker I'll use for two weeks post-op. Stainless steel, sex appeal. Hey baby, come over here and let's test my range of motion.

"Finally," I told my doctor when he gave me the booklet, "an instruction manual to my body. Why didn't I get one of these thirty-two bloody years ago?"

The book has stern warnings not to engage in any high-risk tango or salsa dancing. Lawn bowling: yes. Intercourse that involves "unnecessary bending over:" no. ("What exactly constitutes 'unnecessary?'" Quinn asked.)

It was natural to see my hip as a bawdy house: skin like heavy curtains over the secret creaking of joints. My hip with its red-light-district throb of inflammation when I walk, heartbeat misplaced there. My heart not in the right place, too close to the groin.

The mess in this house is the only part that's distinctly ours. The decorating is mostly a product of our mothers: hand-me-downs from their renovation projects, birthday and Christmas presents. Since I don't work, (not that ball isn't — wasn't — work), there's no money for new furniture. Besides, we aren't an, "Oh look, honey! That sofa! How neo-classical!" kind of couple. We stay away from Ikea and don't mind our couches broken in by other bodies.

My mother, a disciple of those extreme-home-improvement shows, has set out to redirect the energy of our rooms. Since retiring from her position at BC Wheelchair Sports, she has excess time on her hands and plans to use it to bring our house to order. Under her command, our rooms will stand at attention and salute one particular interior-design movement: feng shui, minimalism, art deco. I don't regret the fact that she lives on Vancouver Island.

"Perhaps," she said on the phone last week, "you should start collecting something to tie the house together. Cows, maybe. I had a girlfriend who collected cows and she was so easy to buy for. Or frogs. You can get nearly anything with a frog on it, though I don't know how well dark greens would go with such small rooms."

Quinn's mother worries that any change in decorating might push aside the family heirlooms that she's passed down. Of special concern is the bedside table, which has three generations worth of nicks and chips. Negotiations take place through Quinn or me. Both of them call each other "that woman" as in, "I hope That Linda doesn't assume that she can just have her way with your house" or, "Can you believe That Shelia thinks you have to keep that table just because Old Great-Grandpa So-and-So carved it by hand? It was the turn of the century. How the hell else was he supposed to make it?"

In the bathroom, I scrub the tiles back to their former contrast of black and white, taking a toothbrush to the incisions of grout in between. It takes five minutes to settle my hip into right scrubbing position. I go down slow, as if adjusting to the shock of cold water. The cane, which I've been forced to use for the past year since becoming bone on bone, is impossible to keep both out of the way and close by. Twenty four hours. This time tomorrow.

I imagine the surgeon cutting along my scar and stretching the line that an old surgery drew. The skin there is so smooth, has a pearly sheen. It's maybe the best skin I have.

To replace the hip, they must cut off the leg at the femur and nail in a metal ball and socket. And then I'm "Nolan Taylor: Woman of Steel," but just a little bit. One part indestructible. Four-hour surgery and I'll wake up with the new metal already warmed by my blood, the body knitting it close to the bone.

So much of this cleaning involves motions I haven't had for years: that on-the-knees housework pose that my hip prevents. This surgery, alas, means the end of my ability to play the Cripple Card to get out of chores: "Wax the floor? Whoops, too bad, can't quite seem to bend that far. I guess you'll have to take over, honey."

I remove a little nest of hair from the drain of the bathtub: my blonde and Quinn's brown knitted into a dense clog. There's so much mildew to attack. Every surface has a residue that hides its true colour. Looking in the mirror, I wipe away the smudges over my reflection. A few weeks ago, Quinn wrote, "You look good nekkid" in the condensation on the glass and the invisible-ink traces of the message must be removed. The paper towel against the Windex makes a high squeak: not quite a whine, not quite a scream.

My doctor says that after tomorrow, I'll be almost as good as new, able to wear someone else's walk, someone else's bend. I'm not so sure. I suspect my gait is my body's accent, a lilt picked up from years in the foreign nation of this injury.

In the bedroom, I want categories: socks in this drawer, shirts in that one, all of them folded and tightly packed as if in a suitcase. Everything's in order, ready for me to moor myself to this place. I have compression socks, non-skid slippers, a hot water bottle, and a reach extender. On the bedside table, I stack books into a column of distractions. My aim is to be well-balanced: modern literature to confirm for me that relationships are generally weird and doomed, that love is fleeting, and *Cosmo* magazine for optimistic details and headlines promising simple tricks — sleights of hand — for the best orgasm, the best relationship, the best life ever.

Quinn can take care of the rest: glasses of water, pills, witty banter and constant references to being my naughty nurse; (he threatens to buy a nurse's outfit so that he can wear the cap and I can wear the little white dress after I'm better). I move the phone so that it'll be within my reach. In this bed, I'll heal from the surgery. A clean quilt is its own form of recovering. It's good to mend underneath a blanket with perfect seams of stitches.

Beneath the hung-up outfits in the closet are boxes of photos, medals, old jerseys. I don't have the medals displayed: not even the Paralympic and World Championship ones, not even my All-Star award from the last Paralympics. Once the goal is accomplished, there's no need to be reminded of it. There are many photos that need albums and I'm glad I don't have the time to look at them.

Quinn comes home from work to find me in the living room massaging oil into the rosewood coffee table overtop of decades of other women's polishes. The overload of cleaning products has blanched away the residue we've accumulated over the years, amplifying Quinn's cigarette smells. Usually, I don't notice much. When he hugs me, I usually only breathe in the not-quite-a-smell odour of his office: air pulled through machinery, printer ink left on his hands. Only his fingers keep the traces of cigarettes. The rest of the smoke is filtered and chlorophyll-scented from having to light up away from his building, down the street in a park. Quinn is smoker-skinny, which isn't the same as lean.

"What happened to all the stuff on the mantle?" he asks, meaning the Royal-Doulton figurines and china-faced baby dolls that his mother buys us for Christmas. They sit in a box on the hearth still dulled by a layer of dust that looks like ash, as if downwind from some far-off eruption. She started with young lovers posed as if ready to dance, their faces varnished into a healthy shine, but we've since graduated, (or devolved, however you want to look at it), to baby dolls. Sheila's not one for subtlety.

"I'm tidying up," I say. The living room looks bigger. The walls are white. Even these I've washed, tracing my fingers along wallpaper seams I didn't realize were there.

"I see that." He surveys the room and I stand to look with him: to see each scrubbed part as a whole. It requires effort to unlock all of my stuck bones. I take his arms and put them around my waist, wearing him like an old woman's shawl. Leaning against him, I transfer my weight through his body and don't need the cane. His left hand works its way into the waistband of my sweatpants, down over my hip to hold the inflammation there. Quinn claims to use the heat to gauge today's pain and my subsequent mood, but I don't know how accurate the thermometer of his fingertips can possibly be.

The house gleams with angles I didn't remember it had, the level of cleanliness looking borrowed, someone else's ideal.

"That's cute," he says against my neck. His hair brushes across the skin there, as if cleaning away the afternoon's sweat and churned-up dust. Quinn is shorter than me — five-foot-nine to my six-foot-two — and this is the hollow his face naturally fits into. He's proud of his hair, its ability to trace this warm curve: says it's too long to look like he paid good money for the cut yet too short to look as if it's a lifestyle choice. "You're nesting or something. Are you sure you're not pregnant?"

I promised Quinn that after the hip replacement, after one more Paralympic medal, (gold, thank you very much), we could work on starting a family. No, the word is wrong, more like finishing a family: the body-function baby smell and trail of toys uniting the house in a common motif. Finishing a career, too. Quinn claims that a body built for sports isn't healthy for a pregnancy: my blood too busy fuelling other needs, uterus too jolted by adrenaline, churned with the constant motion of exertion. I disagree, but I've been on the national team for thirteen years and would prefer to have a concrete reason to retire. A new phase, a new cycle.

Wheelchair basketball was its own calendar. Thirteen years on the national team, twelve years without Darren, six medals from major international competitions, nineteen MVP awards from various levels of play. Each year graphed in a measured up and down: macrocycle, microcycle, loading week, unloading week, periodization. My days not just numbered, but graphed. With all those cycles, you'd think the year would chart out curved as energy waves. But no, the graph of the annual plan each year was jagged, the peaks short-lived and sharp. Twenty hours a week for that many years. And this year probably the last. We'll see how this new hip and I take to each other.

"I'm positive," I assure him. "There's a lot to do before we tackle the whole pregnancy thing. Like you quitting smoking, for one. Me recovering from the replacement."

"And I guess I'll have to marry you or whatever," he says. "I mean, I guess I should. Would shut my mom up, anyhow."

Lately I've been stressing the word 'boy' more than the word 'friend' when I think of Quinn; a change in titles would probably be welcome. 'Partner' doesn't describe what we are; it sounds too corporate or reminds me of a training partner, of Darren.

"And we should probably both get checked out," he continues, rubbing the place where my pubic bone should be, waiting to see how long it'll take me to wince and move his hand somewhere more interesting. "We've been together for over a decade and I've never, you know. Gotten you — Hey, do you think I'm maybe impotent?"

"I'm on the Pill."

"But still. You'd think after a decade something would have happened."

"Quinn," I say. "Women on birth control don't get pregnant if they use it right. That's kind of the point."

"Not even if their partners have really top-notch sperm? You'd think with all those swimmers, at least one little champ would get through. Do you think it's the smoking that's doing it?"

"My reproductive system is not a Disney movie," I tell him, smiling a smile he can't see. "The brave little underdog can't win the big game if there's no egg for it to fertilize when it reaches the finish line . . . or however birth control works."

I fit my hand against his and move them both. I can feel the fact that he's smiling in the way his shoulders relax.

"So this doctor thing," I say, "Does this mean thermometers in unpleasant places and us having to time sex right down to the best minute for ovulation?"

I feel new tension in his arms at the word 'doctor': muscle memory activating before his mind. "Speaking of that — right, hmm — bad news. I'm such an asshole; you're going to hate me. I couldn't get the day off tomorrow." He drums his fingers along my hip bone. "Well, really . . . actually . . . my prick of a manager wouldn't give me the time. Said that if I want to be in the running to lead the intranet server project, I had to make a meeting that day."

I crane my neck to see him, but the view's too close and I look away.

"It's all day. You know the government. I can drop you off at the hospital and check you in, but then I have to run. Nole, I'm sorry. But I'll come right after work, probably get there right as you come out of it, and I'll phone the hospital every hour for updates — and by the time you come home I'll have my nurse's hat and I'll be ready to rock in full caregiver mode."

"This is a big deal. They're cutting my frickin' leg off."

"Only for a few minutes. They're putting it right back on again. Tell me again why you wouldn't let your mom come over to do all this."

I untangle myself from his arms and turn to face him. I'm not as mad as I'd like to be. Perhaps the fumes from the polish are somehow buzzing away my anger: cleaning the dark, brooding parts. "Why don't you go shower and I'll finish up and then you can take me out for Greek? I have to stop eating at midnight and you owe me some serious spanakopita, mister."

His arms loosen around me and I don't need the shift of his muscles to tell that he's relieved. "I'll sneak you chocolate once you're better. Really, Nolan, I wish I could be there. And I will, kind of, right? In spirit or whatever." He kisses my neck and rests his head against my shoulder. If he had the height advantage, I suspect he'd be one of those boyfriends who kiss their girlfriend on the top of the head. He leaves and soon I hear the shower upstairs, hissing like a fuse.

I gather up the mess of cleaning supplies — Windex, Javex, Tilex — so many 'ex's. I'm not sure what I was expecting to get out of this. Perhaps I had my own Disney visions of stumbling across old photos and spending the afternoon suspended in a flashback: (Darren, Paralympics, Darren, World Championships). Perhaps I only wanted to make this house finally shed the layer of our combined, discarded skin.

I need a hot shower, an outfit to show off my sport-slimmed body while it still exists, an evening out with unimportant chatter.

A yoga instructor told me once that memories are stored in the hip in the form of tension. She meant the muscles, but maybe the bone too. The hip socket is a good hollow to tuck away what the mind forces itself to sweep out: the ball and socket like a mortar and pestle, a place to crush old, dried hurts into medicine.

2

WHEN I WALKED IN TO PRACTICE pushing my chair in front of me, Darren was alone in the gym eating beef stew out of a can.

"Happy Thanksgiving," I said. "No turkey for you?"

He turned the can around so I could see it. "Eh, Mr. Big n' Beefy is a feast in itself."

"But you aren't going to your parents' house or anything?"

He made his mouth busy with stew. "Ah, that's good stuff," he said. "Mr. Big n' Beefy, chunky style. You are what you eat."

"Better eat a bit more."

"Says you, lightweight. You could do with a few slices of pumpkin pie."

I settled my hips against the snowboard bindings I used as a waist strap. "But I could do without the dinnertime conversation. Every year, my grandma and mom remind me that they were both married at my age. 'This turkey is lovely. Almost as lovely as my wedding dress. When I was married. At nineteen. How old are you now Nolan, dear?' 'Nole is such a lovely girl, why do you think she doesn't have a beau? Do you think it's the limp?' And I just sit there — oh, right. A man. I knew I'd forgotten something. Better buy one at Wal-mart the next time I'm there."

Darren sipped from his water bottle. "You could pick up a guy at Walmart. Those old men in the smocks who greet people."

"I don't know if a Walmart greeter could support the lavish lifestyle I've become accustomed to as a member of the Canadian national team. The free cars, the mansions, the roses and champagne bought by admirers."

He patted my knee. "Don't despair. Maybe you could hook up with one of the altar boys here tonight. Do they say the same thing about Catholic boys as they do about Catholic girls?"

The gym in Our Lady of Perpetual Salvation had been nicknamed Our Lady of Perpetual Smackdowns by Darren long before I got there. His nicknames always stuck in a way that made you forget that a proper name ever existed before. The women who ran the church talked to us in low, sticky voices — enunciating each word as if they'd just learned the language — and called us The Handicaps. We let them because they also charged us a third of the price out of charity.

The gym must have been built in the 1940s for the church's teenagers to play clean-cut games and purge their hormones with sweat and friendly competition. It was built like a war bunker: a place to either do battle or hide from one. The concrete walls were high and windowless and appeared even higher from the chair. Big, circular lights suspended by swinging chains shifted and creaked if there was any breeze, their glow roving like a spotlight.

Some of the bulbs were cracked and others were dotted with flies and they left stained-glass patterns on the floor: mottled textures of light and darkness. The wood was warped and so thickly varnished that the lines on the court appeared to be preserved in amber.

Across the walls, someone had painted murals of children playing sports: girls in skirts and pigtails, boys in trousers and dress shoes. Behind one of the baskets, a Jesus complete with crown of thorns stood with his arms around a crowd of children who all wore skates and carried raised hockey sticks as if to cheer, "Here's the windup. Here's the shot. Re — jec — ted! Jesus saves!"

To warm my muscles, I passed a basketball against a wall to myself. I aimed for the eye of a girl frozen in a frolicking pose, reaching for a butterfly a centimetre past her fingertips; (the church's definition of what constituted a sport was apparently a bit loose). The walls — damp from an unknown source of moisture — made the ball sticky and gave it a scummy odour.

"Ew, Jesus Christ," I said. "I mean, darn it. Look at this. You'd think they'd at least clean off the green stuff." We tried to control our swearing here, though neither of us had recently been in a church for a non-sport purpose.

"Just think of it as misplaced holy water," said Darren. "At least the walls don't cry blood like those statues."

"Just wait until after Cage Match. I'll show you walls crying blood."

"Oh, bring it on. Bring it right on, little girl."

"You bring it on, little man." Darren was a foot shorter than me, though clearly stronger. That night, he wore a sleeveless shirt and I could see the muscles in his arms. There was just enough softness over top that he didn't look vain or mean. I could tell his arms were built from natural repetition, the same way calluses form.

Though I'd started a weight-training program a year before, whatever strength I'd gained hadn't yet piled itself into a visible shape under my skin. I was a different anatomy lesson: could see my ribs, feel the little bone islands of my spine whenever I sat in the hard chairs at school. I was still waiting for muscles. It wasn't that I tried to be thin. I just didn't have much of an appetite.

When it was only the two of us, Darren and I played Cage Match. The ball was never out of bounds and there were no rules, no fouls. Darren created the game to prepare me for big hurts on the national team, but they never came. Neither of us realized that in the games that mattered, people fouled smaller and got away with it.

The brutality of Cage Match was an extension of the basketball we usually played. Our team — called The Handicaps by those on the team and The Holy Rollers whenever we had to put a name down on a roster — was recreational, which granted permission to take a liberal attitude towards fair play. Our Lady of Perpetual Smackdowns, with its dark corners perfect for getting away with an elbow to a soft spot, gave permission too.

Division Two meant that you could play for twenty years, never learn the rules and be proud of that. One guy, Vern, had been around for twenty-three seasons and still professed ignorance when called for a foul. Div Two ball was the whiskey-voiced, slutty older sister of the kind of basketball I would play in Brazil in a few days with the national team, a last vestige of the origins of the sport, when people played in jeans and hurled the ball at the hoop two-handed.

Darren and I were the only ones on The Handicaps who knew the rules. A second-stringer on the provincial team for years, he'd made the national team once a decade before, during a season when nothing much happened. Now, at thirty-two, he was our player-coach.

I was the only national-team athlete who didn't play in Div One. Nobody else slummed it like that. I was the youngest and no one missed my absence in a league full of other national-team hotshots. I didn't miss them either. In Victoria, recreational ball had been all there was. When I made the national team six months earlier, I moved from the Island to the Mainland to practice with the provincial team. I didn't know anyone outside of the gym. UBC, where I was majoring in either History or English depending on my mood at the time, was huge and bland. One more night of basketball was one less night sitting in my new apartment still musky with the smell of someone else's cooking, playing Ani Difranco songs on my guitar for the excuse to swear out loud.

"Good thing you came to us," said Darren when I told him this at the first practice. "Swearing at other people is way better than swearing at yourself."

We usually played Cage Match after everyone left, but that night we had two hours all to ourselves. The parishioners were having a Thanksgiving dinner after a sermon and the gym smelled of gravy and the talc-scented sweat of old women, plus the constant odour of varnish from all those court lines that needed to be preserved.

"If you win tonight, it's only because I didn't want to hurt you right before an international event," said Darren as he strapped in. "Your first big international event. Can you imagine what Tony would do to me if I put you on the DL before you even got on the court?" Foot strap, hip strap, pull the T-shirt out over the belt, adjust the feet, stretch the arms: a ritual in itself. He put a thin band of tape around the three fingers on his left hand. Darren was a walking quadriplegic — C6/7 incomplete — and those three fingers had to be bound to each other for strength.

"Excuses, excuses."

"But really. Let's not devolve as much as usual, okay?"

I watched Darren push laps around the court, the way his body slid in and out of the range of the bulbs, the metal on his chair baptized with illumination then dull again. His hair was dark, but the lights found new hues then lost them.

I watched him. Thought about Brazil. Felt the impending trip in my gut as if I was already on the flight, rising. Thought: ticket, check; uniform packed, check; passport, check; team-issue clothing packed, check; books for plane, check.

"You thinking again?" Darren asked. "I told you not to do that. Your ball."

Though Darren always said that being a cryptologist was boring — all algorithms and acronyms — his job made me nervous. I worried that he had access to the ciphers of my face.

Cage Match. This narrow gym with its high ceilings. The clash of contact. The race for a loose ball on a court where there's no territory we can't go. The jostling the best part, pushing harder because you're being chased, a nudge of elbow against elbow, bone against bone. The repetition of hand against push-rim, hand against push-rim was its own 'hail Mary,' over and over: our bodies asking forgiveness for the limitations of nerve endings and muscle fibres, for being too small or too big or too clumsy.

Darren and I pushed hard against each other, despite our intentions. My arms were still thinking about Brazil. I tried too hard to chart the arc of the ball in my mind, instead of relaxing and letting my body do its own calculations.

At the qualification tournament for the World Championships, I was going to play a kind of basketball where such body contact was illegal, where my flailing would have to be tamed into the fast patterns of picks and rolls, screens and stacks. I watched Darren's back as we chased after a loose ball, the dampness between his shoulder blades spreading in the shape of a chalice.

For long moments, no sound but our breathing and the ball against the floor. I wondered if it echoed into the church on the other side of the wall, a drumbeat backing up the organ, punctuation for the sermon. I imagined all of the candles flickering from the vibrations, the red velvet of the altar throbbing with our rhythm. That night, there was a sermon about gratitude that we could just hear.

"I'm grateful that I can still school you," said Darren when he sunk a shot. And I laughed. I wanted to laugh. I was thinking of Brazil, weeks with older women I didn't know.

Our chairs rotated around each other like gears. Our push-rims clashed: quick sulphur of metal on metal. We didn't apologize or take responsibility for the contact. There was no sorry in Cage Match. There was no sore, either: blood-flush a balm for muscles, nerves humming like struck metal.

"I'm thankful that I can shoot over you," I said and did and the score was tied. "And the Lord spake unto Nolan and said, 'Let there be ass kicking.' And there was. And it was good."

"Praise the Lord, Amen." he said. We hoped no one could hear us, our small sacrileges. Cage Match required different faith.

"Well, I'm thankful that I can still elbow you," he said and leaned in to find my stomach, warm and damp. On the other side of the wall, the choir sang "Amazing Grace" and I wanted it to be a forecast, a sign that my body could move like many voices harmonizing one melody.

When he grabbed my arm during a shot, I laughed big because the gym was huge and empty and I wanted to fill it with sound. He left an imprint. The blood beneath my skin traced out the shape of his fingers and kept them there.

"My autograph," he said.

"A memento to take to Brazil," I said through the cadence of breath.

"War wounds," he said. "So they'll know you're already tough."

Through the wall came a hymn with many octaves of 'Hallelujah' and I tried to time the ball through the net with the word, imagining the choir as our fans when we scored.

"See? Hallelujah. It really is a miracle when you make a shot," said Darren, who found an excuse to trash talk everywhere. Usually, we brought a CD player to practice. Usually, there was no sermon on the other side of the wall. Bob Marley was our favourite. Our theme song: "Get up, Stand Up."

Darren ran his good hand through his hair as he played until it was spiked with perspiration. During Cage Match, he was two inches taller. I imagined our combined sweat mixing with all the trapped liquid in this place, beading on the walls.

We didn't notice that the sermon was over and several parishioners were watching us from the doorway until I tipped Darren's chair forward as we jostled for position and he went down. I was learning how to make him fall without causing harm: contact from the front or sides, never the back. He fell so smooth that it looked like a more metallic version of a somersault: torso tucked in, head protected. Darren was good at falling. He was known throughout the sport for the intensity of his play and his habit of taking out the scorer's table at least once a season. Intensity was the polite term for it.

"Good one," I said. "8.5 for style, 7.0 for technical difficulty." I stopped with the ball in my lap to let him get up, though it wasn't a Cage Match rule. Darren never stopped whenever I fell.

"My goodness," said one woman, suddenly on our court, near the key, "Don't move. We'll help."

"That's okay," said Darren, his smile different from the one he wore in Cage Match, hair falling back against his forehead, "I actually do this a lot." He flipped himself over on to his front and pushed upwards from his hands, going up as easy as he went down. We both practiced this. Often, we timed each other.

One woman, who wore a floral-print dress with stockings so thick that her legs looked artificial, touched my wrist. The lacquered white tips of her nails were stark against my blood-heavy arms. "My dear, you should be more careful. You could have really hurt that boy."

"I know. I'm sorry. I wouldn't want him to, like, break his neck or something." Though Darren was a quad, his break was incomplete and he could walk using crutches and a brace on his right leg. The injury had taken strange, almost arbitrary muscle groups: the three fingers of his left hand, some of the extensors on his left forearm, seemingly random leg muscles — his right leg atrophied more than his left. He was fond of telling people that his break was the only area of his life where he was incomplete.

Darren turned his laugh into a cough inside his fist. The woman nodded. "Or worse. Don't you people have aides? This seems awfully dangerous to be doing unattended."

After the women finally left, Darren rubbed the new bruise on his elbow. He grinned. "Now I have a memento of you. We're even."

"Yeah, sorry about that. My God, those women blow my mind. It's the frickin' 21st century. 'Don't you people have aides?'"

"When she said that I was thinking, like, HIV AIDS and I was going to say, 'No, I think I'm safe now that I've cut down on the unprotected sex.' I guess divorces are good for that, eh?" He poked me in the shoulder. "You really should be more careful, Nole. You might hurt me, poor, defenceless boy that I am. I was worried she was going to pat my head or something. Or pinch my cheeks. I've had that happen."

The women returned later with their own balm for Darren's wounds: two slices of pumpkin pie in an aluminium-foil tin. The food lent the air its light spice and soon even the gym smelled like a new country.

I was already thinking in terms of travel, of foreign atmospheres.

Darren had been trying to teach me New Westminster piece by piece. He considered it his duty both as a third-generation resident of the city and as my player/coach/manager/source of pride and inspiration, (his words, not mine). Since I didn't have a car, he'd been giving me a ride to practice. The first week, he drove slowly so I could find some sort of compass-point in the buildings and streets. In the dark, the city looked generic: all 7-11s and two-story houses on streets either numbered or named after royalty. Only the hills were unique. One road was so steep that it seemed to disappear, as if broken away by some natural disaster.

The next week, he offered to give the grand tour on the way back. He'd lived in New West all his life. He called it The Hole and told jokes like "Why do birds fly upside down over New Westminster? Nothing worth shitting on." Living here for so long gave him permission to mock the place, he said. I hadn't yet earned the right.

The grand tour became several small tours. Every week after Cage Match, Darren took me to a new location and I overlooked the fact that it was too dark to really get a good sense of the place. I liked to drive with Darren. The world shrunk into the manageable size of his Toyota Corolla, just a stain of headlight glare reflecting off the dark shapes of trees and houses.

The night before Brazil, he said he had a special treat in honour of my first national-team competition. Something to remember him by. Previously, the closest we had gotten to the water was the Queen's Park Arenex and the smell of musty ice as we made snowballs from the zamboni's shavings behind the building. We'd seen the high school — two buildings forced together with an overpass — and the World's Biggest Tin Soldier, and the looping tangle of streets in the Massey Heights district, where he lived.

"I'm only going for two weeks," I said. "I don't think I'll forget you."

"Still. Another memento. How's that hand print doing? Think it'll bruise?"

His car had a tape player. He was the only person I knew who hadn't yet made the transition to CDs. That night was Muddy Waters.

"Which is fitting," said Darren, "since we're going to see the Fraser River. Well, kind of fitting. If you wanted to be precise, he'd have to be Polluted And Borderline Radioactive Waters."

I leaned back against the seat and felt the song's thrum in my spine.

"You ready?" he asked.

"For the Fraser River?"

"For Brazil."

I stretched my arms above my head, testing my muscles for stiffness."Oh, yeah, sure."

"I think you're lying, Little Big Girl."

"I think I'm lying too."

"You are ready, though. You're going to play great." He tapped the thumb of the hand that wasn't operating his hand controls, in tune to the music. "I don't even have to tell you that."

We drove over the Queensborough Bridge, over the Fraser River that separated New Westminster from Queensborough, which was also somehow part of New Westminster in a way I hadn't yet figured out. Being from the Island, bridges this size were still strange to me: their arcs a steep learning curve over the problem of fast and dangerous water. I was used to ferry boats with someone else in charge of navigation. Darren parked the car. It was dark and we had to pick our way along the narrow strip of gravel between a ditch and the road.

"There's a pedestrian lane on the bridge," he said. "I can show you everything from there."

I held the pie and we walked. The path was so narrow that we could only move single-file, as if alone, our words smudged by wind. The cadence of his crutches on the ground was reassuring, like the footsteps of an extra person.

On the bridge, only a thin, metal barrier kept us from the drop down to the water. So far down. Lights from barges gave brief flashes of water and logs, but it was too cloudy to see stars. Instead, the pattern of lights from both sides of the river was its own gaudy constellation. It was like being in an airplane, only free of seatbelts and recycled air. It was like hovering, airborne without the need to cross into unknown territory: flight without moving.

"So this, uh, this is everything. There's New West. There's Surrey over there. There's Queensborough." He had to speak loud over the traffic. The constant whirring of cars blurred into a hum of engine noise. He pointed, gesticulated, and I understood. We talked better with our hands.

Leaning against the railing, we ate the pie with our fingers. Darren showed me the hospital, the pulp and paper mill, the brewery. He pointed out the general area where he grew up and tried to locate every house he used to live in. He'd lived everywhere in the city, but never outside of New West.

Back at the car, Darren turned on the ignition so we could hear blues through the window. We lay on our backs on the hood and talked as the coded hoot of the tug boats added bass notes to the song. This new city with its industrial language. The nearby trees were too pruned to be mysterious; the only dangers they could hide were human. Against the innocuous October cold, the hood hummed with warmth.

"It's going to be so hot in Brazil," I said. "I hate the heat. I feel sick all the time in the heat."

"Oh whine, whine, whine," he said, but I could hear the smile in his voice. I turned to look at him, surprised at the proximity of his face, and didn't know if it was polite to look away. I watched him like a nicer version of a staring contest, then looked back to the sky, the lights from airplanes blinking hazy behind the clouds.

3

I READ IN THE NEWSPAPER ONCE about a woman who documented her hip replacement by hiring a photographer to take black-and-white pictures: her surgery classy without colour. There were before and after shots of her naked. A picture of the hip being removed: surgeons with their gloved hands spread over her. The blood looked like a shadow, as if some exorcism was taking place.

When I was younger, I used to hate having my picture taken fully clothed, let alone naked. I only undressed in rooms without mirrors. There were whole spans of time — the teen years before Darren, mostly — when I never once looked at myself naked. Just brief, unavoidable glimpses of skin: parts without a whole. The image of what my body looked like then is not contained in anyone's memory.

Eighteen hours to go, with the door closed in the bathroom and the new stink of bleach everywhere, I take stock of what I know. The trick is to establish a watermark so I'll be able to gauge the changes.

My scar: stretch mark from someone else's hands. It's not quite a line — like the path water finds down a smooth surface — the way it fattens in the middle and appears to silt the pale field of my thigh. I was eleven years old during that operation and still thought of time as chugging forward, no concept of cycles.

For my last surgery, the surgeon stitched my incision with wire to prevent infection. When it first healed, the metal left small dots at the edges of the ragged line, like the character for 'river' in some early language. The scar faded from red to pink to white and the dots disappeared: the horizons of the incision foggy. My doctor says that this bigger surgery will leave a smaller scar. Surgeons, he tells me, can make major changes inside the body without leaving much proof they were ever there.

Inside, from X-rays, I know there's my socket: little half-womb for my femoral head. Bone cornucopia. The formal name for the socket is the acetabulum, a word that holds the fizz of Antacid, the fever-balm of Aspirin. Though most of the damage is in the head, the socket will be replaced as well.

And my growth plate, the part that went wrong in the first place. It's where we grow from, the long bones reaching. Mine's now fused. I think of it as a wafer dissolving on a tongue, a photograph between the pages of a book handled into softness.

I imagine my femoral head as being the size of a fist, though I'm told it's much smaller. Maybe the size of a baby's fist, the pain like some growing thing fighting its way out. The head must be light and chambered as a hive, rough as coral: all these dead homes made by the living.

This is why I need photographs and X-rays. I can't allow myself to think of my body in these puffed-up terms. My hip is just so much bone that can be removed and replaced by a stronger substance. I need to be tethered to my flesh by science, fact, the logistics of the procedure. Healthy or diseased. Damaged or fixed. Metal or bone. This many millimetres of cartilage, that many centimetres of decay. If I don't, my mind will root itself in this rotting part of me and sniff around for sentimental connections.

~

At the last meeting with the surgeon, I asked if he could save the hip for me so that I could see it. He'd finished explaining the procedure by pointing with his pen at the X-ray. This aid was necessary because the language he used to translate my hip was multi-syllabic and derived mostly from dead languages. Dr. Felth isn't unkind, though the smile has been trained out of him. He's white-haired, but not quite elderly, with a British accent that falls short of genuine.

"Ms. Taylor," he said, using my name as a substitute for a sigh. "That's a very uncomfortable question." I was sitting in a paper gown, my legs dangling girlishly from the examining table. He switched off the X-ray viewer and the outline of my hips went dark again, the lesson over.

"Why's that? I'm curious as to what it looks like."

"It's a question of sanitation." He punctuated the sentence with an elaborate furrow of the eyebrows, hinting at the enormity of procedures and protocol, the size and complexity of which only he could fully comprehend. The weight of this knowledge, his eyebrows said, you cannot imagine. He coughed. "We like to dispose of the waste products from this procedure in as orderly a manner as possible." Removing the X-ray from the viewer, he slid it into the file.

"It's bone. It's not like I'm asking for a piece of my skin. Couldn't someone just rinse it off and show it to me? Would it rot? I mean, would it crumble or something? I have this image in my mind of old paper. The way it crumbles. Or Play-doh."

"And then there's the question of you leaving the hospital with it."

"You mean, stealing my own bones?"

He sighed. Again, the eyebrows. "Ms. Taylor, there is a certain smell that the removed bone emits — an effect of the saw. Have you ever smelled burning hair? Something like that. I cannot imagine that you would like it, especially so soon after the surgery."

"I think I could stomach it. When I had the pins removed, they let me keep those. They offered me those. Why can I have the metal and not the bone?"

"Ms. Taylor," he said.

"It was just curious," I said. "It was just an interest I had."

"That's so Margaret Atwood," said Quinn when I told him, referring to a short story she once wrote about a woman who saves her ovarian cyst and puts it on the mantle. Quinn is well-read and has a unique ability to use the names of authors as verbs or adjectives. When we visited the rural acreage of a feminist friend of mine, he named the property the Margaret At-Woods. He refers to a night of heavy drinking as "rocking it Hemingway style." This talent was actually one of the selling points when I first met him.

"You wouldn't be curious?" I asked. "You'd pass up a chance to hold a piece of your bone? It's not like I want to put it in a jar on top of the fireplace."

"Not really but, hey, there's an idea. Tell your mom you found a motif for the house, so she'll hold off on giving you cows or frogs for every major occasion."

~

Quinn drives me to the RCH at 5:30 AM. It's dark, but I know New Westminster well and can feel out its angles like a sleepwalker in her own bedroom. In the car, my stomach shifts each time he turns a corner: no breakfast and the false forest-scent of the air freshener. Driving with someone else at the wheel through this unawakened city makes me feel as if maybe I, too, am still asleep. To dream of being a passenger in a car is a bad omen, predicting passivity, a lack of control. I watch the map of rainwater on the window, all the branching options leading downwards.

Quinn chats bright and eager as if on a first date, his voice sharp with exclamation points: And the intranet server! And the cranky project manager! And the guy beside him at work who thinks Big Country Reeves was just as good as Shaq! Just as good as Shaq! He fiddles with the radio and probes for my opinion on the morning shock-jock commentary (Shaq. Biggest ass in the NBA. Relative merits of this for defensive purposes) — and reaches over at stop lights to touch my leg.

"Don't worry," I tell him the sixth time he places his hand on my knee, "It's still there. It's the hip you have to worry about."

The RCH is only a ten-minute drive from the house, but my whole body feels sensitive, as if someone has already stretched away my skin to get at the bone underneath. I should be looking forward to this.

In the Triage line, he touches my hip by the waistband of my jeans: some strange hollow his hands always find, but mine can never relocate. At night, his fingers often rest on this spot: the last warmth before I sleep. Today, though, his fingertips are cold from the steering wheel and take too long to accept my skin's heat.

"I'm so sorry about this Nole," he says. "I'll be back before you know it. The next time you see me, you'll be all better."

"I'll be puking from anaesthetic." I clench and unclench my fingers around the cane.

"Nole, you'll be fine."

The nurse — pastel smile and bunnies on her uniform — trades enthusiastic comments with Quinn. The weather! The state of our health care system! The price of coffee these days! She eventually asks for my Care Card and I fumble in my purse. It drops on the floor along with my credit cards and several unflattering pieces of photo identification.

"Shit," I say, "God damn it."

The nurse says something that's supposed to be soothing, calls me 'dear' and I think 'deer,' some creature able to use its smooth joints to flee quick-legged.

Quinn — Mr. Normal Hip Flexion, himself — bends to pick up the cards and fix my mess. In only a few weeks, I'll be able to do this for myself. I should be looking forward to this. After the check in — an ID bracelet on my wrist and instructions to report to some floor — Quinn has to leave.

"I'm sorry," he says. "I feel like such an asshole. Do I earn the Worst Partner of the Year Award?"

I link my arms around his waist. "Well, you were in the running, but that guy who chopped his wife up to bits and dumped her body in the woods ended up sweeping it. You missed a good awards ceremony, though. Bill Clinton was a presenter."

He toys with my ID bracelet, his fingers running back and forth against my name. "Did I win any consolation prize? Like a kick in the ass?"

"When the new hip is healed, a mighty kick in the ass can surely be arranged. Imagine the kind of torque I can get out of all that flexion."

He kisses me and I can taste strawberry jam and cigarettes, the combination not entirely unpleasant. "You know I'll bend over for you anytime," he says, "athough now, I have to run. But seriously, Nole, you're going to be fine and I'll see you when you wake up. I'll be all ready to be your caretaker." I imagine Quinn as some old janitor whistling as he turns a ring of keys around his fingers, cleaning my small, bloody incision with a mop and a bottle of bleach. Me: a static fixture that needs dusting.

"Caretaker's for museums and stuff, isn't it? You mean caregiver?"

"Right. Yeah. Sorry. Caregiver. You know how much sense I make without coffee. Either way, I'll wear the nurse's hat."

I smile despite my intentions. "Okay, okay. You get going. They're going to ticket the car."

"No one dares ticket Dr. Love. Hey, hey, that's an idea. Maybe instead of the nurse's hat, I'll get one of those stethoscopes. I'll be Dr. Love, the physician on a mission for the right position. I could have an afro and a big gold chain with one of those snake-on-a-sword things."

"Quinn," I say, trying to make my voice a complaint.

He leans forward and I feel his Barry White imitation against my neck. "Paging, Dr. Love."

My lips rest against his shower-damp hair. The scent is an antidote to my frustration. "Quinn."

"Okay, okay, you're right," he finally says, "Time's up. Now I really have to go. I'll see you in a few hours, Nolan. I love you, you're wonderful, patient and understanding and I'll be the first thing you see when you wake up." He hugs me and I feel, for probably the last time, the familiar jolt of pain when our hips touch.

"Yeah," I run my fingers along my cane: long and thin as a femur but made of steel. "Yeah, I'll see you soon."

"Nole," he says and I mistake the name for the word "go" and am unsure of which one of us he means.

Lying in bed A5 with all my information written in illegible graphs and numbers at my feet, I'm not entirely convinced that Quinn will be helpful after the surgery: the level of difficulty he has with childproof caps, his aversion to blood, the fact that he seems to be drawing most of his caregiver inspiration from porn movies. Does he have basic first aid knowledge? Can he perform mouth to mouth? Isn't this something I should have checked before I moved in with him? Shouldn't this be a prerequisite for adult commitment: the ability to work another person's lungs with your breath?

Once, during a division two tournament, an opponent ran over my hand when I fell out of my chair and the skin between my thumb and first finger swelled in a haematoma, thickened with the weight of blood under the skin. I watched the colour change — green and purples and blues — the injury a mood ring of blood gone astray from the veins. Nationals were a week away.

To cure it, Darren lent me his healing magnet. He placed the disc over the swelling and held it there with a tensor bandage: the magnet matching the lump's dimensions almost exactly. I was sceptical, but the fizz of electricity where the metal and my skin were bonded by sweat changed my mind. It helped, I healed enough to compete, and was impressed that Darren had a solution the exact size of the injury.

It's unfair, though, to make a comparison between the two men: the two ways of mending someone. During the time I knew him, Darren had a concussion, a sprained ankle, a broken nose and countless bruises, jammed fingers and scrapes. His knowledge of his body came from damaging it: testing the limits of his speed and strength and figuring out how to heal himself after he'd gone too far. Like how I know more about my hip than about the parts of me that don't hurt. Like how a scar forces your skin to remember a story.

4

THE TARMAC GLOWED WHITE. The disassembled parts of 200 chairs — Canadian, American, Mexican and Venezuelan teams, both men and women — were piled in a gleaming scrap heap. The tangle looked almost organic: the abandoned nest of some bird, a bramble without leaves or fruit. My chair was turquoise, easy to find since it wasn't the national colours of any country.

Teenage boys, their hair slicked back with Brylcream, smoked against the wall, pleats ironed and starched into the front of their khaki mechanics suits. They watched us and talked in Portuguese, the shape of their words as indistinct as the smoke from their cigarettes. Even though I could never press my tongue into some of the sounds they made, it was easy to tell they were amused by this confusion. To be helpful I paced the pile, looking for a familiar chair, but couldn't find anything.

The humidity made it impossible to forget I was in a different country. Everyone else loved it. The atmosphere made their skin shine, their hair curl. They wore the air like just another uniform, a jersey they'd earned. Tony, my coach, didn't wear a shirt for most of the trip, as if to give his voice the hard authority of the abs that showed through his low body-fat percentage. Except for a childhood trip to Disneyland, I hadn't been out of BC and my body was only comfortable on the West Coast. I felt big and slow. The heat was dense, piling on me like fat.

My roommate, Sue, had been on the team since I was two years old. She was pared down to the essentials. Her hair was almost shorn — a few centimetres of wiry aura — no time for dead ends or the complication of curl. Before I could plan which drawer to cram my clothing into, she'd already organized her entire suitcase into an easy-to-access system and was making tea from a small electric kettle she'd managed to transport unscathed for 11,000 kilometres.

"Are you really going to keep everything in the suitcase?" were her first words to me.

"Probably not," I said and took out T-shirts.

Sue transferred on to the bed, picked up her mug of tea and stirred it with a spoon, straight-backed. "Leave the hangers free so that hand washing — you brought soap, right? — can dry. Fold your clothes — no, Nolan, *fold*, they'll get wrinkled that way — and put them on the top shelf in piles. Then you can take the top garment off each pile without having to sort through. Laundry can go in the suitcase, which I assume you're not going to leave there."

Well, actually. "No. I was just going to put it in the closet."

"You don't want to do that. The wet clothes we'll hang in the closet will drip. I'd say put it on the side of your bed."

I did so and she smiled, sipping her tea. Her mug had a Canadian flag on it. The room smelled of ginger. "If you're nervous," she said, "you should try some of this before bed. It feels like someone's rubbing your belly. Or a shot of Guadalupan rum. Whichever."

When we went for dinner, she reminded me that I'd left my watch under the bed.

"Oh Nolan," she said as she handed it to me. In the days to come, other teammates would mimic her tone of voice, finding the phrase *'oh no!'* in my name.

Otherwise, I didn't have a nickname yet. Most people just called me 'Nole,' which didn't even identify my gender. When they used it on the court, it sounded like an insult, all the emphasis on 'no.'

In Div Two, most people called me either DD or D, both of which were short for Double Dare. The amount of time Darren and I spent together had warranted much notice and speculation by both The Handicaps and our opponents. We'd been weight-training together for three months and seeing each other regularly outside of a sport context since them. People blurred our names together into Dare'n'olan' and winked and stretched the word in their mouths: 'Dare *in* Nolan? Do you think they're — ? So soon after the — ?'

So he was Dare — perfect, considering the risks he took, his willingness to go into the wall for a loose ball — and I became Double Dare. I was never sure whether people were implying that I was twice as tall as him, that I was his twin/clone, or both, but I liked the name. D implied defence, being tough, never letting anyone get an easy shot on you. Vern liked to say that it could be a reference to my cup size. Then he'd look down at my chest, snort and say, "I guess not."

Other nicknames spun off it. Erica Lai became "Truth," and Rob, a twenty-year-old Bif Kid who greatly admired Darren and often stole his jokes became "Promise to Repeat." Though it was too long to use out loud, Rob loved the nickname so much that he made it his email address.

So we were Truth, Dare, Double Dare, Promise to Repeat: a childhood game, favourite of sleep-overs. We were named after a game played in whispers, the sharing of small secrets that seemed important at the time.

You have trained hard, I reminded myself that night as the clanking air conditioner kept me awake. You pushed the chair on training rollers until you nearly threw up. You shot for hours, lifted weights. You skipped parties, ignored homework, made your Victoria friends and Sophia suffer under hours of wheelchair basketball babble.

You are young. You are fit. You are prepared for anything, even well-muscled European women with facial hair. Bring it on. Bring it right on. Not in my house. Yeah, that's right.

But there were no European women — with or without a 5 o'clock shadow — at this tournament. Beyond that, after six hours in Brazil, the only things I knew about the country were Brazil nuts and Brazilian hot waxes. (I planned to try only the former).

I needed a triumphal Disney soundtrack for my motivational talk, unable to muster enough pert and pigtailed enthusiasm. Perhaps I needed cheerleaders: "How do you spell victory?" "N-O-L-A-N!" I needed someone to say 'Nole' with the same encouragement as the word 'Goal."

Before the first game against the US, we had a meeting in the dressing room. Tony gave us the game plan — shut the Big Girl down, prevent the picks, 1–2–2 zone trap falling into a box when we're backpicked, watch the smokin' meatloaf off the inbounds.

"What's a 'smokin' meatloaf?" I asked.

"When the inbounder comes baseline behind your back and gets the open lane because you've guarded the receiver up too high," said Tony. "Do you need me to draw it on the board?"

"Why's it called a 'smokin' meatloaf'?"

Everyone in the circle shrugged. The room was hot, the walls damp as Our Lady of Perpetual Smackdowns. Across the ceiling: a map of cracks. Tony told us to each say something positive about the team. I watched my teammates reinforcing their wrists with tape, pulling their straps tight, the ritual the same in Brazil as in BC .

The general consensus was that people were *so glad to be here* and *just know we're going to do well* and *are really excited for the chance to see everyone again* and *know that everyone's trained really hard and appreciate that just so much* and *think the advantage we have over the other team is that we're all such good friends.* They all *recognize that it's a big change and a challenge having a new person, but we're just so glad that Nolan's here and we know that, even though she has big shoes to fill, she's going to do so well.*

The big shoes I had to fill were Valerie's. The team hadn't had a tall player since she retired two years ago, making do with the quick grit and speed of shorter players to keep their international reputation intact. I knew she wasn't well-liked — most of her nicknames weren't said to her face and contained either the word 'Nazi' or 'ice' — but she was respected and needed.

"I hear you're spending time with Darren," said Sammy after the meeting, taming her dark hair into a thatch of cornbraids. We played together on the provincial team and she'd known Darren for at least a decade. She called him either Dare-Head or Valerie's Man-Bitch. "How interesting. Take her position on the team and her fella."

"She kind of left both before I got there. Or he left her. Or whatever. Actually, who left who? Do you know?"

Sammy shrugged. Her fingers braided without the help of her eyes. After she was done, she collected all the braids into a ponytail. When someone got too close — to steal the ball, to check her — she would shake her head from side to side. Her corn braids — all those strands linked together — had the power to leave welts that unbound hair couldn't. I was in a world where even a hairdo could be a pep-talk metaphor.

I'd always thought that a person only sweated from certain parts of the body: under the arms, along the back, between the breasts. I was used to sweat that left patterns: patterns that spread, though you could always tell where the wetness began and where it was going. The first game was different. My forearms, wrists, biceps were soaked through. Here is the ball, I thought during the first game, the leather sticky with humidity, and here are my fingers holding the ball and here are my hands, which are hinterlands, too far away from my core, numbed by exertion, some vital, encoded message not reaching them. Here are my arms without the topography of muscles, feeling like someone else's borrowed limbs in this gym, on this court, against these players. Here is the number eight on my jersey looking like a racetrack, the symbol for infinity, a closed system with no way out and here is my jersey, which is too new and too loose to look tattooed to my skin and here I am in my first game trying to play the 'post' position, trying to be solid like a stake driven deep into the ground, let them shake against the gate of my body, of my chair. I will be wooden, I tell myself, but instead it is only my fingertips that are wooden and I am only the post in the sense of the word 'after,' a few beats behind the play, my mind looping around and around into ruts, unable to translate itself to the court, unable to keep up.

The American post player, their Big Girl, wears a red, white and blue helmet because she has sustained concussions, her muscles too far ahead of her balance and her mind. And here is the ball, which is maybe damp from my sweat, which is maybe damp from someone else's sweat, which is maybe damp from all the bright oils on our fingertips. And here are the chipped lines of this court and here is my shot missing and here is movement without patterns and my brain is too much everywhere to see anything that could be diagrammed and here I am touching the seam of the ball as I shoot and miss again and look for a seam in the play to slide into and here is the Big Girl pushing past me as if I am a gate, as if I am a stake in the ground attached to oiled hinges and they move past me so greased and metallic as I push along with the Big Girl in this escalating arms race where I do not have the resources to keep up and everyone shouts Jesus Christ Nolan, God dammit, Nolan, but I am a starter so I must finish my shot and since there is no other height on the team Tony continues to play me despite my flailing, my failing and as I push across the court after the play my arms move in their ritual, my fingertips against the smooth push-rims, the movement just another link back through my body and around and around again and everyone is shouting at me different words until they form a scum, a churned foam of noise, dirty as the Fraser, and now the wind has shifted and here is the scent of sewage from the open door, and here is the froth of words building like rapids over me, my arms trying to arc like bridges, and here is another shot scored on me. I can feel the rise of panic through me as if my stomach is thin, strung nylon netting and then I score, but is only a brief reprieve from all I have done wrong and here is the score of the game not in our favour, the final buzzer, and we have lost and it is the first time that team Canada has lost in ten years.

"Well, Nolan," said Tony as I came off the court, and muttered something about teams winning games and teams losing games and no one person being entirely responsible.

After the game, I walked to the local swimming pool to shower. There were facilities at the gym, but this one was up a small set of stairs and I wanted to be alone. The stalls were open, made of cement. Anyone could walk in. I was used to closed stalls, at least a curtain. Outside, children spoke the international, squealing language of water fights. There was no closed door. Anyone could walk in.

The pool smelled like much of Brazil: a combination of coconut tan oil and sweat. My playing pants were stained with the white residue of salt. Inside the shower: cold water on flushed skin. The nozzle only reached my collarbone and I performed tall-girl gymnastics to get my head wet, bending, feeling my game-heated muscles stretch and begin to tighten.

The water was chilled and I wished I could swallow it: wished I could phone Darren and have him lecture me back on to my game. Through the open window, a band set up on the pool deck played a familiar melody in Portuguese. I lathered quickly, the breeze from the door and the window a reminder that they were open. The slight wind sloughed a bubble off my body. It floated, round and pearl-sheened, tinted grey by my sweat.

Halfway through the shower, I placed the melody the band was playing: "Achy, Breaky Heart." I thought of Billy Ray Cyrus with his boots and mullet, his song about a man being broken by a bad, bad woman into conspiring pieces.

I dressed in clean clothes and went for dinner, smiling at the mullet-coiffed band when I left. They'd played the song five times over since I got there. They smiled at me and started again.

On our day off between games, five of us decided to go to an outdoor market. The driver was nervous about the wheelchairs, fearing they would scratch the trunk of his car, which already had three different-coloured streaks of paint on it from other people's vehicles. Once convinced, however, he used the lines of the road more as helpful suggestions.

Sue gripped my arm as the driver swerved into oncoming traffic. Sammy and Wren chatted about bartering customs and handicrafts.

"For balance," Sue said. "Just for balance." Backlit by streetlights, her hair made her face look bigger, like a cat with its fur puffed up in self defence. "I swear, classifiers should accompany athletes in cars. That'll prove I'm a class 1."

The driver made a u-turn across three lanes of traffic and Sue dug her nails in. Her fingernails, though filed down for basketball, were painted with small Canadian flags. "Just for balance," she said. "I feel like I'm going to fall on my face."

When we stopped outside the marketplace, Sue released my arm, leaving a print that shone with my sweat, with her sweat, with the humidity damp as someone else's perspiration.

Sammy and Wren soon left to find whatever small craft made Brazil famous. I walked with Sue. The stalls were lit with many coloured bulbs and her shorn, blonde hair reflected a new spectrum with light each we passed. We didn't talk, walked slow between the stalls and brushed our fingertips against halter tops we'd never wear, pretending that with the right outfit we could speak the body language. Sue would look more natural in the bright clothing than me. She was originally from Texas and kept her love of colour after moving to Edmonton to be with her Canadian husband. That night: perfect posture and a sequined rose on her tank-top.

There was nothing flat about the women who walked past us, but spandex was still the fabric of choice. I suspected that Sue and I were thirty-five pounds shy of beautiful here.

The market smelled of sugar tanned caramel by heat and butter, the aroma a product of rows and rows of vendors selling cakes. They were iced with such intricacy that I expected each one to be lit with sparklers and eaten to mark a special occasion, but they were a regular treat. Young couples shared them, crushing candy roses between their teeth then licking the residue off the corners of each other's lips.

"You know," said Sue as we watched a woman icing a cake, "when I pass you the ball and you miss the shot, I look stupid."

"Oh. I don't mean — "

"You have to know what your range is. I haven't been playing with you long enough to know."

"Those shots were in my range. I was just nervous."

Sue leaned up to look over the stall's plexi-glass. It fogged with her breath. "You need me to get the ball and I need you to score for the team. If you're not going to fulfil your part of the bargain, I have to hold back on mine."

"It's not like I'm doing it on purpose. I'm not missing to make you look bad."

"Just so you know, I won't pass to you outside the key again until I know that you're ready. It's nothing personal or anything."

"I'm ready. I mean, I can make those shots."

Her lips made an expression that was not quite a smile. "You have to prove it with your game, hon," she said, her voice lilting momentarily towards Texas.

In the market, we found three separate kiosks devoted to soccer-themed underwear. We found holy water sold in aerosol cans, which I bought for the Handicaps.

"Your club team is religious?" asked Sue.

"Nah. But we practice in a church. And we're called the Holy Rollers, so. I don't know. They'll get a kick out of it. Plus, one guy's a bit of a Bif Kid, so it might be useful to have some water with miraculous powers for van rides after games."

Sue watched me, then shook her head. "I'm surprised your PSO lets national-team athletes play Div Two. You shouldn't be playing with Bif Kids and two-handed shooters. Isn't it embarrassing?"

The can of holy water hung in a plastic bag on my wrist, the metal canister cool against my thigh. "It's good for me," I said. "I mean, to have someone like Darren around. It's good to have a place where I can kind of just have fun and play."

"Ah. Yes. Darren. How is young Darren Steward? When I first came to Canada, he was just a skinny little twenty-year-old. I used to call him Dare-Bear, which he hated."

"He's doing okay, I guess, all things considered. I dunno how he'll be doing once I start calling him Dare-Bear."

Sue laughed. "Oh, do. Tell him I told you to. Darren's a good man. Valerie was . . . well, Valerie had quite the personality. But Darren was always a good guy. If he didn't have that gimpy hand, he could have had a long national-team career. Smart man."

The others were late, so Sue and I waited near the beach at the edge of the market. Nearby, a man sold ice cream out of the back of a pick-up truck.

"Oh, look," said Sue. "I can't live without mint chocolate chip. My husband always says it's a good thing I have a quick metabolism. What kind do you want? You can't eat ice cream alone."

I ordered vanilla. The vendor shrugged. His hands were scarred and dark as he held the white buckets up to us.

"Vanilla . . .," I said. "You know . . . White? . . . Blanco? . . . The opposite of chocolate? . . . Not cocoa? . . . Un-cocoa? . . . Vanilla?"

"I should learn how to order ice cream in every language," said Sue. "Every place we go, all I learn is 'hello,' 'thank you,' 'where's the bathroom' and 'I'm sorry, I don't speak your language.' You'd think after seventeen years on this damn team, I'd have learned another language."

Eventually, the vendor allowed us to point to what appeared to be chocolate and vanilla. He slid the scoop through the ice cream as if it were a scythe, forearms tight with muscle memory from some other occupation.

I ended up with coconut and grape. Sue got lemon-lime and something that tasted like rum. The only Portuguese word we knew was *'obrigata'* — thank you — so we said it to the man and ate our ice cream.

"Good thing we sampled that holy water," I said. "We won't get food poisoning."

On the beach, girls played volleyball. They jumped so high. I couldn't believe they could jump that high. It was like another form of transportation, that leaping, how their legs brought their arms to the ball in a way that only the very back of their brain could calculate. I licked my cone, my legs heavy and stiff in the sand, and imagined their hose-spray ponytails dousing the heat.

During practice, a hoop fell forward and the backboard shattered into a blue-green wave of glass. It was lovely: the light from the dusty windows and the spray of shards rising. Before games, I would imagine that I had this power: to turn glass into something like water. It was the beginning of mental training, but I didn't know that yet.

There were four more games and I improved through each. My offence, mostly. Defence was harder; those systems needed game experience. I hit eight points, then twelve points, then twenty. It was like years had passed. I emailed Darren at home, finally having something to brag about.

Light from the open door burnished our skin like trophies. I thought it would be easy. How could it not be easy? We'd changed, grown, melded even. Melded in some sci-fi way. The word 'team' could now be used. How could it not be easy? We were a different team playing a different game. Almost like we were living a different life.

I watched my teammates (team mates!) tape up. Beyond them, families were living in cardboard shanties by the pond, but I couldn't see them from where I stood, just my teammates strapping in and taping up in front of the open door, their skin shining. Team Canada may have lost a game, but they hadn't lost a tournament.

It wasn't easy. The Americans were keen as Dobermans and our team was so much older. We lost calmly. They were too experienced to be frantic. It reassured me, but I didn't want to be calm.

We lost and a girl from the American team sang "The Star-Spangled Banner" in a nasal, churchy tone.

"Well, shit," I said. "If I'd known she was going to do that, I would have tried harder." We were all standing in a line, supposed to be at patriotic attention, but everyone turned to look at me. "Kidding," I said. "Only joking."

No one spoke on the bus ride home, except for an Argentinian who sang "Ole, Ole" over and over again, banging his water bottle against the seat. No one could figure out what he was celebrating. We slouched against the seats, the same posture, all of us rookies when it came to losing.

5

AT 10 AM, A FEW HOURS AFTER I GET SETTLED IN, Tony comes by to visit. I've seen him many times in pubs, on airplanes, in foreign countries, but today he looks uncomfortable without a sideline to blow a whistle and yell instructions from. He holds his 'get well soon' card like a clipboard and keeps looking down at it, as if consulting it for stats. I'm glad he came, though, even if his Hawaiian shirt is a bad and searing contrast after hours of beige and mint green.

"Yeah," he says. "Yeah, so. You'll get better soon. The surgery, it'll be a piece of cake. You're fit enough. Did you see the card I got you? See, it says 'get well soon' and there's a picture of a guy buying a well. Kind of funny, eh? Yeah. Heh. I got a chuckle out of that one too."

"Yeah," I say. "That's funny. Thanks. I really appreciate you coming."

"Well. Anyhow." He grips the steel bar of the bed as if it were a cane. "How many hours to the surgery now? Am I your first visitor? I thought you had the replacement yesterday, actually. Guess you don't get many visitors before you even go under, huh?"

"Two or three hours. They'll wheel me down soon to some waiting room place, I guess." I should be looking forward to this.

"Where's the boyfriend?" Tony has never bothered to learn Quinn's name and I've never bothered to remind him.

"At work. He got called in on an emergency."

"Ah." He looks down at the card. Up at me. Down at the card. "Things must be pretty hoppin' in — where does he work? The civil service?"

"Ministry of Arts, Culture, Women and the Environment."

"And your ma isn't coming? I figured she'd be over here in a snap."

"No, no. That isn't necessary."

He drums his fingers along his little belly as if keeping beat to the heart monitor of the patient next to me, as if his skin is stretched taut enough for percussion.

"So, two or three hours, eh? That's not far off. I should let you get some rest." Tony looks kinder now that he has softened.

"Well, if you'd like," I say.

"You get well soon." He pats the metal post of the bed as if it were my knee and I'm glad I'm not the only one who blurs the distinction between skin and steel. "Some of the gals will come by after the surgery in a few days. They send their love but, you know, work and all. Practice tonight. No one could make it."

I watch his hand's attempt to chart smooth passage through his tangle of grey hair. "Will do, Chief," I say.

At 1 PM, half-way through a *Cosmo* article on simple tricks to make true love and happiness last forever, mom calls. I'm not expecting the bedside phone to be hooked up, not expecting the proximity of her long-distance voice.

"I've been trying to get through to you for forever," she says. "All these security protocols. You'd think your room number was a federal secret. 'I'm her mother,' I told them. 'I'm her mother. What do you think I'm going to do?'" I imagine her pacing in our kitchen, tapping out the drum solo in "A Love Supreme" on some nearby surface, which she always does when she's nervous. Her house — the house I grew up in — has small, dense-walled rooms that hold sounds and their echoes well.

"I'm sorry. I didn't know when they'd take me in. Quinn said he'd call during the surgery to update you."

"Put him on the phone. Let me talk to him. I want to make sure." I can hear her fingers, the way they translate the melody of her body on to wood. Likely, she is sitting at the table, looking out at the ocean, at all the distance between us.

"He's out on a smoke break. Should be back soon."

"You're minutes away from surgery and he's puffing on a cancer stick? Get him to call me. I want to make sure he has my cell number."

"Well, actually. There was this thing with work. This meeting. But I know he's got your cell."

"What? You said he'd be with you. 'He'll be by my side,' those were your words. Those were your words exactly."

Mylar balloons are tied to the bed of the patient across from me. I watch them rotate, their half-deflated sheen, the cheery bossiness of the words "Get Well Soon."

"That was the plan," I say. "He got called in. Some big emergency with a crashed server. He had the time all scheduled off and then they called late last night — "

"Couldn't he decline? Isn't that what unions are for? It's ridiculous that in this day and age — What happens when you have a baby? I'm not sure how he'll be able to manage the whole 'till death do us part' bit if he hasn't even covered 'in sickness and in health.' I think it's clear he's failed 'in sickness and in health.'"

"Mom."

"Nolan, this is a big surgery. They're cutting your leg off."

"They're putting it right back on again."

"I think I should come over. That's it: I'm coming over. Your father can drive me to the ferry. It's 12:30 now. I can catch the one o'clock, be there by three, take a cab and be at the hospital by four."

"Oh Jesus Christ. I'll already be under the knife by then and Quinn'll be here. It's really not necessary. I'm perfectly capable — "

I listen to her tapping. Through her fingers hear a saxophone that isn't there, the rising of that sound. "I can't believe Quinn. Can't believe him. I should never have let you convince me not to come over. To go through this all by yourself. You can't be all by yourself."

And then there are two nurses at the door, their expressions hidden by green masks, bodies shapeless under scrubs.

"Okay, Ms. Taylor, it's go time," says one.

"I have to go, Mom," I say. "They're taking me down now. Quinn will call you as soon as he knows anything. Just think — four hours." I recite the itinerary to her — go under at two, if all goes well be awake by six, using a walker the next day and home in another five — and try to keep my voice bright as a travel agent's, though I can feel my words lift as if preparing for takeoff.

"You're nervous," she says. "I can hear it. I should be there. I've been with you for all your other surgeries. Listen, darling, I love you. You're going to do fine."

"It's not like I really have to do much of anything. It's the doctors who have to do fine."

"I'll talk to you soon," she says. "I love you."

"Love you too," I say and in the last moments before I say goodbye I hear her fingers. Through them, I hear my childhood home, the way those small rooms amplify her nails into instruments of percussion. I hear the countertops and the yellowing lace curtains and the condensation on the window and Darwin the black lab and the scent of underbrush and salal in her fur. I hear my mother translated: the Morse code of music.

~

Dr. Taylor:

Of course Linda went. Of course Nolan will be angry. Now there's nothing to do but the breakfast dishes. I want to scrub up like a surgeon before I tackle any task, remove the day's early traces from my hands. The fact of the matter is a guy needs precision right now: to cut along a perfect line, separate something into husk and membrane, pass thread through the eye of a needle.

Nolan's going under and if I believed in magic, I would perform the surgery on a chicken bone in the name of voodoo. Or whatever the word is for positive voodoo. Some kind of spell.

Instead: blues. Baby, *croons the woman singer on the radio,* oh baby. *I spent the first thirty years of my life with that definition of baby: something to whisper into a woman's ear. Though I saw lots of babies in my practice, if you said the word I would translate it into a song.* Baby, please don't go. Take good care of my baby. *All those hits.*

Then Nolan was born with her tiny fingernails and hair so fine I wondered how it stayed on her head. An air baby, picky eater, so pale that you could use her to teach med students each vein on the human body. Surprised you couldn't see right through her skin to her heart, her lungs. She would sleep on my chest and I'd point them out to Linda: antebrachial median, median cubital, dorsal venous arch. Not that Linda was impressed; "What's the fancy Latin word for 'learn how to change a diaper?'"

That fiberglass cast they made of her acetabulum and femoral head I keep on my desk. Turns out she wasn't a good candidate for the surgery — the ortho guy could see that right away — 2:14. Nolan's probably going under right now. As she should be. She's been arthritic for long enough. Bone on bone. And, hell, it's a simple procedure. How hard can it be when you're using a saw? Not like it's one of those surgeries where if you're a fraction of a millimeter off, the patient goes into cardiac arrest.

The fridge hums; the hot water heater clunks into action. Everything on task. The stereo is saying baby, oh baby. And something about love.

There's no reason to be there, anyhow. It's a routine procedure even for seventy-year-old ladies. The fact of the matter is, what good is it to be a doctor if you're not the one making the incision? Decades of schooling and you're still stuck in the waiting room reading about the latest celebrity divorce. Who cares if you know that twenty minutes in they saw the femoral head off? Which is simple too, no harder than sawing a two by four.

I thought groin pull like all the rest of the doctors. Kids get upset at the littlest things. Didn't even want Linda to take her to the doctor. When they brought out the X-rays, I peered over the shoulders of the interns. Something was off — you could tell that right away — but capital femoral epiphisis didn't occur to me. To be fair, it didn't occur to anyone, really. Capital femoral epiphisis. Shit.

She will, of course, be fine. Dr. Felth is an asshole bone mechanic, but skilled at what he does. Linda will phone me the minute she gets out of surgery, though that won't be for another three or four hours yet. Nolan's young and fit — Quinn was right to go to work. He should. In a few years, I bet they won't even keep people overnight. God knows they already send them home with a kit to inject themselves with bloodthinners and a staple remover for when the incision's healed.

"But it's your daughter," said Linda as we pulled up to the terminal. "And you were such a help last time." But what good is it to look at your daughter as they're wheeling her down to someone else's O.R., so pale with hurt you can see every vein on her arm, and know antebrachial median, median cubital, dorsal venous arch?

~

I want to walk down to the O.R., but the nurses insist on wheeling me out on the gurney.

"My hip's not that bad," I say. "I can manage a few floors if we go slow. Even death row prisoners get to shuffle on their own."

"Ms. Taylor," one says. Her latex gloves dull her red nail polish into a pinkish shade. I can only see her eyes: their mascara and liner making them appear smaller. "It's procedure."

I should be allowed to feel bone against bone, nerve ending on nerve ending, the last of my hip's organic sensations. The next time I walk, the hurt will take a different shape and then go.

To be wheeled like this feels like hovering. I look down through the bars at the green-and-brown linoleum rolling by like a field viewed from up high.

The nurses ask distractions: "How long have you been waiting for surgery?" "Are you married?" "Do you have any children?" "What do you do for a living?" "Will your significant other be wanting updates during the procedure?" The word 'procedure' is supposed to be comforting: a quiz instead of a test, corporate restructuring instead of layoffs, 'significant other' instead of 'irresponsible boyfriend who wouldn't take the time off work to hold my damn hand.'

As we wait for the elevator, I spend little time fantasizing about Quinn leaving work unannounced and rushing to meet me just as I enter the O.R. Nor do I think too long about the jolt when he calls my name from down the hall, his dark-suited shape destroying all this pale as he runs towards me. Good thing I caught you in time, he'd say. I could never imagine letting you do this without me.

My thoughts of Quinn are brief: a swoop of fantasy like a crow taking off. It fits, in a way — Quinn, a crow — the darkness of his hair, the way his face makes no effort to hide its sharp angles. Darren is — was — someone I could imagine walking me down these aisles to the O.R. Same dark hair but a redder undertone, rich with curls. Same height, but Darren's frame is softened by muscles. For many floors and hallways, my mind draws and redraws the situation. He would be a patient on a passing gurney and I'd recognize the familiar bones of his face through blood or sickness sweat. I imagine our hands through the bars, hard-earned calluses touching, his fingers rough as sturdy rope, lifeline pulling me to safety. Or maybe he'd read the good luck message posted on the CWBA website and come to find me. He'd reach me so silently now that he's in a chair full-time: his greased wheels without the warning of footsteps. I'd never even hear him coming.

It must be the pre-op sedatives that make me want the comfort of a man who wrapped my hand thirteen years ago with a tensor bandage and tucked some magnet underneath like an amulet. But still, I stay on the image, skimming across it in fits and starts. Fitting, too, since the whole time I was with Darren felt like that: going full-tilt at a low altitude. Fast and low, all the descent necessary in those ways to go fast.

6

DARREN PICKED ME UP FROM THE AIRPORT. I'd been travelling for twenty-four hours and smelled of recycled air, reheated meals served 30,000 feet up. My skin was tight against my bones and my pants were too baggy, making me feel as if I was walking against them.

As I disembarked, a flight attendant touched my arm. "Sorry, sir," she said. "I have to get by here."

It was the bulky team vest, my height. "That's Ma'am," I said. "I'm a chick."

"Oh," she said. "Oh, yes, of course you are. I'm so sorry." The belt of her uniform was cinched so tightly around her middle that she looked like the generic woman symbol on bathroom doors. I wasn't sure whether to be insulted or pleased that my shoulders and arms were finally bulking up.

As we cleared customs, I saw Darren standing in the waiting area amidst glass and steel and natural light, the metal on his crutches reflecting little scraps of brightness on to the far wall. He waved a *New Yorker* magazine in my direction.

"There you are," he said. "First time you've been on time for anything."

I smiled at the sight of him and felt my dehydrated cheeks tighten.

"Well, well," said Sammy. "It's Darren." Her baggage was on the cart I was pushing and I helped her unload it. "What're you doing here?"

Darren shifted the position of his crutches. "Picking up chicks. They're tired from flying, so their defences are down. You should try it."

"Right. That's classy. I already have a chick. How's Valerie?"

"You ready to go, Dare?" I asked.

He rubbed the back of his neck. "I'm kidding. I'm here to pick up Nolan. We're on the same club team and she needed a ride. She doesn't know anyone on the mainland, yet."

People wandered past us, dopey from standing in lines. Sammy nodded. "Nice of you to help our newest Big Girl." Emphasis on the word 'newest.'

"I'm a nice guy. She needed a ride. As far as Val goes, I wouldn't know. You could phone her. You know, like teammates do."

"How long's your parking pass good for?" I asked. "We should probably head out of here."

"Right," he said. "Yeah, we should get going. Nice talking to you, Samantha. Say hi to your lady love for me."

"Yeah, will do. See you later, Dare-head."

It was an unseasonably warm November day and the car smelled of the mud and grass tracked in by Darren's crutches. I rolled the window down to feel the chilled British Columbian sun. Breathed. Darren had the radio on to a CBC interview and, as we drove past cars and stores and cars and stores and cars, I fell asleep to the sound of a civilized argument.

When I awoke, we were in front of my apartment. Darren was reading his magazine, the radio still on.

"How long have we been here?" I asked, stretching out the kink in my neck.

He blinked. "Oh, hey. You were sleeping pretty hard, there. Not long. Twenty minutes, maybe."

"Geez. I'm sorry. Next time, just give me a smack to wake me up and kick me out."

"If you'd started drooling or snoring or something, I would have. I thought about carrying you upstairs to bed but, well, we'd have both ended up concussed."

"You're a good man, Darren Steward."

He folded up his magazine and tapped me on the leg with it. "Depends on who you talk to. Maybe I just like to watch tanned young women sleep."

"I am kind of tanned, aren't I?"

I placed my arm against his to show the difference. He touched the crook of my elbow.

"You get freckles when you tan," he said.

"Yeah," I said. "Brings out the darkness in me."

"The darkness looks good on you." He pulled the switch for the trunk. "You want to go sleep in your own bed now? I'll help you with your bags."

I leaned over the space between our seats and hugged him. "Thanks for the ride, Dare."

His fingers brushed against my shoulder blades. "No problem, kiddo."

"Hey, remind me for next practice. I got something for the team. Something that'll come in handy on long trips."

"Deodorant for Rob?"

"It's a surprise."

"Please God, let it be some kind of deodorant."

Though I'd been at UBC for two months, I still got lost almost every day on my way to class. My year at the University of Victoria had made me accustomed to grass, rabbits and a ring-shaped road that hemmed in the campus and kept frosh from straying too far in any direction.

I had no concept of compass points. At home, I could find anything if I knew where it was in relation to the water, my brain like a dowser's twig. UBC confused me: East Mall, West Mall, Chancellor's This, Queen's That, one-way street here, buses only there. Even in buildings, I got lost.

"Aren't you in my Canadian History class?" asked a dark-haired guy as I walked past him the Monday after I returned from Brazil.

He was lean and blue-eyed. I stopped. "I could very well be."

"Dr. Beauford, right? I'm in that class, but you might not have noticed me 'cause I'm pretty pale and the walls are, too." He flattened against the beige wall and spread his arms against it. "See? Invisible man."

I laughed. The concrete echoed the sound, amplifying it in a way I didn't intend. "Well, I'll notice you in the future. I'll look for a floating shirt and jeans with eyes."

"Good stuff. Anyhow, I wanted to tell you that if you're looking for class, you were about to walk right past."

I sighed. Looked at the door. Down at my schedule. Up at him. "You're right. Thanks. You'll have to excuse me, I'm from the Island and this building alone is about the size of the Greater Victoria area."

He grinned. "I never would have guessed. Where are the Birkenstocks and hemp necklace? You must be undercover. I'm Quinn, by the way."

"Skylark Peace."

"Hah! I knew it! A hippie." I noticed the long, filed nails on his right hand as he adjusted his backpack strap.

"I'm kidding. My name's Nolan. You play?"

He blinked and stared at his hand. "Oh, right. The nails. I'm glad you assumed 'guitar player' and not 'starring in a production of Victor/Victoria.'"

"That was my second guess." I watched students file into our classroom one by one, girls with their clipboards against their chests as if to flatten themselves, guys with headphones on. "I play too. Are you in a band or anything?"

"Yeah, punk-rock. What about you?"

"I just moved here. You're the first musician I've met. But I only have an acoustic."

His pants hung low on his hips, showing a few inches of white briefs, though it didn't look intentional. "So you *are* a hippie."

"Right, you figured me out. And a commie spy too, but shh, don't tell anyone." The teacher walked in, stopped at the door and looked at us. "I think we should be heading in."

"Ah, shit. He sees us. Well, there goes my hope of skipping the dead white guy, Fathers of Confederation lecture. The birth of our great nation! The glory of the railroad age!"

I followed him into the classroom, noting the Bad Religion and D.O.A patches on his backpack. "Complaining about dead white guys? Now who's the hippie?"

He turned back at me and winked. "Not a hippie, just a cultured, sensitive, politically conscious guy. One of the few you'll meet here, I'll guarantee you that much."

When I started playing chess against Darren, all I remembered was the shape the pieces could move in: that the queen was a woman who could go anywhere. She could take the king, but he could rarely take her. Darren had been playing for years and kept notation for every game he played.

"It's like making a movie of the game," he said as he drew a line down the paper the first time we played, separating it between him and me. "Years after the match is done, you can replay it over and over and see what mistakes you made."

He showed me how to translate the game into notation: pawn to C3. D4 pawn takes C3. Knight takes Rook. Queen takes Rook to check.

He was much better than I was. I found it hard to concentrate, to balance attacking with defending. Darren always told me I gave up minor pieces too readily. The older he got, he said, the more cautious he was with his pawns. It was true. I didn't mind giving up pieces, staging bold moves that were too dramatic. I couldn't fool him. I could never fool him. That bothered me, the way his vision hovered sharp over the board, how he'd say, "Are you sure you want to do that?" as I lifted a piece.

I was improving, though, and that night I'd been trash talking him all through the workout in preparation for our match; ("Nolan," he'd said, "I don't think there's trash talking in chess. Can you imagine those skinny, old Russian masters? 'Rook takes Queen. You're mine, bitch.' I can just see it.") He sat on the futon, legs braced apart, the chess table between us. "You know what your problem is?"

"In chess or in general?"

"It's just your endgame. You're always one step ahead of yourself. I think you lose patience and forget to double check your move."

"Patience has never been a strong suit of mine," I admitted. "Can we get on with this?"

"You'll learn, young grasshopper," he said. "Speaking of lack of patience, did I tell you that Valerie's making me pay to have movers send over the rest of her furniture? Can she fit it in her mom's place? No. But somehow it's very important for her to have it right now. Right this instant."

"Maybe she just wants closure or something. To get it over with."

"Maybe she just wants to be a pain in my ass." The foliage colour of his hazel eyes had darkened into brown.

I shrugged. "Could be. Or maybe her lawyer or her shrink advised her to."

"Nah, Val's not the kind of woman who gets a shrink, no matter if she needs it. Which she does, by the way. Anyhow, the point is that if the rusty barbeque is so important to her, she should have taken it when she — Rook to C6 — left me. I mean, if she took the coffee grinder and the Bocce set — I mean, the Bocce set, Jesus — and the stereo. She should have taken everything."

"I guess," I said, even though I couldn't guess. I couldn't even imagine.

He looked around the room and I tried to picture what he saw. Did the futon have two hollows in it flattened down over the four years of their marriage? Was the living room the first room she decorated? Where was he standing when she said that she didn't want to be married anymore?

Though I met Valerie before Darren, I'd only spent a few days with her. The first time was at a national-team training camp. I was seventeen and only knew Sammy and Tony. She wore soft braces on her knees, making her look bionic, indestructible. During warm-up, I watched her move. She sweated but didn't flush. Most of the team gave her a wide berth and Valerie didn't speak unless it was required for basketball. Got boards. I'm in. See number twelve. Switch. Anything she said was shouted, a command.

During warm-up on the second day of camp, Tony asked her if she would teach me some Big Girl moves.

"Show her the dirty tricks," he said. "All the stuff that only one Big Girl can show another."

"I hate that phrase," she said when he left. "Big Girl. Makes me feel fat." She was my height, but about forty pounds heavier, much of it muscle. Her hair was light brown, darker when she sweated.

"Yeah, me too," I said, even though it didn't. "And it sounds kind of. I don't know. Condescending or something."

"Like you know anything about being fat. You're just a little bit of nothing girl."

I looked around at the gym at the basketball lines intersecting with the volleyball and badminton lines until I couldn't tell which belonged to what game.

"Well, come on. Can you catch?"

For the next fifteen minutes, she tossed balls at me as hard as she could, just high enough that I could feel the leather against my fingertips but couldn't catch them. Couldn't catch one. My hands were weak. I couldn't keep anything.

"I was testing you," she would say as another arced over my head and went out of bounds. "Guess you failed. I was testing you. Oh, whoops. You failed."

That weekend, there was a Div Two tournament in Kamloops, my first with The Handicaps. Darren was driving the rental van. Halfway through the trip, the landscape whitening to the point of boredom, Darren proposed re-naming the team the "Sexy Golden Dragons," since our uniforms were gold.

"Both to celebrate the cultural diversity of the city of New Westminster as exemplified by the New West Gardens Won Ton Palace and in honour of the respect and appreciation we have for Nolan's lovely flaxen locks," he said.

"I'm flattered. I would like to thank the little people. Especially Darren, who definitely counts as a little person."

"I pay you a compliment and that's what I get?" He snorted. "No respect. I get no respect around here. Can I continue?"

"I'm sorry. Please do."

"In fact," he continued. "I think we should all get blonde wigs for the next tournament."

"Hah," said Rob. He'd been dozing against the window, leaving a smear of oil on the glass where his cheek had been. Rob was blonde and pink-skinned, proud of his belly because he could rest a beer can on it and drink with no hands. "That's funny. Darren wants to wear a ladies' wig. Is that as close to a real woman as you can get? 'Cause you're little?"

"Oh, big talk from the little man in the back. You go back to sleep and dream of getting a girlfriend."

"That's a dumb name," said Erica. She sat beside me, knitting a sweater for her nephew. "Why do we always have stupid names? I mean, The Handicaps? What kind of a name is that? It's insulting."

"It's not insulting for gimps to call each other gimps," said Darren. "It's like how black people can use the N word. Plus, a little thing we like to call irony. What do they call it? There's a word for it. Nolan, you're in school. What's the term for disabled people using the word 'cripple?'"

"Reclamatory language," I said.

"Right. It's not rude, it's *reclamatory*."

"Okay fine," she said. "I'll settle for The Handicaps. Or the Holy Rollers. That's at least clever. That was your best one, Dare."

"Okay, all right. I was just trying to spice things up a bit."

"Ooh," said Rob. "You're trying to spice things up. 'Cause you're little and you need all the help you can get."

I don't remember the scores of our games. Every game I ever played for The Handicaps has blurred into one long match. The games weren't the point. The national team tournaments meant something, but Div Two was more about drinking contests in the bar on Saturday night.

The first night there, we went swimming in the hotel pool. I watched Darren navigate the slippery tiles on his crutches. On his chest was a Canadian flag, the red faded into pink.

"When'd you get that?" I asked.

"When I made the national team."

"Cool."

He looked down and traced a finger along the outline. "I was around your age. And I knew I wouldn't be there for long. I mean, I'm a class 2 and can't hold a ball in one hand. What're you going to do? If only I didn't have core and leg muscles, I'd be an awesome class 1. Classification doesn't know what to do with you unless you're a cut-and-dried para. Regardless. I digress. I just wanted something to show that I'd done it, you know? I was training four hours a day, didn't eat dessert for two years. All the stuff no one did back then."

I leaned against the side of the pool, my upper-body chilled, lower-body weightless. "Sammy says there's a guy on the French team who has no hand on one side and just a few fingers on the other."

"Yeah? Well, there you go. Good for him." He splashed me. "You going to get a sexy golden dragon tattoo?"

I splashed him back. "You want to look just like me, I know. A little peroxide would do the trick."

"No amount of peroxide in the world's going to make me six foot two." He grabbed my hands — the two fingers on his quad hand surprisingly strong — and we tried to overpower one another.

I linked my foot around his leg and tried to trip him. "My height's not helping me win this little battle."

"Hey," he says, "Illegal use of feet. Class 4s aren't allowed to trip Class 2s."

"No class system in water fights. This is an — " I twisted his arms to dunk him, "an egalitarian water fight. Besides, you're — " He pushed me under the water and I came up blinded by hair in my eyes, "You're stronger. And we're in water, so the playing field's equal."

"Okay, okay," he said. "Truce?" I shook his good hand and he pulled me under again. "Sorry, we class twos have to use every dirty trick in the book."

After we got out of the pool, Erica and I went down to Darren and Vern's room. We sprawled on the bed and watched World's Strongest Man episodes from the 1970s. Men grunted and threw impossibly heavy objects impossibly far distances for no specific reason other than to prove their mightiness. They had names like Magnus von Magnuson.

I lay on Darren's bed and Erica sat on the end in pastel pyjamas with flowers on them. She was thick-limbed and short, her black hair always up in a ponytail. My pyjama pants were loose. They teetered on the edge of my hip bones and undressed me with a slow slide. The elastic stretched lax between the bones, forming a pocket of space. My body with all its hollows that needed to be filled. My head was by Darren's stomach and underneath the chlorine scent we shared was his smell of Old Spice and soap, which was new to me.

Vern sat on the other bed with his shirt off, his big, white belly with its scum of grey hair hiding any trace of muscle. He half-stroked, half-scratched his stomach as if it was a beloved family pet.

"How come no girls want to sit on my bed?" he asked and Erica and I looked at each other to smirk.

"Don't complain," I told him, "You have the pleasure of Rob's company." Rob sat on the edge of Vern's bed. He had spent the evening pretending to be a World's Strongest Man, posing and flexing.

"This bed is too small for any more people," he said in an attempt at an Austrian accent. "I must turn sideways to even sit here because my muscles are so massive, yah, that's right. I am so mighty that I cannot put my arms at my sides."

"Stop laughing, Nole," Darren said "You're making the bed shake." As he spoke, I could feel the vibrations from his stomach.

When I closed my eyes, he poked me in the ribs or tickled me. I squirmed when he did so, probably more than necessary. Once I pressed my hip bone against his palm. When he poked me, I interlocked my fingers with his, at first to make him stop, then under the pretence of making him stop.

"Hey," I said low and sleepy and looked up at him, "Quit that." I didn't let go and he slid his thumb back and forth along the base of my hand. Then he released me. I closed my eyes and he poked me again.

"What are you two doing back there?" asked Erica.

"I'm making her pay attention," said Darren. "She needs to bulk up, learn something from World's Strongest Man."

"How come Darren gets all the girls?" Vern asked. "I mean, really. I'm twice the man he is." Erica and I looked at each other, unable to believe that he was serious. Half of anything Vern said seemed to come from TV movies, like he was practicing to step outside of his role as husband, father, grandpa.

"Maybe in body mass," said Rob, which everyone except Vern saw coming.

"Not my fault," said Darren. "They just sat down here and took the place over and now they won't leave."

"Poor Darren," I said, "It's so hard being you. How do you deal with inconveniences such as having two lovely women such as ourselves — right, Erica? — take over your bed? It's a tough life."

"Right. Maybe we should just leave him all alone."

"Maybe we should," I said, but we didn't.

When we got back to the hotel room, I free fell on to the bed, my arms spread like a semaphore. Erica stood over me.

"You know he's just separated, right?"

"Who? Darren?"

She wandered into the bathroom, "No. Rob. Who do you think?" She began to brush her teeth. "The divorce hasn't come through."

"Why would I care about that? We're just friends." I set out tomorrow's uniform on the floor. It looked like a deflated version of me.

"Anyone who puts the word 'just' in front of 'friends' probably isn't."

"He's frickin' thirteen years older than me. Do you want him or something?"

Erica spat into the sink again and rinsed off the brush. "He's just getting out of a four-year marriage. And they were dating for — how long? I know they hooked up around when Darren made the national team and he was . . . twenty-one, I think. So, like, seven years of dating. So, basically what this math equation adds up to is eleven years of issues. A third of his life."

"But if there was no Valerie? Would you go for him then? I don't want to interfere with anything you've got going on there."

Erica wandered out of the bathroom and turned off the light. "Val was the dominant influence in his life for over a decade. Without her, the Darren we know wouldn't exist. So don't even ask that question. It's irrelevant."

7

THE DAY BEFORE I WAS INJURED — (The Injury, my mother calls it, capital letters in her mind making the distinction between before and after) — we rode bikes fast through a syrup of light and heat and our mothers let us go further than their senses could track us. My family was on a vacation with Sophia's family through Washington State. Each campsite we stopped at had a general store that also sold fishing supplies, which Sophia and I frequented for the chocolate bars. The chocolate was usually white with age and heat, like a sunburn in reverse. When it melted, we drew runes on our stomachs with our fingers and made each other guess their meaning.

We loved to open the freezer and look at the frozen bait beside the popsicles, loved to chill the hot lycra skin of our swimsuits. We sat on rough surfaces in those swimsuits until the bottoms were picked like goosebumps. All of our clothes smelled of wood smoke and charred marshmallows.

That summer, we knew our bodies by their reaction to heat, to sun. The need for shorts. The need for swimming. For sunscreen. The need to jump across the river on our bikes and race each other up the hill. Running barefoot through gravel callused our feet and we were proud of the way the outdoors didn't hurt anymore.

There was a river and it was fast. The water was clear but its motion blurred the shapes of the sharp rocks underneath, blunted them. My body was a new creature viewed under water, wavery and distant. My numbed limbs didn't seem to be mine.

I liked being weightless: the contrast of the warm rubber of the inner-tube tires we floated on to the chilled water, so cold it hurt in a good way. We would lie on our backs and let the current carry us down a small drop that we thought was a waterfall. Sometimes we did it with just our bodies: the rush of water down the front of our swimsuits depositing bits of leaves that we had to peel off our skin afterwards. Other times, we used Sophia's swan-shaped floater with its sweet, rotten scent of hot rubber. Often, we flipped off. Though Victoria was probably less dangerous than the campsite with its cliffs and little rapids, no one watched us the way they did back home. No one needed us to check in. We smelled dinner — Alphagettis with white bread — and followed it home.

All day, we rode our bikes fast and disregarded small injuries. It didn't hurt when we bumped on a rock or a stick. We wouldn't let it hurt. Only afterwards, roasting marshmallows, would we find the river-colour of bruises on our arms and legs. We were anaesthetized by the medicine of cold water.

~

The elevator has acoustic guitar music piped in, the nylon strings tinny amidst all this steel. Quinn's promised that when I'm better, he'll take the Gretsch out of storage and we'll invite some of our more musical friends over like we used to. For years, we did it every Friday night before Clara and Alex had the baby and Jamie got promoted. On someone's porch or in our living room, we drank beer until our fingers began to slur. I miss playing with Quinn, sussing out the rhythm he's building, finding my own space between the drums and the fiddle. When I'm better, there may be time to learn lap steel or the mandolin. I should be looking forward to this.

When I met him, Quinn played in a metal-rock band and his voice still holds the roughness caused by those years of practiced screaming. Now he's growing into blues and jazz.

"Old man music," he often says during car rides as he finds himself enjoying Ornette Coleman and John Coltrane on CBC. "Un-frickin'-believable. I've grown into a skinny white man who likes jazz and actually owns a copy of Harry Smith's Folk Anthology. Where's the distortion gone? If I get into this enough to, like, start calling him Trane or wearing a turtleneck, you take me out back and shoot me okay? Right in the temple. Right there. Bang."

I once tried to teach Darren how to play guitar. The heater in my apartment broke and since I couldn't reach my landlord, Darren came over to see what he could do.

"Okay, pass me a screwdriver," he said. He was sitting on the floor in front of the heater, his crutches leaning against the wall.

"I actually don't have one."

He turned to look at me, smiling. "You really are a chick, you know that?"

"You finally noticed."

Another smile. "Okay, Miss Fix-It, pass me a penny." I searched through an old cookie tin that contained anything remotely related to mending: Band-Aids, tire irons, spoke wrenches, a set of Allen keys, Aspirin, a box of Smarties. "What kind of tools do you have around here? And what the hell kind of tool is that?"

"That's not really a tool. It's a capo. For the guitar. If you want to change the key so the chords are easier or whatever, you can pop this puppy on."

After loosening the screws by twisting a coin against the groove, he removed the back panel. Inside: an incoherent jumble of pipes and wires. Darren's job made him good at systems. He stared at the heater — rearranging the parts in his head, finding the incongruity — then used his hands to enforce his mind's logic. The grime on the pipes brought the lines on his palms into sharp relief.

"Play some mood music, then. Come on. Do you know 'Smoke on the Water'?"

It was impossible not to look at the heater and see intestines, a heart, the grey coils of a brain, though I suspected that my body couldn't possess such order.

"Everyone knows 'Smoke on the Water.'"

I played while he fixed. At first, the cold made my fingers stupid, but soon they warmed and my speaking voice undressed into a song. I did some ballad about leaving, which I was young enough to still find powerful. Most likely Sarah Harmer's "Dogs and Thunder," which was the saddest song I knew at the time, back in the days when I thought death was sadder than love.

"Hey," he said. "That doesn't sound like 'Smoke on the Water' to me. Nothing I can possibly relate to Valerie tonight, please."

"I'm sorry; I forgot." I rested the guitar against the wall.

"I was just kidding. I like it when you sing. It's calming or whatever."

Later that night, I gave him lessons. He'd fixed the heater, so I leaned against the warming grate, feeling the motor's small, instrumental vibrations. Darren sat between my legs, his narrow lower body accommodating my lack of flexibility.

"Okay," I said. I placed my fingers over top of his. The height discrepancy left my mouth at the level of his head and as I spoke, my breath shifted his hair. "You've got your low E, your high E, and in between there's A, D, G and B. A full octave, right?"

"Right," he said, and I could feel the static of his words between his shoulder blades and was surprised to find voice somewhere other than the mouth. "An octave. Okay."

One by one, I took his fingers and placed them on the strings. It was lucky that Darren's numb fingers were on his strumming hand. He could hold the pic with the two functioning ones. "Here's G chord. It's pretty basic. See, try strumming."

His left hand moved down the strings. I imagined the guitar's vibrations against his stomach. "That's harder than it looks," he said. "How do you go up the strings? I don't quite have the hang of this up-stroke bit." He skimmed his thumb along the woman curve of the guitar's edge.

"Easy there. You're going to crush the pic." I touched his hand, the white-knuckled thumb and pointer finger, the rest of them curled against each other.

"With my quadriplegic death grip?"

The heater's hums met the throb of Darren's voice met my own voice and I felt them in all the hollows of my body. Against my back: the metal pipes with their human heat, the slats of the vent against me like a staff bar. Against my chest: Darren's warmth, his dark hair brushing my chin, the bumps of his spine trailing unfinished against me.

When we reach the Pre-Op holding area, the two nurses leave, handing me over to another set. The gurneys are parked in a row, separated by canvas curtains. Someone coughs, someone else whimpers. All around me, other patients communicate the details of their hurt or sickness. There are no walls to hold in the sound, the edges of the room indistinct and shifting. The curtains swell and bend like sails, like the flag of some foreign country and the sedatives make me sway along with them as if I, too, am travelling.

A new nurse arrives with news that there's been a car accident and my spot in the O.R. has been bumped to tend to these emergency cases.

"How long, do you think?" I ask. "A few more hours?"

"If that." The nurse has a red tattoo of a Japanese character on her upper arm. It slides in and out of view of her scrubs as she moves across the linoleum. I like this nurse, this sign that she can take needles as well as give them. "It shouldn't be that long. Don't worry; you'll be in and out of there in no time."

"If some guy named Quinn McLeod is looking for me, will you let him in? He's supposed to come at 3:30. Do you think he'll get here before I go in?"

"I'm sure you'll be under by 3:30. It's 1:45 now. Don't worry. Won't be long." I feel the IV in my arm, taped there, the pressure almost comforting since I can pretend it's someone's hand. The nurse injects something into my IV.

"This'll help you rest up," she says.

"Considering I'm going to be spending the next four hours unconscious, I think I'd rather do less resting and more running around the room to burn off steam."

The nurse — Terri, her identification pass says — smiles as her hands fix my IV. "If you could run around the room, dear, you probably wouldn't be here right now." Atta girl, Terri, I think. The drug sounds like Valia or Velia, an exotic girl name, someone who might wear bright colours and go dancing often.

And so I sleep and when I do, I have either the dream or the memory of the dream. I'm nineteen, a front door opens and I step out into a long hallway. It's one of those dreams where I am both me but also out of myself: able to slip through my membranes and float above the room, go above and beneath my skin like a hand skimming the surface of water to test if it's right. I don't know where I'm heading — my mind an eager, tamed animal bounding behind — but my body predicts everything.

I follow her — me — her past a kitchen: a loaf of bread on the counter open, wrapper blued with the light of the digital clock on the nearby stove. The bathroom's steamy from recent use, the smell of soap and cologne, the mirror fogged and my reflection in it as if I'd been smudged. The hall opens to a living room and Darren is there. Posters of foreign countries are on the walls. I knew somehow he'd never visited them, that he just liked the colours.

The room is tilted: big and ambivalent with a grey light that settles like dust on the posters, the desk, the couch, on Darren, who stands with a hand for support on the couch's arm. Over his shoulder, he's spread a blue and pink baby blanket, the kind used for catching spit-up. He talks to someone in another room and my mind cleaves and spreads, in both places at once.

In the living room, the couch is covered with toys. A teddy bear, its ear stiff with spit. A rattle and a set of bright plastic rings. In the bedroom, there is a round woman with white curls that accept the light's hue. She's maybe sixty-five or seventy. She bends over the cradle near the bed, humming from the back of her throat. An old song: gospel call-and-response without the reply.

In the dream, I know that this is my child in the blankets, that I am leaving or have left and am happy to be back in this place though I know it will be the last time and I try to speak to Darren, to watch the baby. The child is a girl. I know that somehow. I can feel my shadow shape fit the dark spaces of the house, floating unnoticed in both rooms.

Darren smoothes the blanket over his shoulder and calls to the old woman.

"I'm ready," he says. "Okay. I'm ready."

The first time I had that dream was the week I met Darren when I didn't know anything more than his name and the fact that he was my player-coach. I woke up in my new apartment, trying to find a familiar shape in the darkness and locating only the squares of unpacked boxes: angles and angles and silence and angles. I was used to a familiar story of night sounds that repeated themselves over and over throughout my childhood: owls, wind, bushes, mice, water. My parents lived near Cadboro Bay, so close to the ocean I could hear the shush of pebbles against water like even breathing. I listened for some sound to anchor me to a familiar place, but could only make out a truck rumbling by, the tires taking a drag of the wet pavement. The dream was so vivid that I had to touch the sheets to convince myself I wasn't floating.

Now, I can't quite remember what it felt like that first time I went to Darren's house and found it was the same as in the dream. The same posters, same couch, same big windows with their indecisive light. I have that dream maybe once a year, though now I suspect it's just the memory of the dream: photo of a photo of a photo. Each time, the details blur like an old tattoo. Dreams like this are apparently quite common, a phenomenon studied by scientists. Despite our city living, it seems, our subconscious remains peyote-tinged and animal. I'm not psychic, though. This is the only such dream I've had. Besides, the rest of the dreams I've had about Darren since have never come true.

~

There was no fixed beginning and I can't possibly remember where I was when the injury started. I was playing in the river that week, I know that. We visited various campsites, but the river was the same. Sophia and

I played a game that involved us cast as either adventurers or models, sometimes model-adventurers. The river was a set, a prop, and we would either pretend to conquer it or arrange ourselves on its rocks like women in beer commercials, the water all around us meant to make our suntans shine. My family had brought a Bocce set and we stuffed the balls down our bathing suits to make breasts. They wouldn't stay put — gravity and the rapids combining to peel them away from our little buds of nipples and float them down our stomachs and into the water. We hated the fact that we weren't old enough yet.

One night, I came out of the river with a limp, as if the water had fixed everything about me but one, small spot. Achilles or something. I walked with a new swagger, my body rearranging the pattern of my limbs as if to accommodate the addition of hips and breasts, some invisible ballast that required a new balancing act. When I stretched to put on my sweatshirt — that moment where I breathed the smell of my body and the scent of wood smoke and foliage caught in the weave — I felt the pain in my hip and thought that it was just growing. I was getting Hips. Maybe it would be this side first and then the other. Next would be Breasts. I had a vague idea that anything that involved change had to hurt a little in a way that you could complain to your friends about in school bathrooms while applying Lip Smackers in warped mirrors.

The new hurt was a little, round ache — the shape of a mole, maybe, a birthmark — and my parents, too, blamed growing pains or a groin pull. My mom said, "Oh darling girl," and my dad smiled as if he was embarrassed whenever I limped, as if the problem was something pubescent, menstrual in nature. Sophia and I made jokes, loving the word 'groin' in groin pull: Groin pull, huh? What've you been doing? What's his name? We didn't know the specifics of what I could have possibly been doing to strain this warm, secret crease. I was eleven. I got quiet. Even then, I had a high threshold for pain and had always been proud that I wasn't a whiner. That I could take it. After a few days, my foot wouldn't turn completely straight. When asked about the limp, I said it was probably getting better, maybe tomorrow: tomorrow I would be good.

Soon, I dragged my leg behind me as if it were made of some denser substance, too heavy to carry. The pain had spread to new territory, changing the landscape of me. When I lay down in the tent, I could feel every curve of the dirt, every pebble, all of it amplified into my hip.

I carried the shape of it inside of me for another week as we followed the river through Washington State and back again. I was proud of how little complaining I did. Sophia went into the water without me and I sat on the shore feeling the new throb.

When I had to get out of the car on the ferry ride back to Victoria, I couldn't walk unassisted. My mother and father stood on either side of me to ease the weight from my body and we sang "Lean on Me," complete with snapping and harmonizing. My dad sang each chorus in a different voice, ("Like Bob Dylan, now!" "Like Nina Simone!"), and when I laughed I could feel my hip change the sound and was surprised to find my body connected in some way other than "the hip bone's connected to the leg bone, the leg bone's connected to the knee bone," that old song, that way of naming your body like a map.

They couldn't get me back in the car again. As all the passengers tried to offload, I was still standing and holding the car door. The kids in the van beside us pointed at me: fingers leaving smears on the windows. SOS, I imagined them writing. SOS. The teenagers in the car behind listened to angry rock.

"Nolan, you're too old for this," said my mom. "Come on, look at the cars. Don't be silly. Look at the cars."

Everyone's headlights were on and I could imagine myself backlit, a crackly aura. People honked, too, all the different octaves. Some swerved around us and I felt the octane-scented wind brush past my face.

I tried to fold myself into the car — the good leg first and then the bad — but my body shifted so hard that I expected there to be a big, cartoonish sound. The pain was structural, basic as marrow and so concentrated that I looked down at my leg to check for swelling or blood, a shard of metal piercing me from outside that could be removed, a wound to staunch. It was only when I looked at my mother's face that I realized I was screaming.

"Good news, Ms. Taylor," says Terri, "We have a table."

"Sounds like a restaurant," I say. "Such service. Taylor, table for one. Quinn didn't come, did he?"

And then I'm being wheeled again, the blankets around me lifting and the chill from the rest of the hospital sliding up and down my legs, against my hip. We pass many brightly coloured signs, double-doors, pastel prints on the walls whose subject matter I can't discern. They push me through the doors into startling light, a room that's all steel. Four orderlies stand around me.

"They're going to lift your blanket on three and transfer you on to the table," says Terri, raising her hand like a conductor, "Are you ready?"

"Sure."

"Okay, one, two, three." They lift me on to the table and I feel its coolness against my thighs, then against the rest of me as Terri removes the hospital gown and replaces it with a blanket. Her tattoo is visible as she helps the doctor lay out all the tools, its colour the brightest hue in the room. I imagine it means happiness, peace, love. I imagine it's a sign.

At a sink at the side of the room, Dr. Felth washes up, his hands brownish-yellow with antiseptic. He turns and smiles at me.

"Ms. Taylor," he says. "See, Larry, this is the one I was telling you about. The one who wanted to keep the femoral head. Do you have any last-minute questions? I know these drills and saws might look a little scary, but the procedure — I've told you this — will leave relatively few scars. That's what most people are worried about: the scars. We'll go in through the old incision and probably close it up a little. We work out of smaller and smaller holes these days."

Larry, the anaesthesiologist, chortles. "Keep the hip," he says. "That's a first. We've never had that one before."

He wears a bandana with palm trees around his head, but the lights — so much light — find even the most fledgling hairs on his chin, his arms. All around me: steel and posters advocating safety and hygiene.

The anaesthesiologist flicks my hand to bring up a vein, his rhythm roughly four, four time. Terri tells me to breathe deeply, to sing some song inside my head to distract myself and I hold the side bar of the bed as my mind finds a Lyle Lovett song, that one about *sing me a melody, sing me a bruise, walk through the bottomland without no shoes.*

Quinn learned it for me before we'd even started dating, though he hated country. After our Canadian history class, we got into a discussion about who was the better songwriter: the lead singer of Bad Religion or Lyle and I'd used the song as an example. At the end of the conversation, he invited me over to study for our upcoming midterm the next day at his apartment.

"The grand tour," he said as he cleared away *Guitar World* magazines and *Vancouver Sun*s from the couch. "This is the living room slash rock-out practice space. Here're our amps, which double as a specially designed pizza-box stand. Oh and, hey, I have to show you something." He picked up his electric guitar, an old Fender with sharp edges and many other bands' stickers all over. "I was listening to that Lyle Lovett guy. I think you're right about the lyrics."

"You guys are called The Cripple Killers?" I pointed to the drum kit with the band's logo: a punk pushing some guy with a blanket over his legs out of a wheelchair.

Quinn nodded. "Yeah. We used to be the Beaver Eaters, but some clubs wouldn't put our name on posters and shit."

I touched his elbow. "Now, do you actually kill cripples? I'm curious. And what kind of cripples? Are we talking physical, emotional or what?"

"Nah, uh, that's kind of just the name. I dunno, Ralph thinks it's edgy. Or, like, controversial. We were going to go with The Babykillers, but it was taken." Quinn poked his thumb in and out of the hole in his sleeve.

"I just think it's funny. A socialist punk band with a social Darwinist name."

"Well, we wouldn't really hurt, uh, physically challenged . . . physically disabled . . . whatever you call them . . . people."

I looked at him: the square of hair shaved under his lower lip a swatch of proof that he could actually sustain a beard, the three shirts he wore to pad his frame. "Yeah, I know. You don't look like the cripple-killing type to me. I play on a team called The Handicaps."

"Oh yeah? What sport?"

"Wheelchair basketball, actually."

Quinn stepped back and looked at me. "What? You're in a wheelchair?"

"Yes, I'm in a wheelchair. It's a hard life. Makes it really difficult for me to stand here and talk to you."

Quinn blinked. "Oh. Oh, yeah, I'm stupid. I'm sorry, I just — So you play wheelchair basketball, but you walk. Isn't that a little, like, mean or something? To the people in the wheelchairs?"

"You're the Cripple Killer."

He rubbed the back of his neck. "Oh geez."

I touched his arm. "I'm just kidding. Lots of able-bodied people play wheelchair ball and I have a bad hip, so I can't play stand-up."

"S'cool. Well, not about the hip, but — Hey, I'm really sorry about the band name. We really don't mean anything by it."

I placed my hand on his. The guitar calluses matched my own. "Quinn, it's cool. Don't worry."

"Is there any way I can possibly salvage this situation by playing you the Lyle Lovett song I stayed up half the night to learn?"

He unplugged his electric and played the song. I was impressed. His voice was softer than punk metal, better suited for lullabies than screaming. *Sing me a melody. Sing me a bruise. Walk through the bottomland without no shoes.* I think it's blues, actually. Sing me a blues, but bruise is more apt, the word like the mark left when a man's mouth is first learning how much pressure your skin can take, leaving its shape in some hollow against your neck: a kiss you can wear like a locket.

"Deep breaths, Nolan," says Terri. "We're going to count down from ten to one together and by the time we reach one, you should be asleep. Are you ready?"

I nod and my fingers reach for the steel and find her hand. With its pressure, I can feel my guitar calluses and my basketball calluses and all the places I have been changed. The light here is so exact.

Sing me a bruise, I sing in my head. Sing my skin tender. Free my blood from the logic of veins and let the song leave its shape on me. And it's wrong, childish, to want a lullaby, a melody, a blues, but I imagine the anaesthesia as a bottomland, some place where the stage lights lend your skin their brightness and your feet are sticky with beer and liquor and cigarette butts, sticky like they want to stay in one place and you sway with someone, holding them sweaty and gentle against your best pair of jeans. Or you can go fast, flail your arms, your body breathing and swimming.

I've been under before. It's not like sleep. It's dark and quick and you don't remember afterwards, don't feel as if any time has passed. There must be music in a place like that. There must be either music or water to go in so quickly, for time to go so fast.

Once, as a friend of mine was going under, the doctors were playing classical music to help them concentrate. This woman, who'd never raised her voice or held any strong opinions on music, sat up and shouted, "Fuck the Bach, let's rock," before going down to some place where maybe she could.

The first doctor's name was Dr. Domier. He wore bike shorts and shook my hand while still wearing his helmet, as if to reassure me that his day-to-day life was more dangerous than my injury. Dr. Domier explained that there's a growth plate on every joint that widens to allow the bone to grow. As he talked, he used his hands as models. The socket was a cupped palm, the way you hold something wild and injured. The hip was a fist. When he said that my growth plate slipped off part way and would have to be pinned, I imagined it as a wafer from Sunday school back when Nana took me to church, how I spit it out when it stuck to the back of my throat. I thought of plates of the earth shifting like we learned in science, my own private geology. He left and when I fell asleep shortly after, it was not falling, it was being pushed asleep by the morphine and I tried to keep my balance but fell anyway.

I was scared of the needle, didn't want be put out, hated the sound of the phrase 'going under.' The operating table was cold and I looked up at the big light, wondering how it managed such brightness without heat. The nurse held my hand and we counted down together 10, 9, 8, 7, 6, 5 and then I was out, then I was under, and it was such a blink-quick 'out' that I thought it hadn't worked. That was the first surgery.

~

And they count *10 mississippi* — more proof that there is water in this place — *9 mississippi, 8,* like in weight training, counting down the reps and feeling the lactic acid burn fizzle its way through every muscles, the push to get one more in. And that moment after the last rep when it's over.

"Nineteen and twenty . . . ," said Darren as he did sit-ups with his feet against the wall, the image on the front of his shirt — a man with a trombone to his lips — wrinkling as he moved, the musician suddenly aged.

"I think I'm getting fat," he said and poked his abdomen. His voice lifted at the end of the sentence, half a question.

"You are not." I was beside him, also doing sit-ups, trying to force all the small abdominal muscles on task. Belly-button against the spine, squeeze the PCs, what my trainer calls the girdle muscles: quaint undergarments worn inside.

"I think I am. You know, pretty soon I'll have to round up to forty instead of down to thirty. It's that age."

"In three years. Come on." I finished the set and watched him. We were each on our own mats, our territory easily defined.

"Still. It's all about the metabolism," he said. As his torso raised with each sit-up,his sweat and oil shined in a bright shadow the shape of his body. Two middle-aged women chatted as they worked out: the Lycra-against-Lycra scuff of their thighs as they passed.

"And then I said to Harry," one said. "And then I told him."

The sound system was on low. Techno: a woman singing the same line over and over to a beat that was supposed to mimic the heart. Indecipherable but probably about love. At the front of the gym, little fluttering sounds of the desk guy rearranging magazines.

Darren pinched the fat, though he had to round his shoulders to gather even enough for his fingers. "See? Look at this." His stomach. Freckles. The fuse of hair that started below his bellybutton.

"Lie down," I said. "It doesn't count if you hunch over." I moved towards the space between our mats. As I knelt, my hip seized: my heartbeat relocated there. I could feel the mat's edge imprinting my knees. "See?" My fingers. His stomach. "See? I can't pinch anything." My voice came from a new, lower part of my throat. Not husky, more like the sleek core after the husk is shucked away. I heard the desk guy pace around the front entrance. Darren watched me, maybe intently, maybe unsure of his intentions. Or maybe that was my own expression.

The weights that the women used clinked. "I couldn't believe it," one of them said. "I couldn't even believe he did that." They weren't as far away from us as they once seemed.

"See? Trust me. You're not fat," I said. My hand didn't pinch, but didn't move. Strange, I thought, that a handprint forms in Cage Match — brief contact — and not here, this long slow merging of our temperatures.

"You're very convincing," he said. "You should work with anorexics." We both tried to laugh. The movements of his laughter — small, forced arches of his belly — pushed his abdomen into my fingertips. I watched his freckles: the constellation of his skin up-close.

"Yeah," I said.

"Yeah," he said.

"So, yeah," I said and my hand made its unimaginable slide downwards, underneath his two elastic waistbands, my fingers following the dark line down to another texture. The warmth of my inflammation migrated away from my hip. I didn't even kiss him first.

Darren said my name like a new word, a better nickname. On the poster on the wall: a cartoon drawing of a man and a woman with their skins peeled off, their muscles defined and drawn in bright colours for instructional purposes.

"Seven mississippi, six — " I go under and am glad that Quinn is not here, since I don't trust what name I will reach for when I wake up.

8

NO ONE EVER TOLD ME ABOUT THE SILENCES, the time to fill. In movies, relationships went from witty banter to sex scenes and back again. After the "incident" at the gym, after I'd wiped my hand off on a towel and two elderly ladies had come by moments afterwards to compliment me on the service I was doing working out with disabled people, there was a car ride home where we both nodded our heads in time to the music, the action mirroring the yes, yes, yes I was trying not to think.

"Why don't we go out for dinner and talk about . . . ," he gestured obliquely, "this?" As he pulled up in front of my apartment complex, I could hear sirens, a man and a woman arguing as they passed.

"You don't have to try to be a gentleman," I said. "If you don't want it to happen again, say so. If you do, then it'll happen again. No need for sit-down dinners." The trip to Brazil had left me in a basketball frame of mind. I wanted clarity, order: winning or losing team, good pass or turnover, hit or miss.

"Can we just do this properly?" He ran a hand through his hair and I could tell he was sweating because of how it stuck up and stayed there. I wondered if there was a more proper way to give someone a hand job in a public place, if he was critiquing my technique or just my timing.

"Look, I'm sorry," I said, "I shouldn't have . . . been so forward. I didn't really mean to."

"No, it's not. I mean, it's delicate. It's kind of a delicate situation, that's all."

The next night, he took me to one of those restaurants where the waitresses are required to submit a head-shot with their resumés: well-decorated and poorly lit. The table had a chess board inlaid in it but no pieces. On the wall behind Darren, there was a moose head wearing a party hat.

I wore a shirt that showed off cleavage I didn't have, having used a technique of Sophia's that involved sweeping dark eyeshadow where cleavage should be to create the illusion. Sitting across the table, Darren shifted in the silence. He'd added some gel to his hair and it changed his silhouette, spiked and crackling. Likely, he was trying to appear taller. We'd never been this face-to-face.

Darren's thumb traced the seam between a black square and a white one. "So," he said. "So, Brazil, eh? Wanna tell me more about that?"

"Yeah. Brazil."

"So, besides getting your ass handed to you by the Yanks, how was it? I mean . . . well . . . you know what I mean . . . As an experience . . . "

The waitress came by for our drink orders. She had thick lip- and eyeliner, as if her face could be cut out along the line, disassembled into parts and rearranged.

Darren wanted herbal tea. When I ordered Diet Coke, he looked up from the menu at the word.

"Do you know what aspartame does?" he asked after she'd left.

"Rots your teeth, your stomach, your brain, probably causes cancer in some way. I think we've been over this."

"And converts into formaldehyde inside your body," he said. "Briefly."

"Great. It'll pickle me and I'll live forever. Like the soda fountain of youth or something."

The waitress arrived with our drinks and Darren said nothing, sipped his tea and allowed the scent of steeped herbs to argue his point for him. "You don't agree with Coca-Cola's human rights record, yet you still buy their product. How is that? Explain that to me." His tone wasn't mean; he was merely gearing for a good mind fuck. Point, counterpoint. Parry and thrust. Emphasis on the "thrust."

I smiled, letting the bubbles find their way up to the roof of my mouth and absorb into the soft skin there, then swallowed. "Not that this isn't fun and everything, but are we going to actually talk about the fact that I jerked you off in front of two middle-aged women wearing spandex or are we going to continue to dissect my drinking habits?"

Even in the dim light, I could see Darren's blush. He looked up at the waitress who was standing behind me, waiting for our orders, and said, "I think we'll need a few more minutes."

I lacked patience with these rituals, had no experience with them. I'd inherited my mother's blunt nature and wanted to get to the bottom of things, unsure of whether or not men were capable of the biting subtext of girls and everything he was trying to tell me was somehow contained in his opinion on diet pop. All this was new. I wanted rules to follow: when he says this, do that; when he touches you there, touch him here; when he's recently divorced, give him this amount of time to get over her before you put your hand down his pants.

When the waitress left, I looked over at him. He was laughing silently, trying not to let the sound escape, his whole body hunched.

"Touché. You're great, Nolan, you know that?" he said. "I never know what to expect from you."

~

Before it happened, you didn't want to think of sex with Darren as The First Time. That seemed too much a sudden girl-to-woman before and after, quick as an injury. Pain, you could do. Been there, done that, had the morphine-based drugs. Girls who'd only had surface wounds would, of course, cry — were almost expected to cry — but you were used to inside hurt. You wanted to feel like a wily vet, inexperienced in pleasure but well-versed in its potential side effects. Nervousness was underneath this: worry about your ability to perform. Since making the national team everything — school, relationships, what video to get at the store — seemed like a big game needing mental and physical preparation.

It'd been only two weeks since you'd been together. Well, not really together-together. More like fouteen days of doing the same thing you always did, except that sometimes you fooled around on the living-room futon or in his car. The term seemed right to you — fooling around — since it was all less serious than you'd imagined, more laughing. Or maybe you just felt a little dumb, unsure of where to put your arms and legs. Sometimes it was that.

"It's like we're teenagers," he said when you started out on the weekly drive after practice and ended up going back to the garage of his house and reclining the seats back, him unhooking your bra underneath your shirt. The window was open and the garage smelled of wet concrete and gasoline.

You didn't state the obvious because nineteen felt so close to twenty and he was already skittish. Every time you put a hand on his thigh, you could almost watch some hand-wringing corner of his mind calculating how long since the separation, how old he was when you were born. So you tried to ease him into it, tried to make him forget, tried to make him show you everything. You still weren't sure if this was a relationship or if the decline of his marriage had just made him sex-starved. You weren't sure whether or not that mattered.

The thirteen-year age difference seemed appropriate as well, easy to validate with countless historical examples: John Donne and his teenage bride, Woody Allen and his step-daughter. Those worked out well, didn't they? The women on the national team had taught you to defer to age and experience and there seemed to be little point in groping against some other virgin.

As for sex: no reason to wait. You'd picked a course, would follow it to its logical conclusion. Mostly, however, the trip to Brazil had made you tired of inexperience in all areas of your life. You wanted to get the first time over with, sure it would never be any good.

There'd been a documentary on the origins of basketball and you both ate yogurt-covered ginger — Darren extolling its virtues in aiding digestion — and then you talked until 3 AM. Provincial politics, club-team politics, same old stuff. Around three, he kissed you with the taste of gingery heat in his mouth and before you knew it, you were opening the condom from your purse, the one they gave you in the new student orientation at school along with a map of the building, a pen and instructions on how to build a dental dam, all you apparently needed to survive university life. It was the first condom you'd ever possessed for purposes unrelated to pranks.

He was sitting on the futon in his briefs, the TV screen flickering against his flushed face. The muscles in his chest and arms tensed when you brought out the condom and he rubbed the back of his neck, said, "Nolan, are you sure?" and you said, "Yeah. Uh huh." And he said, "No, really. Are you sure? We should wait," and you said, "Yes. I want to. Jesus Christ." And he said, "Sure, sure? This is a big deal." And you said, "Yes. Final answer," and were surprised at your impatience. Nineteen years to get a kiss and now you can't wait a month before you fuck the guy? You surprised yourself, your appetites: such a bony, inflexible girl usually, pale-mouthed and dressed down.

Darren nodded. "I want to," he said. "I mean, obviously I want to. I just don't know if I should want to." He seemed dazed, perhaps too much blood diverted from his brain, as he led you into the bedroom. Old wheelchair parts were stacked in a corner and there were brighter spots on the wallpaper where Valerie had taken paintings.

You loved seeing him naked, though, once he finally calmed, tracing the muscles on his chest with your palm, sometimes your mouth, knowing all the names. The bicep, the deltoid, the sacrum: that finger of bone crooked in a come-hither motion that reminded you of an old pick-up line where you beckon a man with your pointer finger and say, "Come here, I have something to tell you," and when he does whisper in his ear, "If I can make you come with one finger, imagine what I can do with the rest of my body." You'd always loved the word, too: sacrum. Bone named sacred. The rest of your anatomy felt poorly translated, the Latin giving no insight into its use. With Darren, you wanted to rename every bone, fibre, muscle in your body. The lower part of his abdomen was softer, as if something vital was underneath, wrapped up for safe keeping.

When he saw you looking at his legs, you enjoyed his blush, where it started and how it spread down his neck.

"I know," he said. "Chicken legs, eh?"

There was no way to say that you enjoyed the aesthetics of them, pared down to exactly what they were. Instead, you said, "Just makes what's between them look bigger, that's all." And he laughed and you loved — loved — the power of making a grown man blush and laugh nervous.

He didn't touch your legs. At first you thought he was just translating what felt right on his body on to yours, but he had full sensation. Valerie was the one who had pain and numbness in her knees and hated being touched there.

"Tell me if it hurts," Darren said against your chest, his mouth against your nipple as if he could speak the words into your body, bypassing the mind. As if someone could speak right into the pain and neutralize its acidity with all the basic parts of the voice.

"The hip or the . . . other?"

"Both."

He was gentle, trying so hard to be gentle, his hands like the fine brushes used by archaeologists to excavate anything that could be damaged in the process of revealing it. Your skin felt light: powdered dust and rock being swept away to get at some clue underneath. You looked down at your pubic bones jutting against your skin like the find of the century.

"I'm sorry," he said whenever he touched your leg or knee. The movements of his fingers were still dictated by all the apologies he had made to Valerie over the years. All the apologies he was still making.

"My legs don't hurt. It doesn't feel bad when you touch them."

Looking back, you could never have imagined the first time with anyone but him. His disability made him exactly right: narrow lower body fitting between the acute angle of your legs that the inflexible hip caused. Something about your bodies fit, though it was no position you'd ever heard of. You couldn't bend and he could bend too much and together you found a right angle. His wide angle and your narrow one evened to a perfect degree: the human equivalent of the Pythagorean theorum. This was a sign that you were spending too much time with Darren, the tendency to reduce human experience to a mathematic formula.

It was this, too: you were young and he was so much older and when your foreheads touched, your teenage sheen of oil matched the skin where his hair was beginning to recede, bright and smooth as scar tissue, and this was right. It felt entirely right, maybe because you were relaxed, tensing only the moment he entered you, or maybe because he came shortly afterwards, his apologies directed at you now.

When it was over and your nerves had calmed, you felt disappointed that it didn't really hurt. Maybe it was just the adrenaline. Probably you were turned on, part way to invincible, and tomorrow you would feel it. You'd read that some scientists speculate that the G-spot is natural pain relief, since the baby's head hits it on the way out the birth canal; maybe all arousal was like that. Mostly, however, you blamed the hip. For the first time, you felt a little sorry for yourself, as if the disability had taken something. It suddenly seemed a shame that sex wouldn't be your first big hurt, that it wouldn't be demarcated from all the rest of your girlish pains, that the hip had shifted your sense of perspective. Now that it was over, you no longer felt brave and sage in body wisdom, just a little let down. The whole experience was okay. You didn't even bleed.

Now, thirteen years later, you're surprised that you remember these thoughts and not the mechanics of what actually happened. You can't play the scene over in your mind, just remember parts of the whole. A leg, a mouth against your breast, Darren's face when he came, the expression reminding you of Cage Match.

"My God," said Darren as he laid beside you, "Look at yourself." You expected there to be bleeding, some mess, but instead he propped himself up on his elbow, legs trailing down behind him like something recently unearthed, bone unburdened by muscle. "You're beautiful. Just look at yourself."

And so you did: a girl splayed and displayed, legs slightly apart, breasts falling out to the side to show the high hills of ribs, pubic hair all glossy with light. You felt almost voyeuristic. Who looks? You thought. Who really looks?

Then you went to the washroom one at a time, closing the door. When you came back to bed, he pulled the blankets up against your naked back — it felt new and good to be bare against the sheets — and you flung an arm across his chest as if to keep him there. Thought: if I can make you come with one finger. Thought: if I can make you stay with one finger. Then he slept and you dozed to the smell of old potpourri in the quilt and woke too soon before it was morning to find him watching.

"Hey," he said and touched your eyebrow, smoothing a hair into place. This is a man who knows my eyebrows, you thought. My eyebrows, even.

"Hi," you said. "My name's Nolan Taylor. Pleased to meet you."

He laughed. "Darren Steward. Glad to make your acquaintance. I've heard a lot about you."You watched the freckles on his bicep, trying to map them into your memory. There might not be a second chance; this is a man you should learn quickly.

Darren made microwave popcorn for breakfast in bed. It was all that was in his cupboards and you imagined him sleeping there alone the next night, the kernels sticking against his skin to remind him of you.

"Did you know that slave women used to sew ciphers into blankets to help each other along the roads to Canada?" he asked as you lay with your head against his chest, hearing the churn of his stomach, his breathing settling against his heartbeat.

"Really?" Where your head rested against him, your hair grew damp. One ear heard his words, the other heard all of his subconscious rhythms and you hoped that between the two languages, you might almost understand. "They did that with the blues too. When they sang about my woman treats me so low, they were really singing about the boss."

You'd read that in the olden days, people read the pattern of blood a virgin left on her bridal sheets like a fortune. Perhaps you were shedding ciphers everywhere. This was back when you thought every mystery was really just a code, that somewhere beneath your confusion was an agreed-upon set of rules that you only had to decipher and everything would make sense.

Darren told you about a biologist who fell in love with a woman cryptologist during World War II, learned her trade to please her and ended up breaking the German ENIGMA code. You told him about school, some project you were working on and he told you about Caesar, the first man to use ciphers and said that the trick to cryptology isn't the message — which can be public — it's the key that has to be kept secret.

"Like in ball," you said. "Like keeping someone out of the key."

"Yeah, almost," he said. "I guess you could say that. Actually, that's a pretty good comparison. You let them have the whole floor, just not the key."

You liked to listen to his words, the language of him. The language of men. You'd read about how male brains are different from women's, how men's conversation patterns are different from women's, how sex is a profoundly emotional as well as physical experience. Lying there with him, however, it seemed that you were well-read only in the sense that Darren could read you easily. You were well-read and it prepared you for nothing.

Often, Tony videotaped training camps, games and practices and I always hated it when he made us watch the footage. I'd cringe to look at myself wheeling across the screen, every motion appearing to be incredibly hard work. I couldn't bend from the hip or the back very well and this robbed me of the swoop of arms that everyone else had. I was hunched, red-faced, and watching a clip always made me ashamed to wear the exertion so blatantly, as if my body couldn't seem to keep quiet about what it was experiencing.

This is what I thought about the next day at provincial-team practice. I'd left Darren's house early that morning when he went to work. I'd started to hurt inside and this pleased me at first, though the novelty soon wore off. When I got home, I took a long shower, skipped class, popped an extra anti-inflammatory though I didn't know if I was swollen or just torn, and spent the day playing all the chick music I knew: angry-woman rock though I wasn't angry. As I walked into the gym that night for practice pushing my wheelchair, I half expected my freckles to rearrange themselves into a pattern that spelled out my guilt, for the scarlet-letter sex flush to reappear under the practice uniform.

So I wasn't surprised when Sammy commented that my limp had changed. She was the only one in the gym.

I wanted to get there early to strap into my chair and see if pushing hurt too.

"Is your hip extra sore or something?" she asked. "You're walking funny."

"I'm a gimp, what can I say?" I tried to shine my voice bright as a shield.

She laughed and I was surprised to hear it, since I'd never used words like that in front of her. She was a class 1.5; I was a class 4: the 'more disabled than thou' hierarchy had yet to be established. "Fair enough, not like I'm one to judge. But you *are* walking weird."

My brain didn't want to tell. My brain knew that I shouldn't tell. My brain knew that wheelchair basketball is a small, small community and Sammy had known Valerie longer than she'd known me. My brain knew all this and yet I was crying, unable to stop.

"What?" asked Sammy. "What, Nole?" For the first time, she said my name right, without the 'oh Nolan' sigh.

"I'm fine," I said. "I'm sorry. I'm fine." I wished I was as fierce as Sammy: her cornbraids and game face.

She touched my shoulder. "Hey, hey, it's all right. Don't cry." Her hand wasn't soft but it was warm and I was surprised at this. Neither of us were gentle women. Both of us were teammates in only the loosest sense of the word.

"It's been a strange week," I said. "Maybe I'm just tired. I'm sorry."

"Did anything happen? With Darren or someone from your rec team?" Panic changed the shape of my face at his name and she caught it. "I meant a fight or something. But. Oh. Okay. All . . . right . . . then."

Sammy's not a dumb woman and people had been gossiping, but still I shook my head. She touched my arm and said, "Does Valerie know about this?" She didn't say it unkindly and I was almost glad that there was no point in lying anymore. I shook my head. My body was a decoded key. The message was never safe.

"Kind of hurts the first time, doesn't it? It's been awhile since I've done the hetero thing, but I do remember it hurting the first time. One more reason to switch to the ladies . . . " The beads on her cornbraids clinked against her earrings as she shook her head. "Kidding, only kidding . . . But, yeah, you're pretty young. I'm assuming you were a — "

I nodded, wiping a hand against my face and feeling the salt of tears sting the splits and cracks on my palm. "I'm not sore enough to cry," I said. "I'm sorry, I'm being dumb. I'm sorry. I feel stupid."

"Nah, you're not. I'd say you're more stupid for sleeping with him in the first place than crying about it. I understand the crying."

When I got home, my mother called. I was expecting Darren, so I let it ring twice before picking it up; (I'd read to do that in a magazine somewhere).

"Hey honey," she said. "Do you have exams before Christmas?"

"Yeah, soon." I looped the phone cord around my finger until it went numb.

"Because I got some cheap flights to Fernie. It's Granny and Grandpa's wedding anniversary, so we're going to Sparwood. When's Christmas break?"

My mother is from a town called Natal, which no longer exists. It was a mining community in the Crowsnest Pass right by the Alberta border, a twin of the town Michel. I used to think that it was spelled how it was pronounced — na tell, no tell. As a child, all of my Barbies lived in Na Tell, which was always either the past perfectly preserved, still back in the days of horses and pinafores, or some secret land like in "The Lion, the Witch and the Wardrobe." In my mind, Na Tell was behind the mirror, somewhere over the rainbow. I never imagined coal dust or cold. Never imagined that most of the houses were painted red because the mining company got that colour cheap.

My mother would tell bedtime stories of the grocery store with the grape pressing machine and all the local men dancing themselves stained in the vat on wine-making day. This I found greatly appealing. Food and mess. I was a skinny kid, always hungry. My mother would make cinnamon toast as an after-school snack and tell about the baker in Natal who cooked bread in a kiln and wore suspenders and how his wife would roll the dough in cinnamon and sugar and hand it out raw to local children who would smell the yeast as they passed by from school. This was before I grew up mouthy, wanting to be glib: all talk, no meat. She would tell me about feeling the dough expand in her stomach, pushing from satisfied to full. To this day, I associate the yeast stink of the brewery nearby the Fraser with being full. I know where people get the expression "bun in the oven."

She would tell me, too, about what happened to Natal, although it wasn't exactly a bedtime story. In 1964, a BC cabinet minister drove home from Alberta and declared Michel-Natal too dirty to welcome tourists from the

Rockies. That year, the government announced that the towns and everyone in them would be moved to Sparwood. By 1968, people were given an ultimatum: sell or have their water and electricity cut off. Wrecking crews came in and spray-painted X's on every house that was to be demolished and O's on ones that could be saved, until the whole town resembled some child's game, maybe some bureaucrat's game. People thought that they could go back and packed too lightly. My grandfather, who was a musician in the local band, left behind his prized accordion, planning to get it the next day. My mother remembers watching the wrecking balls with her first boyfriend, seeing the bakery go, the floury plaster churned up against coal dust, Natal going down violent as a birth. For this reason, my mother jokes about being pre-Natal and post-Natal, having lost the shape of her home before I changed the shape of her body.

"I don't know, mom," I said. "I'd have to check."

"Well, you let me know. I'll book you a ticket. You don't mind spending Christmas away from home?"

"Nah."

I could hear her walking towards the sound of a TV. "Talk to your father," she said. "He wants to talk to you. Ed, talk to your daughter. She doesn't think she can get time off for the reunion."

"Hi honey," said my father. "How's my little girl?" My father has always reminded me of a sitcom dad, his sweater vests and refusal to admit that I'm over seven years old. When I talk to him on the phone, he's usually watching TV; I associate him with canned laughter somewhere nearby. "Keeping out of trouble?"

"Keepin' busy," I said. I always said.

"Well, okay, that's nice. How's school?"

"It's fine. How's work?" He was a doctor, a G.P. with his own practice.

"Same old, same old, sweetheart. I'm going to pass you over to your mom again. She wants to tell you something about soap. Some soap she saw on TV. Like magic, she says." This is the conversation I've been having with my father ever since I moved out. I had it when I was nineteen and even now, thirteen years later, we repeat the script over and over.

After my mother hung up, I phoned Sophia, who was at school in Newfoundland. She loved the water but hated the west coast and St. John's was the furthest she could get from her parents without having to apply for a visa or pay American dollars. We often talked on the phone, though there was little to talk about. I didn't drink much, went out even less, and she liked raves and told me more than I ever wanted to know about being on 'shrooms, smoking weed with out-of-work fishermen, how many fingers her boyfriend could put in her. This was how close we were. Sometimes I worried about her, imagining her dancing with thick boys, their large hands and beer scent.

It was eleven PM in St. John's when I called and I listened to her trying to push her other friends out of the dorm room so she could talk. I heard them down the hall, calling for her to come out the bar with them, always somewhere in the background.

When I told her, there was silence, so I told her again.

"Darren?" she asked. "That old guy? The one in those pictures? Oh my God, you're like Lolita. Nole-ita!"

"Not that old. He's thirty-two."

"Nolan," she said. Sighed. "Nolan, honey, he has math-teacher hair."

I crunched an undercooked broccoli. "What do you mean, math-teacher hair?"

"Old, 1975-math-teacher, open-your-books-to-page-115-to-learn-some-algebra, boys-and-girls hair. It's trained to grow in a style that wasn't even fashionable in the '80s. Plus, he's been divorced, so he's crazy."

"He does have his masters in math."

"See? Exactly my point. And when did he get his masters? When you were, oh, in diapers."

"It's only a thirteen-year difference. He couldn't be my dad."

"Well, was he good? I'm assuming he's gained a lot of experience in the process of becoming divorced and old."

"Yeah, I mean, he obviously knows what he's doing."

"Not that you could tell the difference." She sighed. "I'm sorry, he's just . . . not who I would choose for you. Did it hurt?"

"Not really."

"But you're sore today?"

"Yeah."

"Gonna do it again?"

"I think so. If he wants to."

"I wonder if old guys have much of a sex drive. Maybe once will do him for about six months. Hey, isn't he, like, a paraplegic? Can they . . . you know?"

"He's a walking quad."

"How can you be a quad and still walk? Where do you meet these people?"

"His break's incomplete, so part of his spinal cord wasn't severed, which means he seems fine in the sex department . . . I think it depends from person to person . . . I know some paras who are real sluts, but that doesn't mean they can . . . You know, I don't remember being this critical when you made out with that thirty-something fisherman guy who gave you weed."

She laughed. "Touché, but I didn't sleep with him. Oh, Nolita, Nolita. Listen, I have to go. I'll call you tomorrow. I'll be more supportive when I'm feeling sorry for myself about a bad hangover. Tends to soften me a bit. I love you, babe, even if you do have shitty taste in men."

I'm sure that during those weeks, I did more than spend time with Darren. True, my life was scheduled between workouts and he was usually a part of those, but there was school. I moved through the hallways dreamy, as if drugged by the scent of sex. The act had gotten into my lungs like nerve gas and each word felt sticky as I spoke it.

It wasn't love — maybe it was, maybe it wasn't, probably it wasn't — just that my body had mutinied. In history class, I sat in the back row, chatting with Quinn and his collection of friends: girls whose smiles glinted with metal, skinny boys wearing all black. During lectures, I tried out the idea over and over again in my mind. I had sex. I. Had. Sex. With Darren. I may do so again. My notes were an odd collection of facts and opinions lacking context. *In 1856, the war started. Cartesian Dualism unsolved. CocaCola-fication of the world instead of armies.*

Throughout class, I stared at the boys in khaki, the girls with frizzy hair and sweatshirts, the bar stars and blondes with thongs visible above their low-cut jeans and wondered how many of them had been laid and how they ever managed to hide it. I couldn't imagine most of them nude, not even Quinn. He sat beside me, drawing caricatures in the margins of my notebook between copying notes in his own. As he squinted to copy down the prof's handwriting on the whiteboard, I watched him: his jawbone, the crook of his nose, his eyebrows, which were scant, lighter than the rest of his hair, just enough to mark out the ridge of bone there. And the scar on his left ear, which I would later learn he got as a kid falling through a sliding glass door. It healed smooth as soapstone, as if someone had sanded away the curve.

Quinn leaned over and scrawled a doodle of our prof's head on a Rambo body, writing a speech bubble that said, "Life is futile and meaningless. Surrender to an alternate conception of reality or you shall be destroyed," then, "The Post-Modernator demands your presence at The Pit for a night of punk-rock debauchery. 7:30 tomorrow."

I smiled and wrote, "Love to, but I may have plans. If I'm free, I'll be there."

"Any groupie-like behaviour will be rewarded with nachos and pints."

"Do I have to throw my bra on stage? They cost good money."

"No, no, your charming host for the evening — that's me! — will be happy just to see the bra still on your body."

I stared at the black ink on the white paper and was pleased by the simplicity of it. I didn't have to guess what he wanted. It was refreshing to be around a guy who could smile without being sardonic.

9

QUINN:

What I'm missing: scale, perspective. I don't know why I thought this whole deal would be small. Maybe I only understood the procedure, (saw the bone, replace it, in and out), and not the recovery, (tubes, quiet, machines the only noise).

Nolan's still and it's a bit freaky. Linda more than makes up for it — must have been those cigarettes — she hasn't stopped moving since she got in the door. Up and down in the chair. Outside for a smoke. Pace around the waiting room. And drumming her fingers on whatever hard surface she can find. You could mistake the sound she taps on the side of the bed for deliberate music. Some childhood lullaby, maybe, but it's too fast. Linda paces, adjusts tubes, touches her arm as if to make sure that she's still warm. She is. When I held her wrist, I felt her heartbeat, though maybe it was my own. Not sure how to check a pulse.

Nolan's still and Nolan's never still. Even in bed she's a thrasher: fights the blankets, sometimes me. She's the master of the midnight kidney shot. But now the nurses have posed her deliberately. I think Snow White, Sleeping Beauty. It's only when I see the machines that I understand. It's good to know the names and I'm glad I accompanied Nolan on the pre-tour: PCA dispenser, Incentive Spirometer, Continuous Passive Motion Machine. Here's her heart rate, there's her blood pressure. Her heartbeat through that little box is the best music, my new favourite song.

At the office, I crossed one leg then the other, tapped the pen on the table, flipped the charts. Her hip seizes after fifteen minutes spent in one location and my body repeated the process. A last-ditch attempt at sympathy pains. Nolan's still and I inherited her pacing.

"McLeod," said my boss, determined not to use my first name. "Is something the matter?"

"My wife's having some pretty major surgery," I told him. She goes under and now I'm using the word 'wife.' Like when a guy you hardly know dies and suddenly he was your good buddy.

"Why aren't you with her?" Eyes doing a great imitation of concern for the benefit of the big wig at the head of the table.

"Because you told me I couldn't have the time off if I wanted the job, which I need," I said. That was the wrong move. Well, fuck, it's the truth, though I guess I could have pressed it, taken a family day or whatever it's called. But hours in the hospital . . . that smell . . . the possibility she might cry. Not that she would. Nolan doesn't cry unless it's for basketball. I mean, she'll be unconscious for most of it anyhow.

And now, Nolan: still. Her fairytale blonde hair: Rapunzel, Rapunzel. Arms at her side in a way she never sleeps. Her heartbeat loops through those machines and mine's erratic from caffeine, nicotine, pacing. It's not that I don't have rhythm. I do, it's just not like anyone else's. Mike and them would ride my ass all the time during rehearsal. What time signature are you in? Hey Quinn, one and two and three and four and. If you can't match someone else's rhythm, you'll always play alone, my man. Come on. Say it with me now. One and two and three and four and. One-e and a two-e and a three-e and a four-e.

I take deep breaths, want a smoke, try to slow my heartbeat to match hers. One and two and three and four and.

~

Maybe you thought that such a large physical change would translate into one in the mind: metallic logic grafted onto your bones, that the anaesthesia would dredge up the kind of clarity that eludes you in waking life. This, you realize now, is too much to expect of cobalt-chrome and sutures. Not enough of your body has been replaced and, regardless of all the sports clichés you know, doctors can't make nerves of steel yet. Instead, you come to feeling as if everything is a complex math equation and you're trying to solve for both x and y: maybe 'ex' and 'why.' This is why you like music, the simplicity of its math: only so many octaves, so many frets to work with, only so far your fingers can go.

When your eyes finally open, there are two blurred shapes standing over you. Every cell feels shrunken and puckered as a dried-up contact lens. You wait for your vision to click, for the two figures to congeal into one, but it doesn't happen. Most likely, this is some sort of recovery area, since a nurse is immediately on-hand to read all the charts, machines, and vital signs. You try to decipher them, but can't focus, don't have a scale to place the numbers on even if you did know what normal is. She smells of breath mints and latex gloves, bends down and becomes clearer than the two figures who talk incomprehensibly.

"Good evening Ms. Taylor," she says. "You're up. I'm going to need you to rate your pain on a scale of one to ten, ten being greatest you can imagine."

It's hard to scan your body, let alone rate it on such a scale. Pain is slippery; it's hard to pin down and dissect. You want to ask if we're talking broken-arm pain or broken-heart pain — all these categories are blurring and it's important to be clear on your terms — but someone in a bed next door cries out and the nurse says, "Hold that thought, sweetie. I'll be right back. You spend some time with your family," and disappears.

"Hey, honey," says the first shape and of course it's Quinn and he's made it, he's here and you're glad. His palm is damp when he takes your hand — moist and cool — and you're so parched that you want to absorb him through all the prophetic lines on your palms, the connection between you and IV. When your grandmother first met him, she called him a "tall drink of water," and now you know what she meant, though you still have the height advantage.

"You were under for a long time," says your mother. She's come despite your wishes but you can't manage to be angry at her. Speaking is impossible; your body is separated into you and I — x and y, maybe — and doesn't obey. Nausea bubbles up, causing you to retch and another nurse to bring a metal pan in the shape of a half-moon, curved like an organ. You can't help but think in terms of flesh recast in metal.

The pan is cool against your cheek and Quinn says, "Oh, honey. Oh, you're sick," and maybe he won't be so bad at this caregiving, caretaking thing after all because he's taking care not to tangle the IV or the tube of oxygen in your nose or let bile get in your hair. Your mother says, "There, there," and she, too, strokes your face and you think 'where? Where?' which reminds you about the hip, the change, and you try to locate the exact spot where the surgery occurred, but your drugged body is imprecise and determining what you feel is like catching leaves out of a fast-moving river.

The new nurse smells of baby powder and you wonder what ward she is fresh from. She smiles, says, "Ms. Taylor, you did very well," and you're not sure if she's talking about the surgery or the vomiting, neither of which you had much control over. "I'm going to leave this pan here in case you get sick again." The metal fits perfectly against the curve of your face. It rests at the temple and through it you feel your heartbeat, as if it is a conch shell and the ocean is nearby. Still, this shifting, this sense of travel.

"So," says Quinn. "How does it feel to be part brand new?" Though he's still holding your hand, he's beyond your line of vision.

"Like the worst hangover ever," you say. Think you say. Your mouth is dried and unreliable.

The nurse brings ice in a Dixie cup. "Now then," she says. "Did you think about rating your pain?"

"I don't know. It's a bit hard to — It's not like the Richter Scale or anything. I don't know. Eight point three?" You wish there was some wavering needle hooked up to one of these machines that could tell you exactly how to feel about everything.

"Smart-ass," says Quinn.

"Let's just say four," says the nurse. "Does four sound good to you?"

When she leaves, Quinn rubs a sliver of ice across your cracked lips and you suck the ice and part of his fingertips, eager to get at this water. He's been eating chocolate; you can taste it along with the sustaining tang of salt. The nurse brings a heated blanket and you're swaddled — this is how it feels to be part brand new — and your mother smoothes it and says, "The hospital coffee is horrible, dear. Quinn agrees with me." So this explains the slight caffeine tremor in her fingers. It's embarrassing to be waited on like this. You want to say something hardy and brave, but instead allow them to tuck the blankets in and brush hair from your eyes.

When you close your eyes, it's easy to tell whose hands are whose. Your mother's are well-trained by years of nursing many sicknesses, schooled in the ways of making small hurts better. These, however, are not small hurts and when she rubs your shoulder, it seems as if her hands are dog-paddling, trying to keep afloat in this new scale. Quinn's more tentative. He knows your body, its odd eddies of tension, the shifting pressure points that training brings. He's afraid, maybe, that you've changed beyond his capacity to help, though his hands are well-meaning, meaning to make you well.

"The coffee is very poor," continues your mother. "You can almost taste the gears in the machine, for Chrissakes, but the cinnamon buns, they're excellent." She leans over — her hair on your cheeks - and lowers her voice. "Quinn picks off the raisins, you know. For some reason, he thinks cinnamon buns are better without the raisins. Perhaps his mother makes them like that. I do have a recipe — from *Chatelaine* or something — oh, it doesn't matter. Remind me later." You picture your mother and

Quinn, their attempts at newfound solidarity, and know that they've spent the past few hours in the coffee shop, the gift shop, the waiting room. They've numbed their lower extremities in plastic chairs, forged some sort of bond over Reader's Digests. "How's the nausea?" your mother continues. "Dr. Felth said you won't feel too bad for today thanks to the drugs. It'll be tomorrow when you really feel it. We met a woman whose sister is having triplets. Can you imagine? Triplets? Quinn bought me wine gums at the gift shop when he went out for a smoke."

You open your eyes and see that she's wearing a silk scarf and a vest made out of a patchwork of fabrics. The scarf — its blues and greens — blends with the vest's little scraps and makes even her boundaries shift. In this fluorescence, her hair appears blonde again, like yours. You can smell cigarette smoke and you're not sure from whom, probably both of them. Your mother quit a decade ago, but Quinn hates going outside alone and can be a bad influence.

"Yes," says Quinn. "It's been quite a day." He gives one of those smiles that you can read so easily that you wonder how he manages to get away with them around other people. "Your mom's been telling me all about her experience with menopause. Apparently, primrose oil is quite good."

"Yes," says your mother. "For the night sweats. It doesn't help with the dryness in sensitive areas, though."

Quinn is a good man. Quinn is a very good man.

Then you sleep again and the dreams you were expecting from the anaesthetic come, though they're of no help to your waking life. Just fragments. You're riding in a school bus in Mexico. All the houses you pass have Christmas lights and these small points in the dark make the landscape look pixilated, like Lite Brite. You reach out the window, pluck the bulbs off passing houses and rearrange them into letters and numbers at high speed and when wild dogs chase you, you hold out a bulb still glowing in your hand and entrance them into stillness.

In another, a ferret breaks into your house and turns your TV to a home cooking channel and when you walk out of your bedroom, he lunges for your jugular and grows huge.

Halfway between waking and dreaming, this strikes you as strange. You'd hoped for some direction, easy metaphors of roses or flying, of walking uphill or waking up blind. Though you suspect Freud would have something to say about the ferret, there seems nothing to interpret and make use of. How can you trust the mind, its Hollywood illusions and surrealist plot-lines? How can you ever explain any of it?

And you have that dream again: Darren, the apartment, the baby. The atmosphere is the same — tilted angles, ashy light, twinned mind — but for the first time in thirteen years its details have changed. The apartment is your current house, and Darren is Quinn and the old woman is you, the way you look today. Not round, not white-haired, not even post-natal, since you're naked in the dream and the borders of your stomach are still defined by muscle tone. You want the old dream, the one worn soft and familiar. You have no patience for this new, updated version, this low-budget sequel.

Maybe that dream was stored in the marrow of your discarded hip and is lost. You can almost see it: a sticky film of memories over your organs, all the cells a celluloid reel. You've read that women don't compartmentalize their emotions the way men do, so surely everything that's happened can't be stored in the heart or the brain alone. Maybe each ache was really just an old memory translated into bone.

As you come out of sleep, you feel more grounded, as if someone has soldered your parts back together. Certainly, you can feel sparks, hot bursts like liquid metal stuck under your skin.

~

An unplugged electric guitar greets my return to consciousness. Quinn sits finger picking my guitar, I'm back in the hospital room, the walls faded against the colourful balloons and flowers on the bedside table.

"I restrung the Gretsch," he says when he notices me awake. "I'm trying to get the strings to settle. I left it here for five minutes to get a Coke and when I came back, they were all out half a step."

The heaviest of the painkillers are beginning to wear off and my hip, too, has shifted a few notches of sensation, feels too tight then too loose, won't settle.

"They came in to change your dressing. Did Doctor Felth tell you that he sewed you up with wire? It's so cool, Nolan. It looks just like a guitar string coming right out of your body." He strums down the strings and I can tell they're already out of tune, a pleasant discord to the rubber-soled footsteps and intercom pages. "That's how I got the idea to bring in the Gretsch. It's like they sewed you up with a high E string." I can feel it, too, a plaintive E-string whine near my incision.

"Thanks," you say. "You're good."

He looks little-boy pleased. "I had to do something and, even better, I was playing 'Stairway to Heaven' and the old broad who was beside you — she was asthmatic, would have kept you up for ages with all that wheezing — complained and got herself moved, so now you have a room to yourself. Don't worry, though. I convinced the nurse about the healing powers of music and she came around."

"Turned on the Dr. Love charm, did you?" He's wearing a suit without the jacket, his office-guy belly visible against the dress shirt.

Quinn beams. "Damn straight. Think I should bring in the amp and we can try for your own ward?"

"That's what I like about you, honey. Always thinking."

"Thinking or drinking? How come this hospital doesn't have a bar? All high-stress places should have bars. Like, schools and court rooms and stuff."

I stare up at the ceiling, trying not to look down at myself. "I don't know if I like you seeing me all gross like this."

I hear him lean the Gretsch against a table and scoot his chair up to my bedside. "Like what? The incision? I thought it was cool. Like the Operation Channel or something."

"All of it." The corners of my mouth starting to crack when I talk and I search for a glass of water. "You shouldn't have to see me all smelly and drugged-up."

"What do you want?"

"Water."

He stands, fills a styrofoam cup up at the sink in the room's bathroom and brings it to me. "Can you raise your head a bit? I know it's hard with the traction and all these tubes." I do so and he tips water against my throat. As I drink, I see my body half-hidden by a beige blanket that looks as if it's meant to duplicate my skin tone. I'm tangled in tubes: an IV, an oxygen tube, a catheter, heart monitor, as if all my complicated innards have been opened along with my hip and I'm wearing them on the outside.

"Is that better?" he asks and I nod, leaning back against the pillow. It's matted with hair.

"I'm sorry," I say. "I just feel . . . exposed. And gross."

"You underwent major surgery. It's kind of to be expected. Oh, hey, look. Sue and the girls from Edmonton sent flowers and so did the BC Wheelchair Sports office. That chick who works there called, too, but I think she's just trying to recruit you for some coaching thing. I told her you were a bit preoccupied. Sophia phoned from Newfoundland. I told her you died on the table. She didn't think it was very funny. Called me a little prick bastard, which I fully deserved, even if the 'little prick' part is obviously inaccurate."

"What coaching thing?" The mention of anything basketball-related reminds me of how little thought I've given to muscular atrophy, reduced lung capacity, any of the problems associated with being still for too long. I should be restless under the mantra of "a body in motion stays in motion," that science turned pep talk. When I couldn't remain in one position for more than fifteen minutes, my old hip was its own conscience, prodding me if I grew inert, never letting me settle. I worry that the comfort this replacement will bring might make me static.

"Canada Games, I think. Because you have your Level Four coaching thing. She said they'd let you pick your manager if you agreed to coach."

"Anyone I wanted? There's not much of a choice. People just want a free trip. Don't want to do any work. Hey, you think Darren Steward would be up for the job?" It's the first time in at least five years that I've spoken his name out loud and the words feel as raw and exposed as my body. I can almost hear the wound behind the name, but Quinn doesn't appear to notice.

"Do I know him?"

"He's from back in the day." I didn't mean to bring Darren up. It's as if my mental filter has been hooked up to a catheter that channels my thoughts outside, beyond my control. Maybe too much of my body is busy coping with the hip and has sacrificed other areas in order to serve its flashes and throbs.

"Oh, yeah. Yeah, I think I remember. Isn't he that guy you used to practice with at that church? That team with the politically incorrect name."

"The Handicaps."

"Right, right. The Handicaps. He was that short guy — like, shorter than me — who kept crashing into things, wasn't he? The one with the weird job and the wife who used to play ball too."

I look at the heart-rate monitor, all my vital signs broadcasted in blinking red. "Ex-wife. He was a cryptologist, if memory serves. Smart guy." If my heart rate rises above a certain level, a nurse will enter to check on me.

"Ah, yes. God, that was ages ago. Back when we first met. He was always a bit of an asshole to me."

I close my eyes, willing both my hip and my mouth to shut up. "He wasn't that bad."

"Yeah, maybe. I dunno. It was a long time ago. What made you think of him?"

The view behind my eyes grows complicated with honeycombs of light. "Who knows? Probably just something this stupid surgery has stirred up."

"Your mom's in the hallway on the phone to your dad, by the way. I think she's relating in intricate and explicit detail how she saved the day by arriving in the nick of time to comfort her poor daughter, who was all alone, abandoned by her good-for-nothing boyfriend. I want the record to state, however, that I was here twenty minutes before her. At any rate, she should be back soon." I hear him tuning the strings, the note sliding into place with the turn of the peg. "I'm going to suggest that she go back to our place and sleep, maybe ask her to bring back our foam pillow to make this damn chair a bit easier on the old ass bones. One more night sleeping here and I'll be classifiable. You want anything? The nurse said you could bring a quilt from home."

"You can go home if you want," I say. "I'm fine here."

"Nah, this is the life. I get to enjoy delicious powdered eggs and don't have to do the dishes. Once you check out, I might just come back for some pampering. I think some of those nurses like me."

Sleep prods me, its pull and push and pull. Even behind my eyes, I see the red-light throb of the heart monitor.

"I'm going to sleep now," I say. "What kind of drugs are they giving me?" I'm surprised by this, the moments of lucidity followed by sudden tugs back into unconsciousness. "Play me something."

"What do you want to hear?" he asks. He plucks the high E and then turns the peg, plucks it again. "Maybe something you could flamenco dance to? You look about ready for some high kicks."

He's right, in a way. I hate being tethered to this bed and all my muscles want to get up and stretch themselves. Maybe there'll be time for dancing when I'm better, though I've never liked clubs with their braggy shows of skin and coordination.

I enjoy moving to music, though. The night we took possession of the new house, I made Quinn slow dance with me in the living room. The stereo was the first thing we set up. We ignored the boxes — both the ones that contained unpacked belongings and the ones we were planning to use as furniture — and turned up Nina Simone. It had been a long day and we were giddy from the chocolate milkshakes we ordered with our White Spot takeout, from holding the new keys so tightly in our hands that we could see the impression on each others' palm. At first, he tried to twirl me around, but I couldn't bend enough to be dipped or to duck under his arm, so we settled for high-school-prom-style hugging in a circle. When I rested my head against his, I saw that his hair was powdered with all the dust our moving in had kicked up, held there by sweat. We were wearing the new house, swaying inside it.

"This is kind of nice," he said against my throat and I could feel the words' vibrations inside my body as if they were mine. "It's like I'm fifteen, but I'm not making myself sick from my cologne." I couldn't stop thinking about how the living room was ours. The kitchen I could see beyond Quinn's head, the hallway, all of it was ours. It was strange to own the spot I stood in. We stayed like that until Quinn stopped moving and I felt his body slump, pressing hard against my chest, and I realized that he'd fallen asleep against me.

Quinn's never minded dancing. He has rhythm, limbs that behave themselves. Even if he had no coordination at all, though, I suspect he'd still be a good sport.

Darren claimed to have no grace or style, that the only reason he was good at basketball was because it's a thinking game. Like chess, he would say, like cryptology, like anything with a set of rules. He would refuse to even sway to music, though his lack of leg muscles made him flexible as a dancer.

I only got him to dance with me once, a month and a half after we'd started dating. (If you could call it dating. If you could call it anything). That Friday-night dance when we were coaching at BC Games, the year they were being held in some snowy town hard-hit by the decline of the forestry industry. Crepe paper and balloons had been hung overtop of the 1960s institutional architecture and elderly women in safety vests served punch and commented on how music had changed since their generation. On the walls, streamers were gathered into limp flowers and stuck beside banners that boasted of hockey, lacrosse and curling championships won in the '60s and '70s. The banners went up to 1984 then stopped, as if the town had collectively stopped winning.

The DJ played a mixture of country and rap and we watched teenagers trying to grind to a techno remix of "Cotton-Eyed Joe." One of our players — a good-looking fifteen-year-old with CP — had two slim girls in tank-tops gyrating on either side of him, one for each crutch. Darren and I sat with our backs against the wall, feeling the music's throb through the concrete. He was trying hard not to sit close to me, though every few songs he would lean over to complain about the music.

I watched as Howie, one of the able-bodied players, made his way out of the crowd towards us. Darren liked to say that Howie's disability was his mother, who made him wear a helmet whenever he played and phoned me three times the week before the Games to ask how aggressive the level of play would be. Now, he was pink with exertion, his glasses fogged from the combined sweat of a few hundred teenagers.

"Wow, this is something else," he said, shifting from foot to foot. "I've never been to a dance before. This is my first one ever. I stood beside the speakers. I've never stood beside speakers before. They're really loud, but really cool. I wasn't going to dance but the rhythm just got to me and I couldn't help myself."

"If you've having so much fun, then why're you over here?" Darren asked.

Howie shrugged. "Slow dance."

"You should ask some lovely lady to dance," he said. "I'm sure Nolan'll dance with you. Not often you get partnered with a good-looking blonde."

Howie took his glasses off, wiped them, put them back on and looked at me.

"Don't worry. It's not hard at all," said Darren. "Asking's the hardest part and you already know that Nolan will say yes. Here, I'll show you. This'll look a little silly because Nole's an Amazon Woman and I'm just a little fella, but don't worry. Everyone looks stupid dancing. Basically, you hold one hand." He interlocked fingers with me and I could feel the scuff of callus on callus. When he dropped his crutch, the weight of his body transferred through my arms and into my core. "Now, put the other around her waist — " He dropped the other crutch, hooking the two good fingers in the belt loop of my jeans to keep himself upright. "And you're set. And you have the added advantage that your legs work. No swaying to the beat now, Nole, I'll fall on my ass."

The music ended before we started dancing, the female singer stretching the word 'love' out until it was more a syllable than an idea. We stood in the silence of couples letting each other go, dancing without movement.

"Well Howie," said Darren. "Maybe next song."

"Is this one good?" asks Quinn. He's fingerpicking some Led Zeppelin tune, a break-up song.

"Yeah. I like that one. Or what about some Lyle Lovett? What about our bottomland song?"

"Picky, picky," he says. "Okay, one theme song coming right up." And he plays "Walk Through the Bottomland," the song in my head turned suddenly outwards, projected beyond my body.

Just before sleep, I open my eyes and see that Quinn's mouthing the words and I follow along with him. *Sing me a melody. Sing me a bruise. Walk through the bottomland without no shoes.*

"Hey Nolan?" says Quinn when the song ends.

"Mmm?"

"That's a weird name for a job, isn't it? Cryptologist. You'd think with the crypt, it'd have something to do with death."

"Mm hmm, guess so," I say and fall asleep to the throb of my surgery — the rhythm a cipher needing translation — my whole body open like an unsealed vault.

10

THE GYM AT OUR LADY OF PERPETUAL SMACKDOWNS was being used for the Christmas concert and we arrived to find the stage set in the nativity scene and parents sitting in rows of wooden chairs. The room smelled of wet coats and pine from the little Christmas tree in the corner. With all the chairs and decorations, the church seemed mortal-sized. The crepe-paper garlands had already grown soggy from the walls' moisture and parents were fanning themselves with programs.

"I guess they don't need a half-time show," said Darren.

"Guess not. This sucks. I was going to get you to fix my tire."

"And I was going to give you your Christmas present."

"Special Christmas Cage Match bruises?"

Little boys dressed as shepherds watched us, their gaping mouths bright from candy, until their mothers hustled them away. "Nah. We could fix the tire here, though. You got a tube?"

"In my bag."

We sat by the altar, in front of all the candles lit for the sick or the dead or those needing remembering. Darren spread out his tools on the plush red carpet: Allen keys, spoke wrenches, a pump, tire irons. I looked up at the tapestries of saints, the stained-glass windows, the lit-up Virgin Mary statue with her palms extended.

"You can call me Saint Darren, patron saint of flat tires," he said, spreading his callused hands in a benevolent pose.

"I thought saints were supposed to be celibate."

"Hope not. I think they just need to perform miracles. And teaching you how to fix anything definitely counts as a miracle."

"Hey, I fix lots of things."

"Sure, you do."

"I do."

"Okay, whatever. Fine. Now, pay attention. Zen and the art of chair repair. First step: remove the popped tube." He coaxed the tread over the lip of the rim with tire irons and pulled out the damaged tube. "Be gone demon," he said as he tossed it on to the ground. "We shall exorcise this wheel, cast out its damaged soul."

"Amen and hallelujah, brother," I said. It was too dark to see the patterns on the stained glass window. The room felt like it had shrunk to the radius of the candle glow. Us in the middle. The smell of lemon polish, wax, incense.

"Will the congregation please open their hymn books for the singing of "May the Circle Be Unbroken," Darren said. He held the wheel in front of him and spun it to make sure it was true. The metal reflecting candlelight made its own stained-glass patterns on the walls.

"May the circle be unbroken, by and by Lord, by and by," I whispered in his ear. Where had that song come from? I had only the faintest memories of Sunday School: colouring baby Jesus in blue, a lady with big hair giving me a peppermint candy for being able to name the apostles, feeling guilty that I'd taken the answer off a nearby poster. And yet, this song. The church had drawn it out of me like our warming bodies were drawing the scent of waxed wood out of the pews.

Darren squirmed at my voice so close against his ear. "Look at you, practically a choir girl. Now, come here. Run your hands across the inside of the rim. Make sure the puncture wasn't caused by a rough patch on the metal." I leaned over and his fingers guided me along the circumference. Cool metal below, Darren's hands above, my fingers pressed between the two. "Feel anything?"

His hands in light: the ulna bones. The spokes. The few loosened spokes and Darren's mangled pinky. Some injury I couldn't explain. "Nothing to do with popped tires."

"Excuse me," said a woman standing at the door. "What're you doing in here?" The gash of light from the door didn't reach us at the dais.

"Just fixing a tire," said Darren. As he spoke, he took the new tube from me and pumped a bit of air into it. "We didn't want to disturb your concert."

"Well, I'm sorry, but you'll have to leave if you're not here for religious purposes," said the woman. She walked down the aisle. Reflections from the wheel turning in Darren's hands illuminated parts of her: a nose, an eye, the wreath brooch she wore on her blouse. It was Margaret, the church administrator.

"Come on Maggie," said Darren, "you know us. We're not trying to wreck the place. Nolan here just popped a tube." He slid the tube on to the rim, deflated it and used the tire irons to get the tread back on before she reached us. "And I'm kind of the expert on chair repairs, so I thought I'd teach her how. It's actually quite simple." It was quick and smooth as a miracle, though there was probably already a patron saint of small repairs, quick fixes. This was a job that Darren had done many times over and was only slowing for my benefit. I couldn't learn at his speed.

"I suppose you'd have to be good at mechanics to play a sport like yours. All that crashing around. If I was your mother, I would make you wear a helmet."

Darren pumped a quick burst of air into the tire. "Wouldn't want to wreck my hairdo."

"Well, yes, anyhow you really have to go. I don't have to tell you that this is a place of worship, not a mechanic's shop."

"No room at the Inn?" asked Darren.

Margaret didn't smile. She fanned herself with a program and the candles sputtered. "You gave me a bit of a scare. Sitting here like that. I'm sorry, but it's time to go. You'll really have to leave."

"Sure, no problem," said Darren. "We don't mean any harm. We were just looking for a place to sit."

I was mute, made my hands busy by packing his tools away. As we left, I turned back to look at the dais and imagined how she must have seen us: two dark shapes, candlelight, the stripped wheel glowing between our hands.

"Whatcha doing tonight?" I asked him as he pulled up to my apartment complex. "You want to come in?"

Darren shrugged. "I don't know. It's my stupid company Christmas party tonight."

"You should go. Will there be drunken debauchery?"

He snorted. "You obviously haven't met very many cryptologists."

"No, I haven't. Does that mean 'yes' or 'no?'" The windows had fogged up and all I could see of my apartment complex were little halos from the Christmas lights. Darren didn't say anything.

"So you're going to go?" I asked again.

Darren shrugged again, "I guess so."

I took my time looking for my purse and keys. "Okay, well, I'll see you in a couple of weeks then. Unless you want to drop by tomorrow to get your Christmas present."

"I guess you could come," said Darren, staring at the haze out of the window. "I mean, if you really wanted to. It wouldn't be much fun for you, but I guess you could."

"Do you want me to?"

For once, the car didn't smell of our sweat, the only spice in the air coming from Darren's cinnamon gum. He traced his finger through the condensation into the shape of a star. "Doesn't matter to me. Either way. I just don't know how much fun you'd have."

"I'd like to meet the people you work with."

"Okay. Well, okay. I guess that's that, then."

"But if you'd rather go alone — ?"

" Meet me at my house in twenty minutes? We'll take my car."

"Can you make it thirty?"

Darren sighed and his breath blanked out the star he'd drawn. "Nolan."

"Fine, fine. Most girls need an hour to get ready, you know. I'm low-maintenance."

"Okay, whatever. Just hurry."

"Listen," said Darren thirty-five minutes later on the car ride over. He'd been doing this more and more and I hated it. The tone, good grief. As if the wonders of the natural world were about to unfurl before my very eyes. Like the narration of a documentary. Listen: the hollow-throated thrush emerges from her nest and emits a rare mating cry. Listen: you can hear the universe spinning. Hark! The king: he comes. Long live the king!

For the party, he'd added a festive red and green tie to his work outfit. The tie wasn't gaudy enough to be funny. It was just ugly and I was young enough to have definition of fashion narrow as my skinny little hips. (Practically pre-pubescent hips, not the kind to be caressed at company Christmas parties). The tie bothered me all the way to the party, even though it was Christmas and I was supposed to feel charitable.

"Hey listen," said Darren, and turned down a skanked-up jazz version of "Oh come all ye faithful." It was music performed with a wink, like the saxophones were stressing the word 'come.' "These guys — the guys I work with — aren't very, what's the word? They're not very social, guess you could say. There're some things you probably shouldn't talk about."

"You as in the population in general or you as in me?"

"Bit of both," he said. I was beginning to think that the Little Black Dress was a mistake. It appeared to be a good choice when I took off my coat, but perhaps his expression wasn't good-stunned. "Like, okay. American foreign policy. You might want to tone down on the anti-American rhetoric. Some of these guys are Yankees."

"Yankees who like Bush?"

At the stoplight, he made broad gestures and I wished he'd pay more attention to his hand controls, less to illustrating his stammering. "No, no of course not. They're American, not stupid. We complain about him all the time. It's just — "

"Then why can't I — ?"

"It's just different," he said. "It's just different, okay?"

"Any other particular subjects I should avoid? I could just smile pretty and answer, 'That's too much for my poor little brain to figure out. What do you think?' to everything."

"You don't have to be sarcastic. It's the lowest form of humour, you know. I forget who said that. Someone said that."

"Fuck," I said, stamping my foot down like I was in the driver's seat, hitting the break.

"Well," he said mildly. "There's that."

"What?"

"The 'fuck.' These people are professionals, Nolan."

"Why don't you just take me home if you think I'm going to embarrass you so much?"

"Because what's the point of having a trophy girlfriend if you can't show her off?"

"Darren — "

"I was kidding. Kidding. I'm sorry. I want you here. I was just trying to give you the heads-up. These people aren't exactly in your peer group. Come on. I'm sorry."

"Neither are you." I looked at my reflection in the car window, pale and girlish, splintered by trails of rain. My lips were chapped, refusing to be defined by lip-liner.

"I'm on your team, though kiddo," Darren said as we pulled up to the building. He turned off the car then squeezed my hand, our bitten nails together, all our ragged edges.

The party looked like a business meeting, except that there was a red and green sign that read "It's Christmas!" on the far wall. This crowd certainly needed reminding. The men all wore business suits and most of the women had on office attire. One guy wore a Santa hat. No one had the part James Bond, part Einstein look I imagined whenever I thought of cryptologists. A conference table by the far wall contained a tray of store-bought cupcakes, a bowl of potato chips and half a shrimp ring. Beside it was a garbage can with a bow on it filled with ice and bottles of beer.

"And this must be the lovely Valerie," said the guy in the Santa hat as he wandered over to us. He was the only one who wouldn't have fit in on Wall Street: shaggy hair, a hemp necklace, beer in one hand, cupcake in the other, and a blob of red icing on his nose. "I'm Rudolph," he noted, pointing to the icing. "You know. The red nosed reindeer." He attempted to shake my hand, realized both were full and shrugged. "Hi."

"When he's not playing reindeer, he's known by his alias, Ken. Ken, this is Nolan. She plays basketball on my team," Darren said.

Ken snorted. "'Basketball' on your 'team,' eh?" He appeared to be of the school of humour that believes that anything can be made sexual, and therefore amusing, by putting quotations around choice words.

"Yeah," said Darren. "My rec league."

"Your 'rec league,' eh? I bet you're sure doing some wreckin'. Hey? Aren't ya? Old Rudolph knows some reindeer games when he sees them." He gave Darren a hearty pat on the back. "Good on ya, Stewie. Didn't think you had it in ya."

"He calls me Stewie because of my last name," Darren noted as he absorbed the impact of Ken's backslap with his crutches. "Nolan and I are friends. She didn't have anything to do tonight, so I thought I'd keep her busy."

He keeps me 'busy' all night long, I wanted to say, but instead nodded.

"Stewie," I said. "Good name. I'll have to use that."

"You're a tall one, aren't you?" Ken asked me.

I looked down at myself. "Wow, you're right. I am tall. Those human growth hormones must be kicking in."

I could see Darren cringe. "Ken's in media relations."

Ken nodded, the blob of icing sliding down his nose to his cheek. "I like to tell people it's another form of code. I'm probably doing more encryption that the whole lot of you put together. Business-ese. I speak it well."

"Nolan and I are going to go get a beer," said Darren. "Or rather, I'll have a beer. She'll have a Coke so I can get sauced."

"Sure it's not because she's under legal age?" asked Ken, chuckling as he wandered off.

An hour later, Darren was standing in a little knot of men discussing something to do with his trade, his face a festive shade of alcohol-induced red. His tie bobbed up and down as he gestured and the men gestured back and every so often someone would exclaim, "One fellowship posting and he thinks he's the king of fucking England!" or "Damn straight! Preach it, brother!" or "So, I told him, 'you call that an algorithm?'"

"That's a cute dress," said a woman who was suddenly beside me along with four or five of her friends. She was plump and had a lacy blouse that made her look like a potpourri sachet. The scent of wine and Chanel added to the effect. "It looks like something you would wear, what does my daughter call it? Out 'clubbing'. Or to the 'raves.' Is that what they call them? Raves?"

"I'm probably not showing enough skin to go clubbing," I said, touching the high neckline of the dress. I tried to dull the edge out of my smile.

The woman gave me a kids-these-days expression. "I'm guessing you're not an employee?" At least this was a code I could speak.

"I'm here with a friend."

The woman smiled. "Would that friend be Darren Steward? Of javascript securities fame?" I hadn't known that: javascript.

I nodded.

"You must be Valerie, then." Clearly, I needed a name tag that read "Hello: my name is Not Valerie." "Hello: my name is The Much-Younger, Scandalous New Girlfriend."

Or maybe I just needed to be sleeping with someone who wasn't embarrassed to be seen with me.

"I'm Nolan," I said, trying to remain in the Christmas spirit. "Darren and I play basketball together."

All three women smiled at once. They looked like toy nutcrackers opening, their smiles were so wide. "Ah," said one. "I see. Don't you get your toes run over by the wheelchair?"

"I'm sorry, but isn't that mean to the people in wheelchairs?" asked another. "Couldn't you just take the ball and run with it?"

Wheelchair basketball was something I could talk about. Able-bodied participation in disabled sports? No problem. Classification system? Got it covered. The formal name for what Darren and I were? No clue. I was still a secret and didn't really mind. Of course I would be Darren's secret. He was a cryptologist, for Christ's sake. He dealt in secrets. Besides, the idea of keeping our relationship under wraps appealed to me. It has a certain romance-novel, movie-of-the-week flair to it that made me feel darker, curvier even: as if I was a film-noir girl waiting under a streetlight for a man in a trench coat, smoking a long cigarette that screamed 'phallic symbol.'

People only keep secret information that they care about, I reasoned. Secrets were important. Secrets were kept.

The air outside was swollen with the prospect of snow as Darren and I walked to the car.

"Okay, so you give me a run-down on what I'm allowed to talk about but you fail to mention that not only have you not told anyone you're fucking me — which I understand on account of the May-December thing, don't get me wrong — but no one knows that you're not married to Valerie anymore? Explain this to me."

Darren was concentrating on not slipping on the tiles and I walked beside him to give him something to grab onto. He had the comforting, yeasty smell of beer. "I've been legally divorced for a week. One week today. Sorry, I didn't have time to print off the engraved announcements to update everyone on my marital status."

"But you haven't lived with her for over a year."

"So? That's not divorced. What if we got back together and I'd already told everyone we were divorced? How awkward would that be?"

"Oh, I don't know. Maybe half as awkward as seventy-five percent of the people in there calling me 'Valerie.' Did she never come to these things?"

We got into the car. I slid the driver's seat back and turned off the hand controls.

"And I am not just 'fucking you,'" said Darren as he watched me. "That sounds so vulgar."

"No, you're right. We're just friends. No, actually I'm not even your 'friend.' I'm your teammate."

I pressed the gas too hard and the car lurched. Darren gripped the armrests. "Jesus," he said. "Calm down."

"I'm calm. This car is a bit —"

"It's a delicate situation," said Darren. "It's just delicate, that's all."

We sat in a crouched silence, him cringing whenever I braked or took a corner, me gripping the steering wheel until my hands went numb. A gritty rain that couldn't decide whether or not it wanted to be snow spattered on the window. "Jingle Bell Rock" played and Darren leaned back, trying to relax into the beer he'd drunk, the carols, the *hush hush* of the windshield wipers.

"We're playing reindeer games," said Darren as I pulled up to his house. "Maybe that's how we can put it. Fucking Ken — what a guy."

"I'm not coming in," I said, handing him his keys and pulling my own out of my purse. "If you want your Christmas present, you can come over tomorrow. And I'm talking your Christmas present, like the one wrapped in paper, not your 'Christmas present.'"

There was a girl in my History class who I went for coffee with once or twice. Probably some others in my English classes. I remember huddling under someone's umbrella and being too tall, the rain dripping down my neck off the umbrella's tines. There were girls in thrift-store chic and a friend of Quinn's who wore cat collars as jewelry, who liked the same grrl-rock singers as I did. I remember bad cafeteria stir-fry, good chai lattes, a trip to the *Rocky Horror Picture Show* and after-parties for Quinn's band where I sat on a couch petting someone's frightened rabbit and some guy offered to adjust my chi.

I would meet girls through class projects and go for hot chocolate after school to bitch about the prof. Sometimes we would go out for dinner before whatever university play or art exhibit we were supposed to review for English class. But the conversation never went off-campus. I didn't know what to say to make them take me to the bar, to call me when they broke up with their boyfriends. We exchanged email addresses and never saw each other after the final exam. The girls I met lasted only as long as the semester.

Quinn tried to give me female friends. After our History final, he invited me out to celebrate. It had finally snowed and everything felt brief and shifting. The brightness of West Coast snow wouldn't last. The girl from back east didn't care but the rest of us were giddy.

"Think there's enough for snow angels?" one girl asked and we decided to drive to a field where we could roll. We were drugged by the temporary weather.

The girl with the cat collar was driving and Quinn had called shotgun. I was beside a girl who I remember only because she was wearing a short skirt and her knees were purple with cold, and a guy who kept cracking his knuckles. We were knee to knee, shoulder to shoulder, as if attached like paper dolls. Our boots left their mark on the cat collar girl's love letters and homework assignments.

We stopped for Tim Horton's hot chocolates and someone made a liquor store run for peppermint schnapps. As we sang Christmas carols, the girl in the skirt drew obscene drawings in the fogged windows, touching Quinn's shoulder to make him look.

I don't remember these people's names, what we possibly talked about. They seemed young to me, leggy as kittens as we ran through Queen's Park, fell and willed the snow to stick. It didn't — all we got was the mud underneath — and Quinn tackled me and looked for enough snow to rub in my face. I fell with him by the playground, the rowdy primary colours of the jungle gym and swingset muted.

"Say I'm cool and I'll let you up," he said, holding my hands down by the wrist. His hair was wet and I liked the boyish way it stuck to his cheeks. The ground didn't smell; my whole respiratory system was big with snow odour.

"I'm cool."

He pinned both my arms with one hand. "Ha ha. Very funny. You're very funny." He traced a football player's war paint across my cheeks with mud. He smelled of peppermint and wet wool and I wanted to warm him by a fire.

"I'm very funny," I said.

"I'm not going to let you up until you compliment me." His thighs kept me there. I wasn't used to men with strong knees and hip flexors. I squirmed, claustrophobic under his muscles. There was nowhere to look but his face. The falling snow was dizzying, the trees too far off. The short-skirt girl stood over us, her purple knees muddied.

"Tell Nolan she has to compliment me," said Quinn.

"Why don't you just let her up? We're going soon. It's getting too cold here." The word 'cold' reminded him. He began to shiver.

"I'm immune to cold," said Quinn as he let me up. "I'm Quinn the Eskimo. You haven't seen nothin' like the Manly Quinn."

"You're supposed to call them Inuit," said the girl.

"It's a Dylan song," I said, the snow melting on my eyelashes blurring Quinn's face.

"Right." Quinn stood to let me up. "For your musical knowledge, you have won your freedom. You got lucky this time, punk." I used the opportunity to grab his wrists and daub mud on his nose and he chased me past the short skirt girl. People were too busy commenting on the flurries to notice the way my bad leg dragged in the mud.

Everyone's limbs were useless in the cold, so the playing field was even.

The cat-collar girl drove us home, taking the long route. Quinn sat beside me in the back and pointed out the Christmas lights, which floated in the snow haze like constellations.

"Thanks for inviting me," I said as the cat collar girl dropped me off.

"Need some help getting out of those wet clothes?" Quinn asked cheerfully.

"Goodnight, Mighty Quinn."

"Was that a compliment?"

"A compliment and a Dylan reference. I'm two for two."

"And I didn't even have to beat it out of you."

"Okay, okay," said the short skirt girl. "Let's get going."

The car pulled away from my apartment slow and noisy as a train. The windows were rolled down and someone was singing.

11

THE PAIN IS LEAVING, MY MUSCLES working themselves supple around the new hip. Now it's only the mundane, humiliating details of getting well. A bath, for example. I wanted to wash off both the antiseptic and everything the antiseptic wards off, but I couldn't stand the thought of those nurses and their gloved hands, industrial-strength soap. Quinn volunteered.

"Are you sure?" I asked him. "I'm too sore and stoned for anything remotely fun."

"I'm not all about sex," he said, looking surprisingly hurt.

Hunched over the walker, I feel brittle. My lower back aches in the familiar pattern. Years of hip inflexibility have taken their toll, wearing the space between the facet joints away, amplifying an old injury. Some hurts can't be fixed so easily. Some hurts can't be repaired at all. Quinn stays beside me, holding the hospital gown closed, propping me up, talking to the nurse who flanks the other side and offers constant instruction.

"Walk this way," she says.

"If I could walk that way, I wouldn't have needed the hip replacement," I say. This is an old man's joke — one my father has told — but Quinn and I laugh. I'm morphine-loopy; he's just nervous.

"Make sure she doesn't bend too suddenly," the nurse continues. "She can't touch her toes or lean forward at the sink. And, whatever you do, don't leave any soap residue inside the incision. The risk of infection is very high at this stage."

"*She* can hear you," I say. "*She* takes instructions well. I'm sore, not stupid." Already, I'm cranky with the thought of dependence, remembering those days when I was a teenager and orthopedic surgeons used to look beyond me to ask, "Now, Mrs. Taylor, how's your daughter's pain level been?"

The nurse coughs. Quinn tightens his grip on the fabric of the gown, as if to rein me in. "Well, sorry," I say. "But really." Silence would be the better option. My mouth is unreliable at the best of times.

"I'll show you how to use the lift to get her in the tub. Even though she could probably get in by herself, we don't want to take chances." I'm not sure who 'we' is. Probably her and Quinn, a little union of caretakers. The word is right — care taker — Quinn's grabby hand on my back, the nurse snatching bottles of shampoo off the shelves.

The shower room is white and easy to wash. No mildew on the canvas shower curtain, nothing organic: steels handles, red buttons, levers and pull cords to summon help. Help is everywhere, easily attainable, and I don't want it.

"All right," says the nurse, after giving Quinn a rundown on the lift. "I guess you're set. I'll be outside if you need me. There's an intercom attached to that button."

Quinn nods, the nurse leaves and it's just us. The white room makes me forget the backdrop, lending the sensation that we're not attached to any setting, like the stage in some minimalist play. Quinn McLeod playing the role of Dr. Love. Nolan Taylor debuting in the role of the needy little invalid.

"Okay," says Quinn. "Ready to rock?" He rolls up the sleeves of his dress shirt and tries to tie his hair back with a rubber band. Though it's too long to keep out of his eyes, it's too short for a ponytail. "I need a hairnet or something. This mane won't be tamed."

I try to raise my arms to loosen the gown's ties, but the movement sets off a reaction down the dominos of my spine: "God dammit."

"Hey, hey," says Quinn. "Let me help you there." He stands behind me, sweeps my hair to the side and undoes the top tie like we've just come home from a party and I need to be released from some confining dress. I breathe, imagine we've been to Quinn's office party and my fingers are numb from cold and apple cider, our bedroom eerie from the pall of the moon reflecting snow.

The hospital gowns are probably more complicated than any garment I own. There are actually three: a blue cotton one on the front, an overlapping green one on the back "for modesty," (right, modesty), and a flannel overcoat to insulate me. Quinn picks at the knots on the ties and frees me.

"Thanks," I say. I shrug all the garments off my shoulders and let them slide against the muscles that are already retreating. I know that it takes three weeks for significant muscle loss, so perhaps I'm imagining this. I hope I'm imagining this. Maybe it's dehydration or the effects of the drugs. Quinn gathers the hospital gowns, tries to figure out how to fold them neatly and eventually gives up and tosses them on the chair. His fingers can play complicated solos, but folding a T-shirt has always been beyond him. When he has a big meeting and I'm feeling particularly house-wifey, I iron his shirts and he loves to watch me steam and press, steam and press. Maybe he imagines my hands performing such a job on his skin, smoothing away the wrinkles and imperfections. The sanitized air is lukewarm against my breasts and realize that I've felt naked since the moment I put the gown on.

"Ready?" asks Quinn, touching a smudge on my shoulder that turns out to be a bruise. How do these bruises get there when I haven't done anything?

"Yeah," I say. "Let's get this over with."

Quinn pokes my arm. "At least it's not an enema."

"Right," I say, and want to apologize, though I'm not sure for what. We use the mechanical lift, a sling that swings to one side, to get me in the tub. I know I could do it myself, but Quinn likes new toys: a lever to crank, a button to press.

"See, what I'd do is attach a small-block Chevy motor to this baby," says Quinn as he looks for more towels. "If you want to lift, say, a 300-pound heart-disease patient, you're gonna need something with a little growl in it. Know what I mean?" What he means is that this business makes him uncomfortable and he's unsure of what to say.

I've been naked countless times with Quinn, but this new incision, my matted hair, the yellow antiseptic wash brings out my shyness. The water in the tub immediately turns toxic as Fraser River sludge.

"Want to empty the tub and start fresh?" I ask. "The water already looks like nuclear frickin' waste."

"Sure. Nolan's bath. Take two," he says and reaches underneath me to pull the plug, letting the water swirl and burble back down the drain. As we wait for the tub to fill again, Quinn holds his hand up to my sore, unwashed leg, matching the nicotine stain to the antiseptic coating that the brief submersion didn't clean.

"I'm going to quit," he says. "I'm going to get those patch things and the gum. Can you do both? The patch things and the gum? Or do you have to pick one?"

"I don't know. But that's good. That's really . . . good." My mind feels shifty from opiates. "Any reason why now?"

Quinn shrugs. He leans over to peel the white tape from my incision now that the water has softened the glue. It comes off with the imprint of my skin. I leave so many traces. "Being here. Just thinking. I don't know. I was up in the nursery looking at the newborns while you were sleeping." He shrugs again. "I don't mean I want one right now, right this minute. I mean, we'll wait until you heal, of course, but." He shrugs. "I was just thinking. Just putting it out there."

"Okay, well." Underneath the bandage, the stitched incision is crusted with blood, the skin around it white and puffy from being covered so long. It's skin that wants to breathe. "That's a good start. That's . . . good. So you think . . . we should start trying soon . . . or . . . ?"

"Yeah, well, I mean. How long does it take to get pregnant? At least six months, right? Less if you're younger, which we're not. And then nine months. So you'd be healed by then, right? A year and a half?"

"Definitely, yeah." I've handled this surgery well. Why not get pregnant? We've talked about it for so long. It was, after all, one of the reasons for quitting the national team. "So do you think we should? Because I'm already off the Pill for this whole thing." I gesture to my hip.

Quinn isn't looking at me. He's touching the stains on his fingers almost fondly, as if he'll be sad to see them go. This is assuming that nicotine stains disappear. "We could. Yeah, I mean, see what happens, right? Maybe this isn't the time to talk about it. How long did it take us to decide on buying that house? Three months? This seems like a decision that should take longer than fifteen minutes."

The tub fills and I'm surrounded by warmth that's impossible not to see as amniotic. Quinn turns off the tap. "For sure, for sure," I say. "And under these meds I think I'm not even legally allowed to sign a contract, let alone decide to get knocked up."

Quinn laughs, the sound escaping easy as smoke. We go well together, Quinn and I. Why not a baby? "Hey, you want me to take my shirt off so you don't feel so exposed?" he asks.

"Lean over," I say and unbutton the shirt. If I can't undress myself, at least I can manage him. His stomach, its lack of muscle and scant hair, is a comfort. The shirt releases the scent of cigarettes and soap and cologne and sweat and that top note of his skin. Quinn is the scent of home in this white, white room. He looks at me, his expression the absence of a witty comeback.

When the tub fills again, he cups his palms and scoops water over my tangles, anointing my forehead. In his hands, the drugstore shampoo and liquid soap are so much a balm. Even this water, despite its dissolved minerals and Fraser-River gunk, could be a salve.

I close my eyes every time he pours water over my head, each minor submersion. It almost makes me forget that he wasn't here when I went under, that it wasn't his hands washing the anesthesia brain-fog over me.

"Just pretend you're one of those ancient Queens who had other people bathe them," he says. "And I'll be, like, your cabana boy. Or man slave. Dr. Love at your service." As he applies the shampoo, he holds the back of my neck. His name reminds me of quinine and he must be the right man to treat this drug-induced not-quite-a-fever. His hands are rough as medicinal bark found in some ecosystem I would love to walk through.

"You know, I bet I could do this myself."

"Oh, don't start that. Think of the homonym in the word 'patient.'" Quinn is of the firm belief that grammar can be used as a pep talk. Life is a verb! Patient is a homonym! Now, Trying is a noun. We are now Trying. "Good thing you look like hell. I might want to jump in there with you and the hip would be out of its socket in no time."

I laugh, feeling the sound snarl against my bed-ridden muscles. "Thank you, Dr. Quinn, Medicine Woman. Okay, let me do some of it," I say. "I feel like such an invalid."

"As opposed to just a gimp?" He lifts his hands and I scrub deep against the scalp. Medication deposits traces on my growing hair and I want to scour myself to the root, make myself clean in preparation for Trying.

"I weren't still high on morphine, I'd have a snappy retort." I want this bath to give me back my edges.

"I don't mind doing this, you know," he says as he soaps my chest. I don't even flinch when he touches my nipples. His hand feels so much like my own that sometimes I confuse which is which. Yes, we have certainly been together for thirteen years. Yes, it has been over a decade. "And not even in a sexy way. It's kind of like when I saw you naked for the first time. Although, that was sexy. But, no, I mean. That same . . . " He shrugs. "I dunno. I don't even know what I'm saying today. Don't even pay attention to anything I say. I'm just out in left field. Hell, I'm not even in the field. I'm camping behind the stadium with the radio on 'cause I couldn't get tickets."

I scrub my face with the wash cloth, making my skin pulse with irritation. Quinn was much gentler than I'm being. "I'm glad you're doing this," I say. "If I have to be bathed by someone, I'd much rather it was Dr. Love than Nurse Perky."

"Dr. Love . . . On call to attend to your every need." His hands are red from the water and soap and the colour hides the nicotine stains. He wipes a hand across his forehead, leaving a line of bubbles. "But, seriously. If we can be serious. I dunno if we can. But seriously, I'm glad you let me do this. I didn't think you would." Scooping water in his hands, he rinses my chest. "You can call the newspapers and tell them to stop the presses. I was serious for once. Once in thirteen years. I didn't have a bad run, did I?"

The way he swabs the incision, so careful to avoid the metal wire. The way he knows my calf muscles are sensitive and says, "Is that okay? Is that okay?" as he washes them.

The way he uses his hands and not a wash cloth. We have been together thirteen years. My relationship with Quinn has never felt like years, more a series of small moments strung together. Quinn is ideal in short sprints of good intentions, bursts of time the length of a laugh, a song. And, yet, who writes a song about bathing their girlfriend when she can't stand? Who writes a song about changing her dressing? I know that in ten years, I'll remember this moment, not the long drought of time I spent waiting to go under without him.

"So, the baby thing," I ask as he wraps a towel around my shoulders. "Are we officially Trying? I mean, as soon as I'm . . . "

"I think we should," he says. "You're the most Trying person I know." He offers his 'man walked into a bar. Ouch.' grin. Then he hugs me to him, enough pressure that my wet body leaves an imprint on his clothing, as if he is an imprecise mirror. He drums a ba-dum-pum-shiii bad-joke punchline riff on my shoulders, uses me for music.

It took three weeks for Quinn to get bored with the business of healing. It was fun for him at first, the hospital especially. I think he liked the noise, the constant stimulation, the student nurses whose names generally ended in 'i' and their eagerness to help with crossword puzzles.

"As much as I'm glad you're not one of these girls," he would start many sentences with. "As much as I wouldn't want a girl like that every day, you know what I mean?"

"That's their job," I would say. "They probably go home and whine about you."

"Yeah, but they'll bring you jello whenever you want it. You better watch out. I think the one with the short red hair likes me. She keeps touching my arm."

He loved the new gadgets with their moving parts. The Continuous Passive Motion machine that gently moved my hip for me to prevent stiffness, the device that allowed me to put on socks without having to bend over.

"They should modify that sock thing so that really fat guys can put condoms on," Quinn kept saying. "I bet that would sell. Hey, you think there's money in that? That would totally sell, I think. I'm getting sick of the Ministry. Let's start a business. We'll call it PhatMember, Inc. With a 'ph' so we sound hip."

He showed off by doing wheelies in the hospital chairs. One would think that spending thirteen years with a disabled athlete would have worn the novelty off wheelchairs, but this isn't the case. When the kids of the guy next to me came to visit, he'd race them up and down the hallways, around the nurse's station.

"Oh, Mr. Taylor," Tammi or Sandi or Cindi would say, hands on hips, "What are we going to do with you?"

I would wonder what it meant that he so easily accepted my last name and didn't correct them that he's Quinn McLeod. Then he'd be on to the next task: playing poker with me for Smarties, serenading the elderly women with show tunes so that the nurses would let him keep the Grestch, getting coffee and cinnamon buns for my mother when she came. Quinn has always balanced an endearing line between arrested adolescence and ADD.

It was hard to get bored in the hospital. My teammates came by with flowers, homemade cookies, wine. The determined cheerfulness held up even when Quinn's mother, Sheila, came to visit.

Sheila arrived fresh from the hair salon, smelling of bleach and lavender shampoo. She's the kind of women who looks rich, but isn't: her yoga thighs and trophy-wife cheekbones. She was young when Quinn was born — twenty-one or something — and whenever she enters the room my mom puts one of my pillows over her lap and smoothes her hair.

"Well," she said, surveying the scene. "You look fine."

"Doing pretty well. Nice to see you, Shelia. Thanks for coming."

"I thought you'd probably have more than enough food and gifts, so I brought wine. My husband made it in our basement." She produced three plastic cups and a bottle of the wine they gave us for Christmas.

"You must need a drink, Linda," she told my mom, opening the bottle. Weird: the smell of booze against the disinfectant, both of them with their antiseptic properties. My stomach still hadn't settled since the surgery. "It must be tough watching your daughter here. When Quinn was in the hospital for a broken arm — remember that, honey? — I bit my nails until they bled."

"I don't know if you're supposed to drink in here," said Quinn, fingerpicking on our contraband guitar.

"Darling," said Sheila, patting his thigh. "There are different rules for mothers."

She and my mother spoke in oddly loud voices, like stage actors projecting from their diaphragms. Perhaps they were simply exorcising the memory of those deep-inside shouting muscles used in previous hospital trips:

gripping the bars of the bed with their feet in stirrups, getting us out and bringing us home.

I closed my eyes and when I opened them again, the conversation has veered someplace else.

"Oh, *yes*, dear," my mother was saying, "Our children are a *beautiful* couple. They age like *wine*. Just like *wine*. Like this wine, in fact."

"Oh yes. Like *wine*. Or good *furniture*." Whereupon Quinn, sensing the disaster of the Great Home Decorating Argument, steered the conversation back towards what beautiful, shining people we are.

As the visit progressed, Sheila and my mother harmonized Supremes songs with Quinn playing backup and me keeping beat on the bedside table.

Maybe next year we should have our Christmas dinner in the hospital: the pale walls, the needle cart passing by to put our problems into perspective, the furniture free of our stories and arguments.

Quinn:

"This place smells like a Brazilian grocery store," says Nolan as we walk past an alley. "No, really. They're called supermercados. The ones I've been to look clean, but there's this smell. Maybe the meat? They have these huge jars of bull's balls. The same with Turkish grocery stores: that smell. I don't know what they're called, since Turkish is a bitch to speak. I couldn't even pronounce 'hello.' Kept trying, even got the tour guide to write it out for me, but my mouth couldn't even produce the first sound. Like, physically couldn't."

Nolan may have sniffed the grocery stores on every continent, but this knowledge isn't helping her work up much walking speed. Two weeks post-op but we've yet to pass the old guy across the street whose fedora is so big that he probably can't see more than half a foot in front of his toes. I'm using him as our pace car.

"Mm," I say, "bull's balls."

"They're supposed to be really good for you. Nothing like a dose of bovine semen to get you through the day." She's swinging her arms like we're out for an easy ol' constitutional, but look down at her legs and you can tell that she's concentrating. "The way I'm going, I could use some, I think. Shit."

Nolan's retired and now the stories from the road are coming out. Did I know, by the way, that she was groped at a Turkish massage parlour and two obese Irish guys did the full colour commentary on her massage, thinking she couldn't speak English? I did not. Have I heard the one about that time in China when their bus broke down and an entire contingent of the People's Army stopped to push them into the nearest village's mechanic's shop? Why, no, I hadn't. Maybe the fact that she's either bedridden or slow-moving is bringing out the need to brag about travel adventures.

"I think I'll stick to Red Bull," I say.

"Well, you know what it's like being in a foreign country, how the smells are what assault you the most."

"Does California count as a foreign country?"

She puts her arm around me, more as a mobility aid than a loving gesture. "Sure does. That place's a different planet. You've been to Mexico, too."

"Yup."

"That's what we should do. When we come into some money, let's go on a vacation. We'll sit on a beach. A nude beach. And get drunk and sunburned."

Talking requires part of her concentration, so we slow down and the old guy passes us. The way she's walking now, I can't imagine us on any kind of beach: Nolan with her limp and incision, me with my desk-job belly hanging over my shorts. I know there's no reason to think this way. We're young, she's fit, I'm naturally slim. (The stomach's not that bad, really; a few weeks at the gym would cure it). Hell, Nolan's the kind of blonde who causes riots in dark-haired countries. And every man becomes better looking when he plays guitar. That would be great: a beach, my guitar, the surf and sky a poetic word like 'azure.' Cerulean.

Still, it's easier to picture us on a cruise ship wearing matching T-shirts. Maybe it's the way we're shuffling arm in arm. It's not fair, I know, and it'll pass. In a few weeks, she'll be out power-walking. It's just a weird time. All kinds of strangeness I didn't expect. Like, what kind of medical system thinks it's okay to send a patient home with needles to inject herself in the stomach with blood thinners? What kind of medical system doesn't take into account that Nolan might get woozy at the sight of needles and I'd have to do it, even though my hands tremble when I've had too much coffee and the first few times I felt a little dizzy myself? How can that be routine?

I'm not trained. I can't be expected to know. What if you miss the vein? What if you get air in the needle and the bubble goes to her brain? What if the tip breaks off in because you jabbed it in at the wrong angle? What if you measure the wrong amount? People talk about finding a woman you can grow old with, but no one says anything about the ones who make you feel like you already goddamn are.

~

It's been a month since the surgery and I've memorized the bedroom. Five steps from the bed to the bathroom, four to the window, twenty-seven to the kitchen. At first,

I counted this room out in 'one more step's, translating the floorboard into the length of my gimped shuffle. Everything required thought, conscious effort. No crossing my legs, no bending forward to get the toothpaste from the sink, use the grabber to reach everything; hey, where're you going without that walker, young lady? One foot in front of the other, drag the stiff, scarring skin, the bone healing around the screws driven like prospector's stakes into the marrow. All I wanted to do was weight train.

Now, I'm not thinking, just walking. It's been a month and too much linen and pills and that awful needle they make you jab yourself with and too long of Quinn easing himself into bed to not disturb me. Three novels, countless hours of television and so many chick magazines that when I enter the room I can smell the perfume samples. But now, my gait has worked itself pliable again. I healed fast, my impatient muscles working overtime to replenish. I'm fit. It makes all the difference.

We've been back to the doctor twice. Yesterday Dr. Felth took the metal wire out of the incision, grabbing hold with fancy pliers and yanking until the whole length of it came out like a magician pulling a scarf out of some kid's ear. He doles out pill samples like card tricks, parlour games. Guess which one will take the edge off. Keep your eye on the swelling, ladies and gentlemen. The incision is now a scar, neater than the old one. Better handiwork, more definite edges.

I'm bored with recovery and so is Quinn. And now, all the important changes are going on inside so he can't even chart their progress. No more putting antibacterial gel on the incision and taping gauze over top to keep the wire from tangling in the sheets. After all his talk, there was no nurse's hat when I get home, though he has kept up with the Doctor Love shtick.

("Honey, can you pass me my grabber?"

"Dr. Love will show you a grabber, baby.")

Plus, we're on to bold new health adventures. Last week, Quinn quit smoking and figures it's his turn for a little TLC. I have sympathy but no empathy. It's like dieting if you knew you could never eat again he says; but I've never dieted. He's never been under and I don't know what it feels like to crave something you can reach for but aren't allowed. Quinn needs something to tire his fingers. If I were well, I would buy him stress balls, chewing gum, pack little candies in his lunch. Instead, I can only listen to him pacing, tapping a Morse code or a blues riff on his thigh, looking claustrophobic and lonely for something people can't provide.

"You're driving me nuts," I finally said yesterday, reaching for his shirt with my grabber. "Come here." Least romantic pick-up line I've ever used, but still we have the first post-surgery sex two weeks before the manual says we should. I'm stiff but we follow the diagrams.

"Is that okay? Are you sure that's okay? I'm sorry, did I — ? Is that okay?" he kept asking. "Wait, wait, wait. This says the person who was operated on can be on top, but this one says no woman on top. Don't they cross-reference these things? Is that okay?"

I grip the nicotine patch on his back, trying to press the medicine into him quick. He needs a fix and I'll do what I can, but I listen hard as if my body is a new house and I'm trying to figure out: heater? Old flooring? Burglar?

"Yeah, it's fine. No. Wait. Hold on. No, yeah, it's fine. Go ahead."

The sex seems like a coed naked version of "Go Go Go Stop."

Still, he's cranky. Some nights, he just sits on the bed trying to inhale the second-hand smoke off Rolling Stones CDs or the old 12-bar blues he plays on my Gretsch. *Well, they call it stormy Monday,* he sings, *but Tuesday's just as bad. Well, yes, they call it stormy Monday, but Tuesday's just as bad.* He's so irritable that we're living the blues. I have to ask him to do everything twice. *Well, he won't bring me a sandwich and he forgets about my pills,* I think as he sings. *Yes, he won't bring me a sandwich and he forgets about my pills. My baby's quit cold turkey and it's givin' me the chills.*

I'm done looking at these walls, the room's scent nervous with the absence of nicotine. After the first week, I could tell he was ready for me to be able to get my own damn glass of water.

Now, though the doctor says I shouldn't try activity for another day, I get out of bed and put on my workout pants. It's early afternoon, six hours until Quinn returns from work. Strange that the pants feel the same, though my body's changed. Just a little workout, I figure. If we can have sex a few weeks early and do no damage, working out should be fine.

I could go to the gym and wander along the treadmill, but instead I decide to go to the Quay. I need new smells, the river with its every-day commercial transactions.

I push along the boardwalk just to hear the wooden slats underneath me, the sound like a card in the spokes of a bike going fast downhill. It feels good to be outside, wind through the rotting seams of a shirt I won a decade ago, drying the sweat that collects in familiar places. On the boardwalk, scores of elderly men walk very small dogs. Terriers and wiener dogs mince along in sweaters, though it's warm enough that no human needs a jacket.

I used to think of the next tournament, going fast, playing well, scoring. Now, I imagine those arthritic men trying to ease the dog's scrabbling paws through the arms of the sweater, their infinite patience as the animal flips and twists to escape. Picturing these images gives my mind an outlet as I push, as the old men stop to watch and the little dogs yap and the birds swoop low out of trees over me at the sound, their shadows brief against the pavement. I can't feel my hip and wonder if the painkillers are blocking some vital message. My hands are dirty, but inside nothing sticks. Perhaps this new joint is Teflon, cool and uninterested in the drama of my circulatory system. And yet the back injury remains: a little hot spot the size and location of a discreet tattoo. But working out, finally working out, yes finally working on the inside too.

This is how I used to train, before I got the training rollers. When I first moved here, before I'd even met Darren, I taught myself the city this way. Three mornings a week, I would push for an hour around a loop I found on the Quay boardwalk. It would be so early that the silvery scratches on my chair would glow red and orange with sunrise. Start at the tugboat turned playground, across to the waterfront through the smell of old vegetables and brewer's yeast, past the condos, the woman I saw every morning at 7:30 watering the plants on her balcony in her leopard-print bra and panties, past the memorial benches and the stink of geraniums, to the playground on the other end then back. Playground to playground, punk rock from my headphones an odd soundtrack to the plump mothers and gated condo communities.

Back then, I discovered New Westminster through bursts of scent and blurs of colour and people as I passed. I wasn't planning on staying. Still, I learned the city by what was left on my palms at the end of the day: what stuck to me.

Now I'm going slow, trying to work up a familiar rhythm. I watch a young couple dressed in rave clothes, who've obviously been up all night. They're wet — her mascara is smeared across her cheeks and his hair is wilting without gel — as if they've been running through the sprinklers that operate at every hour of the day in flagrant disregard for the city's water laws. It's been fifty years since anyone could swim in the Fraser River: can't be from that. Darren once said that his parents swam here as children and they were the last generation.

I used to pass children here more than thirteen years ago. Usually, I'd take a water break at the fountain by the playground and watch them run and scream. Those teens, holding hands as the water dries on their synthetic fabrics, were only three or four when I started coming here. The math is inescapable. At least the old people and their terriers and poodles still look the same. Same sweaters, too.

Today, I wheel through mandolin arias and fiddles: complicated rhythms that can only be performed with a band. Folk music needs people, none of that skinny boy with an acoustic guitar shit. My tastes have changed, even if the scenery hasn't.

I want to go fast. I want to make this damn place blur. My heartrate isn't high; I'm not too damp. I'm dumb to even try to work out and I won't press the considerable luck I've had thus far. It's the hip, the worry of wiggling the screws out. Quinn and I have been joking about that, me getting a screw loose to match the few screws loose I already am (ba-dum-pum-chiii), and it's stopped being funny. What's inside me now feels like someone else's property that I don't want to damage.

My hands are filthy. Despite the risk of slivers, I don't wear gloves. Never have. My toughened palms are their own form of protection. I never realize how dirty this damn city is until I see it on my hands. Still, I am moving, moving, yes moving, finally, finally, finally moving: my muscles smoothed from bedrest, new joint silent, grey shirt freckling with rain.

Before he went off to work this morning, Quinn said he had something to tell me.

"Shoot," I said.

He came out of the bathroom fiddling with the knot of his tie. "Oh, well, I have to get going. I'll tell you tonight. I'll make dinner."

So now he's home — with roses (roses!) — and I'm worried. This is clearly worse than his "thai takeout and back massage" errors: getting drunk with his buddies and not coming home until three, the time he broke my mother's antique Christmas ornament. Those, I could forgive. Could forgive instantly. Maybe this whole dinner thing is belated penance for missing the surgery, though the, "Who? Me? I'm such a good boyfriend" expression he adopted as I watched him cook, (wide anime eyes, no real-laugh lines), suggests this is something new. Come to think of it, where was the free dinner for missing the surgery? Quinn's worked up quite a tab in the relationship zen account.

My mind, which has been spinning its wheels too long against the *Cosmo* magazine and daytime television of my life, has had the whole day to come up with all sorts of scenarios. Could be that this mistake's name is Marcie, the petite little receptionist at his work, the one who can really fill a cardigan set and files her nails down to sharp points then glues a little heart or moon on each one. Perhaps that Lauren woman he works with. I thought she was a lesbian, but it could be just a cover. Though, come to think of it, she is married to a chick I've met once or twice — nice woman, too — so Lauren's out. But still, there's Marcie.

Maybe he's started smoking again. Fell off the wagon or something. Forgiven. Instantly, I forgive it all. Maybe even Marcie. Okay, no Marcie but certainly any other transgressions. Strippers, I can deal with. I draw the line at strippers. Or maybe escorts. No. No, escorts. Strippers, yes. Escorts, no.

Of course, chances are that he's thinking of leaving.

"Where're the matches?" Quinn calls from the dining room. He's banished me to the living room while he puts the final touches on the dinner.

"Try the junk drawer," I call. Quinn is not a man who lights candles unless the power goes out or there's a smell in the bathroom, and this whole dinner thing promises to have candles. Clearly, I've done something wrong. Too many crusted scabs and too much bed rest. Maybe I've become uninteresting now that I'm no longer training. I don't have a job. Come to think of it, he was appalled that I knew the names of not one but two hosts of two separate reality TV shows. What was that line from 'The Big Lebowski'? The brain is the biggest sexual organ? I'm atrophying. I'm quoting 'The Big Lebowski.'

"Okay," he calls. "Dinner eez served." The French accent is half-hearted, reminds me too much of French kiss or affairs.

Indeed, there are candles. Scented ones. I smell a rat. A lavender-scented calming-aromatherapy rat. The candlelight finds strange shadows of Quinn's face: places I never thought could darken. His hair is groomed with a hint of gel, though his bangs still hang at his temples. I can't help thinking of curtains descending, a show ending. The hip is silent in the face of this new fear. It shirks.

"I made omelettes," says Quinn, pointing to the plate, even though I watched him make it. An omelette is one of Quinn's only specialties. Mushrooms, ham, cheese, egg: four ingredients. Maybe this won't be so bad. Whatever he did isn't severe enough to warrant getting out a recipe book. He's accented the dish with frozen-food-aisle french fries sprinkled with some kind of herbal mixture. Egg cups hold individual portions of ketchup. Ah, my man. I could just weep. I should save the weeping. It may be needed later.

"Looks really good." I take a bite to silence my churning stomach. "Tastes good too."

"Thanks," he says. He's wearing a black shirt, maybe to hide sweat stains. "I put taco seasoning on the french fries. Did you notice the taco seasoning?"

"I noticed. They're good. You did a good job."

Quinn smiles, but the expression is quarantined from reaching beyond his mouth. "I aim to please." He balls up his napkin. Picks at a mushroom.

"So?" I ask.

"Huh?"

"You said this morning you had something to tell me."

Quinn nods as if he'd forgotten. "Oh yeah. Yeah, I do."

"Which is? . . . "

He looks anywhere but my face. This is a man who has done something very bad.

"Come on," I say, trying to be gentle with him. "Say it with me now: Forgive me, Nolan, for I have sinned. It has been two weeks since my last confession."

A smile fissures his nervous face. "Forgive me, Nolan," he says.

I reach across the table and touch his hand, noticing too late that my sleeve is trailing in the ketchup egg cup. "Quinn," I say. "What's her name?"

He blinks. "What? Whose name?" He blinks again. "That's what you thought? No, no. No, it's not a — You thought I was sleeping around?"

"You brought roses. How was I to know?"

"Oh, God, Nolan. No, nothing like that. I can't believe you thought I was cheating on you. Like I have time to cheat on you."

He stretches back in his chair, adjusts his courage and finally looks at me. "No woman, Nole. I quit my job."

I'm relieved. No, I'm upset. No, I'm relieved. (Wait: is he saying he would cheat on me if he did have time?) I take a breath, which tastes of the waxy candle smoke. "Okay. Right. So, um, isn't this something we're supposed to discuss like mature adults and arrive at a sensible decision after much consultation and deliberation? Like our pregnancy discussion, where we decided to become financially secure to — "

"No, no, I didn't mean to." He's talking with his hands, making broad gestures that threaten to knock over the candles and torch a place we can no longer afford. Between the body language and his words, I get confused. "See, I was in a bad mood because of the smoking — or not smoking, I guess you could say — and, you know that intranet server project? Well, I didn't get it and . . . " His hands make shadow puppets on the walls. "And, well, I guess I had a few words with the manager and perhaps I occupied his personal space bubble in a less-than-friendly manner and one thing led to another and I gave him some specific instructions on where he could relocate the intranet server to. So I don't think I'm going to get a reference from him."

"Quinn . . . " I try not to use his name as a complaint. "We were Trying. Okay, wait a minute. Just so I understand this. Come May, I'm not getting any carding money. No playing, no carding money. Once the new team is selected, I'm off the dole. And if you quit, you can't go on EI, yes? And we have mortgage payments and so we're . . . royally fucked, yes?" My voice is surprisingly calm and I hope he doesn't mistake it for a 'before the storm' tone.

"I hated being there," says Quinn. He looks as if he might cry. In these thirteen years, I've yet to see him cry. This is likely because nothing worth crying about has happened since we've been together. We have been charmed and employed. "I really hated my job. I couldn't do it anymore." Quinn has been miserable: the ties, the paperwork, the soul-sucking fluorescence.

I place my hands over his, silencing the pantomime of his gestures. The curtain of his hair parts as he looks at me. "I'm not mad that you quit," I say, choosing my words like selecting jewelry to pawn, like circling low-budget apartments in wanted ads. "I'm mad you didn't tell me first. How long until you're done?"

"I'm already done. I never went back."

"Where'd you go all day?"

"Nuffy's Donuts. They're licensed."

"And did you smoke your lungs out all day?"

"I smoked my lungs out. All day. And drank from 10 AM to 1:30 PM with a gentleman named Chester — I kid you not, Chester — then slept it off on a park bench and woke up to a little girl hitting me with a Barbie, saying, 'Is he dead? Is he dead? That's so cool.'"

12

IF IT WASN'T FOR THE STREET LIGHTS, I wouldn't have known that a town even existed. The buildings of Sparwood seemed to be just another surface for snow to collect on. The cold was different from the west coast. Gentler, somehow. It couldn't find your bones as easily.

"You're planning on behaving yourself, aren't you Ed?" asked my mother as the taxi dropped us off in front of my grandparents' house. "None of this 'Crazy Connors' business."

"Good as gold," said my dad and rolled his eyes at me. "When your mother got pregnant with you, Granny and Grandpa wouldn't talk to me for a year, until we got married. Those were the days."

My mother swatted him, then held on to his arm for support on the icy walkway. "You just have to be nice for one week. Do you know how much re-education I've had to do with Nolan thanks to your side of the family? 'Now, honey. Just because Grandpa Taylor says that black people can run fast because their heads are more aerodynamically shaped doesn't mean it's true.'"

"Okay, okay."

My mother winked at me. "You'll thank me the next time you meet a nice black man."

At first glance, I thought the far wall of the entrance room was a mirror. It was wall-to-wall with framed photographs. Most of them were people I'd never met, but there were some shots of my mother and a few of me as a toddler. I stared at a head-shot of her taken on her wedding day, trying to match the curves of her face up with my own reflection. It didn't work. I had too much of my father's jawline.

Nana put her hands around my waist in greeting, as if measuring me for a dress. "Skinny little thing, aren't you?" she said. "You take after me. Not like your mama. She has those gorgeous hips. I told your mama — I told her that if you give her a boy's name, she'll grow up with no curves. Flat like this." She slapped a nearby table with her palm. "Do people often mistake you for a boy?"

I looked at my mother, who was blushing. "Sometimes. When I'm dressed in baggy clothes," I said.

"Sometimes, she says." She slapped the table again and a collection of miniature porcelain shoes vibrated. "The girl says 'sometimes.' You need a sandwich." She put her hands around my waist again then turned back to my mother. "Ah, don't worry. We'll get some breasts on this one yet. Ed, put those parcels and suitcases down there. You don't need to strain your back."

"See where your mother gets it from?" my father whispered as we headed into the kitchen.

There were more photos in the kitchen, hung on a wall that had either been white or bright yellow and was now a dingy in-between shade. I stared at all the frames: my mother and her sister as babies, my grandpa in front of the mine, Nana holding up a prize-winning jar of spaghetti sauce. You couldn't look anywhere on the walls without seeing someone else's face. The whole house was a tribute to our inherited cheekbones and height.

"Sit down," said Nana. "Those little legs don't look like they could hold you for long. Let me get you something with meat in it. And you too, Ed. You're looking thin."

"I'm biking to work now," said my dad.

"Get your husband a beer," said Nana, and my mother actually complied.

Nana was skinny like me. She wore two sweaters in the house and thick work socks under crocheted slippers. Age had softened her, pillowed her bones with wrinkled skin, but she carried a wooden spoon around like she meant it.

"She is a pretty girl, though isn't she?" she commented to no one in particular as she cut thick slices of bread, added butter and mayonnaise and piled on the ham. "Do you have a fella yet?"

"I'm sorry?"

"A suitor. Are you going around with anyone?" She set the sandwich down in front of me.

"I'm single."

"She does talk an awful lot about a boy named Darren," said my mother. "He plays basketball with her."

Nana stood behind me, waiting for me to eat the sandwich. "Are you sweet on him, dear? Is he crippled too?"

"He walks on crutches," I said. "We're friends. He's quite a bit older than me."

"Nothing wrong with older men, darling. They don't need as much training."

"Oh God, mom," said my mother. She patted my leg. "Would you be Darren's first girlfriend if you went out with him?"

I took a bite of the sandwich. The butter and mayonnaise slid down too easily and my fingers left smears no matter where I put them. "Of course not. He's thirty-two years old. Plus, he's recently divorced. They separated a year ago."

"You should go out with that poor man," decided Nana. "Who will take care of him now that his wife's gone?"

"I'm not dating Darren," I said and gulped the full-fat milk to hide the blush, even though it was true. I wasn't dating Darren. We were 'together' only behind closed doors: the loosest sense of the word. It was more of a backroom deal than a relationship.

My dad stood off in a corner with my grandpa drinking his beer. "I don't want to hear about this," he said. "Can we change the subject to something that doesn't involve the thought of my daughter dating?"

"Men," said my Nana. "Darling, there're some lovely dill pickles in the fridge. Get your husband some before he faints from shock. It may be the new millennium, but men still cringe to hear the word 'daughter' and the word 'sex' together."

My mother and I were sitting at the oak table after dinner, watching the new mountains. In Sparwood, I could feel the border between BC and Alberta, the lack of humidity making my skin pray for rain.

"Looking forward to getting back to that little team in the church?" she asked.

"Sure. I guess so." I was stirring non-dairy creamer and sugar into the coffee I was trying to learn how to drink. I hated bitter tastes — Darren's gin and tonics, my mother's coffee — but was trying to adjust my palate. Coffee drinking felt like a skill I should pick up, since that meant coffee dates, which meant debating leftist politics and jazz in little cafés somewhere in Europe, wearing basic black and carrying my possessions on my back. Or so was the plan.

"That Darren guy," said my mother. "He's quite a nice young man, isn't he?" She drank her coffee so black that you could almost see the ulcer it was giving her.

I stared down into the mug, away from her, unable to see my reflection in the milky liquid. "He's not really young," I said. "He's thirty-two."

"That old? Really? Maybe I've just never gotten a good look at him."

I leaned over my mug and inhaled, loving the smell as much as I disliked the taste.

"So what's wrong with him?" She stood and opened a cupboard, as if looking away for what she figured would be a raw story.

"You mean the divorce?"

"The divorce left him on crutches?"

"Oh, you mean the — Yeah, he was in some kind of accident when he was a kid. On a playground."

That was basically all I knew of Darren's injury. He'd told me once during some conversation about his father. Before, I hadn't asked. Hadn't really thought to ask.

"My dad's just weird," he'd said. "I think he's probably still guilty about the whole 'me becoming disabled' thing. We talk about math and leave it at that."

He was five, walking with his father through Queen's Park. Darren Steward Senior was some type of scientist. In the pictures I later saw of this time he had a buzz cut and wore a tie even on Sundays, though it was the mid-1970s. It was one of his few days off work. I imagine it was Fall, like in those Hallmark card ads where there's a father and his son crunching through the leaf-scattered woods in boots and coats, their features pinked with cold air and familial love.

Darren says his father was never one for games that required exertion. His Christmas presents were usually gadgets you could take apart and explain. That day, however, they decided to go on the see-saw. Here, I imagine his father's geek-skinny body turned lanky with the task, his long legs propelling his son up higher and higher. Likely, he'd never made anyone laugh so hard in all of his life; (this is not a stretch. I've met his father).

This isn't my story. I wasn't there, wasn't even born, but I still imagine young Darren's hands against the metal handle, the link between ground and airborne numbing with cold. When he first got on, maybe he traced his finger over the initials and obscenities carved into the seesaw or written with felt marker. At eight, he was probably more interested in the obscenities than so-and-so's initials surrounded by a heart. I imagine all the love and hate messages blurring into pure motion: up down up down up down up.

His father could see that he was having a good time. Maybe he was remembering the early days when he would bounce his infant son in his arms to make him squeal and gurgle. Maybe he was enjoying the simmer of lactic acid in his calves, remembering that his legs worked. So his father went higher. Not too high, said Darren at this point in the story, just higher. And Darren started bouncing off the seat. It felt like a horse, he said. It was fun. He remembers laughing, maybe coaxing his father on.

But his hands were cold and numb and they slipped off. When he told it to me, Darren was only interested in the math, the numbers and forces that had to line up, the physics of it all. If he'd held on for half a second more he would never have played wheelchair ball, but instead he went up, further than the see-saw, and fell backwards. I imagine him going up, the wind lifting his shirt, filling out his child-skinny chest. I try to picture him like that the moment before the descent. He came down wrong. Landed where his neck met his upper back. It was such a small, stupid thing. There wasn't even the Hallmark drama I imagine it with. Just a boy and his father on some Sunday that could have been any Sunday. His father knew enough not to move him and sent a young mother running through the woods for the ambulance while her little girl sat by Darren and curled a strand of hair around her finger again and again; he remembers this. It's about all he remembers.

His father was afraid to touch him. He walks because his father wouldn't touch him. The paramedics put on a collar and strapped him to the board and because of this, Darren has an incomplete break and can walk. He's still amazed at what messages the break has intercepted, what strange, almost arbitrary muscles have been lost.

He has just enough function to walk, but not enough to walk without the brace on his right leg and crutches. Just enough hand and forearm strength on his left arm to use those crutches, but not enough to catch or shoot a basketball. His right arm is his only unaffected limb.

It was such a small thing: a see-saw and then the lucky coincidence that his father had taken first-aid training as part of his lab certification. Some people we knew were injured diving off cliffs or crashing motorbikes or getting run over by drunk drivers. Not me. Not Darren. Our big stories aren't big at all. Such small, small hurts.

Christmas came in the form of two plastic snowmen with glowing red eyes that sat on my grandparents' front steps like dogs guarding the gates of Hell. Nana refused to let my father hang Christmas lights out of fear for his bad back. There was an artificial tree that smelled of burnt rubber and impending electrical fire and every time my mother passed it, she would sniff the air like a cat, sigh and question Nana about replacing it.

"It's been fine for twenty years and it'll do for another twenty," Nana would say. "Christmas is about family, not pretty things."

"It won't be about family if we all die in a massive inferno," my mother would shoot back, which would make my Nana chuckle and go into the kitchen to check on her mincemeat.

There was nowhere to work out and I had no idea how to fill those hours. I wondered what people who aren't athletes do to keep themselves occupied. Since the semester had ended, I wasn't even a student anymore. The change in atmosphere made my hip ache: the weathervane of my arthritis sharp and reeling. I was forced into relaxation: lying on the couch trying to hear 'The Price is Right' over a continual loop of "Please, Daddy, Don't get Drunk This Christmas," which was one of my Nana's favourite songs.

Eventually Christmas came and the house was stifling from the pots boiling on the stove and the friends and relatives who came by. Their wet coats and scarves steamed in a pile and a teenage mother — some second cousin of mine — chased her little boy around the house to wipe his cheeks. I was sick of the noise and the heat and my Nana's perpetual attempts to administer doses of sausage rolls and desserts laden with whipped cream.

"Now who are you?" people kept asking me. Old women with blush like Santa Claus' cheeks, middle-aged men with long hair and overalls.

"Nolan," I'd say.

"Oh, yes? And who do you belong to?" It took a while to figure out what particular lineage they were after. I was Ed and Linda's daughter, Frank and Mary-Jean's granddaughter, the second cousin once removed to some guy who kept patting my knee. Most everyone in the room was related to me just enough that they felt justified in making suggestions on how I could get some nice curves.

By mid afternoon I escaped to the porch and its scent of varnished wood and snow. The sliding glass doors were fogged, the Christmas carols muted. I breathed.

I'd borrowed my dad's cellphone on the pretext of calling Sophia in Newfoundland. She hadn't come home for Christmas and I felt guilty for missing Darren — who

I saw nearly every day — more than Sophia, who I hadn't seen in months and wouldn't see until April. Still, it was Darren I called.

The cellphone reception was poor and as I waited for him to pick up, I looked out at the trees fattened up with snow, the sharpness of their branches gone. Darren's voice sounded sleepy.

"Merry Christmas," I said.

"What? Can you speak up?" The phone was staticky, which didn't surprise me in this place where touching anything metal would give off a spark. I imagined Darren's braces and crutches in this cold: the minor bursts they could create. The snow blanched my hair; the static made it fly.

"Merry Christmas."

"Who is this? I can't hear you. Valerie?"

"It's Nolan." I almost shouted. Nolan, daughter of Ed and Linda, granddaughter of Frank and Mary-Jean, second cousin once removed to some guy who kept putting his hand on my knee.

"Oh, Nolan. Nolan. Hey, you. Merry Christmas. I can hardly hear you."

"I just phoned to say Merry Christmas. How are you doing?"

"Bah humbug. Just like any day of the year," he said. "You coming home soon?"

"You're cutting out," I said. "I have to go. Love ya, babe." I could test out words like 'I love you' because of the bad connection. I hid them under electronic snow.

"Nolan?" he asked as I hung up, his words minced by mountains and rivers and cities and all the distance between us.

Darren bought real wine, adult wine, and taught me how to let it breathe. We were celebrating my return from Sparwood and the end of Christmas. Not that the season had actually come to Darren's house. His Christmas tree was a little Charlie Brown artificial number. It was bare because Darren has originally decorated it with candy canes, then decided that they might attract rodents so took them down.

"No mess," Darren bragged. "You almost wouldn't know Christmas had come at all. No clean-up, no wrapping paper, no leftover turkey."

"I like leftover turkey."

"Yeah, me too."

The windows and doors were closed and I wondered how the wine could breathe in this place, since sometimes I had difficulty. The odour was what I imagined dead skin would smell like. The wine tried to change the scent of the room but couldn't. Despite the locked doors. Despite the closed windows. Despite how the panes were so fogged that the rest of the world had been frosted away. It wasn't even raining, but we were shut-ins. The lack of air vents made me feel claustrophobic, since I couldn't see where fresh oxygen was flowing from. The rooms needed more greenery to compensate for all our wasted breath.

Regardless, I was flushed by good wine. Before Darren, I hadn't been a big drinker. Still wasn't, really. I drank when the opportunity arose, which usually happened when Darren bought wine with dinner or Quinn treated me to a beer. I'd completely skipped the "shared mickey of vodka poured into a Slurpee" stage of alcohol consumption and graduated right to this: glass held up to the light, Darren pointing out the top notes. I learned how to taste wine before I learned how to drink it.

"I think women like having sex with disabled guys because they have more control," said Darren as we sat in dimmed-light silence on the floor in front of the coffee table. The disassembled dinner in front of us — takeout veggie sushi with little tongues of ginger on top — was the one chaos in the place.

"Probably. Once they realize that disabled guys can have sex. I've been playing ball for six years and I'm still not sure how high paras do it."

Darren shrugged. "How would I know? Strap-ons? Really talented mouths? It's not a problem I have, you may have noticed; don't even have any sympathetic nervous system damage. All systems go. I can feel everything." He tapped his leg. "Well, not everything. Reduced sensation in my legs — the left more than the right — part of my pelvis, the back of my left arm and those three fingers. But not bad considering I could have ended up a sip-and-puff quad."

"What do you mean 'reduced?' What does that feel like?" I'd just assumed he had everything, since he could feel his Cage Match bruises.

He glanced down at his legs then took a last swallow of his wine. "Well, the message is getting there, it's just . . . fuzzy. Pins and needles, but not quite. It's like I'm dipped in wax. Or like I'm wearing a really thin piece of clothing I can never take off."

"So when I . . . "

"You should go harder," he said, swirling the wine in his glass. "When you touch me, you have to really touch me. You know?" So this was what the conversation was building up to: a performance critique meant to be gentle.

"I'm sorry," I said, since it seemed like something I should apologize for. "I didn't know." All these months with him and he'd felt like he was still wearing clothes. All these months and he'd never even felt naked around me.

"No, no. Don't be sorry. Here, I'll show you what I mean." He set his wine glass down on a coaster and scooted his chair towards me. "It's like this." He ran a finger across the sleeve of my shirt, then eased the shirt over my head. "As opposed to this." The same finger along the now-bare spot.

"Okay," I said. "Point taken."

"You try."

"This," I leaned in to kiss his neck. "As opposed to this." I sucked the spot, charming the blood to the surface, adding a hint of teeth.

"Quick learner." I felt the hum of speech through my lips. "But I can feel there."

"Shut up," I said not unkindly, and kissed him to make it happen. "This," I said. "As opposed to this." His lower lip between my teeth. "And this," I said, and then I was undressed and he was undressed and I wanted to make him naked for real. "And this."

The thought should have been funny — Darren encased in a rubber, half-body condom, the ultimate safe sex — but I was too angry at myself. All those wasted times I'd touched him before. I wanted to make him feel it the way Valerie made him feel it. There must be a difference between that and making him hurt the way Valerie made him hurt.

He wanted me to take control and I did, though it was like being asked to solo when you've only ever played rhythm. But it was something like a cure, me on top of him like that. The opposite of necrosis. My bones found angles that shouldn't have been possible. I played him harder than Cage Match. It was good to make that living room a ruin of shed clothing and half-eaten food.

Him pale in the frosty light those days when his living room curtains were still open. Me making full use of our height discrepancy, lording it over him. But it was me getting hurt too. I felt so much: my hand flung against the side of the coffee table until the wineglass tipped and I looked up the moment before it fell and shattered and fuck the wine, the glass was breathing. Every shard. Breathing. Our bodies struck like flint, the first fire, and beneath me his bones found no peace against the hardwood floor and I hurt him like this too. And I held his wrists down willing him to bruise someplace visible; I stopped at hickeys, just teased the blood but didn't let it stay there, the first trick I'd mastered so he could keep me secret.

The shards of wine glass made a landscape of the table. They hummed and bounced but didn't fall. But I watched that wine glass fall. Reached out to either catch it or push it over and touched that smooth, cold rim and saw it the instant before it fell. Before it was falling. And it was like that when I came for the first time: a moment, then movement; a moment, then falling in reverse. Little bird flutters. A light touch that made my whole body hunch.

And me and him and the first time when the Pill was the only thing that stood between us and pregnancy. No latex between us at all. My body making use of all my sensation and all he had left. My body showing what nerve endings are for, realizing what he was missing. The scent of the room changed, the house around us breathing like wine.

Darren lay beneath me and I reached down to sweep the hair off his damp forehead.

"Feel me now, asshole?"

13

NONE OF MY TEAMMATES HAVE SHOWN UP since the hospital, but the woman who works for BC Wheelchair Sports phoned, offering me both the Canada Games coaching job and another one in public speaking. I'm gainfully employed, but Quinn says it doesn't count considering that it's related to wheelchair basketball. Sports, he maintains, is not a job. Not at all. Retail is a job. Human resources management: a job. Waitressing: also a job. Anything related to sport, which is fun, is not a job. He's a recreational athlete and so believes that work is something performed trapped inside wearing some sort of unflattering uniform and sport is something done to forget that you have to work. My lines between work and play are smudged.

Besides, this is a public-speaking gig: preaching the gospel of sport to eager young converts. I imagine myself as some sort of waitress, a morality waitress dishing up inspiring messages with a side order of My Life Story, all shiny as hashbrowns. Not that playing wheelchair basketball is inspirational. I'm disabled. I play disabled sports. Really, it's less inspirational. Only ten percent of the population has a disability. Right away, that's ninety percent of the competition taken away, maybe more since a lot of that percentage involves old people who aren't going to be competing for your spot on the team. Had I made the WNBA dragging my gimped hip behind me up the court, I would be inspirational; (considering my gait, I would actually be on the verge of miraculous).

The woman in charge of the public speaking job phones while Quinn and I are reading on the couch. Well, Quinn's reading. I'm lying down with a cold cloth over my eyes. For the past week, I've felt tired and vaguely nauseous. Not right. My worry is that the new hip's become infected. Every morning I inspect the scar for any tell-tale streaks of red. I could have to go under again only weeks after I've healed. I could have to do this all over again.

The woman, whose name is Jennifer, is big on Your Story: How You Were Injured.

"I just think that you people . . . well, athletes like you . . . of course you guys are athletes . . . have a real message of hope and inspiration to give to the children," she says. I make a face at Quinn, who puts his *Guitar World* magazine down to eavesdrop. "Now, let's see here, the woman from your organization said that you aren't in a wheelchair. Are you legally disabled?"

"Illegally disabled, actually. On the lam." This was the wrong move. Morality waitresses don't use sarcasm. Quinn mouths the words 'illegally disabled?' at me and I roll my eyes.

"I'm sorry? What?" Jennifer asks.

"I do have a physical disability, but I can still walk. I have arthritis. I just had my hip replaced, so I don't use a cane anymore."

"Oh. That's too bad, dear. It's really too bad. When working with the, um, special needs athletes, we find that those who are in a wheelchair are much more popular with the children. Especially the guys who're missing a leg. Children love to see the stump. They just love it."

"We actually prefer the term 'disabled athletes,'" I say, since what I want to tell her would get me fired before I even started. "I'm more into giving a sports-related talk than a 'look at how disabled I am' talk. I don't actually have much to say about my disability."

"That's fine, dear." This woman can't be more than a few years older than I am. Dear. Fucking 'dear.' "I'm just saying that you'll have to work hard to make your message effective. To convey to the children what you've learned."

Considering that I drink Diet Coke despite the health warnings, have never gotten over my fondness for men with loud guitars and am still fantasizing about a relationship I had thirteen years ago, I'm pretty sure that I haven't learned any profound life lessons in my thirty-odd years on earth.

"I could bring a gold medal or something to show. I think it's important that people know that wheelchair basketball is played by able-bodied and disabled people alike. It doesn't really matter if you walk or if you don't."

"Oh, yes, yes. Of course."

I put up with the "dear"s, write down the details and I'm employed, the sole breadwinner.

"What the hell was that about?" asks Quinn when I hang up. His hair has grown longer since he became unemployed and has a Farrah Fawcett fringe to it.

"That job," I tell him. "Doing talks. That'll be some money coming in."

"Is it regular? Like nine to five? With benefits? I'm guessing no."

"It depends on how many talks they book me for. But, who cares? It's cash and we need cash, even if it means having to put up with the world's dumbest woman."

Quinn sighs and rubs the back of his neck like I'm giving him a headache, though maybe all that hair is weighing him down. "But it's not regular. And it's during the daytime so you can't get another job on top of it. One of us needs to get a steady job with benefits."

"And one of us is trying to make money how she can. The other is sitting around reading *Guitar World*."

Quinn stands. It must be nice to spring to your feet like that: to get mad with your whole body. "Nine years, Nolan. I did the nine to five thing for nine years." Ever since he lost his job, he's looked spring-loaded. He even lies on the couch like a fireman waiting for an alarm to go off.

"I know," I say. "But I'm doing the Canada Games coaching job too, so that'll be more money coming in, though not right away. I think it's just a per diem."

Quinn paces. "All stuff that distracts you from getting a real job. Do you even have a resumé?"

"What's wrong with you? I'm trying. It's not like the magic job experience fairy is going to come down and take care of the decade I didn't work for."

Quinn holds up his hands. "Fine," he says. "Fine. Whatever."

"And what the fuck is this about you being Mr. Sole Breadwinner for nine years? I didn't ask you to work. Until this year I paid my way."

"With athlete's assistance," he says. "That's not the same thing."

"Oh, right. Because obviously everything I've done for the past thiteen years wasn't hard work."

"I didn't mean — You didn't work for it with a job. That's what I meant. It wasn't nine to five."

"No, it was 7 AM to 11 PM." These are the times I wish I was completely healed. The dramatic effect of stomping out is dampened by my shuffle. Quinn watches me with balled fists. I go into the bedroom and ease myself down onto our bed. Minutes later, I hear the door slam and the car start.

"And since when does being in a cover band count as legitimate employment?" I call out, fifteen minutes after he's gone.

There's too much time to think, to spin a whole web of sticky tangents and connections. Time to weave enough rope to hang myself many times over. Quinn is like Darren because. Quinn is not like Darren because. I am like Quinn because. A woman could drive herself nuts with all these similes.

That's the appeal of basketball. The game's edges are distinct: a line that divides on-court from off-court. Comparisons stop. A game is like a game. And try as they do to draw metaphors, (game is like war; game is like love), they always fall short. A game is not war because no one lives or dies based on the outcome. No countries fall, no hordes invade over a lost match, (soccer fans aside). A game is a game is a game is a game.

At Quinn's work, they did teambuilding exercises, bringing in women with exclamation-point pumps to say a department is like a sports team and we all know there's no 'I' in team. But the comparisons fail. They slide right off. A game needs nothing to explain itself. A game is whole, a complete universe.

It doesn't work to say that sport is life's essential struggles smelted down to their pure iron, that they bring out all of mankind's strengths and foibles, victories and defeats. Basketball is this: five people on a team trying to put an inflated ball of leather or rubber into a hoop. In wheelchair basketball, no shot is ever heard 'round the world.

Two hours later, Quinn's still not home. Well, fuck him. Really. Darren's phone number is still in our phone book. I've been transferring it into every new address book we've owned, though I didn't think I would ever phone him again. Now I sit on the bed so nervous that my arms tingle as if I'm having a heart attack and one phone call can do what ten years of anti-inflammatories shown to cause aeortal damage didn't.

"Hello?"

"Hi. I'm looking for Darren Steward . . . ," I say, my voice high as if I'm much younger. "This probably isn't the right number . . . "

A pause. "Speaking." I wonder if he has call display and would call me back if I hung up.

"Oh, yeah, hi. I didn't know if you'd moved or not? This is Nolan . . . Nolan Taylor? We used to — "

"Is that like Bond, James Bond?"

I breathe. This, I can do. Point, counterpoint. Parry, thrust. I'm glad he interrupted me, since I wasn't sure how to finish that sentence: We used to — We were once — "Kind of. Less gadgets, more bionic parts. I got the hip replacement a few weeks ago, so I've got some steel in me. Well, cobalt-chrome."

A pause. "Would it be corny to say that you always had a bit of steel in you?"

"I dunno. I'm not sure how these conversations are supposed to go. I hadn't gotten past the 'I know I haven't seen you in thirteen years, but . . . ' part."

"Yeah, I was kind of wondering . . . " He speaks like his words are Lego blocks and he's pressing hard to make them click into a sentence. "I was kind of wondering how you could get beyond that . . . "

"Lemme try, okay? I know I haven't seen you in thirteen years, but I've been hired as a coach for the Canada Games and they've told me to pick a manager and no one else wants to do it and I thought of you."

He laughs, the sound nervous, almost a giggle. "A manager? That's definitely not the worst reason you could be calling me. I was thinking you wanted to take me on a talk show because I had some kid I don't know about and he wants to see me." He laughs again, the breathy sound scraped by the receiver. "Jesus."

"Nah, nothing as dramatic as that. I know it's kind of a weird request. Hell, it could very well be the T3s that are making me do this, but we could meet for coffee or something?"

"I don't drink coffee."

"Oh, well, okay. No worries. I just thought I'd ask if you were interested."

"No, I don't mean that. I get ulcers. So I drink tea instead. Some kinds are better than other. Earl Gray is bad for some reason. But anything with peppermint is good. Or ginger. We could meet for tea."

"Okay. Okay, yeah, tea then. At a Starbucks or something?"

"I don't like crowded places. You can come here. I haven't moved. It's just the same. I'm better at home. Tuesday at noon would be best."

"Tuesday at noon," I repeat. "Yeah, I can do that. So, I'll see you then? Tuesday at noon?"

"Tuesday at noon," he says like a goodbye and hangs up.

Grocery shopping is too much. The aisles: so long now. Choosing melons: what a chore. This recovery thing isn't agreeing with me. In the freezer aisle I see my wavery reflection, tangled hair and sweatpants and am shocked. That's not me. That's some housewife with four screaming kids, a dog, and a cat that just had kittens. When I get to the front door, my arms doing a domestic version of weightlifting with grocery bags, I want to close my eyes to avoid my image in the glass. This is as close to training as I get: the Safeway workout program.

A pentatonic blues scale comes from my living room. This isn't my doorbell chime. No, it's Quinn. Quinn with other people. A band. My partner has assembled a band. Who knows where he found these people? It's been years since I've met anyone new. How'd he get so friendly?

They sit in my living room and eat seven-layer dip. When did Quinn learn how to make seven-layer dip?

"Nolan," says Quinn. He's cheerful. The music has warmed him. Who cares who's employed doing what? We have blues, we have rock, there's enough for everyone. "Come and meet the guys." The guys. Quinn doesn't just have friends, he has Guys. Why don't I know these Guys?

"Wow, she's really tall," says one. He's about forty, fat but with fashionable glasses. "You're pretty tall aren't you?"

I look down at myself, my big-girl arms still balancing the groceries. "It appears so."

"You don't have to do that," Quinn hisses at me. "You say that line about the 'human growth hormone kicking in,' I'm going to kick your ass." He takes the groceries, sagging a little under their weight and calls over his shoulder as he heads to the kitchen: "Nolan, this is B.B. His real name's Evan."

I reach over to shake his hand and B.B. gives a fat-man chuckle. "They call me that after the blues guitarist."

"They both have diabetes," Quinn explains. "That's why we call him that. And this is Roger, our drummer, and Mike, our vocalist." Roger and Mike are entirely average. Average height, weight, hair a plebian shade of brown, no noticeable scars or birthmarks. Roger's fly is partially unzipped and Mike wears flannel, that's the only difference. No idea how I'll tell them apart the next time I meet them. This could be why I don't have Guys.

"Hey," says Mike.

"Hey," says Roger.

"Where'd the crackers go?" asks Quinn from the kitchen and I shrug out of the conversation and go to help him. I can make crackers and cheese! I can be one of the Guys!

"Where'd you meet these people?" I whisper.

"They're professional musicians." Quinn's shifting from one foot to the other. These are moods I usually love in him. Not today. I want a nap. "They have a couple of house bands. Their rhythm guitarist just left and they're looking for a new one and they want to audition me."

"Wow," I say. "Paying gigs?"

He nods. "Yup! Well, after the audition period. They think I'm just right, Nole. Just right for them." He appears to have forgotten the 'what constitutes a real job' lecture. We'll talk about the possibility of him getting a day job after The Guys have gone home.

"Where do you meet these people?' I ask as I slice some cheddar and put it on a plate with the crackers. What I mean is: are there any left for me? Some Gals?

Quinn shrugs. "I network." He networks. "I kind of stumbled on to it. Long story: friend of a friend introduced me to B.B., turns out Mike saw The Cripple Killers back in the day and thinks he remembers me from that other band I used to sit in on. You remember Eve of Destruction?"

When we return to the living room, The Guys are playing some old blues standard — "Can't be Satisfied," I think — and Quinn picks up my Gretsch and slides in. He seems to know right where everyone is. So friendly, my husband-type-person. On the same page as everyone else. In the right key.

I put down the plate and B.B. nods his thanks — or maybe he's stressing the downbeat of a set of triplets. I want to play in a rock and roll band. No, I want to play in a chick rock band. A growly one. Lots of spangly skirts and high boots and thrusts with my new hip. The orgasm-face solo pose, screaming into the microphone, lights and makeup melting under them. Quinn wants me employed. That's the job I want. Where do I find such women? Such Gals. I want to be on stage, all of us looking at each other during the pause before the downbeat, right before the punk-girl scream.

Darren:

Nolan's voice has a roughness to it that grates against the ear like a cat's tongue. It's deep, but a voice that fits her frame. A woman over six feet with a squeaky voice: that would be ridiculous. Valerie's is lower too, those rare times she opens her mouth.

So I keep talking, holding the phone against my shoulder with my ear, and I feel this good, good warmth and I think, geez, I must be glad to hear from her. This must be what people mean when they say that someone makes them feel warm all over. Who knows how a person will react to these things? Who's ready for their ex-whatever-the-hell-she-was to phone out of the blue, thirteen years later? How does the body prepare for that from an evolutionary standpoint? I mean, this isn't a problem our ancestors ever had. And the phone's so new, historically speaking. It changes everything. Takes away that eighty-five percent of information. The body hasn't figured out how to cope, that's the problem. It's slow: needs generations. It's not in our muscle memory yet.

I thought the warmth was maybe some reaction because, hell, I'll admit it. I was thinking about that time. In the gym. Those days, it was only math that saved me . . . and even then it didn't work for too long. "When she was born, you were thirteen. Thirty-two minus 19 is 13. When she was born, you were 13. Thirty-two minus 19 is 13." And then she put her damn hand down my pants and — I shouldn't have, I shouldn't have, I know I shouldn't have — but I let her and it felt like the best gunshot ever. What can a guy do? Your body takes over. Screw Descartes: moments like that, your body's the only thing that exists. Your mind goes. That day, Nolan taking a little breath, sliding her fingers against my belly button and down. Like a great wound. Nolan's rough hands: cat-tongue fingers, cat-tongue voice. Nolan's rough hands — though you wouldn't want them down there for too long; they feel like bloody sandpaper. Her hands, though. The best gun-shot ever.

I was still talking to her. Didn't even feel shame, almost a clinical detachment. I said something about Starbucks and watched the puddle spread on the floor. And I felt that warmth down into my sneakers and was glad for the reduced sensation. Who knows what able-bodied people feel at a time like this? Though, I mean, this isn't the first time. I guess I got up too fast, shouldn't have had three cups of tea one right after the other. There have been other problems since the neck surgery and the doctors did warn me about this. Quads age in odd ways. I mean, used to be that a broken neck meant death; it's only been in the last sixty years we even survived at all. We're a new species. No one's sure what to expect from a quad.

I hung up, glad I could sever my mind from my body like that and Nolan couldn't have suspected anything. Proud of my focus. Valerie was in her room. She didn't see, didn't hear. I cleaned it all up and threw the rags out and threw my clothes out and mopped and bleached and Valerie was napping. Probably napping. I cleaned naked, stripped right down, my thighs all sticky and the slight air letting me feel the difference, hoping to hell she wouldn't come in and wonder what I was doing. I settled on telling her that I spilt tea all over myself and didn't want to get burned. Then I had a hot bath and went up to bed and Valerie was still napping, so I didn't need the excuse. Or whatever she was doing. Christ. All this means a trip to the organic foods store for maybe some cranberry juice or ursa ursu (and a haircut probably, too, if I'm meeting Nolan, a shave wouldn't hurt either, a new shirt might be too much). Nolan might like the carob oatmeal cookies they have at that place too. It's getting more and more difficult to have a body.

Though I'd heard that Darren's in a chair full-time now, it vaguely disturbs me. Most people with his disability choose not to walk using crutches and braces. It's cumbersome, tiring, leaves you with a robot walk that people can't quite slot into able-bodied or disabled and so decide you're stupid. A limp suggests sickness or age. So most choose the wheelchair and some don't get to choose at all. But Darren walked, limping in a way that grated against his bones. The body wasn't made for crutch-walking but he kept lean — less load to carry — and lifted weights and he walked.

Now, Darren has finally become practical, made the rational, economical decision and I'm weirdly disappointed, though who am I to judge? Me, who chose this new hip.

"Nolan." He says my name like he's been practicing it in his head. "It's good to see you." I can't look at him. Eye contact feels like trying to force two same-sided magnets together.

Instead, I focus on the room. He was right. The place hasn't changed much. There's even still a picture of me on the coffee table behind photos of people I don't recognize. We're at some breakfast joint. In Kamloops, maybe. All breakfast places feel the same: hashbrowns and misspelled menus. Yeah, it was Kamloops. Erica took the picture. Darren's head is tilted towards me and my face is skewed, caught the ugly moment before laughter. I wander over towards it as Darren locks the door — (he's always done this; it's always made me nervous) — and pretend to examine all these anonymous people.

The frames are dusty in the corners, cleaned by someone's fingertip. Most of the photos are old, the melatonin blanched out of everyone's skin tone. The sun giveth, the sun taketh away. People's edges seep into the background and make them look like ghosts.

No time to think of ghosts because Darren is here: pale but here, graying but here. I watch him as he toys with the wand on the blinds, avoiding my gaze. He's gained weight, but the borders of his old body remain, just smudged, blending against the old wallpaper: a chiaroscuro of skin.

I'd wondered why, after thirteen years in the same city, we hadn't run into each other. It felt like a sign or something, but looking around the room I realize that it wasn't anything remotely cosmic; Darren obviously doesn't leave the house very much. The place has an antique smell. The air is curled around the edges, parched in the sense of the word parchment. The windows are open, but it doesn't appear to make much of a difference. The occupants never track in new smells and the house has grown bored with itself, huddled around the TV waiting for new stories.

"It's nice to see you too," I say. "Dare." I tack his name on at the end as if I've just remembered it and am not sure if it's right. My gaze won't settle: the blinds, the dust motes making shards out of the light that survives through them, the photos, the familiar couch with a new afghan, anything to distract me from his face.

Luckily, the house is dark. A grotto, cavern, and Darren has grown hunched to fit in. Maybe it's the wheelchair bulking the forward muscles while their opposing partners grow slack. Maybe he's spent too much time hunched over small things: fine print, equations.

He says nothing, watches my eyes adjusting to the light, to the time-travel that has taken place. There's no evidence of a woman's touch besides the purple afghan, not even the scent of body lotion, no photos containing her face.

"Being here," I say, trying to find a word I suspect doesn't exist: some cross between strange and uncomfortable and nervous and yet.

"Yeah," he says. Finally says. Finally speaks. His chair is the red of a sleeker machine: fire engine, Corvette. It's the brightest colour in the room, the one thing new. "I've got the tea ready."

I head towards the kitchen and its new smell. Not like earth tilled from a farm, more like the same soil after it's been tracked into the city and ground into the concrete. Earth that has become dirt. Herbs, most likely: something clean and vital lost in the transition to pill or powder form. I think of Darren's spaghetti sauce on the stove, how it used to simmer. Where is Valerie?

"I don't know how long I can stay," I say, forcing my vision from the cluttered table, the full sink, to his eyes.

The table is the same. The counters are the same. The lace curtains are the same. His eyes are the same. Maybe not. No, yes. The same.

He nods, smirking like he's found a metaphor that can sum up our last interaction. "Will ginger do? I'll spare you the taste of the medicinal stuff."

"Ginger's great. Been awhile since I've had ginger tea."

On the kitchen table — a table I have had sex on, the knobs of my spine chafing against the seam where the leaf could be put in — are bottles and bottles of herbal medicine, a plastic mortar and pestle, a blender.

"Sorry about the smell," says Darren. "Between me, Valerie and my mom — she's sick now — there's a lot of medicine in this place."

"How's Valerie?"

My vision flicks between him and the books on the counter. Broad, tanned men in tight shirts proclaim that You, Too, Can Love Juice! Shakes for Movers and Shakers! Better Blending! Juice for the Health of It! Darren never used to be the type of guy to read books with exclamation points in the title. Maybe his eyes *are* different.

"She's at her mother's place."

"Oh," I say.

"Visiting," he says.

"That's good."

He's silent and I wait for a moment to insert Quinn into, but he doesn't return the question. Come to think of it, I'm not sure if he knows about Quinn. He must know about Quinn.

"So," I say. Think: sew. Imagine my nerve-taut voice like a needle through a silence that needs mending. "Canada Games."

Darren conjures two mugs from the dark cupboard. On one, there's a faded BC Wheelchair Sports' logo, an old one. He looks at me and the steam from the kettle further blurs his face. "Wheelchair sports are like the mafia. The only way out is death. People keep trying to recruit you back in." He looks pleased that the sport that has left him alone for so long is finally paying attention.

"We don't like to lose people," I say. "The community's too small."

Again, that smirk that wants to be deciphered. "No one wants to lose people." He stops against the window, his hair tangled with cloudy light. "I don't know, Nolan. I've been away so long, I don't think I'd be much help for wheelchair repair. Who knows what's happened with the technology. Do the chairs still have wheels?"

I forget to laugh. "They're simpler if anything. Invacare changed its stupid name and dumped that camber insert system. So no more bent tubes. And the All Courts have fewer adjustable parts — less nuts and bolts — and most of the frames are fixed." My hand gestures come close to knocking over my mug. "I'm sorry, I'm going on and on. But, yeah. Much easier. I'm in an All Court now, myself. A fixed-frame titanium with Spinergies and offensive wings. Well, I was."

The tea's ready. He takes the cups and tea-bags over to the table and I carry the kettle. "That's harder when things go wrong, though," he says. "You take a big hit, it's not like you can fix the toe-in, toe-out. It's the whole frame that's bent. It's a structural problem now." He's settling back into the language of the sport.

"The job's the same, though. Change tubes. Smack bent wheels against walls. Tighten some screws. Not rocket science. And fourteen-to-twenty-four-year-olds don't change, really. You still need to keep them in line the same way." The ginger-scented steam opens my pores.

"Brute force and cold showers?"

I laugh, have a deja vu sensation of laughing here before. Right here, leaning against the counter, a mug of tea in my hand. "Pretty much."

"Been awhile since I've had any experience with the 14–24 demographic." He looks at me, makes what could be too much eye contact.

"Yeah, probably around the same time I was in the 14–24 demographic."

"You still look like you are," he says. "Or maybe I'm just seeing the old you."

The skinny nineteen-year-old me from that photograph has been scarred on to his vision like a computer screen left on too long. He can't see my wrinkles, my Big-Girl arms, the grey hairs highlighting my blonde. This is time travel and it's fine by me.

Darren sips his tea and stares into the cup like he could read the leaves. "You know, I think this whole manager thing might be good for me. Can't say Val will be too pleased about it, but I guess I don't have to tell her right away. Wait to make sure that I like it, you know?"

14

TO CELEBRATE OUR SURVIVAL OF CHRISTMAS with the relatives, Quinn took me to Chuck E. Cheese's. I wasn't born on the mainland, so the place wasn't part of my childhood mythology, which Quinn felt was unforgivable. He treated the excursion like one of those Make a Wish Foundation trips: poor denied little Island girl given a last chance for childhood cool.

As we pulled up to the place, I could hear screams and pinball machines. It sounded like the most fun massacre ever was going on inside.

"I can't wait to see this place at adult height," Quinn said. "I was going to suggest we try it on acid but, my God, our heads would explode."

"And I have to get drug tested," I said.

He shrugged. "Well, yeah, there's that."

If ADHD had a headquarters, it would be Chuck E. Cheese's. Constant fucking stimulation. Lights! Loud Noises! An ice-cream bar with twelve different kinds of sprinkles! Mechanical gophers to be hit on the head with large mallets! This was child heaven and adult hell but we weren't either. I followed Quinn in a daze.

The idea was to trade dollars for Chuck E. Cheese tokens, plunk the tokens into game machines, and earn tickets based on how many points you scored in a game. I figured I would be good at the basketball simulation game, but I wasn't. Smaller ball, different height, the pressure of competing for those damn tickets. I choked. In an hour, I'd lost fifteen dollars and only had enough tickets for a small plastic ring.

I enjoyed watching Quinn bent over his skeetball machine, though. He wasn't especially strong, but he was a determined little bugger. Squinted eyes, thin smoker-boy shoulder blades knitting together. He was wearing designer jeans, the kind that someone else fades, and a T-shirt that proclaimed his love of New York despite the fact he'd never been there. And he was taking the whole skeetball thing very seriously while pretending not to. Although who was I to mock skeetball when my rent was paid by putting a ball through a hoop?

As he bent, his pants slipped down a few inches, revealing tighty-whitey underwear at least a size too big. I hoped that was an appropriate metaphor for him in general. Hip outside, but underneath the endearing male equivalent of granny panties. I was big into metaphors that year: all those English classes.

Quinn's skeetball mastery had drawn a crowd of little boys who were skinnier than him. They flanked the machine and cheered him on and fed the tokens into the machine so that he'd be ready when the game started.

"It's not just about the arm," Quinn would tell them. "You have to throw with your whole body, that's the trick. You have to be loose, but ready." He smiled like a zen master, despite the sugar-high surroundings. The little boys were still, watching and nodding gravely, and shied away from the grown-ups in cartoon-character costumes who came by looking for photo opportunities. By the time he was out of quarters, he was sweating. He gave each boy a strand of tickets the length of his arm and they ran off, powered-up again by the flashing lights and the candy counter. With the leftover tokens, he bought me a plush Chuck E. Cheese doll.

"Five-inch plush toy," he said gallantly as he presented it to me. "Now that's worth at least a blow job."

"I'm a top-shelf kind of girl," I said. "Twelve inches and over."

It wasn't a date. I wouldn't let it be a date. I pretended not to notice when he leaned over to kiss me in front of my apartment, dodging his mouth.

"That was fun, Quinn." I said. "I was humbled to witness a skeetball master at work."

He laughed. "Next time I'm taking you on man-to-man. Or, woman-to-man, whatever. You're mine."

"Ooh, fighting words. We'll have to do that again." I stepped out of the car. "Thanks for taking me. Maybe Chuck E. will be good luck for the essay writing."

"Considering you haven't done the reading, I think you need all the Chuck E. luck you can get."

It wasn't a date but I still put the stuffed toy on my dresser so that it overlooked my bed. It wasn't a date but I still hoped that maybe Darren would see it, despite the fact that he rarely came to my apartment.

~

At practice, Darren and I were always on opposite teams. With the Handicaps, there was no 'us' to describe what Darren and I were. This was the good part of our relationship being secret. Also, the bad part. He tried so hard not to play favourites that sometimes he confused it with playing nice.

"Hey, smarten up," he'd say if I missed a pass or an easy shot. "What the hell is that? What's wrong with you?"

Our Lady of Perpetual Smackdowns was still decorated for Christmas when we arrived for our first practice of the new year. We wheeled through glitter from drawings of Christmas trees pasted to the walls and cotton balls from Santa's beard. The gym's moisture had made the decorations crisp and curl, as if the Holidays were in the distant past.

"I feel like I'm dragging behind twenty pounds of shortbread," said Rob as he warmed up.

"You probably are," said Darren.

"Shut up man," said Rob cheerfully. "At least I've got a nice little girlfriend serving me Christmas treats. You got anyone licking your candy cane? You gotta get back in the saddle, my man."

"Mind your own saddle," said Darren. I looked up at the rafters where a red balloon was wavering from light to light, passing across each lamp like a miniature sunset.

"Man of your age can't afford to wait too much longer or you won't have a saddle left. Bad enough you're a quadri-fucking-plegic. What about Nolan? I bet she'd be more than happy to trim your tree. Wouldn't you, Nole? Wouldn't you, heh?"

"Nolan's nineteen," said Darren. "Rob, you want to go white? I'll stay dark. We'll get this thing started."

"Nolan can decorate my Christmas tree any day," said Vern, who was changing into his practice jersey and taking a long time of it. "I dressed up as Old Saint Nick for the grandkiddies a few weeks ago. Wish I still had the costume. She could sit on my lap."

"As if I hadn't learned my lesson from countless lecherous mall Santas," I said.

"Ho ho ho, Merry Christmas little lady," said Vern. "You want to find out how to get on old Santa's naughty list?" He patted his lap. "Come here, Nolan."

"No thanks."

"You know she's nineteen, right?" asked Darren. "Okay, Rob go white with Nolan, Erika and Max. Vern can be dark if he'd put his damn shirt on, I'm getting a bit sick of the impromptu belly dance, thank you very much, and I'll take him with Ed and Larry."

After practice, Vern stood at the door of the disabled washroom with his shirt off, arms on either side of the frame as if to mimic the Jesus-on-a-cross painting on the nearby wall.

"Lookin' good Nolan."

"Yeah, thanks."

"You gonna come in? We could close this door."

"Hadn't planned on it."

"Had a dream about you. Did I tell you that? You were naked in high heeled shoes. Big glittery ones. And a smile. Just a smile."

"It's going to stay a dream. Clichéd dream at that."

Darren appeared in the doorway of the gym, diluting the sweat on his face and neck with water from his water bottle. "Ready for Cage Match?"

"Ah, Darren. Now there's a red-blooded man. Don't you think Nolan would look good naked in high heeled shoes?"

Darren blushed and I was glad his face was already camouflaged pink from practice. "We have an anti-harassment clause in our code of conduct that prevents me from answering that question. You read our code of conduct lately?"

Vern smiled, his grey hair beatific in the light. "I must have read a different version than you. Maybe I read the version that's wondering why you can stroke her thigh when she's going in for a shot and I can't make a few harmless jokes."

Cage Match was harder that night: no caress to his fouls. Throughout our sexual relationship, it hadn't changed much. There was some knowledge I wouldn't let myself use: his sensitive spots, his quad hand. Sometimes I thought he went easy going after a loose ball in the area I couldn't bend far enough to reach. Cage Match was usually a strange kind of playing fair.

The after-practice car tours were getting shorter, too. Maybe Cage Match *had* changed and it was just another kind of foreplay. It was one-on-one, after all. Maybe it was inevitable. Regardless, the Darren Steward Tour Company seemed to be emphasizing New Westminster's best makeout spots.

"Show me something," I said as we got into the car that night.

He raised his eyebrows.

"No, really," I said. "Show me something. Some place in New West I've never been."

"New Westminster's not exactly a great cultural mecca. I'm running out of locations." I'd given him a Discman with a car hook-up for Christmas, and the CD sat spinning between us. Through his crackly speakers came a Lucinda

Williams mixed CD I'd burned him. His music tastes were good, but narrow. Old blues, a bit of country, Dylan, the Stones, Miles Davis. Darren liked the standards, the most popular of every genre. I wanted to give him a woman with a hard blues voice so he could see who I wanted to become.

"What do you think of Lucinda?" I asked.

"She's . . . different. I like her, though. What genre is she?"

"I don't know," I said. "That's why I like her. See? She's good driving music. 'Car Wheels on a Gravel Road.'"

He nodded. "I think I need to listen to this a few more times to really get my head around it."

"I've got more for you when you're done with her. You heard of Bonnie Raitt?"

"I could take you to the rose garden in Queen's Park, but it's too cold to get out of the car for long and nothing's growing. Where else could we go? Let me think. We might have to branch out into Burnaby. You probably know this place as well as I do now."

"So it's another bedroom tour then?" I asked.

"Don't sound so enthusiastic. I want to take you to Friendship Gardens one day, but it's not safe to go at night. And we could go to Woodlands, but again . . . not at night. Does Vern bother you?"

I looked out the window: up Sixth, across Eighth, past McBride Boulevard. The quickest route to his place. "A bit. I keep telling him the shut the hell up. Like, I don't care that he says stuff, because I'd let you or Rob say those things, but I don't like that he won't stop, you know?

"I don't know if I'm in a position to talk to him about it. I should be. That's my job. The coaching part, I mean. I just don't know if I'm hypocritical or not." He stopped the car outside of his house, but we didn't get out. He rubbed his hands along his thighs, then toyed with the lock on his brace, and I put my hand over his to stop his fidgeting.

"Don't be dumb. If I asked you to stop, you would. Right? Wouldn't you?" He nodded. "Right. You would. So that's totally different from making crude sexual comments when the person's asked you to shut the hell up. It's apples and oranges. I'm a few years past jail bait, anyhow." I read his fingers: the swollen knuckle on the index, the mangled pinky, the slight tremor in them.

The car's interior bulb made his face all glasses and receding hairline. He sighed and squeezed my hand. "How'd you get so smart in nineteen years?" he said, leaning over to kiss me.

"It's like this: you're allowed to ask to see me naked in high-heeled shoes; he's not."

"I wouldn't want to see you in heels at any time. Bad enough you're like eight feet taller than me."

~

I don't remember most of the training camps. Hotel rooms, cabins, bus rides, airplanes. I even forget who exactly was on the team that year. The roster changed each season and most of the women back then seemed to be a different species altogether. The Adults. Not adult like Darren because he was something else. I'd seen his tan lines and could locate his more obvious fissures: Valerie, his failed athletic career . . . It didn't take a genius. Regardless, I'd mapped him. These women were real adults.

By January I'd finally settled into some sort of routine with Darren, worn a comfy little groove in my life that could be called a relationship, when I had to leave for a training camp in the States. The timing was bad. Valerie had only recently discovered that Darren was 'seeing' someone. She just didn't know who. I suspected that Sammy had done some hinting.

We were staying at a sports centre for the physically disabled in Georgia, posh from a user-pay medical system and many $1000-a-plate charity dinner auctions. It was named after Franklin Delano Roosevelt, America's most famous cripple. The place was like a summer camp: same log cabins that smelled of being boarded up for winter, same blonde people-person women with gravity-defying ponytails. The path from the gym to the cabins was spruced up with little white bridges over carp ponds, the kind invalids might have been pushed over for their daily constitutionals back in another era. The locals were bundled up, but the climate didn't pass as cold. We could still sit out on the porch without our fingers going numb. Walking from the cabin to the gym could be done without a jacket.

With the team and away from Darren, I had to remember how to be body-shy again, how to dress behind closed door and pretend that I was still a rookie of anything relating to private parts. I was bad at it, wearing the lie like too much makeup. Makeup, like lying, must be learned at a young age and the window for both had closed even at nineteen. No concealer, no concealing.

I was sharing a room with Nikki, who didn't have any trouble in the makeup department. She knew what shadows a woman should keep and which ones should be conquered with foundation and blush and eyeshadow and special moisturizers for around her eyes or between her breasts, (her decolletage, she called it). Nikki wasn't very popular with some of the women for this reason, not to mention that she signed thank-you cards for supporters with a little heart over the 'i' in her name. She lay on her bed in her sports bra and jeans, her belly brown against the white sheets.

I was supposed to use the cabin as a chance to bond with my teammates. I could hear what everyone else was up to. Sue was singing in the shower in the next room, something about blue eyes, her Texan accent surviving the walls and hiss of water. Two of the other girls were discussing one of the guys from the men's team.

The cabins had good acoustics and me without my guitar. I wanted some sort of stringed instrument: to play the blues into the firefly sky, jam with crickets and their washboard backup. The nights were asking me to sit on the cabin porch and rock in both senses of the word: let an old chair keep time. Mostly, I wanted to be good at something. During practice, my fingers and brain were speaking two different dialects. My hands were rough in all the wrong place. All that year I felt body stupid.

Nikki flipped through a magazine and the scent of perfume samples added to the odour of jerseys hanging to dry and shower steam. I was lying on my bed composing an email to Darren in my head. I did that sometimes when I was nervous: wrote the email then imagined his response. The springs on the mattress reminded me of my bones, anchoring my fantasizing to the present.

"You got a boyfriend?" Nikki asked me and for a moment I wondered if I was speaking out loud.

I looked up at the ceiling. "Not really. Do you?"

"Trevor from the men's team. You didn't know that?"

"I didn't." I shrugged. "He seems cool." I'd never met Trevor.

"Too cool sometimes. He's pretty metrosexual. Big into the waxing." She winked at me. "Everywhere. I mean, what the hell, he can't feel it anyhow. Might as well. Not like me. I frickin' wear my shoes too tight and I'm spasming all over the place."

I picked up my own magazine and flipped through it so she couldn't enjoy my expression. "Yeah, might as well. That's what I would do if I had no sensation. Get tattoos all over."

"Too bad there aren't any guys your age on the men's team. We've got to hook you up with someone."

"I think I'm fine."

"I bet there are lots of guys who'd agree that you're damn fine. You're a little blonde thing. You should be rolling in men. Literally, rolling around with men. Who could we hook you up with? Let me think. You do like boys, right? You're not a dyke?"

"Nah. More partial to the men over the boys, though."

Nikki laughed and there was laughter from someone eavesdropping in the common room. "Atta girl."

The showers at the workout facility in Georgia were communal and I was the only shy one. I didn't even like changing at my gym in front of women I didn't know. There were no curtains or dark spaces here, just a line of showers, the hiss of water, and everyone transferring from their wheelchairs to folding shower chairs.

Strange to be soaping up in front of other women, women I knew: the trails of shampoo fingering their necks and chests as it slid down, the scars bright as soap froth. The way skin stretches around a scar, making room for it. I tried not to look: their nipples, bruises, tattoos. I tried not to look: the stomachs folding as they bended, someone humming, the shush of razor against foam. Instead, I stared at my own tanlines, conscious of where my clothes used to be.

A bruised knee from being tipped during the first game against Mexico, scratches from someone else's nails taking a dirty swipe at me during a shot, a little ache from a friendly fire incident in practice. Sammy tossed me a pass and it slipped through my hands, hitting my breast bone with a pain louder than my lungs, a weird kind of heartache. Nothing extraordinary. I couldn't go fast enough yet to hurt myself properly and most opponents were still giving me a rookie's grace period.

Everyone was in the common room and it was supposed to be team building. All the little clusters. A moth swooned with light love and fell dead at my feet. There were mice in the walls and the barbeque outside creaked in the wind, wanting fire, meat and good weather to work with.

Darren had taught me how to play Hearts because it was a team favourite and he said he hoped it was the only mind game I would have to play with these women. He still took Valerie's side in decade-old fights, I could tell. He only knew her side of the story.

We were silent. Five hours a day of basketball and no one wanted to talk about it anymore. The American team had come for a training camp of their own and we'd won an exhibition match. We'd erased the loss in Brazil and were now on the right side of 'you're only as good as your last game.'

I played a silent game of Hearts with Sammy, Wren and Sue. The cards thrown on the table fit against the slap of branches on the window. It was the wrong season to be here. This was a summer place.

"Nolan, hold your cards to your chest," said Sammy, wanting to play fair. I was always showing my hand.

"Sorry."

I'd been dealt a bad hand and was trying to go for control. The silence helped. No one realized I was doing it and let me keep picking up hearts thinking it was a rookie mistake. Darren had taught me the math and strategy of it, but I still wasn't sure if beating them was an appropriate rookie move.

"Well, shit, you slid right under our radar," said Wren after the hand was over, though I wasn't sure if it was admiration or not.

"Good one, Nole. Bet you learned that from Darren," said Sammy. "Apparently you're learning a lot from him." She winked theatrically.

The room became communal again. Everyone turned to look.

"You and Darren Steward? Like, the former Mr. Valerie Steward?" asked someone. "Aren't you a little young?"

"I wouldn't call it dating," I said. There was no 'I' in team, no 'secrets' in team and no 'lying about your ill-advised sexual relationship with someone's ex-husband' in 'team.'

"What would you call it?" asked someone. This was supposed to be bonding. Tony had explained it as a web, all of us connected by invisible threads that would hold us up no matter what. I wasn't sure if I was supposed to be a spider or a fly in this particular metaphor. My teammates weren't being unkind. This kind of gossip was supposed to make us stronger.

"I don't know." I didn't know. It wasn't a boyfriend-girlfriend thing, we weren't really friends. There was no good word. There was no good excuse.

"Oh come on, Nole," said Sammy. "No one cares you're fucking Valerie's ex."

"She was such a beast," said someone else. "Good ball player, but a total beast. I nearly beat the shit out of her after she got pissed off and threw a ball at my head during a practice. He must be happy to have a chick who's not a psycho."

"She had her moments," said Nikki. "She was nice when you caught her in a good mood. Really smart."

"We're not just — I mean, it's not," I stammered. I wished I could spin a cocoon around my full body blush. The hair falling in front of my face was bright as a web, but without the strength. "I like him. He's been really good for me." My heart was beating hard; embarrassment was apparently good cross-training. I wondered if it would improve me in the same way.

"I'm sure he has," someone said.

There was slumber party laughter and the room smelled of summer camps, even though it was the wrong season. I laughed with them, thinking this was maybe how bonding was supposed to go.

I went to bed worried that night. Everyone realized and soon Darren would know that the secret was out. The little bruises didn't hurt me, the ache in my chest had been replaced by a heartbeat that wouldn't settle. I was up all night nervous, my heartbeat pulsing like an injury.

Darren:

And of course Valerie picks this place to meet, precisely because of the staircase. She knows that Nolan's at a training camp, so now was a good time to phone me up and ask for some box of photos she can't live without. (Who needs photos of me when we're divorced? Doesn't divorced mean you don't want to be looking at pictures from the good ol' days?) Also a good time to mention that someone's told her about my "new little girlfriend," which means Nolan and I will have to have a discussion when she gets home about the confidentiality required for our situation.

I have memories of walking into Lucky Strikes Lanes, actually. Real walking. My mom took me here for a birthday party. I was maybe four and wanted the gift for myself. It was a truck. I remember that. A little firetruck that squirted water out of a hose. The stairs smelled of something I couldn't name then and don't want to guess at now, (not that I need to guess, it's the bar downstairs and the old people upstairs). My little legs, the big stairs with their carpet and odour, my mother coaxing me to hurry up, something about a clip-on tie that had caused tears earlier in the morning. I probably remember walking up the stairs because it was the first time walking was hard. Kids have such an easy time of it.

Anyhow, it doesn't take a masters degree to deduce that the box of photos is of secondary importance. She wants to meet me because she wants me to have to park my car on a hill in the rain and struggle up stairs, I'm sure. Valerie wants to make me earn it — whatever 'it' is — wants to make me feel it. Maybe this is some kind of healing metaphor: life a long stairway and her with new knees. Rapunzel, Rapunzel, me struggling up this tower. I'm used to stairs, not so much with dealing with ex-wives.

The staircase still smells of the bar below, the "Thirsty Duck," which Nolan said was an allusion to a blues song about if rye whiskey was an ocean and I were a duck, I'd swim to the bottom and never come up. I thought only literature was allowed to have allusions. Regardless: some of those guys down there haven't surfaced from whatever booze ocean they're floating in. It's two PM *and they're bloated like drowning victims.*

At the top, I see Valerie standing and talking with the woman at the counter, who's spraying the shoes from an aerosol can that smells like rotten baby powder, even from this distance. When the counter lady points at me, Valerie smiles like I'm some knight who's overcome an ordeal to get to her. Clearly, this was the plan. The meeting's plot is apparently drawing heavily from bodice-ripping romance novels.

The lady at the desk nods her approval and I'm glad that I go with Nolan to the gym. I like the way she's changed me; people comment on my arms these days. That's Nolan's doing.

"Want to play some before we get down to business?" she asks, all amicable. And of course I don't. I'm not built for bowling. Such simple physics but the gravity just doesn't add up. Skinny legs in braces. Big heavy bowling ball. One gimp hand. Val has new knees and she's showing them off. This is apparently her own cross-training. Or maybe it's just a sport, since she's not competing anymore.

She's wearing a black sweater that shows off her cleavage, proof that she's trying. No T-shirts, big coats, sweatpants. A sweater that tight is like nudity for Val. This is a special kind of flattery, which is why I'm risking certain humiliation and possible concussion.

"Okay," I say. "But you'll kick my ass."

"We won't place bets."

On the first try, Val throws a strike. She's picked the right location to meet. Nachos and friendly competition. And we look damn good next to some of the bowling lane regulars, the ones who were probably here when I was four years old. Have to say, though, alcohol suits the teenage girls stumbling against their partners in the lane next to us. Their booze-shiny cheeks look well-scrubbed. They laugh and coax the ball with their whole bodies and hang onto their boyfriends' pillowy jackets for support. It's because of Nolan that I'm noticing these girls. They never used to be in my range.

"Hah," says Valerie. Grey slacks too. New, maybe bought for a job interview. A chance she may be working. Maybe bought for me.

"You going pro?" I ask her.

She laughs and it's a misplaced sound. "That's Special O," she says and gives me a wink for old times. "But if Paralympics ever adds it, I'm in, baby."

Was 'baby' something she ever called me? Maybe an inside joke we once had. We had a lot of those, but it's easy to get rusty without use. Easier still to confuse the jokes I have with Nolan.

Valerie stretches her arms above her head so her breasts rise against the sweater. She has arms that could carry someone out of a burning building. Even now. Nolan has focused her. Whatever, it's a school-yard competition, but at least it's some sort of game. A game means rules and rules make sense out of Valerie's limbs. She knows how to move in a game. She knows what she has to do.

I step up to the line and Valerie is quiet, showing off how well we do silence. She stands behind me, watching as I try to pick up the ball with the good arm without falling. Her nervous posture: I can just tell no one's touched her since I've been gone. You could do a forensics investigation and she'd be free of fingerprints.

"The wings here are good," Valerie notes. "And the woman who works here makes baked goods when she's stressed and her kid's a little shit so she's always bringing me in these little cookies she makes in the shape of cupcakes. She keeps trying to hook me up with this guy who stocks the pop cooler. He's not bad looking, but I'm busy with my online courses."

I lean on the crutch with the bad arm and get ready to throw the ball with the other. "Ah." Despite the woman's baking, Valerie's lost weight. Not so much that I can notice, just that she moves like her clothes are looser. Like she knows.

"Here, I'll show you," she says. Valerie doesn't ask. She never does. Just walks right over and stands behind me so close she's like a brace that breathes against my ear. Her sweater smells like an old lady's attempt at fresh and clean.

And then the silence. She puts her hand on the ball, bending with those shiny new knees, supporting me. She doesn't need permission.

"You know it's going to go that way because of how you compensate, so you need to flick your wrist the other way," she finally says and we move together and ball rolls right into the gutter. Valerie shrugs and steps back and I've lost my scaffolding again. The air is all smoke, old carpets, nachos.

"Just a theory," she says.

"I can get you that box of stuff by the weekend. They're rat-proofing the attic right now, but they'll be done by Wednesday. I know right where the box is. And my lawyer sent over a fun

and exciting home video about dividing assets, which we're apparently supposed to watch. We apparently have to do a better job of keeping track of what goes where."

"There a problem? With rats, I mean."

"Nah, but tis' the season for rodent infestation and I've been meaning to get it done for awhile now. It's an old house."

"That and you're a bit phobic," she says, perhaps referencing the great 'Camping in a Field' disaster from three years ago. It's not a phobia if they're actually trying to get into your tent.

The nice part about when Valerie and I were together was that I could blame every sound in the room on her. After we separated, every floorboard squeak or pipe clang was a rodent. I knew what sounds were mine and everything else was up for grabs. Everything else was an infestation. I couldn't sleep. I checked each corner for droppings, even though I didn't want to look. Good thing Nolan came along and I had someone else to blame the noise on.

"Well, whatever. Those things jump and if I'm going to share my bed with something, I'd rather it have two legs." The bowling ball on the wood floor is punctuation and I hope it erases the use of the word 'bed.' The woman at the counter glares, but she won't say anything to the poor disabled guy in case destroying her floor is my brand of Overcoming Obstacles and Adapting to Life's Challenges.

"And how is . . . Nolan, or whatever her name is?" This is how she always refers to Nole. 'That girl: what's her name again? You know, that little bit of nothing girl.'

"She's good. Nervous about the Paralympics, but she'll do fine. I think she's just having a hard time fitting in. Well, you know those women can be kind of — "

"Incredibly cliquey? Ruthless bitches?"

"I don't know about that. I think it's just what happens when you put twelve driven women in a room together." I sit down at the computer console that keeps track of the score. The click of buttons, the easy code of the program, the competency of it all. No heavy objects or lines to step over.

"I'd say they'd eat her for breakfast, but she wouldn't make much of a meal." She stands behind me, hands on my shoulders. "I'm going to assume we're done with the bowling. I don't think you're cut out for America's favourite past time. You can drive me home. It's on the way. We can hammer out the rest of the details when you bring over the photos." Valerie doesn't need permission. I'm supposed to sell the car and pay her half. I'm supposed to sell the house but she's settling for a pay-out even though her lawyer says she could take me for all I'm worth. ("He's not worth much," she told her, looking at me as she said it and the lady lawyer smirked behind her working-professional lipstick. "He needs all the assets he can get." And yet, which one of us is employed? Which one of us is dating again? Well, Nolan and I aren't exactly dating, but still.)

"We just bowled one frame," I say. "Are you sure?"

She laughs and touches my neck with just one finger, all of my small hairs damp with sweat, and it's a gesture older than sex, the punchline to every inside joke we have.

"I didn't know you liked Lucinda Williams," says Valerie as we drive. The rain shadows and headlights make a home movie on her pale cheeks. Her dark hair, not quite curly. Tangled enough that my fingers used to get caught.

"It's not mine, though I do like a few of the songs. That one about lonely girls. Someone told me that a refusal to listen to women's music corresponds with an inability to listen to women speak."

Valerie smiles and the expression is not entirely unkind. "Your new girl some kind of feminist? Or do you have a shrink now?"

"I think she was teasing me. Nolan likes this kind of stuff: anything that comes from the blues. She's not a bad guitar player." Embarrassing to realize I'm still at the stage in a relationship where Nolan's name makes me smile a little. "Whatever, it's all in the name of self improvement."

Valerie looks out the window, "Well, well, you've come a long way since your heavy metal phase." By which she means: that time at nationals when we got drunk off Jagermeister and sang AC-DC while jumping on the bed — I was drunk enough to think I could jump — and I fell and cut my forehead and she called it my headbanging era. By which she means: any road trip from 1988 to 1992, that party in Quebec, the time she posed as my attendant to get into a concert. Everything she says is a game of 'name that tune.'

"I'm all grown up. Or something." I pull up to her mother's house. It's dark, so it's impossible to see if anything's changed. There's a first date moment when she looks at me before getting out of the car.

"Goodnight, baby," she says and touches my knee as she leans down to get her purse. She knows exactly where I can feel it.

"Night Val," I say and take the long way home so I can listen to Lucinda Williams, so I can drive to the edge of New West and get out and listen to the CD while laying on the car roof and look up at the loose alliances of stars.

15

DARREN:

Nolan never saw the in between. With Val, she either got the on-court explosion or the off-court brooding. Shouting or silence. When Val was at her peak, I used to love her coming away from a game with her voice still hoarse from screaming, whispering little calm things in my ear. But Nolan's never known any of that. Just her brooding. She'd call her Mrs. Rochester. Or 'your psycho ex-wife.'

Nolan likes literature and poetry, but it was ruined for me. Dr. Livingstone. Ninth grade English. Must have made him feel he was born into literature, a name like that. Or maybe that he could never make his own: too much a character in someone else's story. And he had to enter a profession filled with teenagers who knew just enough about literature to drive him to the brink of a nervous breakdown with constant, "Dr. Livingstone, I presume?" If it'd been me, I would have forgotten the PhD and called myself Mr. Livingstone so no one would make the connection.

Kind of guy hockey players wouldn't approach to ask a question to unless someone else went with them. Used a ruler on the desk like frickin' punctuation. "Now," whack, "we can glean from this stanza that the speaker feels" whack, "gentle longing for his homeland" whack "and familial love for those left behind" whack.

Made us memorize Robert Frost's "Birches," telling us, "You won't understand it yet, but it's a good poem to have in your pocket for when you're older." Like it was the poetic equivalent of cab fare on a Saturday night. So — whatever — I memorized it, thinking I'd get the extra marks and it would fall out of my mind-pocket the minute class was over, like the date of the Treaty of Versailles or pi after the third decimal place.

The words feel nice against my mind, like rosary beads, though it took me years to understand that damn poem. Maybe I still don't, though I got a Robert Frost for Complete Idiots kind of book and went through it line by line. With poets, you're never sure what they're trying to say, since part of poetry is trying to make everything more complicated. You can't just say "I love this woman" or "I'm sad my mom died" or "life's pretty crappy." That's not what poetry is.

But, anyhow. Birches. I like how he goes on about wanting to swing on a birch tree like when he was a kid and needing to escape and life being 'too much like a pathless woods where your face burns and tickles with cobwebs broken across it and one eye is weeping from a trees having lashed across it open.' And I like how he keeps trying to escape from what's going on by these pretty little digressions, describing the trees like women and ice storms and what not. And then he says, "but I was going to say before truth broke in with all her matter of fact about the ice storms." No use! Life just keeps rearing up and won't let him take off on tangents. Kills me every time.

So now that poem's what I think when I'm trying not to. It's what I thought during the first game of my short-lived national team career, what I thought when Valerie was walking down the aisle and I was trying not to pass out from the heat and the smell of all that old woman perfume. (If I was a poet, I would talk about the white birch tree of her body swaying through the heat shimmer like she was bending, all those veils and lace encrusting her in the softest ice ever). That's what I thought my first night alone. 'But I was going to say before truth broke in with all her matter of fact about the ice storms'. 'Earth's the right place for love, I don't know where it's likely to go better'. A reminder I needed. My first night alone, I started to think about it more: the guy, how he couldn't escape, how the trees weren't really women and the truth always broke in and the boy who eventually wrecked the whole forest for good. Turns out, it's a fucking depressing poem.

I should be practising for job interviews, working on the old can-do smile. Hello, my name is Nolan and I am a — I was an elite wheelchair basketball player. The centre for Team Canada. The Big Girl. The Post. Now, I am a . . . former elite wheelchair basketball player: the post-Post.

I'll have to go back on the Pill. We have no money and no money means no baby, maybe even no house. Neither of us are employed, (since the public speaking gig apparently doesn't count), so there'll be no baby and this is a disappointment. Not only because it means I'll have to get a job — a pantyhose and yes-ma'am kind of job, no probably a 'would you like fries with that?' job considering my qualifications — but because my body feels without purpose. I'm used to that little red pulse of me that I draw out, charm to the surface. There are so many sports clichés about heat — she's on fire! Hot hands! — and I miss my embers. And pregnancy, I liked the job description: the idea of an egg that grows like a muscle, making sense out of my blood by putting my nutrients to good use. The feminist in me is cringing already. I want purpose, so I'm having a baby? I'm not a woman who can be still. I can't decide if it's a legacy of the hip or of sport, my inability to stay put. Push the barbell. Grow the muscle. Push the chair hard. Push the chair far. I'd be great at labour. I'm a woman used to pushing.

Quinn's adopted my Gretsch as his own and sits in our room for hours earning his calluses again. He's cleaned it up and put in a new bridge, which I didn't think it needed, and round coil strings instead of my flat coil ones, which makes my grungy blues guitar sound oddly chipper. Not that I'm an expert in gear. I've never played on stage and Quinn plans to. He's tuning with other people in mind.

"My back's sore," I tell him as we're reading in bed.

"'Wasn't the hip replacement supposed to fix that?" He doesn't put his book down.

"It could be that I'm walking differently now. Got time for a massage?"

Quinn shows me his fingertips, scabbed and ragged. "I would but I've played too much today."

"Just on your left hand."

"It's all coming back, though. I keep remembering licks I thought were gone forever. Just wait — B.B. and the guys are already impressed. A few more weeks of this, I'll be money. Thirty-two isn't too old, I don't think."

"So we're talking professional musician now?"

There's a silence, as if I've jinxed him by speaking the dream out loud. "I think so," he finally says. "I figure now's the last time to try, right?"

Quinn's a musician now and this is how it's going to be. He's breaking his fingers in like leather. He's going for thick skin, getting rid of the soft touch. This is how it's going to be: my sinews replaced by steel strings, any electricity between us channeled into the guitar. My guitar. The round Gretsch is like a better me: bigger hips, a mouth that says only what he wants it to, such a cheerful tone now.

"Okay," I say. "No worries."

"Okay," he says and tests his fingers with an air-guitar solo, playing the space between us like an instrument.

Darren takes the back roads, still thinking them a short cut no one else knows about. In some places, the pavement has worn away to reveal cobblestones. It looks like someone has scrubbed this city so well that the past has emerged. The shocks in the car are bad and our voices shake from the broken pavement, as if we are on the verge of tears.

We're supposed to be checking out the gym for the tryouts, but the music is low and good and in the car we don't have to look at each other. The silence isn't right yet and our bodies still want to fill it with motion: his fingertips on the steering wheel, my knee keeping time. The gym was open until five and it's six now. We've driven through a tank of gas, two CDs and a Tim Horton's drive through run for glazed donuts and chamomile tea. New Westminster doesn't seem big enough that we could lose this amount of time in its streets.

His mother's heart is clogged, he says. Or, rather, her arteries. And she's lived in New Westminster all her life, wanted to get treatment at Saint Mary's Hospital. But Saint Mary's has closed down — provincial cutbacks — and New Westminster's lost another Saint, even if it was a dirty one with no emergency room. Her arteries are clogged and her valves are weak, says Darren. He looks straight ahead and is probably glad for it. The streets can't hide how talking about her changes his voice.

"She's getting old," he says. "It's hard to — I mean, she's always been healthy as a horse — and my dad's never been one for cleaning the house. And between the two of us: I'm so tired these days. That's what they don't tell you when you become a quad: the rate all the working bits wear out. Anyhow, it's little things like that. Meals. Chores. Valerie's been good about it. Pretty good, actually. Mom likes her enough."

"You could get a maid service. Someone to come once a week to make sure your mom doesn't have to overexert herself. Because you've got to take care of yourself too."

"Yeah," he says and flicks at the radio. "Maid service. That might work."

We approach the forked on-way to the Queensborough bridge, the traffic thick but fast, like blood. Maybe this is what his mother's heart valves look like: a poorly constructed on-ramp, a bridge a few lanes too narrow. I'm in the mood for metaphor: what is a heart if not a bridge? What is a home if not a metaphor?

The gym's closed by the time we get there, so we don't leave the car. It's early December, the kind of chill that should be warded off with a lit fireplace and thick socks. The little heating vents try to ward off our breath fogging the windows, but fail except for a small flame-like spot near the middle. The car is no protection. There's nowhere to stretch our legs or curl up under a blanket.

"The school's new and it's too small already," says Darren. "Look at those portables. It hasn't been built even two years. But there's wireless internet access and . . . something else that's supposed to be state of the art. I forget. Supposed to be the very best in everything." Outside, a juice box shines with frost. A chocolate bar wrapper looks lovely without colour.

It's a little like one of our old tours: nearly night time, a good song on the stereo, locked doors and landmarks viewed from a distance. I don't think we ever had the windows down, even in the summer. Darren's driving a different car now, but it smells the same. The smell must belong to him.

The nausea is the only difference. For the past week I've been sick and there are two possible causes: hip infection or pregnancy. Pregnancy seems doubtful. Between the amount of chemicals and radiation my medical history has left in my body and the amount of chemicals Quinn's post-secondary education has left in his, we're not exactly Mr. And Mrs. Fertility. If the hip is indeed infected, I could have to have the replacement all over again or worse, be stuck with no hip at all.

"We should come up with the selection criteria. Then we can say we accomplished something."

"Ergonomic chairs. That's what it was. Save those young backs."

"But it's too small?"

Darren nods. He turns off the car, unbuckles and faces me. "Too small. So selection criteria. I'm thinking speed, skills, commitment to training, works well in the systems and lineups . . . What else? What do you think?"

"I think I need to throw up," I say and unlock the door, unbuckle and stagger out into the playground towards a garbage can. The air is good. Its chilled scent of rain and pine needles is the only medication I need. The wind holds my hair back. For a moment: that deep calm after sickness before the nausea starts again. I'm finished before Darren can even get his chair out to follow me.

"Jesus, Nolan. You okay? You want the window down? Get some air?" he asks as I slide into the car again: so smooth, this new hip.

"Must have the flu or something. I'm okay."

He touches my arm with his bad hand — the three curled fingers tight against each other — and I feel the old jolt of contact even through my nausea-clammy skin. I'd hoped adulthood would've changed my hormones enough to make me immune to Darren. I wanted to be reconfigured. "You're tough. We could go back. Do you want to go back?"

"Nah. Selection criteria. I like what you said, plus maybe . . . game knowledge, court vision, fits into our lineups . . . "

"Right. You sure you're okay? You're pale. I've got some flu-be-gone tea at home." He raises his arm as if to touch me again, then distracts his fingers by tapping a pen against the steering wheel.

"I'm fine. I'll just lie down when I get home. Don't worry. But thanks." Outside: a new school and old trees. Familiar bridges with new exit ramps. A new car, but I touch his knee to make a point and our circuitry is the same.

~

Dr. Benson, my GP, is a sports specialist and I wonder if she'll still treat me now that I'm no longer on a national team. The walls in the examining room are white with framed photos of athletes in the midst of competition, their faces pained and spastic. The photos are so bright I feel like I could step back into them, my first Paralympics, my second, my third.

"Nolan," says Dr. Benson. She's a former marathon runner, her body lean but the skin around her face stretched from resisting the wind too long. "Long time no see. Weren't you supposed to come for a check-up two weeks post-op?"

I shrug. "I felt pretty good."

She punches me on the shoulder. I like a doctor who can deliver a good punch when it's needed. Usually, it is. "Did you learn exactly nothing about your body from being an athlete? You underwent major surgery."

"Yeah," I say and look at the contorted face of a runner pushing his rib cage at the finish line. "Sorry."

She sighs. "How's the hip holding up?" I sit in the chair in the examining gown resisting the urge to cross my legs.

"Pretty good. Surprised I haven't ruined it yet."

She peers at me over the file. "Me too, actually. Knowing you. Any fevers? Infections? Red streaks? General feeling of unwellness? Because one infection and you're basically screwed, to put it medically." I like this doctor for her bedside manner and refusal to hide behind terminology. "How're you feeling in general?"

"Actually, that's kind of what I — I'm tired and really nauseous, even though I've done dick all — I don't know — It could be just stress. The new hip. Quinn losing his job. Me trying to find one. Oh, speaking of which, I need a new prescription for birth control. We were Trying, but since we're broke . . . "

She makes a note and I'm glad that her writing is illegible. "Uh huh. I see. Is there a chance of you being pregnant?"

"I don't think so. We've only had sex four or five times since the hip replacement. Plus, he's unemployed now."

Dr. Benson smirks. "Right. You can't possibly get pregnant if your partner's unemployed. Just like you can't get pregnant if it's your first time or if you keep your socks on."

I'm beginning to rethink the idea of choosing a GP based on sense of humour. "Yeah, yeah, I know. But we're in our thirties, so it takes three to nine months. I read that somewhere."

"Should. Doesn't mean 'will.' Listen, I'm going to give you a pregnancy test before I prescribe you the birth control pills. You're on ortho-tricyclene, right? Next time — and I shouldn't have to tell this to a woman your age — use a condom unless you're absolutely sure you want a baby."

All the couples we know tried for years and years. You'd think it was some kind of Olympic sport, the way they trained and took time off work to consult experts. Some part of me was looking forward to that, used to the notion that anything I want is hard work. It would have been familiar territory. Swap a heart rate monitor for an ovulation thermometer and we're off to the races. Maybe I don't want this? Maybe I just wanted more time.

I had the idea that trying to get pregnant would be like waiting in line. When I was young, some well-meaning adult told me that when a mommy and a daddy want to get pregnant, they send their wishes up to Jesus and wait and hope and if they're good and ready, He sends down a baby. For most of my life, I've had an image of people's hopes standing in some customer service line-up. The hopes are dressed mundane as the people who do the wishing — sweater vests, pants with skinny ankles, tasseled loafers — but their faces are puffy yet disturbingly cheery like children's show hosts after an all-night bender. They wait in line in a room with old linoleum and signs that say, "Four menstrual cycles from this point." At the front, some angel or God-figure — bored and cranky, wearing overalls and a name tag — takes frequent breaks and sighs often. Teenagers on skateboards muscle to the front of the line every now and then, impatient to see what all the waiting is about. No one complains, they just smile and the teenagers wander away dazed, holding their skateboards against their stomachs.

It pleases me now to think of teenagers this way, all them one monolithic, disrespectful group. It's a sign that I've forgotten enough of what it was like to be young that I'm ready to become a mother.

Still, it happens too quickly. Two months off the Pill, a few post-surgical sex acts and bam. I was hoping for a little leeway, for time to sort out some major questions. For example, will listening to the haunted, untethered voice of Robert Johnson during pregnancy make the child grow up with a high sheriff or a hell hound on his or her trail? Will listening to alt country turn my baby into a wanderer? A red-neck? A cowboy? I could listen to folk, but I wouldn't want the kid to grow up arrogant as Dylan. Plus, I've always preferred early folk of the 'takin' my cheatin' woman down to the river and layin' her low' variety and this can't possibly be healthy for a growing fetus. Probably it's not even healthy for me. Jazz is too sexy and no good mother would expose her growing child to a music form that is reported to be named after the jasmine perfume worn by prostitutes in the brothels of New Orleans. Maybe some Howlin' Wolf or Muddy Waters, hope the kid doesn't figure out what a 'mojo' is, let alone how you get it workin'. Maybe I should learn to stomach — ha ha — pop music, but this can't be right either. The kid might grow up frivolous and that would be the worst. This is the kind of thing that books can't tell: how to tune our connection to right pitch, how to strike the right umbilical cords.

Quinn's been hell-bent on this whole musician thing and I'm becoming a less and less suitable candidate for 'girlfriend of rock star.' But still, he's my . . . partner, boyfriend, significant other, better half. There's no good word. He's my Person. In the eyes of the law, we're some weird combined entity. We share assets. Some of his assets are right now cooking in my uterus.

I've heard about women wrapping up the pregnancy test stick and giving it as a gift. I've even been subjected to the home video of Alex when he found out that Clara was pregnant. Him opening the box on Christmas day and being puzzled then elated. Hugging! Crying! The

Christmas tree sparkling in an oh-so-merry way! God bless us everyone!

Christmas is still three weeks away and I'll never keep the secret for that long. I'm also not sure that Quinn would like to receive anything I've recently peed on as a gift. And besides, video evidence could prove traumatic to the poor little kid at a later date. It's too easy to imagine myself consoling some angsty thirteen-year-old; "No, honey, your daddy always swears like that when he's happy. It's good screaming." Video won't work.

I could take him out for dinner to a place where he can't bolt. Tell him over dessert, hope he doesn't get suspicious when I refuse the wine. Or I could just sit him down for a mature and rational discussion and do the old, "I have some good news and some bad news. Which would you like first?" routine. Bad news: I'm knocked up. The good news: you're the father. (Or is that the other way around?) Good news: I'm pregnant like we wanted. Bad news: we're broke. Bad news: I don't know if being pregnant is good news or bad news.

Unfortunately, I'm a terrible liar, so I'll have to tell him soon. I wear the lie on my face, in my body, that little half smirk like the tear in the wrapping on a Christmas present. He'll probably notice the instant he steps into the house.

When I hear the key in the lock, I freeze as if I've been caught breaking and entering.

"Hey hon," I call, wondering if this is the routine: if I usually call to Quinn when he comes home or if that's something I saw on TV. Times like these, I forget what's normal.

"Hey," he calls, and wanders into the kitchen. I fling myself into a Sear's catalogue pose by the table: Girl Without a Secret Modeling Something Innocuous and Tasteful.

"What's up?" he asks, scrounging in the cupboards and finding a bag of Oreos.

"Oh, not much." I'm sure he can hear it. What's up? I'm knocked up! We're knocked up! "What about you?" I pretend to do dishes, washing the same knife over and over.

"Was just jamming with the guys. You should hear us, Nole." He sits on the counter top and opens the bag, twisting an Oreo, licking the icing off, then leaving the cookie part and taking a new one. What kind of a father figure is this? What will he teach this kid about frugality or good nutrition?

"Oh yeah?"

"Yeah. We're fucking A plus. B.B's written this great song and asked me to solo in it and I just stayed within the classic Albert King box, but it still sounds really rocking. He's got this software that's amazing. You can layer and overdub whatever you want, so I came up with this bass line that just slides right underneath it. Smooth. He's going to email it to me. You can give it a listen. Cover band no longer, I'm telling you." He twists off another cookie, licks the icing and stacks the leftovers in a neat pile by the sink, his skinny legs swinging off the countertop. Those running shoes: is he ten years old? So much for being on the same wavelength. So much for him being my better half . . . or any part of me, really. He's my pre-operative lower body right now, not working at full speed, not getting all the connections. Shouldn't he be picking up on this by some kind of sexual telepathy? Doesn't he know where his assets are? What they're doing in other people's uteruses?

"Aren't you going to eat those cookies?" I ask. "Isn't that a waste?"

He blinks, pausing mid ramble. "Do you want them?"

"It's not about whether I want them or not. Those are perfectly good cookies and you're just throwing them away."

Quinn peers down at the cookies, then picks them up. "Jesus, what's your problem today? You're a bit cranky."

"I'm not fucking cranky. We're on a budget and you're wasting two thirds of those damn cookies and — " This is when the tears start. These are new. I'm not a crier. Quinn's seen me cry probably five times since we've been together, all for basketball-related reasons. Where are these coming from, the tears? I feel as if I own a whole new face.

Quinn stares at me, holding a cookie in each hand. "I'm . . . sorry if my snacking habits offend you . . . ?" He scoots off the counter, head tilted right and then left as if the tears are an optical illusion.

I try to speak, but the tears have moved from my face to my throat. He touches my hand. "Nolan? . . . What's wrong? Who died?"

I wish I was small and could curl against him. "No one," I sob. "No one."

He massages my shoulder. Maybe the tears are some weird muscle reaction, a knot that needs to be worked out. He wrings my shoulder as if it's a towel he's trying to get dry. "Hey now . . . what's wrong? Don't cry . . . what's all this? . . . "

"I'm pregnant," I blubber, the words all soft and squishy with tears. No lead up, no smooth preamble, not even a knock-knock joke. His hand on my shoulder tenses, then relaxes.

"No, no," he says. "That's all you're worried about? We only tried for two or three weeks. It's harder than that." He massages my shoulders again. "Don't worry. You can't be. Remember when Alex and Clara were trying? Remember how long that took?"

"Guess we had a bit of beginner's luck," I say. Quinn's hand leaves Oreo smears on my white shirt. He sits down at the kitchen table beside me, his knees giving out a little, and shakes his head. "I'm sorry," I tell him. "I didn't know how easy this would be. And by the time you lost your job, we were already . . . you know . . . "

Quinn tries for a wry smile but somehow falls short. He looks almost scary, distorted. "Don't be sorry. It's not like you did it alone." He rakes his hand through his hair, but it falls right back, obscuring his eyes. "So . . . is this a good thing or a bad thing? 'Cause we wanted a baby. I mean, we were Trying, right? We did this on purpose. It's just . . . things are different now. Financially."

He looks up and I wish I could kneel between his shaking legs and hug him, that we could be some intertwined creature with the strength of many. But I can't bend that way for another two weeks.

16

I RETURNED FROM THE STATES WANTING Cage Match. Everyone knew that I was with Darren, even Tony. The joke was that I was absorbing Valerie's on-court knowledge through some kind of sexual osmosis. Maybe I was channeling her ghost. Weird that it was some kind of initiation, though. I became included in conversations even beyond the topic of sex. It was assumed I knew what every nudge-nudge and wink-wink meant. And Sammy was right: no one really cared. Everyone was sleeping with someone else in the wheelchair sports community anyhow. I was linked now by degrees of sexual separation.

I wasn't sure that I liked new camaraderie. While we were warming up for a game, Nikki asked me if my hair had ever gotten caught in Darren's brace and even the American girls laughed. I didn't want those images in people's minds. Darren, I suspected, would be furious. I had cracked easier than a cipher, was less trustworthy than math.

When I returned, it was near Valentine's Day, a holiday I'd forgotten. Valentine's Day was a holiday for those whose relationships could be described in a Hallmark rhyme scheme: not us. "You couldn't be prettier/ You couldn't be sweeter/ You be my Humpbert, I'll be your Lolita."

The foyer of Our Lady of Perpetual Smackdowns was filled with the artwork of Sunday School children, who had made hearts out of glitter and construction paper proclaiming that Jesus is Love. The foil sparkles were picked up by my front wheels, tangling with the gunk there. This was likely the only glitz I was going to get from my Valentine. Somehow, the by-products of every celebration these children had ended up in my front casters.

Valerie was over by the sidelines getting into her chair. I didn't recognize her right away. Though she'd gained weight, she still looked smaller than I remembered. I only knew it was her by Darren's reaction. He was doing a big belly laugh that struck me more like a Santa Claus imitation than the real thing. And she was Santa laughing back and everyone was making some attempt at jolly. For two Big Girls, we were practically opposite in looks: her dark curls to my placid blonde. She was Big; I was a Girl.

"Hey Nole," said Darren. "Welcome back. You've met Valerie, haven't you?"

Valerie wheeled up to me and extended a hand. "Hi, I'm Valerie Steward."

Her hand was smooth: definitely an off-season palm. "Nolan Taylor. We've met before. At selection camp a couple of years back."

Valerie smiled. "Right, right."

"I thought you'd retired," I said.

"Funny how you miss it. It's been a while since I've been in Our Lady of Perpetual . . . what did you used to call it, Dare? Our Lady of Perpetual Smackings?" An elastic couldn't contain her hair. It had not just body, but personality. And not a particularly good personality at that.

"Smackdowns," said Darren. "Right." He dusted the soiled glitter off his palms. "Should we get on with the Smackdowns?" He strapped in, pulled the T-shirt over the strap, fixed his feet.

"We still call it that," I said.

I thought on-court would be easy. There were rules for fouls. We knew exactly how close we could get to each other, how we were allowed to cross paths. Valerie and I were on opposite teams. Big Girl to counteract Big Girl. Usually, it was Darren's job to neutralize me. With Valerie here, however, the teams were immediately lopsized. The team with Darren was always too good. The math didn't work anymore.

"I'm so out of shape," said Valerie. "I don't know how long I'm going to play."

"I bet you haven't lost it," said Darren, almost by rote. He was likely well practiced from years of 'no, honey, you're not fat.' She was, though, and this pleased me. The chair proved that she was out of shape. It was a reminder of her old measurements and I was delighted at how backrest and side guards couldn't contain her. Her belly almost obscured the buckles of her hip strap.

"I'm sure I'll want to drop dead within five minutes. You should be on my team, Darren-Honey. I'll just yell 'man down' and you can pick up the slack."

Erika and Vern laughed, Darren nodded and off we went.

For the first time, Darren's on-court presence didn't make a difference. He shied away from the ball, letting us have our one on one. She tried to full court press me, but I was faster. I tried to full court press her, but she had better chair skills and wouldn't be pinned. We weren't used to having someone our own height to contend with. I watched the space between her breasts darkening with sweat. The stain was the size of a man's hand and I tried not to think of all the shadows Darren's hands had cast across her body over the years. Eleven years. I'd known him for ten months.

Twenty minutes into the practice, neither one of us had scored. We blocked each others shots, spun around each other's chairs, keeping ourselves out of the play.

"Do people still do the spin-out drill?" asked Valerie. "You would benefit a lot from that. Even if it only helps you move your hips within the chair, it'd be worth it."

"I do the spin-out drill twice a week," I said.

"Ah," she said and smiled. "Well then."

Every retort I could come up was some variation of either "Do people still diet? You would benefit a lot from that," or "Yeah, well, maybe I'll improve my hip movements fucking your ex-husband." Instead, I smiled. "Thanks for the tip, though." That was the only time she spoke on-court.

Halfway through the practice, she was on a fast break and I was racing to catch up. I passed her, going faster than I'd ever had at a practice like this one. Valerie translated into good ball. Valerie went hard. I got my chair in front, but she didn't stop. We collided. The mice in the rafters above skittered away at the sound. No one usually made an impact big enough to worry them.

I skidded sideways across the floor, unable to hold her. She moved me aside as she went up on her front wheels. Her head ended up in my chest as she fell and she smelled of the potpourri sachets that were still in Darren's clothes drawers.

"That's a foul," said Valerie.

"You smoked me. It's a charge."

"You didn't give me time and space to stop." She had great hazel eyes, green with anger, the kind someone would never get tired of looking at.

"The time and space rule went out two years ago. Now it's just whoever has chair position. You're either across the path or you're not. New rules."

"You just swerved right in front."

"To establish chair position. I got there."

"Can we just keep playing?" Darren asked, though he was supposed to be the referee. He hadn't been pushing the chair hard, but his face was flushed. "You okay, Val?"

"I'm fine too," I said.

"Is this true about time and space?" Valerie asked.

"I didn't see the play."

"But in general?"

Darren shrugged. "It depends on how the ref calls it. No one's really used to the new rules."

"Yeah, and if the ref calls it right, it's either 'the defender has chair position' or 'the defender doesn't have chair position,'" I said. "I had position. She's not even debating that. She moved my chair sideways. That's a foul."

Darren held up his hands. "I didn't see it."

"How can you not have seen it when all you're doing is sitting around watching us?"

"We'll give the ball to Val because it's her first time out of retirement. Let's go."

There was no Cage Match that night. Though Valerie left the gym early, brushing her finger against Darren's shoulders as she walked out the door as if to mark him with her sweat and the metal residue from her pushrims, neither of us asked.

The gym was silent, the swinging lights hunching over us like carrion birds, the rafters alive with wind and mould. My sweat dried quickly and the workout flush faded, though the adrenaline stayed. We sat side by side and took our time packing up. Vern left without asking for sexual favours. Rob left without teasing Darren. Everyone knew.

"Well," said Darren finally. "You coming with me?"

I went back to his place because I suspected that if I didn't, Valerie would. She still had a key and a hundred reasons to come over in the form of boxes left behind. She was there in the old bottle of Midol in the medicine cabinet, the writing on the back of photos and the little notes Darren had stowed on the top of the fridge to remind him of dentists' appointments that were years past.

The CDs I'd burned for him for Christmas had been relegated to the back seat, along with the CD player itself. He didn't like the flashy technology: the way it made the music hiccup. And it was harder to go back to just the right place in a song when you're waiting at a stop light. Darren liked music the way people liked tobogganing. He'd fast forward a song to its crescendo when the singer is just about to go crazy and take the guitar and drums with him, then go sliding down as the song descended. He'd do it over and over.

"What's that?" he'd often ask me at a particularly difficult solo. "How do they do that?"

He was impressed by geometry: how the pentatonic shapes made sense of his favourite blues noise. He'd fixate on a few measures and tap them our on the steering wheel.

"Now this is music," he'd say. "Now this is real goddamned music."

My Christmas present to him apparently wasn't real music because the Bonnie Raitt and Lucinda Williams and Michelle Shocked were all gone. Howlin' Wolf narrated the drive home. It was just as well. I mouthed along the words to "Killing Floor" — *I shoulda quit you a long time ago — and* looked at him when I said it. The Blues were better than silence. Son House said once about how the only true blues songs are the ones about what happens between a man and a woman. It didn't matter what tape was in the player. Our conversations on the ride home were the same song over and over.

"It's not an exclusive club, Nolan," Darren finally said as he fumbled with the lock to the house. "Valerie's a good player. She has every right to be there."

"Fine, then. Make her sign the code of conduct and then enforce it. She doesn't get to go flying all over the court because you don't want to make her learn the new rules."

The key finally gave. The house was darker than nighttime. "You were both right."

"No, we weren't. We're following two different sets of rules. Eventually she has to follow the same ones as everyone else."

"I got a kitten," said Darren, as the lights went on and a small puff of fur leapt for my shoelaces. "Did I tell you I got a kitten?"

"It appears so," I said.

"I figured someone besides me needs to take up space around here."

"She's not taking up much space now," I noted. I picked her up and she fit in my cupped hands.

Darren's house was over a hundred years old and he was the first person to ever live in it alone, he told me. Always families, not a single spinster aunt or grandmother waiting out her final years. This house was never passed down through generations. It didn't belong to any one last name. People raised children here and then moved on and someone else filled the rooms with sound.

"It's a big house, that's why people want to have families here," he said. "Too hard for just one person to take care of. It's easier for me because I've gotten rid of a lot of things that could collect dust and I vacuum often, but can you imagine being some poor crippled-up old woman trying to keep up with this place? All these little nooks and crannies. It's made for an era when you'd have eight or ten kids as slave labour."

We moved through the dark into the kitchen. The kitten shirked from the light, burrowing her head in my armpit. Darren made tea and I sat at the table with the kitten on my lap. She snuggled as close to my heart as possible, greedy for warmth. "So, what, you bought the cat so she can work the vacuum cleaner once in awhile?"

Darren reached over and scritched the kitten's ears. She made a cooing noise, like a bird or a baby, as if she was so young she hadn't decided what animal she wanted to be. "Nah. It's just not a natural thing to live in a house this big alone. This is a house that thrives on people. It needs them."

The kitten had lovely lines of grey and black and white and dots you could connect with your finger. "Ah, I see. I see. It's just the house that's lonely?"

"I'm not lonely." He got up to fill the cups with water and ginger tea bags. "If that's what you're insinuating."

"But the house is lonely?"

Darren frowned and the kitten licked at his finger. "I don't know. I'm not lonely. I don't know why I bought the damn thing. I just figured it would be good to have someone else living here. Someone to chase out the cobwebs and rattle the ghosts."

"You're not all alone. I'm over here all the time."

"Yeah, but you don't live here. Even when you sleep the night, you're a guest. You leave the next day."

He was right. I'd been involved with Darren for four months now and still didn't have a toothbrush here. I wasn't trying to conquer the house with feminine hygiene products in the bathroom, but it made sense that since I spent more time at his house than my apartment that I should leave some mark on the place. When I left, the house shed me entirely.

"What's her name?" I asked. She was sleeping with her head resting on my forearm. Darren stroked her head with his pinky.

"I could never get a cat when Valerie was here. She's allergic." The news made me like the kitten even more.

I may have been a stranger in the house, but at least it didn't give me an allergic reaction. "Why does it bug you that Valerie comes out?"

"Because she's all 'I'm Valerie *Steward*, oh Darren-honey, play on my team.'"

He laughed. "Quit the falsetto. She doesn't sound like that. I'm kind of flattered. You're both jealous. Not often that two lovely ladies duke it out over a middle-aged quad."

"I'm not jealous. I just don't need those kinds of mind games."

"If I were you, I'd put up with them in the interest of getting a chance to play against her. She can play you in a way I can't. Just pretend she's some Big Girl from the German or the American team."

"What'd you name the kitten?"

"Morse. Because she looks like Morse code. I'm just calling her Morris."

"Do you know how many cats are named Morris?"

"Yeah, but how many are named after the code?"

I stroked the dots and dashes on the cat's fur, a cipher without a message behind it. On my arm, there were scratches that Valerie had left when she fell, lines I didn't have to read between.

At provincial team practices, we shared around women's magazines. The routine had started on airplanes, but gradually it had become an on-land bonding experience. Darren disproved of them in general. He'd seek out their bright covers like a father searching for drugs, then read their titles out loud: "Create More Motion with Love

Lotion . . . Sex Toys for Good Girls and Their Boys. Why do you need sex tips? Let alone sex tips delivered like a Dr. Seuss rhyme . . . all this corny alliteration and slant rhyming. 'Have you done it in a bus?/ I have not done it in a bus/ Do you use the HandMaster Plus?/ I have not used the HandMaster Plus.' Come on, Nolan. You're smarter than this."

"Oh, relax," I'd tell him, taking the magazine out of his hand, hitting him with it, and tossing it on a pile beside my history readings. "Woman does not live by Foucault alone."

I showed up at practice the next night with two new magazines for trading.

"This one's boring. It's all makeup tips," I said as I handed the magazines over to Sammy. "The *Cosmo*'s not bad. A few good suggestions."

Sammy was changing into her practice jersey. "Learn anything to try out on wheelchair basketball's answer to Pierce Brosnan?" She stretched and her ribs were stark without ab muscles, pushing against the skin. The pattern was like the slats of a fence and I wondered how it would feel: the texture of bone and its absence.

"Not really. Between the leg muscles he lacks and the hip flexion I lack, I'm pretty sure *Cosmo*'s not designing their position of the month with us in mind."

Sammy laughed, the beads on her cornbraids clicking against each other. "Amen, sister. But least you can read it for the girl on guy action. I'm still waiting for the issue devoted to lesbian paraplegic sex."

I began taping up my wrists. Sammy put her shirt on: again, musk or cologne. "You need your own magazine," I said.

"I should write a how-to manual. I really should. Good idea, kiddo. You're way more fun to bug about Darren than Valerie was. She was so damn secretive. All 'there's a reason they call it my *personal* life.'"

"Well, she's not being secretive these days. She comes out to the rec league practices. I bet she flirts with him now more than she ever did when they were together."

"You get a chance to play against Val? Even if she's out of shape, she's still one of the smartest players in the game. You can learn a lot from watching her."

"Watching her flirt with Darren?"

"Nolan, honey. I know you're only nineteen, but come on. Let's grow up a little bit, here. Play nice with Valerie. Learn a few tricks of the trade. Go home and try out every position in the Kama Sutra with her ex-husband."

~

Darren:

Mid-afternoon how long ago? Maybe thirteen years ago? A long, rainy stretch of days in January with no holiday in sight. Nolan spread belly-down on the living room floor with her schoolbooks in front of her, legs up and knees knocking together in a Lolita pose. Chewing on a pencil, even, her tomboy calves swaying. I could almost imagine her in white, lacy socks and Mary Janes, though even little girls haven't worn those for decades.

I was working in an armchair that smelled of wet dog despite no dog being present. So, yes. Nolan in a schoolgirl pose, one of the first times I realized that I didn't have to entertain her anymore. We didn't always have to converse or show off. It was nice. It was just that: nice. It was exactly the time on a Sunday afternoon when I wanted someone around. We were doing our own thing, but it was better to have her there.

"Fuck," she muttered and shifted. Her hip clicked; I heard her bones. Old woman bones, a knitting-needle sound. She winced and rolled over, then gathered her books up and went to find an easier chair.

"Want some tea while I'm up?" she asked.

"Sure," I said.

"Earl Grey or Ginger?"

"Surprise me."

And off she went. No wonder she didn't make sense. A school girl playing my old lady. A teenager choosing to spend her Saturday night over chess and mint tea and get up in the morning to dash off her homework. She should have been one or the other: a woman my age who'd always been there and knows me by heart or a younger girl with easy bones.

I went to Darren's gym five days a week: usually with him, but sometimes without. Even though the desk guy knew me by name and one of my calves had grown slightly bigger than the other thanks to the imperfect cycles of the elliptical machine, I still didn't feel like a regular. It was a gym aimed at the older crowd and there was hardly anyone in my age range or tax bracket. At nineteen, I was entirely too old for the awe I possessed towards the change rooms: the complimentary hair-care products, the towel service, the women who wore scarves well and could get away with a pant-suit, even one with shoulder pads. In the change room, they conversed about children while dressing under fluorescent lights. It was so easy for them. They treated their stretched-out nipples as if they were simply brooches or Remembrance Day poppies. I was a different level of naked. My ribs were not yet submerged and I moved as if with extraneous bones, scaffolding waiting to fall away.

In the workout rooms, I could use Darren to blend in. People usually thought I was his attendant, despite the fact that the roles were reversed. Plus, a bench press machine was a bench press machine no matter where it is and I knew my way around. In the change rooms, however, I was on my own. I dressed behind the shower stalls, but was fascinated.

In the gym, the mirrors were warped and my shape wavered across them, reflection arbitrary. I could hardly stand to watch myself. Instead, I spied on the regulars. They all knew each other and I'd overheard talk of a coffee-date group. I named them by their accessories: Led-Zeppelin-Shirt-Lady, Lycra Woman, Girl With Racquetball Skirt Many Inches the Wrong Side of Appropriate. When I was bored during cardio, I would invent occupations: married rich, married rich, mother of two who gave up a career in publishing to pursue domestic happiness, married rich then divorced, high profile stocks and bonds investor who owns acreage in the Fraser Valley with hopes of getting back to her farm girl roots.

Darren was trying to tell me something, but I was too busy eavesdropping on some of the "regulars" talking about their grandchildren. I loved their helmets of white hair and Red Door perfume. They smelled like an old, glamorous movie.

"You listening, Nolan?" Darren asked. We were side by side on the ground doing bench presses with free weights. He would only work his good arm when I was around, but I'd catch him struggling with the 20-pound weights on the other arm when he thought I wasn't looking. The muscles on his weaker arm had grown, but they looked misplaced: a bicep with no tricep, the left side of his good hand bigger than the right. The muscles he could change looked like creatures under his skin, as if they didn't even belong to him.

"Yeah, sure."

"I was just saying that you should switch up the angle of your bench press. You're up to fifty pounders. It's getting too easy." He had a forty-pound weight beside him.

"Tony said to change the tempo."

"Just because he's your coach doesn't mean he knows everything."

I lay down on the mat again. The women beside us had learned to work just hard enough that they could still laugh. I never saw them weight train and imagined that they grew their muscles hoisting bags of soil for tomato plants or holding grandchildren above their head and making them fly.

"He has a degree in human kinetics."

Darren shrugged. "Well, whatever. You do what you think is best."

After the workout, I went to the change room to shower. Usually, I showered at Darren's place, which meant I would emerge smelling like his soap and shampoo and spend the whole day feeling as if I was in borrowed clothing. That day, however, there was no time. We were going straight from a workout to a movie — a rare time we left the house — and I would have to shower at the gym.

When I entered the change room, the women had just finished getting out of the shower. The steam's heat had made their breasts pink as infants and they dried them as lovingly. The curves of their bodies were easy gradations and I could only think of my pubic bones and skinny legs: the sharpness of me.

I tried not to stare, though sport had taught me to compare and contrast. I thought of my body like a series of trading cards: her hips for my strong shoulders, her breasts for my waistline. I wanted to come out ahead, to have the best collection. This was the way I knew myself: the bicep straining during preacher curls, the hip aching after practice. Only with Darren did I ever feel united: knit together with nerve endings.

It was strange to be showering in such a well-lit place, my skin wet and iridescent. As I left the shower stalls, I had to pass by a room of mirrors. The regulars were applying lipstick with brushes so small they could be painting miniature portraits. They wore scarves like my mother. In the mirrors, I saw my body from behind: the shoulder blades pulling the smaller muscles in tight against them, the ribs like the hull of a streamlined boat.

When I got to my locker, a woman whose workout outfit had a sequined flower on it was changing beside me. She wasn't one of the regulars.

"Are you a cheerleader?" she asked me. "You look like a cheerleader."

"No. I'm a basketball player." I turned away from her and did up the clasp of my bra.

"You could be a cheerleader. I think I used to be a cheerleader." The regulars had turned to watch. They appraised me and I imagined what they saw: a girl so pale steam couldn't brighten her.

"You think?" I asked.

"I think," said the woman. "I'm not sure. It was a long time ago."

When the woman left, one of the regulars smiled at me. "I think someone needs to adjust her meds. You look more like a basketball player to me with that height." And that was the first of many times I walked naked through unflattering light.

17

QUINN:

I mean, come on. I was nineteen. Girls with piercings in surprising places wanted me. They flashed lip-metal smiles and ate nachos at my shows. And nice-girl girls too, smart girls playing dumb. Why did they smile and squeal and make suggestive tongue gestures with melted nacho cheese? Because I was the man. Why did girls who usually dated smarter, richer guys touch my shoulder and stand close in the hall? Because of me, the man. Nineteen years old.

The Fender Strat, the leather jacket, the slim hips, the "Fuck the police" patch on my backpack. I was nineteen. I was fucking punk rock, baby. And Nolan was so uninterested. Not cold . . . distracted. And she was tall, which made her seem mature. Yeah, her height: I felt like Napoleon looking at a map of Russia.

Hell, we just kind of . . . forgot to break up, Nolan and I. I mean, we get along, right? And she's pretty in an angular, sporty way if you like women whose arms are bigger than their legs, (which she didn't have when we started going out). And she gets along with my friends, if not my mother, who doesn't get along with anyone. It's not like we fight often or she nags me or whatever. We have a few stock arguments, but I mean, she's great. Nolan's great. We're both basically easy to get along with.

Plus, for all these years she's been traveling a lot, preparing for World Championships, Paralympics, calling me on crackly phones from places where I could hear chickens in the background. And then we graduated and became employed, (well, I did), and it was like six or seven years had gone by and we'd somehow gotten over the five-year hump. We're like those cartoon characters who can walk on air until they look down. All these couples who work on their issues and read self-help books and talk about their feelings. We just kind of . . . stayed together.

And this, too: I never met anyone cool enough to break up a six year, seven year, ten year, thirteen year relationship over. Not that I didn't have crushes on certain women, (oh Marcie and your cardigan sets!), or fantasize about parts of a whole. I either never had the opportunity to follow through or I just . . . didn't.

So, sure. I got lucky first try. Picked a winner, though I know Nolan thinks I've sowed my wild oats, gathered my rose buds while I may, whatever that poem is. But I haven't. Some high-school make-out sessions, a religious girl I dated for a month or two in first year who wouldn't tolerate much of anything, a party where a drunk chick let me put my hand up her skirt, but besides that, it was just her. In second-year university I waited for Nolan. Not sure why I did that. Probably my idea of either a romance or a challenge. And now, there it is. Thirteen years of her.

But what happens to those wild oats, those rose buds? Everyone else picked the best ones, that's for sure, and the rest have bloomed, wilted and wound up in potpourri sachets for old women's lingerie drawers.

It's like sexual accounting. The average Canadian man will have sex with seven women over the course of his lifetime. That's like science or sociology or something. Seven women. It's like paying your taxes.

And say you forgot to pay your taxes, oh, thirteen years ago and you finally pony up. That money doesn't count to the current fiscal year, right? No, it counts towards the year you missed. So what about those six women I forgot to have sex with? Well, buddy, you've got to pay your dues. Doesn't count as infidelity. In fact, it probably makes a relationship stronger because those doubts are gone. You know what's out there and it's more dimpled and saggy than you expected.

Because once you're married or have a kid, the window's over. That's a whole new animal. You get married, your girlfriend gets knocked up . . . it's totally different. That's mature, adult. Real life, baby. Then you're breaking something set in stone by law or biology.

A threesome might work, of course, but Nolan's pregnant and the window on that's already closed. You can't ask your pregnant wife-person to have a threesome. She's pregnant. She's the mother of your child. That would somehow be like having sex with the Virgin Mary.

It's not like I really want anyone else. No one in particular anyhow. There's tons of stuff I'd change about Nolan, but basically . . . we match. We work. We're fine. But, really, I worked damn hard to get her and when you put it out on paper, she's not something to get excited about. I mean, come on. With the bad hip, she's not exactly going to be a gymnast in bed. She's just not very . . . bendy. And she's smart but not driven career-wise and plays a weird sport no one watches. Still, it took a lot of effort to date her. And then she seemed to know everything about sex the first time after I finally (finally, finally) convinced her.

Eight or nine months of sucking up, two months (two frickin' months!) of dating and then her in my bedroom with the windows open and me looking down to see her skin all flushed and lit, the gravity spreading her breasts into nothing. And me, feeling short and clumsy and looking at her ribs, (her ribs of all things), just a skinny kid amazed by the shape of her bones.

~

The biggest disappointment is that the limp hasn't gone anywhere, just the pain.

"You will probably never walk normally," says Dr. Felth. He's rolling a leather cup in his hand, a memento from some exotic vacation. I've brought no X-rays with me and he needs something to do with his hands. "After twenty-odd years of limping, it's all you know how to do. You've never walked properly in an adult body."

My last good steps were taken with a child's frame and my body doesn't have the muscle memory now that it's earthbound by breasts and hips. They wouldn't let me keep the damaged bone and this limp is my one souvenir. It's in my mind, in the muscles that have grown wrong in compensation. My gait is my body's bad habit and I've read that personality is nothing more than a series of habits, the same steps over and over. Skin sheds, hair grows, scars fade, this limp is in me deeper than flesh or bone. It tells me that the bionic hip hasn't changed anything. There's no cure for what I am. I'm above science.

"So I'm pregnant," I tell Dr. Felth. "Is that going to be a problem?"

"Really now?" he asks, British accent disappearing in surprise. "That's wonderful news. Certainly explains why you've arrived here without X-rays."

I blush. This must be what they mean when they say that pregnant women glow. It's constant embarrassment. And I still haven't told my mother yet.

"Thanks. But is it going to be a problem hip-wise?"

Dr. Felth taps his leather cup with his pen. "Well, it won't make things easier, that's for sure. Pregnancy causes all sorts of muscular imbalances even in able-bodied women. And there is a risk that labour may damage the hardware. We'll monitor it. You keep up with the physio." I don't mention that physio is fifty bucks an hour or that we're both unemployed or that I don't feel right going to physio for any injuries that aren't game-related. "Here," he says, putting down the cup and going to my file folder. "Let me show you something."

He puts an old X-ray up on the screen and I stare at all my ghostly bones. "See where there's some arthritis on L5 on your spine because of when you fractured it? That's exactly where the baby's going to press on. You take care of that, okay? That's going to be a trouble spot. Plus, the new hip. That's a lot of pressure to be putting on a prosthetic device that hasn't fully healed yet." A hundred thousand years after I die, people will be able to read this baby on me. All that will be left will be my bones tattling about my life's traumas and childbirths. This what they'll know: that I was female, a Big Girl, that my hip was necrotized thanks to an improperly pinned growth plate — or maybe they won't have that detail, just wonder how I got an old person's disease so young — that I have a back injury, though they'll never know who caused it, and that I was pregnant. My skeleton will say nothing about Quinn; he hasn't gotten bone-deep yet.

~

The house is too full of our bills and Quinn's rehearsing. Everyone else on the street has put up lights and most yards have plastic snowmen. One family has even spray-painted the dead grass white, so it appears that our house has missed not just the season but an entire weather system, (though I'm sure we'll be feeling the effects of that guy's white Christmas in our garden next year if we're still here).

I visit my mother just for an excuse to ride the ferry. I want to breathe in some place where the wind moves fast all the way through me, inflating me like a scarecrow. I've lost weight since the pregnancy — morning sickness that lasts through all three meals — and it feels like my clothes aren't even my own.

I stand on the deck but the air smells of french fries and the perfume from the girls beside me. I move locations, but even without people the wind carries the odours of fuel and fish. Seagulls hover above us, but the wake's velocity won't let them scream.

In my parents' house, there's an old couch I like, one I've worn down to fit me over the years. I had hoped for this couch, a hand-knit blanket and the herbal-tea smell of my mother's pantry. Instead, she picks me up at the ferry with a list in her hand.

"I've worn out the rest of my friends," she tells me. "Drained their shopping marrow to the core. Some people have the stamina, some don't. I figure you must have my shopping genes in there somewhere."

"I'm actually just getting over a — "

"What's your budget for this season, dear?"

"Sixty bucks."

My mother sighs. "Quinn's still not employed."

"He wants to try other options. Something in music, maybe. A band. I don't think he's talking about stardom — well, I don't think he's serious. Maybe he'll settle for the production side."

The radio's off. My mother hates to be distracted when she drives. She lets the silence write its own hurtin' country tune. "Well," she says. "Sixty dollars, then. It's a good thing you don't have much in the way of close friends."

After an hour, I'm ready to pull the cripple card to get home. I won't have this excuse for too many weeks longer.

"Oh look at that," says my mother when I tell her I'm ready to pack it in. "The Rubber Tree! And it sells condoms! Isn't that clever? I have a friend who's just gone through a divorce and she needs some incentive to get back at it."

The woman at the front desk of the Rubber Tree has long, frizzy hair with an excessive amount of beads around her neck and skirts around her ample waist. My mother, too, has scarves. They flow behind her as she bustles about the store, blending in with the palate of condom colours.

"Look Nolan!" says my mother, "Coloured *and* flavoured condoms." She lowers her voice at the last word, as if we weren't in a store devoted solely to the selling of prophylactics.

I am an adult and therefore should be able to handle my mother flapping around a box of Wet n' Wild Cherry Flavoured.

"Didn't have that in our day, did they?" says the woman at the desk.

"If they did, I never tried one." She studies the box. "Thank God for the hippies."

"Oh, you can say that again," says the woman, beads clicking against her chest. And before I know it, my mother's in a detailed conversation, complete with hand gestures and flouncing of scarves, about how their generation made the world safe for peace, love and designer condoms. The conversation is an anti-aging formula. The more she talks, the more I revert back through my twenties right into my preteens when the mention of me K-I-S-S-I-N-G in tree with a member of the opposite sex was cause for a full-body blush.

"But, really," says my mother. "Flavoured, I can understand. Flavoured, I can deal with. Great idea. But coloured condoms? Now, you have to tell me what the line of thinking is here. Because, in my mind, a coloured condom is of little use considering where it's going. I mean, there's not exactly a great light source up there."

There are some conversations that should not take place.

"It's for foreplay. Spice," says the woman. "But, you're right. Hardly useful. But I guess you do what you can to get people into them. No matter if it's flavoured, coloured, ribbed for her pleasure, ribbed for his pleasure, or has bells and whistles."

"Myself, I think it's just overcompensation," says my mother, winking theatrically at me. "A man uses one of these, he's obviously trying to distract the woman from, well, the size of the prize, I guess you could say. I would never be, you know, intimate with a man who wore one of these."

The words 'mother,' 'condom shop' and 'size of the prize' should never appear together. Not in the same sentence, not in the same room, not in the same universe.

"Nolan, does Quinn use these?" My mother and the desk woman look at me.

"No, we don't really — "

"My daughter's been with the same man for thirteen years. God knows how she keeps things interesting, considering that she has this problem with her hip where it doesn't bend more than thirty degrees." She beams at me. "Oh, honey. That hip replacement must have done wonders for your intimate life."

"No kidding, eh? Those hip replacements," says the woman. "They're really something else, aren't they? But I never thought they could spice up a sex life. I wonder if my husband could get one for that reason. Mike needs all the range of motion he can get, let me tell you."

My mother laughs. "Don't they all, at that age? But Nolan, really. You should be using protection. Sometimes birth control isn't enough."

"You know," I say. "This lecture is coming about two months too late--."

"I'm not lecturing. Am I lecturing?"

"Because Quinn and I have stopped using birth control."

"But honey. You could get pregnant." She punctuates the sentence by knocking over a vase full of condom

Christmas trees on sticks. The woman at the desk giggles nervously.

"That's kind of the point," I say and the desk woman bustles over and begins a very intricate, almost zen-like process of condom-tree arranging.

"You don't have a job. You're not married. Do you even plan to get married? Did you make this little decision before or after Quinn lost his job?" I decide not to tell her that we made the decision while I was high on opium-based painkillers. Her face is red and it's impossible not to make a comparison between the shade of her cheeks and that of the condoms on the box.

"Before. And by the time he lost his job, it was a bit too late to call the whole thing off."

The woman at the desk looks up, brandishing a condom-Christmas-tree-on-a-stick like a magic wand. "Oh, congratulations! That's so exciting!"

"No, no, no. Wait," says my mother, her scarves undulating as her hand movements get more elaborate. "You can't be pregnant. You're not married. Neither of you are working. Wait a minute. You're pregnant? You're going to have a baby?"

"That's kind of what pregnant means. Geez, mom, you're a condom connoisseur but you don't know about the birds and the bees?" The attempt at humour is misplaced. My mother glares at me.

"No, but I know what the word 'irresponsible' means. You never think things through. And Quinn. He's not ready to be a father. He's barely ready to admit that he's never going to be a rock and fucking roll star."

This was unexpected. Too many "Baby Story" episodes had convinced me that this would be a time for pink-cheeked squealing and tears of joy, not angry gesticulating with condom boxes.

"Quinn's held down a full-time job for nine years. He's just going through a . . . phase. He didn't know we were pregnant when he quit his job. And I'm looking for work. Plus — come on — what's this about marriage? We've been together for over a fucking decade." So much for the liberation bestowed upon us by the decade of free love.

"Don't swear at your mother," she says and turns to the desk woman. "We'll take one box of the red condoms, two of those Christmas tree things and a package of the ribbed."

"And yes," I tell her as she grabs me by the arm and escorts me out the door, "we have used coloured condoms. The novelty wore off quickly."

When we get outside, I glance down at the bag in her hand and begin to laugh.

"This isn't funny, Nolan," says my mother. "When you're up at 3 AM with a screaming child you will realize how not funny this is."

"No, it's just . . . " I gesture to the bag. "It's just that one of us is post menopausal, the other is pregnant. What exactly are we going to do with these?"

~

Dr. Taylor:

Linda says it's such a pity: only one man and now she's good as married.

"I know I learned a lot from playing the field," she says as we sit on the porch and drink coffee. "I was ready for you, when you finally came along . . . my knight on his Vespa scooter."

And I'm the only one who knows, outside of probably Sophia. We'd gone to one of Nolan's games and as they were warming up I saw that man — likely a triplegic, incomplete — touch her fingers against the wheel. With his good hand, I guess, stroking her thumb as if it were the leaf of some fine bloody hothouse plant. Just a touch, and then she blushed. Amidst all the warm-up music, clash of chairs, people counting out the number of lay-ups scored, I noticed what he was doing to her fingertips. And, of course, the way he looked at her. I'd been worried about the wolf pup teenage boys.

But it was him, this guy maybe only fifteen years younger than me, one affected hand, a walking quad. He had to be over thirty, probably the same age I was when Nolan was born. Odd to see that: him stroking her fingers like me holding that infant on my chest, amazed at her downy eyebrows.

"Oh, they're just friends," said Linda when I pointed it out, her voice hoarse from screaming. "That Darren guy, he's not unattractive, but with his condition I don't know if he could really, well, you know. Even if he wanted to."

And, of course, I've never told.

Teenagers stink and this pregnancy has given me a prima donna nose. The tryouts are being held in a high school that smells of b.o., perfume and rotting lunches forgotten in lockers even though there are no teenagers present. I touch the walls and expect them to crumble away under the saturation.

"Can you smell that?" I ask Darren as we walk through the halls. He's got the ballbag around his neck as he pushes, his nose in old leather. I carry the electric pump, a clipboard, papers.

He shrugs. "Not really. What am I supposed to be smelling?"

"Teenagers. I already feel sick and no one's started sweating yet."

"You're not pregnant or anything, are you? You've had the 'flu for like a month."

I don't say anything. I've long ago given up lying to Darren.

We get to the gym and the odour is different: all these kids and their tryout-camp nerves. It's good to smell someone else's anxiety instead of just my own. We probably should have gotten here earlier to pump their tires and ease their fears. The janitor must have let them in. These keener kids banter and shoot and dribble faster than a heartbeat.

Darren drops the ball bag and we stand outside the doors. "You are, aren't you? You are."

"I don't know if you're supposed to tell people before the second trimester. It's supposed to be bad luck." I set the clip board by the ball bag and some helpful mother takes them both in without being asked.

"I guessed. I won't tell a soul. Are you excited? Had you and . . . what's his name again? — "

"Quinn."

"Had you and Quinn been trying long?"

"A week. Maybe two."

"Shit."

"I know."

"I guess you really will be a Big Girl in a few months, eh? How far along are you?"

"Three months. I think. You know me and math. Three down, six to go." I don't know who started it, but we hug and I can bend so well now that my face ends up in his neck and he smells like Vicks VapoRub and herbs, medicine you take just by breathing.

Darren:

I count to ten. I count forward and backwards. While Nolan banters with the kids and our knees touch — she's so careless with her limbs these days now that she has that new hip — I count down then back up again. Easy math. Simple task. Loop the numbers around my brain like a bridle.

We sit against the gym wall as the teens scream and flirt and scrimmage around us, their pheromones disguised as cologne and imitation perfume. Nolan's tried to make the practices scent-free — her pregnancy nose and its easy access to her pregnancy stomach — but there's no hiding these bodies.

Breasts a little bigger even under her T-shirt: likely she doesn't have to fake cleavage anymore. Stomach swollen as if she's eaten a big meal. Not fat, really. Mostly she just looks nauseous. I count from ten to one, from one to ten. When I see birches sway from left to right across the line of straighter, darker trees . . .

The new Big Girl is eager to please. She laughs too loudly when the short Bif Kid boys touch her knees to make her miss a shot. She's trying out for adult, but she doesn't know the dance steps yet. She's trying out for the national team this year and is expected to take Nolan's spot.

Nolan doesn't even excuse herself when she leaves. I know she's going to puke or going to get air so she doesn't puke or going to get more orange peels, which her mother swears will help. I hold down the fort. That's my job.

I give her fifteen minutes, then go check on her. Not my job, but I do it anyways. She's in the nurse's room, rubbing an ice cube along her cheek. The ice melts and simulates tears, collecting in her ears. She's pale and I watch her veins and count 10, 9, 8 and try not to think of her blood heat and body warmth and count 7,6,5 (like girls on hands and knees who throw their hair before them to dry in the sun) and count 4, 3, 2 and think of her spread on the nurse's bed, body making short work of the ice and count 1 and count 10, 9, 8, (but I was going to say, before truth broke in with all its matter of fact about the ice storms).

"Hey Dare," she says with her eye closed. She's whispering because she's sick, not because of any intimacy between us.

"Hey," I whisper, though I'm not sick.

"Don't ever get pregnant. I can't take anything, not even Gravol. It's way worse than when I was getting drug tested."

"You look like hell," I say. We're hushed, maybe because the lights are dim. "How much longer do you want to go give them for lunch?"

"How long have they had?"

"Fouty-five minutes."

"I'll stumble out in a minute. Tell them to clean up any garbage and get in a circle."

"Aye aye, chief. Any other commands?"

"Do I smell bad? I don't want to go out there reeking of vomit." She sits up, her hair dark from the water she's splashed on her face. I'm used to seeing her hair dark with so many kinds of sweat: the malt scent of it as she would shake out her ponytail in the car during the drive home.

"Not that I can smell," I say and wonder about myself, though I never used to care, not even after Cage Match when my deodorant was in a froth under my arms. My mother has her own scent now since she's been sick and compensates with Chanel. I bathe until my skin flakes.

"You sure?" She sniffs her shirt. "Those kids stink anyways. Probably wouldn't notice."

I lean in and smell her hair and the odour is of soap and bile and oranges, mostly of oranges, and I count 10, 9, 8, 7 and, "You're fine," I say. "You smell like oranges."

"Thanks," she says, blushing, and I wonder if this is the pregnancy blush or if I've come too close, imagine the radii of our scents clashing, and maybe you should always keep yourself out of smelling distance of a person and count 6, 5, 4, 3 — .

The kids leave but their scent stays along with a few sweatshirts, chocolate-bar wrappers and Gatorade bottles. Darren opens the door to let in the musk of rain on cement as we clean.

"Someone picking you up?" he asks.

"Quinn. I was going to walk, but I feel like crap."

"I'd like to meet your husband — is he your husband? — father of your child, whatever." He runs his good hand through his hair. It's grey and staticky now and stays up even without sweat.

"No, he's my . . . we've never really settled on a good word. Boyfriend sounds so young, you know? And that still sounds weird to say: father of my child. Quinn McLeod, father of my child." I toss an energy bar wrapper in the garbage can.

"You'll get used to it. Well, in six months' time I guess you'll have to."

Quinn is standing by the door, rain on his T-shirt. "Speak of the devil," I say. "Darren, this is Quinn, the, uh, father of my child. And Quinn, this is Darren, the manager of my athletes."

"Nice to meet you," says Darren. "Congratulations on the . . . Actually, can I shake your hand with this one? That's my gimp hand. Doesn't do much for the manly grip."

Quinn shrugs and shakes Darren's hand. I wonder what Darren thinks of Quinn's long nails. "I didn't realize we were telling people."

"He guessed."

"She wasn't feeling well . . . I figured . . . "

"Because I was at my mom and dad's house and I didn't tell them . . . and my mom was going on about a cousin who's having a baby and when are you and I going to — "

"I'm sorry. He guessed and I'm a shitty liar."

"That's fine. I'm just saying — Anyhow, Darren, good to meet you, man. No offence or anything. We should head'er."

Darren picks the label off a Gatorade bottle with his good hand. "Yeah, see you guys later. Nice to meet you."

"I'm sorry," I say as we get into the car. "The way I'm throwing up, people are going to notice. What's wrong with you?"

"With me? We agreed to keep this secret and you told him — "

"He guessed."

"You confirmed his guess, then."

"And here's another little bit of info you can tell Darren," says Quinn as soon as we're in the house and he's behind the shield of his guitar, fingerpicking a melody I don't recognize. "There's no way we can pay our mortgage this month," he says, not looking up. "Or the next."

I sit down beside him and reach over to mute the strings. "So what's the plan?"

"Get employed damn quick or sell the place. Knowing you, I say sell."

"I was looking through catalogues. If I go to secretary school, I can get a diploma in four months. Or I could take computer courses. Something I could do from home."

Quinn pushes my hand away with his pinky and continues strumming. His hair curls a little at the ends and he doesn't look old enough to even think the word 'mortgage.' "None of those will save our mortgage. One of us needs a job right away."

"Tell me again why you can't get a part-time day job? Something in the afternoon. All of your other Guys have day jobs."

"I need to write songs sometime. And I'm still not sure what I'm going to do. I need to look for a career, not a job. Not just busy work."

"Can you write songs after I'm employed? Or, actually — " I put my hands over the strings again. He drops his pic. "Can you not write songs while we're trying to have a conversation?"

Quinn puts the guitar down. "Sorry," he mumbles. He stares at the long nails on his right hand. The hand looks as if it belongs to someone else.

"Is the market good for selling?"

"I don't know. I don't know anything about it."

"We should look for apartments. Or get a real estate agent, or — "

"We should look for work." He stands up.

"Where are you going?" I ask.

"To make you tea and dry toast. You look like death warmed over. Have you been puking?"

"Yeah. That's the only reason Darren guessed, I think. Because I was vomiting."

"Want a bit of honey on the toast?"

"Okay."

Quinn's still sweet, bringing me tea without being asked, inquiring about my day, but a shell has formed around him. He hasn't so much hardened as he has caramelized.

"Did you know that right now the fetus is getting vocal cords?" I ask Quinn as we're sitting in bed, reading. "That's what it says here. Next week the hands become functional."

Quinn reaches over and pats my stomach. "Cool."

"So, if you're serious about us selling the house, I can phone a real estate agent and get the ball rolling."

Quinn puts his book down and looks at me. My angular man: his jawline working hard at keeping his words back. "I thought you wanted to have the baby in this house."

"I did. I do. I do. But I'm just having all these visions of repo guys taking our furniture and our situation isn't exactly looking up and — I think we need to make a decision, that's all. I would feel better if we made a decision."

Quinn shrugs. "No harm in talking to an agent, I guess. If that's what you want." He picks up his book again, then puts it down on the bedside table and rolls over on to his side. "We should get some sleep."

We should, but the house no longer feels good for rest. Usually, these are the moments I like. Night: my stomach settled and lower-back supported by pillows. It's the lower back that's a problem these days. Just months after the replacement, the tang has already returned to my bones. Arthritis with its shifting pressure points.

It's 3 AM and I watch the scene we make in this house we won't have for much longer. The window open, the moonlight making paper-snowflake patterns on our sheets and arms, the air edged with rain.

18

DARREN'S HOUSE GAVE ME DIFFERENT DREAMS. Maybe I just remembered them better because I slept poorly. He generally wanted to spoon, but that was impossible. Our bones didn't match up, all of our hollows in the wrong places, and I needed to move every hour or so. My hip wouldn't let me be pinned down. It was the one part of my body that refused to be domesticated. So I would wake up from Darren's place bleary, drink coffee with lots of his soy milk and cane sugar, and go home to nap. With Darren I could sleep, but not rest. I could dream, but not forget.

In Darren's bed, I never had the recurring dream: him in the living room, the old woman, a baby. I'm glad I didn't. I would have been tempted to tell him and he wasn't exactly a dream-interpretation kind of guy. He said he did his best work when half awake, so the bedside tables on both sides were strewn with notes, none of which made sense to me. Programming codes and grocery lists were as close to dream interpretation as he got.

At Darren's house, I dreamed in Grecian sunlight and primary colours. More shadows. I must have kept him awake all night with my tossing, but he claimed he slept better when I was there. He wanted an arm around my waist, but I nightmare-twisted out of his grasp.

He found me in my subconscious all the same. Darren's breath against my ear gave me dreams of the ocean and Cadboro Bay and the Island. I would wake up all salt sweat and sea longing. His cologne brought images of Vancouver Island rainforest: damp moss, splintered cedar, my mother and her constant, "Is that a blue jay, Ed? Are you sure? Well, is that one a jay? That one up there squawking." When I was at his house, I always dreamed of some other home.

I woke up that night with my hip wanting alone time and his arm flung nearly across my throat. It had been a hard day at training and I was raw from it. My hands and elbows felt so chapped that I expected my skin to recede to the bone.

"Dare?" I whispered. He frowned in sleep and the passing headlights through holes in the curtains rolled across his skin like coins. In sleep, his face was unlocked. I liked to watch him when he looked like this. He didn't wake up, but his fingers moved to find me again. I gave him my hand and went back to sleep and he held it all through the night as if we were dancing and he was guiding me and my sore hip through my restless positions. Maybe that was why I dreamed in tangos that night. On stage in high heels. I'd already had the hip replacement, but they did too much and replaced all of me. The million-dollar woman. I was too bionic to dance; I think I'd read that somewhere. Robots can learn the moves but never really dance. And then I was playing music: a full crowd and my guitar strings snapping one by one. Me sitting in the audience, seeing myself on stage and the light so white I had no features. Even my eyes were gone.

I woke up with a spotlight of sun through a hole in the curtain trained on my eye. Darren had woken up and was looking down at our hands.

"I dreamed I was on stage," I said.

"Good morning to you too," he said. He swept his palm over the base of my hand and it was so parched that it rasped. The kitten, who'd been sleeping at the edge of our bed, sighed in annoyance and went back to sleep. No, it wasn't our bed. It was still his bed. The Darren Steward Hotel. "What were you doing on stage?"

"Dancing, I think," I said. "And then playing guitar, but I couldn't."

"You're just nervous about Paralympics," he said. "Worrying about your ability to perform. Don't need Freud to tell you that."

I released his grip and felt a slight pain in all the places my palm had split open. I usually broke along well-used wrinkles, the creases between fingers. I looked down and they were bleeding. Little stigmatas. During the night, they'd healed around Darren's skin and I had reopened the wounds.

"What's on the agenda today?" he asked as he rooted around for his crutches and got up to go to the bathroom. His hair was all over the place; even his eyebrows were unkempt.

"Sophia's coming home."

"Right, right. The amazing and wonderful Sophia. I've heard so much."

"Thanks for offering to drive, by the way."

"Insert Beatles 'Baby You Can Drive my Car' reference here."

I swung my legs to the side of the bed and my hip clicked. "The Beatles? Who are the Beatles? Were they popular when you were young, mister?"

"Don't even joke about that," he said and emerged grinning from the bathroom. "You don't know who the Beatles are, I won't sleep with you anymore."

I was sitting on the edge of the bed in my underwear, stretching the effects of the previous day's training away.

"Look at that back," he said.

"What about it?" I turned around to look at him.

"It's gotten bigger. You have some serious definition going on. I wish you could see this." He sat back down behind me and touched beneath my shoulder blades. "You're still so skinny you're like a frickin' anatomy lesson. I can even see your teres minor."

"Momma told me never to show my teres minor before marriage."

"Well, you've got a beautiful teres minor, and teres major and a strong set of shoulders." He gave me a quick shoulder massage. "You're growing up."

"I'm filling out. You're lucky I'm a skinny girl or I might take offense."

"Thank God. I'm so glad I don't have to do the 'no, honey, you've got a great ass, don't talk about yourself that way' routine. Hey, what should I wear today?"

I reached over and smoothed his eyebrow hairs back into place. "Nothin' but a smile."

"Well, I'm just — I assume Sophia knows we're involved or whatever, right?"

"Dare, you look fine. And I mean that in the 'damn fine' teenage-speak sense of the word. Wear the running shoes instead of the loafers and your boyish good looks will do the rest."

Darren laughed. "I think I'd need the hair around my temples back to qualify for boyish good looks."

Sophia was going to stay with me for a few days to adjust to the nuances of West Coast life and wear away the slight accent she'd picked up. We arrived at the airport just in time. Traffic had been bad and Darren was tense. I'd put on slow jazz to watch his blood pressure drop, but he still arrived flustered.

"I think that's her," I said, waving at someone who could be a stranger. She'd gained blonde highlights in her curls and about twenty pounds.

Sophia waved, approaching me almost shyly. I accosted her with a hug.

"Look at you," I said, holding her at arm's length like a proud mother. "You look great."

"Look at you, skinny legs. You need to eat a sandwich."

We both used to be bit-of-nothing girls. The weight gain was one more thing we didn't have in common anymore.

"Look at you," she said, then turned her attention to Darren. "And look at you. I'm Sophia, Nolan's sidekick."

"I'm Darren. Nolan's other sidekick." He was standing with his good arm facing her, showing off our weight training.

She gave me a sly smile. "I know who you are."

Sophia returned with a new language. Though she didn't have much of an accent whenever I spoke to her on the phone, the plane ride had brought out the Newfie in her.

"What's up with your bye?" she whispered as Darren loaded her suitcases into the trunk.

"My what?"

"Oh. Boy. Sorry. Your fuck buddy. He seems nervous."

I shrugged. "I don't think he's nervous." She was right, though. Darren fidgeted around Sophia, unsure of how to pose like someone in my age group.

"Well, then he's high-strung."

My plan was to take her to a tourist destination so that the presence of foreigners would make her feel like more of a local. As we sat in the backseat and talked, Darren drove us downtown.

"Wherever you girls want to go," he said. He sounded like a father chaperoning teenage daughters.

"Women," said Sophia. "We're women."

Darren blushed. "Women. Right. I didn't mean anything by it. I was just . . . " He made broad hand gestures.

"Hand controls," I hissed. "Watch the hand controls."

Sophia shrugged. "Just because you're old . . . er doesn't mean we're not adults."

"I know," said Darren. "I wasn't implying that."

"Do you want to get something to eat," I asked.

Sophia nodded. "Definitely. It's dinner time back home. Back east. Back wherever. Let's go eat tons. I'm so fully taking advantage of the fact that you burn an extra 300 calories a day when you're PMSing."

Darren gave me a pleading look, which Sophia intercepted like a bad pass.

"What?" she asked. "You're uncomfortable with women's bodies?"

"Of course not. What the hell are you talking about? Can we lay off the first-year women's studies lecture, please?"

"You don't like the word PMS. You think we're girls."

"Sophia," I said.

"I'm just not . . . most women I know don't . . . There're some things I just don't want to know. Like you probably don't want to know about . . . erectile dysfunction or whatever."

Sophia leaned back into the seat with her hands behind her head. "Sure. Go ahead. Erectile dysfunction. I'm all ears. So, even though you're a paraplegic or whatever, you can still get it up?"

"Darren, hand on the hand control. Jesus."

"I'm a quad. Well, triplegic, if you want to be technically accurate: only three limbs are affected. And I assume Nolan's told you the rest."

We went to Denny's. Sophia was hungry and tired: not up for the grand tour. Darren sat on the edge of the booth. Across from us, seniors were enjoying all-day pancakes. The muscles in his neck were tight, as if they'd been stretched across the generation gap.

"God bless Denny's, eh?" asked Sophia. She had a little handbag, an imitation of some designer that I probably should have been able to name.

"We go to Denny's when we're away for tournaments in Kamloops or wherever," said Darren. "It kind of feels like we're on vacation."

"Exotic," said Sophia. This was her attempt at being friendly, but Darren fidgeted with the lock on his brace. "Nolan, are you wearing a sports bra under that shirt?"

I looked down. "Yeah."

"Jesus H Christ. Way to go all out on the sexy lingerie for your buddy here. I've never understood the point of a bra whose sole purpose is to squish your tits into nothing. Not that you have much in the way of tits, my dearest."

"I think we're ready to order," said Darren to a waitress who was passing by.

"I think he's ready to change the subject. Are you one of those guys who can't say the word 'vagina?'" The elderly women sitting near us turned.

"Sophia. Come on. Can we please not do this?" I said.

The waitress was standing beside Sophia, her pen ready.

"He's blushing," said Sophia. "How old are you? Twelve?"

Darren had his arms crossed over shirt he'd eventually picked out. "Funny, I was wondering the same thing about you."

"You know what, let's just go," I said. "Let's go home. This is obviously not working."

"What? All this talk of vaginas getting you going? Can't wait to get back home?"

Sophia stayed at my apartment for a week. We slept in the same bed, back to back, in the flannel pyjamas our mothers bought us. I preferred sharing a bed with her than with Darren. We each had our own rectangle of space, though she would often press her cold feet against my neck or poke me with her toes to wake me up. The apartment began to smell like someone lived there again: new recipes and herbal shampoo.

Sophia cooked me salmon for the good oils and went tsk-tsking through my closet, then demanded shopping. We went to Metrotown and downtown Vancouver and Sophia talked me into appreciating my legs in a skirt that barely covered my surgery scar.

"You're so hot," said Sophia. "Look at the lines on your belly. Stop weight training now while you still look sexy. Don't become butch. Promise me." She was my personal shopper. I could never translate my frame into the short-girl clothes in stores, but Sophia became my mirror.

We were sitting in the kitchen cutting strawberries for a salad when Quinn phoned.

"Nolan . . . Nolita . . . ," Sophia whispered as I talked. "Is that the math teacher?"

I shook my head, said goodbye and hung up the phone. "Nope. Quinn. He plays in a band and wants us to go."

"Is it an easy listening band because he's forty frickin' years old?"

"Punk. He's our age."

Sophia stabbed a strawberry. "Woah, woah, woah. You're being pursued by a musician? Do you know how high up on the list of sexual hierarchy they are? Is he hot?"

I shrugged. "I'm not exactly single."

"You're not exactly sane. It's okay to fuck old guys when you're going through a dry spell. It's not okay to fuck old guys when a frickin' musician wants to get into your pants. These are the rules. Time honoured."

"I think Darren's more my type."

"And I think he looks like he just stepped off the set of The Wonder Years."

I was a jeans and T-shirt girl, but Sophia was having none of that. She knew my skin tone and fixed it with concealer. She knew my colours and dressed me accordingly. I borrowed a pair of her dress shoes, since I only owned runners.

The pub's coppery light made my skin blush as we entered, college boys cat-calling at both of us. Quinn saw me from on stage. The makeup and the satin skirt alerted him even through the white-out of the stage lights. He gave me a thumbs up mid-song, right before he launched into a solo.

"I'm so glad you came," said Quinn after the set was over. "Were you on some sort of extreme makeover show?" He was sweating and even in the dark I could see his flush. We were sitting at a table with some of Quinn's friends who I recognized from class. Sophia had befriended them all within minutes.

"I've been re-educated," I said and patted Sophia on the arm. "This is Sophia. I flew her all the way from Newfoundland just so she could make me pretty. Good set, by the way. You guys must have been playing together a long time. You all know exactly where everyone's going to be."

"Nice to meet you, Sophia," said Quinn. His fingers tapped out upcoming solos on the table, still plugged in from on-stage adrenaline. "Though Nolan was already pretty damn hot."

I blushed and was glad for the foundation to mute it. "Shameless flattery. You're lucky I fall for that kind of stuff."

"Flattery? That's the way? And here I was just going to get you drunk. Saves me a few bucks."

"He's cute," Sophia kept whispering once he went back on stage, loud enough that all of his friends could hear. "You should do him. Don't you think he's cute?"

During the next set, we danced, the skirt swaying against my thighs. For the last song of the night, Quinn took a long draught of ale to soothe the punk scream from his voice and told the crowd to grab someone to dance with. (I believe the exact words were, "Come on you pussy guys, ask a girl to slow dance if you have the cojones.") Sophia found one of Quinn's friends and I swayed up front like a groupie girl, not wanting to make eye contact with the older men who were sitting at the bar watching me.

"Come on, fuckers," said Quinn. "I want to see some slow dancing." He touched the microphone, nodded to the drummer and eased the band into an electrified rendition of the Lyle Lovett song I'd taught him.

"That hot Nolan Taylor, she just ain't no good to follow a rocker that way," sang Quinn. "Sing me a melody, sing me a bruise," and closed his eyes to find the bruise in the song. The drummer's brushes liked it rough, slapping the snare around a bit, and people swayed and I sang the words back to him. "Walk through the bottomland without no shoes." I looked at all the dancing couples and the music became some kind of silence: people breathing against each other's skin, oblivious to the melody.

"Yeah," said Sophia as the song ended. "You should definitely sleep with this guy."

Athens was only a few months away and thinking of it was like caffeination. Sammy was already getting her Olympic tattoo touched up in preparation. I decided to go back to the Island to visit my family and Sophia, though she'd only been back for a week. It would be good to be a daughter again, to live in a house whose kitchen door was scarred by my mother charting my growth spurts. The anaemic in me craved home-cooked meat.

On the ferry, the wilderness was displayed as if up for auction and the tourists bid with pointed fingers and five-dollar postcards, haggling over the correct pronunciation of the word "Tsawwassen." On the ferry, I had no land line and there was no one to talk to, no Quinn, no Darren, no Sophia. I wasn't anywhere: the islands with their toy trees and doll-house wharfs rolling by, the tourists speaking in competing accents.

The ferry made me pull out the books and get down to business. I sat in the work stations like putting on blinders and finished everything I should have started long ago. It's likely that BC Ferries saved me from failing university.

I'm sure that I must have done more homework than it seems now. My grades weren't terrible. Of course, I don't remember any of the topics I studied now. A couple of floating facts I've used in conversation: the German lineage of Hohenzollern had a habit of accidentally killing heirs to the throne by placing the royal crown too early on newborn soft spots; Fidel Castro almost gave away Che Guevara's guerrilla hideout by sending him countless boxes of asthma medications out of concern; in 1935 the RCMP used machine guns in the streets against strikers on the On to Ottawa Trek. But what to do with those trends?

What time line can I tie them to? I can't make anything from my book learning connect. I have a diploma that's packed in an old apple crate in the closet and a few pictures my mother took of convocation that feature a blonde girl walking across the stage, though closer inspection reveals it's not actually me. I was there, though. I went to school: learned and forgot again and re-learned for the final. I spent so long shifting in those seats that it's strange to have the whole experience summarized as one sentence in my resumé. I was there. I have a degree. Bits of facts, splotches of history, easy to forget as the names of the islands through the windows.

"Take Nolan with you," said my mother as we walked through the door. My father was about to leave, wanting to replace girl-talk with the unquiet silence of a forest; the dog communicating her joy through broken branches and muddy paws. "Nolan, get your jacket. And take fruit." She slipped fruit in each of our pockets: a pear for me, a pomegranate for my father.

My father shrugged and gestured in the direction of the car. "I'll be out here," he said. "When you're ready."

We drove to Mystic Vale, Darwin's pacing in the back seat a blessing, since it dampened the silence.

"So," said my father. "How's school."

"Not bad. How's work?"

"Oh, same old."

"Yeah?"

"Pretty much."

When we got to the Vale, my father spoke in myths. This was the only way we talked. All he knew about my sport was that I was going to Greece. All he knew about Greece was the stories.

The forest smelled as though the organisms couldn't decide whether they were being born or dying. Rotting leaves the winter preserved. My father let me wear his Cowichan sweater, which smelled of Old Spice and dog hair. He was wearing the Gortex my mother had bought him. It was a hunter's jacket, bought on sale, colourful in order to remind other hunters that the wearer was human.

Darwin crashed about sniffing out slug trails. She could be counted on to emerge wet-nosed with twigs in her fur whenever we ran out of words. We would talk then forget to talk and scratch under Darwin's collar to make us remember again.

"Are you a good girl?" my father would say. "Are you going to catch a big old slug for your breakfast, my good girl?"

As we walked, my father removed the bruised pomegranate from his pocket. He split it between his fingers and it cracked like cartilage.

"You have to eat pomegranates outside," he said. "Messy as hell. You look like a carnivore after you've eaten one of these things. All that juice."

The seeds inside were blood-glossy, packed in like honeycombs.

"Guess I've told you about Persephone," said my father.

"That's the one from the underworld?"

"Hades was in love with her. I've told you this, haven't I? How he kidnapped her and took her underground and her mother wept and refused to make anything grow. She was in charge of nature." He broke off a hive of the seeds and passed it to me. "You just have to bite into it. They don't taste like much if you just eat them one by one."

I did. The berries dropped to the ground and looked man-made amongst the foliage: rubies spilt from a necklace.

"Isn't that how they explain seasons? The Persephone myth?"

"Right," said my father. "The seasons. She was some mother, that Demeter. See, now you've eaten maybe fifty berries. That's fifty days in the underworld. Or was that fifty lifetimes? Either way, you're doomed, kiddo. You're going to have to marry old Hades."

The berries popped and crunched in my mouth. I couldn't see my face, but I bet I was tattooed with juice. "Last time I eat fruit with you. Good thing I have a mom who'll save me."

"Yes, that's actually the moral of the story. Call your mother. And here I thought I had it bad with your mom when she's angry you don't call."

"I try."

"Hey, doesn't bother me. I know you're at university. It's probably good to have a little water between you and your old mom and pop."

Darwin emerged with a nose chilled from creek water and a toad in her mouth. She dropped it and it hopped off into the unknown dry land, jittery to find water.

"Is that the toad croaking?" I asked.

"Raven," said my father. "The good old trickster." We walked home through local legends and someone else's gods.

Dr. Taylor:

What do you say to a daughter going to a place you've never been? To a country whose language you haven't spoken since university, and that was the ancient variety?

She talks of her mental training routine, her periodization chart for optimal tapering. Sounds good to me. We walk, Nolan's limp amplified by the forest floor. Darwin crashes along beside us and removes the desire for goodbye advice or farewell wishes. The scenery too: the late-summer light winnowed and sifted and threshed through trees. Forests have a kind of melodrama to them that makes you feel foolish about your own dramatics. The problem is there's so much time. She'll be around for another two weeks and I can phone her whenever I want. And she can call us in Athens, too.

Athens: how do you equip a daughter for such a city? Turns out I don't have to. Someone else — a coach, her teammates, Darren — has taken care of it. These are people who have stood on podiums.

Nolan, of course, seems to grow in light years and no one can talk that way: a quick straight line. We can't travel like light either; we curve and amble, pause at alcoves of stone, places where the tire tracks of boys have worn a firepit, the prints of a deer.

It's good, this stroll: a few stories, the dog cutting boomerang swaths through the undergrowth, going beyond our line of sight, looping back again, the light making it out of the trees and continuing onwards.

19

I'VE ONLY DONE ONE TALK, but already I'm tired of it. The story of my disability is too complicated to be filled with hope and inspiration. Too many big words, ironic twists of coincidence and fate, tangents and side notes. The kids like the little wheelchair basketball demonstration, collectively gasping and clapping when I hit a three pointer.

"Do you hurt all the time?" asks a girl during question period.

"Most of the time, yes, but I've had this condition since I was eleven, so I'm pretty good at dealing with it. Yes? You in the pink shirt."

"Do you cry a lot? Because it hurts?"

"No, no. As I said, I know how to deal with it pretty well. Yes? You in back, behind the red-headed kid."

"My brother broke his leg last year and he was in a wheelchair."

"Oh yeah? Well, he could come out and play wheelchair basketball now that he's better because, as I said, you don't have to have a disability to play. We're an integrated sport. Okay, you up front."

"Are you old and sick?"

"No, I'm not sick — people in wheelchairs aren't sick any more than an able bodied person. And I hope I'm not old. I'm only thirty-two. Though, I guess to you that sounds ancient." A few twitters from the teachers in the back.

Someone should have told me that kids are sadists before I decided to have one. At least they're frank. They don't lower their voices to ask.

"Pregnancy is a team sport," announces the LaMaze instructor, by way of introduction. We all sit in the Centennial Community Centre in a room that smells of plasticine and Elmer's Glue. One woman has brought vegan cookies. I have brought only my inappropriately named "morning" sickness and a very apprehensive Quinn, who so far has not inquired about my talk this afternoon.

"They're not going to show videos of the birth, are they?" he kept whispering as we waited for class to begin. "You know me and nausea. Think I should take a Gravol just in case?" Our lives are apparently changing so fast he's getting motion sickness.

"Think of those around you as your team," says the instructor. "Who would be your coach?"

"My midwife?" suggests one woman. She's wearing pigtails. Pregnancy is an excuse for a lot of things, but wearing pigtails isn't one of them.

"I don't trust this metaphor," I whisper to Quinn. "It's not like I can sub you in to carry this thing for awhile."

"Shh," says the guy next to us, "I'm taping this." He holds up a small tape recorder.

"What? Worried you're going to fail the final?" asks Quinn.

"My fears are completely normal," says the man. He's gotten a head start on the sympathy belly.

"You do know that all you have to do is feed her ice chips and get the hell out of the way when she throws stuff, right?"

"I'm sorry, can I have your attention?" asks the Lamaze lady.

"Well, really," mutters Quinn. "Rent 'Look Who's Talking' once or twice and you've pretty much got the idea."

We can strike these two off our list of newfound pregnancy acquaintances. That was part of the plan: to find other couples having a similar experience. Or maybe that's just what I wanted: Some Gals.

Even though it's the first class, the other women seem to have bonded. They have sleek hair and lip gloss and I have a healthy measure of distrust towards women without split ends.

The Lamaze lady wants us to introduce ourselves. Except for one teenage girl, these women are working professionals, which means they can afford things a decent hair cut. One woman has a business suit well-tailored like a European dictator's. I suspect she has a five-year plan.

"My name's Quinn McLeod. I'm a musician. I play guitar in a classic-rock house band," says Quinn when it's his turn. It's that easy for him: say it and it becomes a reality. Have a dream, join a house band, and suddenly you're the real deal.

"And I'm Nolan Taylor. I'm a . . . public speaker, I guess. I'm a recently retired elite athlete. Used to play wheelchair basketball on the national team." There's a silence. "Even though I walk. I have a bad hip. Actually, used to have a bad hip."

"She's a pregnant lady," says Quinn. "Full time."

"Well, it does seem like an occupation some days," I say. "I'm looking for work."

"How hard are you looking for work?" asks Quinn in the car ride home. "You said you were looking. What're you doing?"

I have my shoes off and one foot up on the dash, trying to shrink my ankles so I can see the bones there again. I wish I could have both feet up, but that's a pose the doctors have forbidden for fear of damaging the replacement. "Trying to pad my resumé. Pretty much all I have as far as work experience is athlete, coach and those few sport camps I worked at. I've been thinking about school. I told you that."

"With what money?"

"Sport Canada will pay for two more years of tuition for me retroactively."

Quinn uses the road as an excuse not to look at me. "Nolan."

"What?"

"Have you realized that you're pregnant yet?"

"You know, yes, I kind of clued in when I was puking up half of my organs this morning. Do you realize I'm pregnant? I don't see you scrounging around for a day job."

Quinn turns off the music. "If we want to keep the house, you have to get more work. I can get something for minimum wage part time, but it's not going to cut it."

"I contacted a real estate agent. Her name's Donna and I scheduled an appointment for this week. Besides, who's going to hire a pregnant chick when they know they'll just have to pay her maternity leave?"

"Whatever. When you were an athlete, you were too athletic to work. Now you're pregnant and too pregnant to work. Maybe it's my turn to be too musical to get off my ass and bring home a regular paycheque." He's rigid, every muscle tense, his veiny forearms taut like guitar strings.

"Jesus fucking-all Christ, Quinn McLeod. We're pregnant. We're going to have a baby. That means that there's no such thing as whose turn it is anymore."

Quinn is silent, using the lack of music to his advantage. My ankles look bleached in this light. The baby is taking all of my colour.

"You want to be a musician," I say. "Okay, listen. You want to play music, right? I want to have a job that doesn't involve the fast-food industry. I'm thinking I could take a two-month course somewhere and maybe get on at a place with benefits and you could get a day job . . . Darren was saying there's a good course at Douglas College — "

"Do whatever you want. We're probably going to lose the house anyways."

We arrive home and Quinn considers the end of the trip to be the end of the conversation. The bones are still hidden in my ankles, as if I've been on an airplane. All the puffiness with none of the world travel.

Quinn's cleaning out the little room underneath the stairs, which we've been using for storage space. There's nothing of real value there: all the boxes I wanted to forget about, jackets from a time when my nationality was emblazoned on every warm thing I owned, tennis rackets, McDonald's Happy Meal toys, those Christmas ornaments we'd been looking for.

"Do you want this?" he keeps asking me, bringing me objects that smell their age: dust and mould, crumbling rubber. "Will you miss this or can I just chuck it?"

Soon, the entire contents of the storage closet are in a pile in the main hall.

"I know it looks bad," says Quinn, "but things have to get worse before they get better."

They don't. Quinn piles everything unsorted into boxes then wanders off and I inherit the work. It's me who will have to sort our history into save, sell or discard. I will pick up Quinn's slack. He's all tight shoulders and tuned strings these days, while my calves grow soft from lack of cross-training.

Even with the new hip, bending is difficult. For the first time, my stomach brushes against my legs: the weight and slope of me. Having this belly brings a strange heat — I think of humidity, August, a cloudy day on a porch swing waiting for thunder — and a pulse in my back. The good hip's a bit achy, but it's mostly my back. Some days, standing in front of the mirror, I can hardly bear to touch my stomach. I rub in body lotion to prevent stretch marks and my fingers are surprised at how much space I take up.

The room under the stairs will be his from now on. A studio, he says, though I suspect he just wants a door to close. Nonetheless, he's got his practice space, a little cave for his music to hibernate in. The concrete provides good acoustics, the small space making his music big.

"It's perfect, isn't it?" asks Quinn as he shows me his handiwork: a bare bulb, a stool, a Jimi Hendrix poster, his guitar and amp. "It's all I need." What I need: him to be employed or at least play with the door open. There's not enough room for two in there and he's borrowed my Grestch until his Gibson is fixed, though I'm still not sure what's supposedly wrong with it.

"Yeah, and if you get that civil service job you can afford a new amp. The one I found on Workopolis."

"Eh, this one's good for now," he says and shrugs. "We'll see what kind of coin I can make as a musician. This baby's enough for me for now." He pats my Gretsch and looks satisfied.

What about the other baby? I want to ask him, but he ducks back into the Rock Cave. I pull up a chair and bend over boxes. Have we ever thrown anything out? Anything with possible sentimental connections is stored in our bedroom closet. This is just a chore, none of the "remember when?" of spring cleaning. How did we let our house get like this? So full of junk we don't want.

"Do you want this?" I keep asking Quinn, more for the excuse to knock on the door. "What should we keep?"

~

The belly gets me to the front of the university admissions office line and entitles me to not one, but two, scotch mints in the glass bowl on the counter; (I'm breath-freshening for two).

"You'll find our school is very accommodating," says the woman at the desk. She's dressed in a style I wouldn't even know where to shop for: clothing in pinstripes and careful shades of pastels that suggests everything she wears has been tailored just for her. "We have a mandate to help women like you: subsidized daycare, parenting classes."

"Like me?" I imagine a whole room full of recently retired, recently healed, recently pregnant women: all of us thinking ourselves to be specialty items. Girls adapting to metal and stretch marks.

"Young mothers. Women under twenty-five. Our school takes pride in being non-judgmental and offering working solutions. See? You'll notice that right here on the pamphlet. 'Working solutions.'"

"Oh," I say, "Well, thank you. That's . . . good to hear." No reason to correct her. When I was twenty-five, I'd just come back from the Paralympics and Quinn and I moved in together. I help myself to another scotch mint.

She gives me a course catalogue and a pamphlet on their "Ready, Set, Grow!" daycare program. The course catalogue features a girl on the cover, book in hand, staring off into the clear campus sky. She appears to have a pregnancy glow, though probably that's just the vim and vigor of youth. Something like that. I have less the pregnancy glow, more the powdery, drab cheeks of a cold-and-flu symptom, though sometimes the thought of the baby — something new, a real, live person — gives me flutters of excitement similar to my first day of university.

I sit in a coffee shop, sated by the simple carbs of a muffin, and weigh my options. Anything I'd be interested in taking — The History of Reggae, Films of the Future: a Jungian Perspective on Science Fiction — is unlikely to lead to gainful employment. The whole 'lifelong learning' bit has left me without a resumé. In between training sessions, I read, took adult education classes, (painting, which was less Victorian and relaxing than I thought it would be, and bird-house making, which I was discouraged from taking again for my unwillingness to follow the class colour scheme), and learned how (and how not) to make sushi. I can play guitar: acoustic and electric. I've been to fourteen different countries, three Paralympics, four world championships, know the basics of five or six languages and have racked up enough Air Miles that someone from Air Canada sends me a hand-signed card at Christmas. Still, I'm not qualified for anything beyond the personal greeter at Wal-mart. Employers want to know where thirteen years have gone. I need something I can write down on paper.

The application form sounds like a nosy aunt at Christmas. It wants to know my goals, dreams, ambitions, course of study, a prospective graduation date. My future must be mapped and slotted into boxes. It all seems vaguely familiar. I remember doing this when I applied to UBC and know that I lied shamelessly. Well, probably it wasn't really lying: a combination of embellishment and changing my mind. I was young enough to do that, confident that I could make things up and stumble into the perfect occupation, like falling in love.

~

"Do you think I look pregnant?" I ask Darren as we get into the car.

"No," he says without looking at me. "Definitely not. You know, you don't have to ease yourself into the car like that. You're only, what, five months along?"

"I think that's a legacy from the hip. You forget: I'm not used to it yet."

At the light, Darren looks at my belly. I cross my arms over my mid-section. "It's just like you, Nole. You're on the provincial team; you want to make the national team. You're on the national team; you want a gold medal. You're pregnant, you want to be in the third trimester right away."

"You think I'm looking forward to having something the size of a watermelon pressing against my bladder? I already have to pee every fifteen minutes. Thank your lucky stars that you have a penis, buddy."

Darren pretends to look down to his lap and nod his gratitude. "Thank you, lucky stars . . . and Y chromosome. Though I swear I have the bladder of a pregnant woman anyhow. Quads age in crazy ways."

"I'm serious. I only have a small window of time between being gimped up and thoroughly being knocked up. Don't think I'm not going to enjoy it."

The market is good to sell and Quinn and I hope selling our house will pay our rent until money becomes steady. Quinn does a lot of hoping, but not a lot of home shopping and Darren has stepped in so easily to pick up his slack that it's hard to follow the chain of events back to how he ever got involved, considering that he's never even been to our current home. Something about expertise and a second pair of eyes. Regardless, he's been taking notes. Donna has shown us a few properties already today and they were good enough. Not great, not terrible, just other people's homes. We'll take one of them. Eventually. Today, though, it's too hot for decisions. It's a rare heatwave day, a shock of thirty degrees in the middle of an overcast March.

Donna meets us outside the house. "Welcome to Port Moody," she says, pronouncing it "Part Moody" as if she were describing the civic character. Her makeup is very precise: highlights, lip liner, eye liner. In the war against middle age, the boundaries have been drawn, the territory staked out. She looks like a former Miss Part Moody. Definitely, former Miss something. As she fumbles with the house key, I invent a whole life for her. Wore pastel gowns on parade floats through small towns, the wind resistance making a mockery of her up-do. Was a single mother and named her first daughter Crystal or Ruby, hoping to remind her that she is precious but instead dooming her to never be taken seriously. Sharpened her can-do smile selling Avon.

"This is a great suite," she's telling Darren. I'd forgotten about the house and its suite. Darren had gotten out of his chair, much to the surprise of Donna, and walked down the stairs while I followed carrying the chair. So far, the only thought we've given to the house is the five steps that prevent it from being wheelchair accessible.

It's a building easy to forget about: the same as every other on the block. White. Door in the middle. A window on each side. The kind a kid would draw with a crayon. And it's much smaller than our current home. "It's so spacious inside. Perfect for the little one," Donna is saying. "And just wait until you see the closet space."

I scowl at Darren. "I thought you said I didn't look pregnant," I hiss, trying to make my voice lithe and feline.

"You told her you were expecting when she asked why you're selling, dumb ass."

"What?" asks Donna.

"Mr. Steward was just calling the poor pregnant lady a dumb-ass," I say.

"Mr. Steward is sorry. He's not used to Ms. Taylor being neurotic about looking fat."

Donna smiles and pats his shoulder. "Better get used to it. That old body never comes back." The two of them stare at me and I want to ask what about Donna's old figure, what about the shoulders Darren used to have?

There's no good sunlight in the suite. The only view is of the feet of people walking by. Despite the big rooms, I can't imagine our furniture here. The rooms smell like a lung infection waiting to happen.

"Do you have anything more . . . above ground?" I ask. "I'm feeling a bit claustrophobic."

Donna pats my arm. "That'd be the hormones talking." She reaches out to put a hand on my belly. "You've got quite the little bump there for such a slim woman. You're hardly showing from behind."

"Actually, that's probably the part of me talking that doesn't want to live like a mole."

"It's just that this property has a back yard and no balcony, perfect for kids. It's important when renting a property to think of its potential say a year down the line. We can get the owners to put in a ramp very easily. You didn't tell me you required wheelchair accessibility."

"We don't. I mean, it would be nice, but Darren's not living here. He's not my . . . spouse or anything. He's just — helping."

"This place isn't bad," says Darren as we follow Donna outside. "The yard's big. And you're right, you don't really need to worry about wheelchair accessibility."

"The next woman who puts her hand on my stomach is going to get her boob grabbed. That's my plan. I'll say, 'Wow, your breasts have adapted remarkably well to middle age. What are you? Let me guess. 38D? No? Am I close?"

It's so hard on these walk-through tours to tell what the place really looks like. It's too crammed with a stranger's furniture, the light bent by someone else's suncatchers. How can we tell whether or not we'll fit in this place? Harder, still, since Quinn's not here, sleeping off the effects of last night's gig. When we looked for our last house, he spent hours staring at hot water heaters and knocking on walls, listening for something.

"Now the backyard is big — you'd be allowed to share with the owners — but there is a pool," says Donna as she concludes the tour. "That's probably a draw-back, given that before you know it the baby will be crawling around. But I'll leave you two to snoop around unless you have any questions." We don't and soon she's gone, her heels clipping along across the exposed aggregate.

"I guess it's a risk with the baby," says Darren. "Days like this, though, you really want a pool."

I sit down at the pool's edge and dangle my legs in the water. My skin itches so much I might as well be wearing wool. Darren transfers on to the ground beside me, holding my shoulder to lower himself, and his hand is soon damp with the sweat that collects by my hair. It's easy sitting like this, our feet in cold water, bodies unsure of whether to be hot or cold.

School is still in session and in a few hours children will come by in their bathing suits to cannonball and scream, but right now it's only us and last night's spider casualties that haven't been scooped out of the water yet.

It's hard to remember how we end up in the pool — the cool slip, my sundress darkening — how I end up buoyed. Water gives my body amnesia: my spine and belly forgetting the weight of me. I float, laughing about something with Darren, unable to even remember what the joke was.

Darren takes his off his shirt. He's shy with his new belly and can't stop staring at mine.

"Need to get swimming more," he says, cupping his stomach where it rests over his shorts. "Hard to tell which one of us is pregnant."

"Nah."

"I float more now. I've been in a chair so long I think my bones are losing density. And the lack of muscle I guess." I watch his legs and imagine the bones hollow as wings. Even his belly has a lightness to it. In water, we feel almost airborne.

"Saves you on floatation devices." We move to the shallow end to sit on the steps and he won't look at me, swishing his bad hand back and forth through the water. The numb fingers move like fronds, brown against his pale stomach.

"I should have kept up with the walking, I guess. It was probably a mistake to stop. But, gravity, eh? Gets to the point where it takes you three hours to go grocery shopping."

"I don't blame you. I know all about gravity."

He glances down at my belly. "Bet you do."

"On a day as nice as this, I'll settle for any apartment."

"I'd take the second one, myself. South-facing windows will give you the most light. And it's got air-con. Not big, I know, but the price is decent, especially since heat and hot water are included." As he talks, he swishes his hand back and forth, the current creating a tide against my belly. "Yeah, definitely the second one. If it were me picking. Though you wouldn't get this pool. Not that you'd want it with the baby."

We sit in the shallow end on the steps, our hair drying to frizz, clothing lightening. Our speech is picked clean of innuendo. Here, the only angles are the bones of Darren's three fingers, his hand that cannot make a fist.

Back home, the house is showing off. Begging, maybe. This is the kind of light I like. All I want to do is stretch on the sofa in front of the window and absorb the sun's good vitamins. Today, the rooms feel right. The house is a body after exercise, sun moving through it like pheremones. I should go to the gym. The doctor said they could set up an exercise program for "people like me," though I wasn't sure if this meant disabled people like me or pregnant people like me. Probably pregnant. Now that the hip's gone, am I still disabled?

I never fit into that category anyways. I walked. I was never sure whether or not that counted. When I told people I played wheelchair basketball, they looked at me like I was getting away with something.

So, yes, I'm pretty sure I'm not disabled anymore, some kind of better. This is apparently what able-bodied feels like: dis-disabled.

Quinn's playing under the stairs again. He stays there for hours then emerges hunched over and squinting. The floorboards hum when he plays. The stairs . . . are alive . . . with the sound of music (la, la, la, la). With Quinn's perpetual soundtrack, I feel like someone in a musical. I waver between wanting to burst into song and burst into tears.

Quinn's locked under the stairs and I want to be with him. This'll be the one benefit of moving to a smaller place; maybe the lack of a practice space will make him want to get a job. This isn't estrangement, I have to remind myself. He's just working. Something like that. He's growing as an artist. Maybe that's the same as maturing. Either way, he's doing a job like everyone else.

Everyone except me: a public speaker waiting for a public. I need a new job. I need a Real Job, something to fill in the blank in the phrase, "I am a ____." How can I possibly remain as a public speaker, fitting my life story into half hour segments with time for questions? How can I possibly own the story of my sports career when I'm not even disabled anymore?

I listen outside the door. Quinn's playing the blues, lots of bends and slides and hammer-ons so that the notes are shifty, hiding something, too quick to mutate. The amp's static and the muffling walls give his music a baby-monitor quality and I can't help but picture him in this house's concrete womb, gestating.

This seems fitting. The baby has begun to move in little blurts of music quick across my abdomen like grace notes. Quinn plays my guitar and the child plays me with connecting notes, with her body that has never cried out before. She's pure music, this kid, her whole body a sound, something between a noise and a breath.

~

Quinn says that the sonogram will make the whole experience more real for him. Between the sickness, the fatigue and the brand, spankin' new breasts, I don't have this problem. As we sit in the waiting room at the Royal Columbian, he bounces on the balls of his feet, either from excitement or the desire to test out some new rhythm he's been working at. My knee jiggling is more a product of my overfull bladder. You'd think that if that machine's strong enough to see through my skin and muscle and fat, it would be strong enough to zoom right past the bladder.

I haven't been here since the replacement and my hip remembers, aching out of nostalgia. I should be able to bounce along with him.

"Do you have a family history of birth defects?" asks the technician.

"No, pretty much everything else, though. Cancer, heart disease, diabetes," I say.

"Dementia, arthritis, scoliosis," adds Quinn. "And your disability is a birth defect that just took ten years to appear, right? The weak growth plate?"

"Was. It was a birth defect, I guess. I don't have it anymore." I shrug. "We have a family history of everything. And we're worried because I've been exposed to a lot of radiation since I was a kid. X-Rays and CT scans. All that jazz."

"Right," says the technician, making a note. "You should probably take those issues up with your doctor." We must have a strong faith in science bringing this child into the world.

I've been in this room for X-rays before and it's strange that they're focusing on another area now. The bed for the ultrasound machine is cold and calms the inflammation in my lower back. It gives me hope: the machine soothing the history of my bones.

The technician squirts the goo on my belly and flicks on the monitor. The only shape I can make out is the new ball and socket and the screws that hold both into place, my new hip floating through cloudy organs.

"You've had a replacement," notes the technician. "That should be interesting down the line. Is that the Birmingham hip?"

"Yup. They figured it would last the longest, since I'm so young."

"There's the fetus," says the technician. She looks like a nurse, except for her anti-radiation apron. The apron is silver and makes her look bionic. The Termi-nurse.

"Between the X-rays and the heavy metals found in the bloodstreams of some people who've had the Birmingham hip, if this baby has three heads, I know who to blame."

The technician gives me a 'they don't pay me enough to laugh' smile. Quinn leans over to look at the screen. I'm holding his hand so tightly I feel his heartbeat quick through my palm. "Okay, you're going to have to help me out with this one," he says, "because I can't tell the kid from her kidney."

The Termi-nurse giggles. Oh, sure. Quinn gets the little laugh. People always laugh around him. He wins them over as if by luck, like finding a silver dollar in an old-fashioned birthday cake. "Well, I'll show you," she says, touching the screen with a pencil. "Here's the fetus. This is the heart, the lungs." She smells of patchouli, incongruous against the ammonia and steel of this place.

"I can see it," says Quinn, running a finger along the place where the technician says the body is. "Look, Nole. Can you see it? That's the baby."

"Sure," I say. "Wow, look at that." Really, the scan is like one of those Magic Eye 3-D pictures I could never relax long enough to have any success in. It's all clouds and static to me. Recognizing your child on the ultrasound must be the first big test of motherhood and all I saw was my new hip, the only part of my body that isn't made of me.

"Now, let's see here, did you want to know the sex of the baby?" the Termi-Nurse asks.

"I'm not sure," I say. Why haven't we talked about this? Why has this never come up? We've known the date of the ultrasound for over a month now. "Do we?"

Quinn stares at the screen, as if trying to make his own predictions. "Might be nice. Would be easier to shop for stuff. I dunno. And it might make it more real, like, to picture the baby as a real boy or girl, not some floating alien-looking thing. I dunno. What do you think?"

"I'm thinking I have to pee, so whatever decision — let's hurry it up. A surprise might be nice, you know?"

"Wasn't the pregnancy enough of a surprise for you?"

"Maybe we should talk about this more. We have one more ultrasound coming up. I really have to pee. Let's just get this over with."

Quinn stares at the movements on the screen. "If that's what you want. Yeah, I mean, sure. There's one more ultrasound coming up. At least. We've got time." I study the monitor: a quick little heartbeat, a frond-like wave that might be an arm. My blurry child coming into focus. "It's probably a girl anyways. Any boy of mine — well, let's just say there wouldn't be any question." He winks at the Termi-Nurse and she giggles.

"Is this your first child?" she asks.

Quinn nods, "Yup." He taps the screen again. "There he . . . or she . . . is. The first in the McLeod/Taylor lineage . . . Kid A."

We look at each other at the same time and laugh. Kid A? Get it? This is the one expression of Quinn's that can always comfort me: when we're tuned to the right channel, have the same song in our head. A radio station of two.

"Can you please contain the laughter, Ms. Taylor?" asks the Termi-nurse. "It's hard to get a picture when your belly's shaking."

"I like that," I say. "Kid A."

"Many couples like to come up with personal nicknames for the fetus. It helps them to connect with the child before the birth." We've been reading the same books, the Termi-Nurse and I. How she falls back on book learning makes me smile. She doesn't get the reference.

"Knowing the sex of the baby would do that too, don't you think?" asks Quinn.

"Yeah, but how healthy do you think it is to name your fetus after a Radiohead album?" I ask. "Isn't that just asking for trouble?"

"Eh," says Quinn, stroking my hand. "We've been asking for trouble since the day of conception. Probably before that, really."

Termi-Nurse tucks a strand of hair underneath her skull cap. She's safe behind her book learning and Kevlar vest. "I'll make a print out of . . . Kid A that you can take home."

Quinn's bouncing on the soles of his feet again, a rhythm I can feel up my arm, and the image on the monitor moves, maybe from me, maybe from him, maybe from the new beat of the baby.

Quinn:

She was a bit on the big side, but that could just be because I'm used to Nolan. Man, fat chicks look solid. Like she was wearing a pillow or a parka: something to protect her from falls or cold or . . . me, I guess. And it was nice being against her skin, like it was protecting me too, (from falls or cold or . . . myself, I guess).

Up in her apartment it's dark and the window's open and on the ledge there are all these ceramic figurines of little kids and puppy dogs and the moonlight makes them glow. Those figurine things are even freakier when they look like they're glowing. The place smells of burnt food and vanilla, which makes me worry that I'll get the scent in my sweat and take it home with me. But she has a nice, girly voice — high-pitched in a way Nolan's isn't — and says she's a social worker and she's just so . . . not Nolan, which is kind of the goal of the whole evening.

"Do people call you Steve or Steven?" she asks and I keep forgetting that's supposed to be my name. Man, I'm such a tool when it comes to all this. How hard is it to remember the name Steve? Good thing I'm not an undercover agent.

Her name's Susan. I think 'Steve and Susan Johnson' and suddenly want to leave. We sound like a cross-word puzzles and church-group couple. But she's definitely the anti-Nolan: soft where Nolan's toned, dark where she's blonde, short and stumpy where she's all legs and angles. I'm on top of her with all these figurines staring me eye to eye and there's a Winnie the Pooh sun-catcher and her breasts aren't erased by gravity. I can't see her bones at all, not even that little basin that forms between Nolan's ribs and her pubic bones. Nolan and Susan (Susie?): it's like the difference between a tree in Fall and one in Winter covered in snow. Or something. Basins . . . snowy trees . . . what the hell. It's weird — God it's weird — to be not doing this with Nolan. I've never had sex with anyone who has normal hip flexion.

But then she starts to sing. Like, not just hum, but sing. Some pop tune about heroes and eagles and true love and spirits soaring like doves or some other cliché. I'm on top of her and she's turning our sex act into Adultery: The Musical.

"So baby put your dove in my outstretched hand," she sings, jiggling a little.

"Shh," I say, stroking her brow. She has the kind of hair that won't fall into place. "Easy there."

"You're my rose, my star, my one command," she sings and I start wondering what the whole dove/hand metaphor's about, since a dove doesn't seem very phallic to me and this situation calls for innuendo. I don't think I was as flattered as I should have been, considering the 'hero' theme and all.

There are obvious questions here. Quality versus quantity? Ask her to stop or wait it out? Is my thirteen-year-relationship worth sacrificing over a woman whose mode of sexual expression is limited to three chords and a fistful of clichés? Name that tune?

This, of course, should be a great, big, juicy sign. Susan sings during sex. Nolan does not sing during sex, unless you count afterwards in the mornings when sometimes she hums when having a shower. But now there's a conundrum: half of my sexual experience now consists of a woman who sings about doves during intercourse. Is that the track record I want? Better if one out of seven women I've been with sings during sex. Then it's just an isolated incident, not the story of my life.

I go home that night and the next day over breakfast I think of this poor woman singing my . . . praises and start to laugh.

"What?" asks Nolan.

"Huh?' I say. "Nothing. Just thinking of something B.B. said last night during rehearsal."

She reaches across the table to stroke my wrist, smiles up at me. "Ah. And here I thought you were laughing at my growing ass. Admit it. I've had a real budgetary increase in the T & A department."

"And you've done wonderful things with the allocated resources," I tell her. I wonder what happened to her belly: if you can still see the bones. This is something I'll have to check "You've got boobs now. I'm like a teenage boy all over again."

And this is the moment I feel real regret because I'd love to tell her. She'd get such a kick out of the whole thing if it'd been a story about someone else. Too bad this can't become some private joke we share like the Dr. Love thing or the Kid A thing. Hey baby, I'd say to her, wanna come over here and sing my praises?

~

Quinn has a degree in English along with his degree in History. He likes to remind me of this in bookstores, though I minored in English. Quinn has rules about books.

Where was I when these rules were being developed? What vital class did I skip? He's not a particular guy, not given to rules, logic, order, but when it comes to choosing books he has a system. Rule number one — and this, he complains to me, is getting harder and harder to follow all the time — is when a book has the phrase "a novel" after the title. Like, what the fuck else would it be? A manifesto? An epic poem? Quinn paces. He lectures. He expounds to nearby clerks. See, if it were a manifesto, an epic poem, a collection of short stories, then you could label it as that. But "a novel?" Chances are that if it's in the damn fiction section, it's a bloody novel. Especially if the words are in italics. These, he says, are books that take themselves too seriously. No, worse: *authors* who take themselves too seriously. Quinn sighs, shakes his head. Authors. Rule number two is nothing with the words soul, body, rose, moon, hope or spirit in the title. Extra negative points — awarded with a deep sigh and a lecture about the State of Literature These Days — to books that combine the two. Example: *Moon Soul*: a novel. Quinn speaks of the State of Literature These Days like people of some other time would say the words "house of ill repute." Like he's the governor of the State of Literature These Days, cracking down on illegal and immoral business. He wanted to be a novelist sometime between wanting to be a musician and starting to work for the government.

We go to Chapters, even though Quinn complains about the store endlessly: multinational conglomerate . . . monopolizing of the nation's cultural voice . . . blah blah blah. I remind him that we're going for the sales and are too broke for morals. Lately, we've also been perusing the self-help rack. Since becoming pregnant, we suddenly seem to be not good enough at anything and I'm willing to take help in whatever form it arrives in. All those well-coiffed people on the jackets, the soothing pastel backgrounds. You can do it! They say. We'll show you how! Quinn is horrified.

"What about this one?" I ask him. It's a book on becoming a new father, supposed to be written with humour and insight, to divulge the things that no one ever tells you. There's a cartoon drawing of a guy with a baby wailing under his arm, which looks like a possible Child Services snatch-and-grab situation if ever I saw one. But still: humour and insight.

"Why would I need a book on that?"

"Because — oh, let's see . . . let me think now — we're having a baby in three and a half months."

He hunches his shoulders, waving the book off. "Whatever. Parenting is a natural urge. You don't need a book. Books make you over-think. The kids of psychologists are the most screwed up of all."

"Says here . . . 'most men think that parenting is a natural urge, but — "

"I don't care what is says."

"I'm reading *What to Expect When You're Expecting*. It might ease your concerns or make you feel more prepared or — "

"Nolan, I don't want the book." People are turning to look at us with pity. They sense our fear. These are people who have no reason to feel sorry for us: an obese man in a stained shirt, a woman with too much makeup and cowboy boots on. These are people who need a self-help section. Not us. We're here for improvements, not help. Adjustments. Tweaking.

"I don't understand why you're being so — "

"And I don't understand why you're fucking nagging me about some fucking book that I don't want and am obviously not going to read." Cowboy-Boots Woman is in full stare mode, her fuchsia mouth open a little, in need of some serious Ann Landers manners.

And then the tears come. I knew they would. And why did I know? Because 'What to Expect While You're Expecting' told me. Like a little warning label on my body. Does Quinn know this? No. Why not? Because he won't read the fucking book. He reddens.

"Jesus, Nolan," he mutters. I pretend to be reading the jacket with furious interest. He lowers his voice. "Nolan. Hey, don't — Jesus Christ. Nolan. Nole." He reaches out tentatively and touches my hand. "Why do you have to — ? Okay, fine. I'm sorry. Don't cry. I'll read the damn book."

"No," I say. "It's fine. I don't care."

Quinn's wearing an old leather jacket he found while cleaning out his practice space, and he smells of lanolin and dampness. He touches my good hip and I'm momentarily surprised that he can't cup my pubic bone anymore. I am without handles, flying off the handle, something like that. "You do care. I'll read it. Come here. Look, it's recommended by Parenting Today and it's written with humour and insight, supposed to divulge all the — "

"I said that. I said the humour and insight bit." With this new hip, it's so easy to bend down to breathe in the smell of him. "I'm not a crier. I don't know why I'm crying."

"Must be your commitment to literature," he says, letting my hair slip in and out of his fingers. "What? Not even a pity laugh? Maybe I will buy this book. We need all the humour and insight we can get."

At the counter, the tears start anew. Nationals are being held today, the first time I haven't gone. Mandy will be there. Lucky thing that my uniform wouldn't fit her or she'd be wearing it. Number 8. I'd once planned to get a tattoo involving the 8 and the symbol for infinity and now I'm glad I didn't. Basketball ends. Basketball has ended. I imagine Mandy doing the figure 8 drill with the behind-the-back dribble. I imagine the smudges her wheels will leave on the gym floor: the symbol for infinity over and over. She will have a career and it will be long.

"I wonder what that Mandy kid got classified as," I say, mostly to distract a brooding Quinn from the memory of my tears. "Nationals are this weekend."

"Does it matter?" he asks.

"Of course it matters. If she's a 4, she'll be competing with disabled people for playing time. If she's a 4.5, she'll be lumped in with all these ABs who've been playing standup for their whole bloody lives."

Quinn shrugs. "I still don't get the whole classification thing. You guys spend your life trying to convince people you can do everything an AB can do, but the minute the issue of classification comes up, everyone's all 'I'm so disabled! I'm so disabled! Look at me flop all over the place!'"

"It's such a screwed-up system anyhow. I'm so glad I don't have to put up with that bullshit anymore."

Quinn eyes me but says nothing. I suspect he's thinking of the end of my Athlete's Assistance money. The last carding cheque will come and with it a notice that my funds have been terminated. This is the one memento I want to keep: frame, maybe. Proof that the accounts are settled. Basketball owes me nothing anymore.

I've applied to the sport-management program at Douglas College and will put the last cheque towards application fees as some sort of good-luck gesture. Everything is being processed, always being processed. Everything is in progress. Kid A is due in July, which means that the pregnancy waiting will end before the school waiting. It appears to take just as much time to approve or reject my university application as it does to turn a speck of an egg into a fully formed human being.

If I get rejected from university, I suppose I'll be a homemaker, though the position appears to demand more than the light vacuuming and dusting when the sun shows too much build up: probably something to do with balanced meals and chequebooks to match. Also, it requires another income to allow us to keep a roof over our heads.

Quinn's making a home under the stairs with my guitar, so I have the rest of the domain at my disposal. When we get home, he tosses the book of the couch, jostles the keys in his palm for a few moments, then says he's going out and will be back soon. After he's gone, I make the bed, put the book on his pillow, then go out into the hallway. If I'm a homemaker, I reason, I have a responsibility to the whole home, even Quinn's secret-garden room. Especially Quinn's secret-garden room.

I hit my head on the bulb and send a shock of light across the ceiling, brightening the Van Halen poster into a guitar-solo spotlight. The room isn't my size, those few crucial inches between fitting in and not. Song lyrics and chord progression charts are duct-taped to the bare cement.

Sheet music, too — not just tab — when did Quinn learn how to read real music? I sit on his stool and trace the notes with my finger. They're ruins, there's magic here and the scrawls are like cave paintings willing long-dead creatures to return. Quinn conjures '70s testosterone rock back into an emo world. That poster of Van Halen on the wall: he hopes for spells and time travel. The room wards me off, my future-tense belly.

I squint at the sheet music and try to remember old piano lessons: Every Good Boy Deserves Fudge. And what was that trick for remembering the spaces between the lines? FACE. I try to tap out the melody on my leg, but it's only his part of a whole. The bare little riffs — I think those are riffs — wouldn't make sense even if I could read sheet music. It lacks a band's logic. If I'm a homemaker, what's Quinn making here?

Years of old coats and unused sporting equipment give the place a nesty smell, but the concrete walls aren't for burrowing. The floor is fissured with patch cords, adaptors and old strings. They warn me to be gone, but it's my damn guitar.

The Gretsch is the one curve in the room, its varnish bright as a woman stepping out of a bath into sunlight. I wish that I'd named her. I pick her up and even now she fits well against me. My breasts still arrange themselves around the curve and the chilled wood feels good against my belly. But the sound: Quinn's tuned it to a different key. Dropped D, apparently. I spend the first few minutes trying to bring her back to open. It takes too long to find my bearings on my own instrument. When I'm done it's still not right, but at least she's tuned in relation to herself.

This is the right place for sound. Quinn picked a good cave. The G chord is fat with reverb and electricity. You can feel the meat and potatoes behind it. And concrete holds echoes well: the room has a long memory.

I try to read Quinn's music — is it rock? Is it blues? Allegra? Bellisimo? A slow groove like Lou Reed on good heroin? Every Good Boy Deserves . . . And Quinn here, living out his little boy rock-star fantasies. Actually, most little boys want to be firefighters or policemen, don't they? Quinn should take a lesson: pick a fantasy that at least involves a good dental plan.

"Whatcha doing?" asks Quinn, his shadow somehow projected on all the walls. I didn't hear him coming. No wonder he gets distracted. In this room, music goes deeper than the eardrum. You forget, the echoes remember.

"It's my guitar," I say, my voice stupid without amplification. "I thought you went out."

"You want the Gretsch back or something?"

I shake my head. "Just visitation rights. Play me something?"

"I don't mind that you're here. I was just surprised."

I nod and the amp crackles as Quinn takes the guitar from me. "I was curious," I said. "You're in here all the time." It sounds too much like a complaint, but Quinn's too busy tuning the strings to his own liking.

"Did you have her in D?" I ask as he tightens the strings.

"Mm-hm."

"How come?"

"Song we're working on."

"Will you play it for me?"

"It might sound a little thin without the guys." He picks out a riff I don't recognize, then strums a few chords.

"Why'd you pick that tuning?"

"Not my choice. So think I should save our song — that Lyle Lovett one — for when I really need it? What do you want to hear?"

"What's your favourite song?"

"At this moment?" Quinn pauses. He brushes the strings with his new nails. "It's impossible to have a favourite. You're putting me on the spot here."

The room's too small for me to stand without hunching, so I sit on the floor beside his chair. "Play me the first song that comes to mind."

He brightens. "I'll play a song for Kid A."

He plays 'Mary Had a Little Lamb,' both the lullaby and the Stevie Ray Vaughn version. He sings to my belly, his guitar as close as possible. Kid A responds: a heel deep under my ribs, dances me an inside bruise. There's still skin and fluid between us. She mistakes the word 'blues' for the word 'bruise' and does her best for a hurtin' song. Quinn plays on. He wants to charm her like a snake. He plays just for her. It wasn't what I asked.

Every phrase between Darren and I should be heavy as a book submerged in water. We should be loaded with subtext; our history is the kind that encourages weeping and fistfights. Once, in a bar, Sophia saw a man that she'd broken up with ten years previously and punched him in the face: one last anger. Darren and I have chosen amnesia, though which kind I'm not sure. Our lens is off: either far or near-sighted. We're either unable to remember the past or unable to acknowledge the present day. The rooms help us recall: bits of old conversations triggered by muscle memory alone.

The walls in Darren's home could maybe be torn apart like a bird's nest to reveal cloth from forgotten gowns, thread for a tear no one mended. That table, his arm just so, the kettle's train-whistle hoot. Darren's happy to see me and I'm happy to see him. Sometimes I wonder why that is. We sit at the kitchen table and make plans that have nothing to do with reality, drawing up defenses and offenses like generals. We drink tea, eat trail mix and figure out how to develop someone else's children.

Darren:

She walks like a slimmer girl. Isn't skinny anymore but her bones haven't gotten the memo. On the table, unable to quiet herself, swinging her legs.

"So," she says, uncapping a pen and balancing the notebook on her lap like a reporter. "Inbounds play."

This's my job: I'm the math guy. She teaches skills and controlled chaos. I do the patterns and repairs.

"Right," I say. "Put Mandy at centre, let Sam and Nick cross to get open for the first pass."

Weird to know her now that she's grown. Weird that she grew up at all: went from nineteen to thirty-two without my intervention. Like she caught up to me. Passed me, maybe. I feel the same age as when I was with her, but I don't look in mirrors long enough to chart the changes.

"Think Mandy has the hands?" Nolan doesn't like Mandy for obvious reasons.

I've never even seen a picture of her in-between years. Nolan is before and after. Nolan is what I look at to tell me I'm getting old. "Yeah, for sure. Or send her over centre as safety. Have her come back if they need her." Nolan doesn't realize she doesn't like Mandy. She should give up her Quickie, give the girl a real chair, but Nolan claims it's built too specifically for her to be of use to anyone else.

"I'd prefer to have her getting the first pass and Nick crossing to get open and take it up the court," she says. "I don't think she has the hands yet to be over half." She taps the pen on the notebook. Is never still. Even though she's pregnant. This is her idea of 'rest.' This is her idea of 'easy does it.'

"Well, okay. You're the coach," I say. She nods, slides off the table and wanders over to the sink for a glass of water. She works all the corners of this house, hating it when I close the door. We rarely leave my home. I've never been to hers. I imagine big rooms, hand-me-down furniture but a good stereo, her boyfriend wrecking the house's order in the name of rock and roll.

"I'll put a question mark next to it. Next question." She touches my hand to get my attention. She already had my attention. "Alberta's fast but has no height. So I'm thinking pack it in, make them earn it from the outside. But do we do the old 2–3 zone or mix it up with 1–2 –2 and have someone hawk the ball and contest the shot? Remind me to introduce the triple switch, though that may be too much for them."

She speaks basketball better than I do. Her hands are all over the place as she talks, looking for a ball to make sense of them.

"Which one can they play best?" I ask. "That's the real question. Mandy would be good in the middle of the 2–3. Not that we have to decide now. The Games aren't until next October."

"Mandy," says Nolan."You really have a type, don't you?"

Thirteen years well up in us like tears.

"You think I'm interested in her? She's a teenager. She's, what, thirty years younger than me. From a biological standpoint, I could be her grandfather."

Nolan blushes a few decades off her age. "You do talk about her an awful lot."

"Because I think you're under-utilizing her. She's the size of a small elephant; you might as well put that to good use."

Nolan shrugs. "I guess she could clog up the middle of the key pretty well."

"No kidding she could. You should work with her. Show her all the Big Girl moves."

Again, the shrug. Swinging legs. "Right. I will. Now, moving along. You think 2–3 zone; I think you may be right." We stick to talking ball, which is a better game than the "remember when?" my mind wants to play. Thirteen years can't be caught up so easily.

20

DARREN:

Wasn't so much the dream that scared me — you can't take full responsibility for the scheming of the brain's reptilian parts — but it alerted me to how often I'd been fantasizing about Nolan getting pregnant while awake. During the thought-breaks I'd take at work, I'd lean back in my chair and stare at the walls of Melinda's cubicle next to me, all her glossy photos against the grey partitioning like they were sci-fi portals and you could step right into the birthday parties, family portraits, dance recitals. I'd imagine lying on the couch with some soft-breathing child against my chest, both of us drifting off. A sturdy little hellion of a kid with Nolan's blonde hair but my curls. It must have been all the estrogen, on account of the two secretaries and three female computer systems analysts nearby.

The estrogen, you know, and me still some kind of animal driven by chemicals and keen sniffing. Or even simpler biology. Darwinism. Survival of the family genes. Survival of the family name. Reproduction: a basic, forgivable urge.

A baby — I even thought of names for him — Nolan pregnant, the dark panelling in the living room decorated with streamers and cake-icing handprints, a photo for my wallet, us waking up at 3 AM *to wailing and Nolan hunched on the edge of the bed with her long hair forward — ("like girls on hands and knees who flip their hair before them to dry in the sun") — saying I can't do this, I can't do this, why won't she just stop crying and me bringing the baby still heaving with tears in to the room quiet, having calmed them both.*

I drew a perimeter around these thoughts. They couldn't leave the cubicle, the chair. They couldn't even go into the hall. That's the best way: lining the dream in chalk like the police do for murder victims, trapping it in a cubicle, anchoring it to the mundane present, forcing the truth to break in with all its matter of fact about the ice storms.

Maybe that's why I was startled when the dream spilled out from the office chair and came home with me like the common cold: something else I'm always getting second hand from the kids of the secretaries. It was late morning when I woke up and Nolan was still asleep with her arms and legs all over the place and I wondered what even keeps her bones together. She slept like a younger girl: always on the move. I know it's the arthritis, but still. I watched her laying there, the covers rejected, an arm flung across her face, her bad leg and its submerged pubic bone. Disregard what pregnancy would do to her athletic career, just think of the body. The pelvis shifting: plate tectonics. The reaction along the spine, the hip. Beyond the bones, too: the skin, the muscles confused by the new centre of gravity. Just think of what I could have done to her.

Which was one of the reasons Val wouldn't have kids. Her knees hurt enough, no need to add swollen ankles and an extra thirty or forty pounds to the equation. There are some things you can't ask a person to do.

"You're being good about taking your Pill, right?" I asked her when she woke up.

"Yes, dad," she said, rolling her eyes in that teenage way that made me cringe. "Could you just wait until I regain consciousness before you talk down to me. It's a little early for condescension."

"I'm not trying to start a fight. I'm asking. Only asking."

"Of course I am. What? You think I'm going to get myself knocked up?" The violence of that phrase, though I guess in her case that's what it amounts to: warping the bones from inside. You'd think Quinn would feel the same way. He knows her medical history better than I do. Plus, the replacement. Those things don't last. They're not as good as the real joint. And I don't even want to think about the possible damage from the hip's metals getting in through the umbilical cord.

"No. I just mean for your sake."

"How very thoughtful."

"Nolan."

"Speaking of which," she hopped off the bed — well, it was slow kind of hop, her hip clicking — and went to her purse. "Baby Pill time. Ten AM. I sure slept." I watched her bend down: the lean spine, the ribs all in order. A place for everything and everything in its place.

"Baby Pill? Who calls them that?"

She shrugged and I noticed the muscular atrophy on one side of her back, ruining the illusion her bones gave. "Me. Sophia, too. Anti-Baby Pills. You don't have to remind me. I'm not going to forget. Give me a little credit."

"I didn't say that you were going to forget. I was just — "

"You're always reminding me." She joined me on the bed again.

"I don't want . . . You're going to Athens in, what, three weeks? You don't need any more stress."

"Don't talk about Athens," she said. She flinched whenever the word was mentioned. Her nervous system. Emphasis on the word 'nervous.' "I'm not pregnant. I'm not going to get pregnant." She took my hand and pressed it to her abdomen. "See? Feel. No baby."

"That's my bad hand."

She took the two feeling fingers and pressed them again. "I know. I know you. These two are fine." She stroked the three bad fingers curled against each other. I could feel her touch through the nerve damage, as if through static.

"I know you're not pregnant, but I would feel awful if you were. And you do forget things."

She dropped my hand and it rested on her belly. I could feel slight movements under skin, though that was just hunger. "I forget my keys. Sometimes I leave my jacket in the gym. Neither of those is going to make me an unwed single mother. We haven't gotten pregnant so obviously I've been doing something right."

"What do you mean single? You think I'd leave?"

"You forget I'm an adult. Just because I'm in school and a rookie doesn't mean I'm not. I'm just a younger adult than you are."

"You're nineteen. Note the word 'teen' at the end of that word."

"That's legal. I'm legal for everything here."

"Yeah, just don't go down to the States."

She stood up and my fingers fell away, skimming her pubic hair. "If I'm old enough to fuck you, I'm old enough to remember to take my Baby Pills. I think it's really as simple as that. Don't worry. I'm not going to make you a daddy."

Quinn was turning twenty, shedding the 'teen' in his age, and I was invited. The party was being held at a friend's house: pool in the backyard, parents out of town, the stuff police reports are made of. All of the furniture had been cleared out away to make room for people, except for a table at the back with a few bags of chips. I'd brought a gift — a keychain with a little skeetball game that could be played during class — and a mickey of vodka. It was two weeks before Athens.

Quinn was sitting on the countertop that partitioned the kitchen from the living room, holding court. He'd been complaining for the past week about having to limit the invitation list, but there were already more people there than I knew. I could have fit all of my friends in the kitchen: maybe a few in the hall.

"Nolan. Nolan, baby, I'm on the prowl," Quinn informed me when I approached him, "I'm going to get laid tonight. Either that or wake up in a pool of my own vomit."

"Maybe both. Just don't count on a second date."

"You're funny," he said. "But not in a nice way."

I drank the mickey quickly, confident that Big Girl could translate into heavy drinker. I wandered between groups of people, looking for friendly banter. Everyone else was drunk, too. It was like a tribe. Though most of us were either over twenty or on the cusp of it, it felt as if we were all teenagers in the same high-school clique. People put their arms around me, girls cried to me before being led away by better friends.

I was outside by the pool when Quinn found me. The pool's light was the only brightness, so the yard had a blue, wavery hue. I was watching a girl swimming, the water enchanting her skirt into silk, her blotchy limbs pale as an angel. I was drunk and the pool seemed to hold healing powers. Quinn was carrying one of the dining-room chairs, which had clawed legs and a red velvet seat.

"Here," he said. "You need to sit." I'd forgotten to rest and my bones were doing the remembering for me. Weeks ago, I'd mentioned that I couldn't stand for more than fifteen minutes and he'd listened. He set the chair down in the mud.

"I booted a drunk guy off it," he said. His shirt was undone, bragging about his 100 sit-ups a day. "I said, 'Hey, this chick is going to the Para Olympics. Show some respect. Give her the damn chair.'"

"Paralympics," I said.

"Right. Paralympics." He put his arm around my shoulder and leaned in. "So I said. So I said to this guy. I said, 'You don't even know what the Para — the Paralympics is. It's like the best competition for the wheelchair people. She's going to Athens, man.' And he was all, 'Sorry, sorry, I didn't know."

"Thanks," I said. I couldn't tell if I was smelling his cologne, his hair gel or the alcohol.

"You know what? I'm going to tell you something." His pointer finger wavered at me like the needle on a compass. "I admire . . . " He gestured and I laced his fingers with mine: his strong grip, the fine hair on his knuckles. "I just think it's really . . . You're like overcoming shit . . . "

My stocking feet were in the mud. "I've lost my shoe," I said. "Must have happened a few minutes ago. Are you trying to get in my pants?"

Quinn looked ashamed. He looked young. One side of his collar was turned up and his fly was undone.

"Well . . . ," he finally said. His cheeks were glossy with booze. Mine were too. We were both teenaged: the same oily sheen of youth. "Well . . . " Every sentence Darren spoke was well punctuated. Quinn and I were rough drafts. Quinn and I were well-meaning.

I kissed him. I was the one who started it. I held his face to keep him still. We were sitting on dining-room chairs in the middle of someone else's dark garden. He was eager. Romance was alive and vodka-flavoured.

"Oh shit," I said as we pulled away, dazed and teenaged. "Oh shit. I shouldn't have done that. I have a — "

"A what? A husband?"

"I can't kiss you anymore."

"You think you're so adult because you're always in pain," said Quinn as I sat in the chair he'd found for me. "You think it's made you grow up too soon. That's the problem with you. You're not mature, just . . . arthritis-having."

"Arthritic," I said. "I'm arthritic."

"Right. Not mature."

"I never said I was mature. Did you ever once hear me say that?" I was yelling. The pool carried the sound over to the neighbour's yard. People who were just showing up in cars stopped to watch.

"It's my birthday," said Quinn. "You can't yell at me."

"I can too. I'm going home."

Instead, I called Darren. His house was closer and the buses had stopped running.

"Oh, good grief, Nole," he said. "Don't drive. I'll be right there."

He showed up in embroidered slippers, the kind that grandfathers wear while smoking pipes. They'd never bothered me before. A crowd on the front lawn watched us go while Quinn was inside, getting sick.

It was inevitable: people asked if Darren was my dad. The grey hairs on his temple were too obvious under streetlights. The slippers didn't help his cause much, either.

"I can't hold you," he said as he helped me into the house. "I wish I could just carry you in, but I can't."

"I'm sorry."

"Don't be sorry."

He headed towards the couch. Hardwood floor in the living room: he was aiming for damage control in case I vomited.

"Sit," he said. He couldn't force me, so he settled for a parental tone. I sat. The kitten — who by now was in a long-limbed stage of adolescences — was on the couch. She trotted over to my lap, licked the crook of my arm once and settled into sleep. She forgave my excesses. Darren went into the kitchen and returned with a glass of water and two Advil.

"Drink," he said, sitting down beside me with the glass like a mother in a medicine commercial.

I took a sip. "I'm sorry," I said.

"Hangovers are caused by dehydration, so drink it all. It's a remedy I've honed over the years."

"Can't imagine you drunk." There was already a blanket on the couch: we'd brought it down to watch a movie a few days before.

"You want one of my shirts to sleep in? I'll make you a bed on the couch."

I drank the water. I did as I was told. "How come I can never leave a nightgown behind? Or a toothbrush?"

He smoothed a hair off my face, more out of annoyance than affection. "It's not that you can't, kiddo. We'll talk about it in the morning."

"Do you have to call me kiddo?"

"Shh," said Darren. He went away and returned and I sat with my unfocused anger, too young to argue, too old to tantrum. "Here, let me help you."

"You undressing me like a mom or like a boyfriend?"

"Honey, you're drunk. What do you think? And I'm not really your boyfriend. I think I'm too old to be anyone's boyfriend. There's not a lot of boy left in me." He touched my shoulder so gently I wanted to hit him.

"I said like. Like a boyfriend. It was a simile. I can undress myself." I struggled with the dress' straps. "Well, okay. Apparently I'm having difficulties. But I can't put on this thing whole sober. You know that when people talk about 'the love that dares not speak its own name,' they're not talking about us, right?"

The dress was no puzzle for Darren. He slid it down my shoulders and I wished I was the one with reduced sensation, hating his condescending touch. "No offence or anything. I just don't want you thinking — "

"Now, if I were a choirboy or a ruggedly charming football player . . . ," I said.

"Nolan." His answer for everything.

"Or a college boy experimenting . . . anyways, point is no one cares that we're . . . involved. It's not a scandalous thing."

Darren turned my wrist over. It was scaly with eczema. "Is that a stress reaction or an allergy?" He skimmed his thumb over the spot, as if to smooth my rough patches.

"Stress, I think." The shirt smelled of him. It was so old that the image on the front looked like a TV show on a staticky channel. It calmed me: the worn cotton, the smell of him disguising my breath.

"Aww, Nolan."

"I don't think you're my boyfriend. Don't think I do. I have no such illusions."

Darren kissed my head. "I'm going to bed. If you put one foot on the ground, you won't feel like you're spinning. Works even with paras without sensation, strangely enough."

"I'm sorry."

"Goodnight, Nole."

"You can say that you love me now. I won't remember it in the morning."

Darren went up to his bedroom and I sat on the couch in his T-shirt, stroking the kitten.

"Pretty girl," I whispered in her ear. "Little monkey-nosed girl." The kitten had a million nicknames: Monkey Girl, Foxy Face, Big Paw Bear. The kitten was indifferent to this. She licked at my eczema as if to exfoliate my rough patches. Darren treated me like a child and I deserved it.

~

What I should remember: training camps, practices, drills, learning the reverse lay-up — the right swoop of the hand, flick of the wrist, a ballerina's choreography — mastering the three-point shot. And the plays: those too. "Pick for the passer, pass for the picker," the inbounds play, reverse, counter, the picket fence, triple switch, high-post offence. I got to know my role. That was a year my body learned by rote. Darren had taken me as far as I could and the rest I discovered through stumbling. Tony gave me handouts, but they didn't translate into game speed. He drew things on the board, but I learned best when Sammy would stop the play and push my chair through the motions as if leading me through a dance step.

This is what I should remember: the form, the technique, the correct angle for a fast break. My body knows them so well. They've been pushed to the back of my brain, tucked right beside walking and breathing.

The on-court is gone, even big games. When that uniform went on, I had the memory of a base creature, a reptile. Shooter's mentality: forget successes and failures.

The new wheelchair arrived in Canada colours. It was a much-needed sponsorship deal, ordered months ago with Darren's help. He'd promised to come with me, but something Valerie-related had come up. I knew because he'd phoned me up to say that he was going to be staying after hours at the office to get a head start on a special project.

"That's nice," I said. "You always work late."

"Well, yeah, you know. I didn't want you to wonder why I hadn't called. Just thought I'd give you the heads-up. You know — to check in."

"Right. Tell Valerie I say hi. I'll see you tomorrow." This was my version of adult and understanding.

The wheelchair measurements were right: fourteen inches wide, twenty-one high. Me in numbers, cast in metal. The new chair was titanium and the bars were thin as bones. Maybe this is what they would make my new hip out of, when it was time.

When I got the chair home, I sat on the floor of the living room with all the furniture pushed aside and my gear laid out. The new chair came with its own tool kit and for the first time I had the right equipment.

The chair wasn't a fixed frame. I wasn't a fixed person: so many variables, so much room to grow. I wanted a little leeway — move the wheels forward, take off the offensive wing — but now each screw was a weakness. I knew all about that. After my first surgery — screws driven into the socket to pin the growth plate back on — I was pronounced cured. I walked. It was October. I forgot the old hurt. The scar lost its pink, fading as if exposed to the sun. Then it was November and the hurt returned and I carried it under my jeans because I was too busy: the school volleyball team, grade seven, a bony kid named Max who dressed like Kurt Cobain and apparently 'like liked' me. It was November and the sunlight was amber and I'd gotten a part in the school production of "Our Town." The limp returned. It forced me off the volleyball team. It forced me out of "Our Town." The doctor said I was fine and I went back a few weeks later and he promised I was fine. He gave me some exercises to do, saying all I needed was strength.

It was December and we'd drive by the doctor's office and I'd fantasize that he would run out of the building waving my X-rays, having found some mistake that could be easily cured. Then the hurt had become pain and the pain had become chronic and the injury had become a disability, but I didn't know that yet. Then it was December and I tried to walk home with my friends — Max's impossibly long fingers poking under my coat to tickle me — but my leg wouldn't move and I tried to force it and fell, humiliated, grateful for the cushion of the year's first snowfall.

We went to a new doctor. He took X-rays and found that the screws that were supposed to pin the growth plate back on had gone wrong and severed the hip's blood supply. My hip was smothered by lack of blood, aging in animal years. I had surgery to remove the screws, (which they gave to me in a plastic baggy like the kind the use to hold crime evidence), and then there were hospital stays and the briny, subterranean physio pool and crutches that rubbed against my new bra. I decorated the crutches with butterfly and heart stickers, which fell off wherever I went. They tried a half body cast that spread my legs apart at ninety-degree angles and I was so tall that the doctor cut up his broken hockey stick and sculpted it between my legs and my mother had to cut my underwear up the seams and put in velcro and my father had to cut a hole in the bathroom door so that I could get in.

But these repairs, chair repairs. These, I could do. It wasn't surgery. I taught myself the simple jobs so that Darren wouldn't scoff. With my Allen keys and new wrench, I disassembled each joint one by one and put a blue daub of Lock-Tight on each screw, using all the torque I had to tighten them good. Each screw was in its place. Such a small competency.

Darren had promised to help me with this, but he was with Valerie. Some dubious meeting. Probably a martini and low-cut dress affair, I decided. A 'remember when' kind of thing. I sat on the couch and stared at the new wheelchair. I would have two weeks to get used to it before the Games. Darren was spending time with Valerie on a regular basis. How long would I need to adjust to this? I waited for the Lock Tight to set and sketched plans for modifications. I wanted to build a foot plate near the back to tuck my sore leg. Darren had promised to help me, but he was out with Valerie. Darren was out and I stayed at home, tending to new metal.

I sat back on the couch and surveyed the room, wondering what I owned. The apartment was rented. The wheelchair was a gift for the price of an endorsement. I was some kind of nomad, wandering across both sides of the water. *And both shall row,* said the stereo. I was listening to the song because Darren liked it and I wanted to memorize the chords and give it back to him with my name scrawled all over it. *And both shall row, my love and I.*

The wheelchair sat on my rented floor on a quilt given to me by my mother. It was bright, the way gifts should be, cocky in its red veneer. I became unsure of the repairs. Likely, I'd done it all wrong, left off some vital screw.

Easy to compare this to the surgeon in his stupid bike helmet, his bookworm thighs forced into spandex. The surgeon was eager as a boy. My injury was a first for him, but he knew just what to do. A group of interns flipped through the textbook. I was something they'd never seen. They should have done the surgery: at least they knew that they didn't know. Didn't someone teach him that in first-year philosophy? Simple Plato.

And Darren. He was so confident he could navigate between the two of us. And Darren, sure he knew me so well.

21

DR. TAYLOR:

"Are you having trouble with hemorrhoids?" asks Linda as we're sitting at Nolan and Quinn's table. "I've read that's a big problem with pregnant women."

"Nope," says Nolan. "But, hey, good to know." She's sitting on a stool with better posture than she's had in years, trying to find the right place for her belly and spine to rest.

"Well, it's true. Isn't it, honey?" Linda pats my thigh. The way that woman can find my nerve endings, she should have been the doctor in the family. Since Nolan's been pregnant, Linda's paid more and more attention to my nerves: their endings, their beginnings, their flashes in between.

When I was a med student, she would hold up the anatomy chart before tests and offer her skin saying, "Can you find the pancreas? Okay, how about the spleen?" And eventually: "The labia? The vulva?" If I got it right, she'd simply nod and say, "Correct." Just sitting at my desk naked, looking studious. "Correct. Okay, Mr. Taylor, show me where the clitoris is."

"In some cases that's true," I say. And, of course, there follows a silence that should be the comfortable, well-lit Sunday afternoon kind, but isn't. "How you feeling, honey?"

"Pretty good." Nolan nods. "Yeah, pretty good."

"Good," I say. And sip my Earl Gray. She's drinking some prenatal tea that may as well have been purchased in a back alley for the way it smells.

"Yeah," she says. "Can't complain."

When Linda got pregnant, she'd lie on the bed and say, 'why do I feel so awful? Why do I feel so goddamned awful?' and even after I told her all I knew and all I'd researched, she would keep with the questions. After Thalidomide, there was nothing to give her. That's why we only had Nolan.

"And you're drinking orange juice?" I say.

She nods, blonder in this light though her hair has darkened since childhood. "Yup. I'm coaching enough Bif Kids to know I don't want one myself."

"I was talking to my friend, Dr. Garramonde — great ob-gyn — and he recommends a C-section, given the recent hip replacement. Is this something you've discussed . . . or?"

"No C-section," she says. This curtness wasn't surprising when she a teenager — my slight and absent daughter a ferry ride away — but she's an adult now.

"But if the baby was in danger, you would," says Linda. She goes to the cupboard, opens a box of gingersnaps and arranges them on a plate, placing a milder spice between us. "Of course you would."

"Yeah, of course," she says.

"But it's a good idea to at least discuss it with your doctor. The fact of the matter is that you might as well be prepared for whatever happens."

"No C-section," she says. "Not unless the baby's in trouble."

I understand the hormones, the whole "pregnancy is a state of health, not a medical condition," argument, but sometimes you've got to use common sense. I had, of course, expected more from Nolan, now that she's round as her mother, belly curved like a lens.

~

We have one more ultrasound before the birth. Twenty years of exposure to radiation thanks to scans and they want to see if any harm's been done using, of course, more scans. The scan's in 4D. Quinn's here but groggy: three hours of guitar playing, two of sleep. He's still wearing the clothes he wore on stage last night with their sweat-and-smoke residue, an odd comfort amidst the hospital smell. I'm wearing my old national-team sweatpants below "the belly". Despite the maternity clothes that my mom's sent over, they're the only thing I want to wear.

"Is that coffee?" he asks as we sit in the waiting room. I'm trying to negotiate a peace accord between my lower back and the chair.

"I'm off caffeine. I told you that. This is tea."

"Will it wake me up?"

"It's ginger root with a bit of burdock thrown in. Might make you feel better." I offer him the mug.

Quinn smells it, takes a small sip, then hands it back. "That's foul, Nolan. Where'd you get that? Some cauldron? It's like a frickin' witch's brew."

"Darren. He's into that sort of stuff. It's for a healthy baby."

Quinn peers at me over a *People* magazine. "Why's he so concerned about our kid?"

"Takes a village, hon."

Quinn rolls the magazine up and taps it on his knee, then against his hand. "Does that village have to include him? The last time Sophia phoned you were at his house and she was all, 'Oh, he's back in the picture?' What kind of picture are we talking about?"

"We used to weight train and stuff years ago — again, something I've told you. He was a mentor. You know, my mom's bringing over some tea when she comes over next. You going to get jealous about that too?"

"The baby shares genetic material with her mother. She has a vested interested. You know, Darwinism."

"You sound like Darren. He keeps saying how I've fulfilled my Darwinian destiny."

"How's his wife these days?"

"Ms. Taylor?" asks a nurse, holding my file.

"Look," says the technician, waving the wand over my belly, (presto chango! abracadabra!), "There's the fetus. You can see quite clearly the eyes, the nose . . . I wish I could tell you the sex — let's see here — nope, you've got a stubborn one here. Crossing its legs. Being a little modest."

"Not even born yet and she's already acting like you," says Quinn. "Stubborn. Won't do what he's told. Now, if he took after me, he'd be showing off the goods 24-7."

This scan is much easier to see. Kid A looks made of wax, as if I've swallowed a doll.

"He's . . . She's . . . it's awfully pale," I say. The baby — it looks like a baby, a real human — gives a dreamy, disinterested wave, shrugging off the suggestion. Who me? Chill out, ma. I'm just floatin'.

"There's not exactly a lot of light in there," says the technician. He zooms in and the face appears bulbous, distorted by the lens and the amniotic fluid.

"It looks like he's walking," Quinn says.

"That's exactly what he — or she — is doing. From about the second trimester onwards, the fetus will often walk against the walls of the womb."

This is great, really. One less thing I'll have to teach her. I'd worried that she would imitate my limp, but Kid A's still three months away from being born and already she's walking better than me.

Lately, I've been dreaming about dancing. I take off the belly and rest it on a chair — there, that's better — and Quinn buries his head in my neck and we sway. It's some teenage slow song and I feel all lungs and legs. He twirls me, starts to tango but I tell him the hip replacement manual says no. In some dreams, it's just me dancing and with my belly gone I can feel cold air through all organs and it's like breathing with my whole body.

The dream with Darren has returned for the first time since the hip replacement: Darren, his house, a baby, an old woman. I share it with Kid A like a first bedtime story. Even while I'm dreaming, I know it's wrong. Even in the dream, I know that Quinn's the father, but still the old woman rocks a cradle, the girl-child cries, the light casts a pallor on everyone's face, there's bread on the counter and tea on the stove and Darren has a feeding blanket over his shoulder and says, "Okay, I'm ready" and when Kid A kicks to wake me up, I wish I could say the same.

Sometimes it's 3 AM and Quinn still isn't home from a gig yet, so I get up and heat milk on the stove — no microwave just in case — and put on all the dreamy songs I know: lullabies for grown-ups. I drink warm milk with honey stirred in slow, standing in the living room with the window open and swaying because when you're pregnant you always have a dance partner. It feels good to shake out my spine a little, shrug the facets back into place. I sway; Quinn isn't home and the moon soothes warm milk patterns against my arms. When Kid A is born, I'll dance with her when she's wailing and sing under my breath against her soft-boned skull, all those downy hairs fluttering with my voice. I'll sway with her and so far this is all I know how to do, despite the books and the prenatal class.

It's almost a disappointment when Quinn returns, his voice loud no matter how he whispers, the bar scent of him making the room jittery. He looks startled when he sees me there and stammers, unsure of where to put his hands.

"We went out after the set," he says. "I'm sorry. I should have called."

I shrug and wander back to bed trying to remember the milk, the honey, the folksy ballads, but the smell of him makes me forget.

"Goodnight Nolan," says Quinn once we're in bed again. "Good night Kid A." My mother's been buying us children's books and he's caught up on "Goodnight Moon." Sometimes we take an inventory of all the items in our room, as if playing I Spy: goodnight half-eaten dish of applesauce; goodnight redundant box of condoms in bottom drawer of bedside table.

We've read them all: Dr. Seuss, Robert Munsch, Shel Silverstein. We may not have the facts, but we know all the best stories.

Quinn:

I told her my name was McKinley Morganfield, since I knew she wouldn't get the reference. Nolan would've gotten it. Nolan would've smiled. Actually, McKinley would be a great baby name if my last name wasn't McLeod. That's something we've avoided. When she's not home, I've been reading that book that Nolan made me buy and it mentions writing down lists of names, making a game out of it. I don't want her to know I'm reading it. I don't need lessons — no one needs lessons, it's a natural thing — but I figure some of the basic facts might be helpful. Anyhow, this Nancy girl asked if she should call me Mick or Kin. I said not Kin because where are we? Mississippi? She didn't get that either.

I met her at The Fox and Raven and it was old-times easy. Even easier, because the whole 'being a virgin before meeting Nolan' thing made me a little too reverent of women. In awe. Now I feel like an old battlefield general, ready to parachute in. I think of that scene in Dr. Strangelove with the guy on the bomb. Sometimes I hum "The Ants Go Marching" as I'm getting dressed to go out.

Nancy slid on over to me in tight jeans with a little bit of pudge hanging over the belt, all healthy as bread dough. I guess her beer smell added to that: yeast. She had these jeweled barrettes in her hair placed in there like some bird had dropped them. I made a point of asking about her job and her parents. When I told her my parents owned a tobacco farm and I wanted to get out of the business, she said I was noble.

Nancy's apartment had hardly any furniture in it because she'd just moved here from Manitoba. There was a chair in the middle of the room that she was trying to sand and repaint and flecks of this burnt orange colour had been tracked all over the bed, which reminded me of those detective shows where they find the murderer based on one little fibre or wood splinter. I wanted to flatter myself into thinking I'd be her first heartbreak on the coast, but I don't think she's that kind of girl.

Had this weird dream that night. Kid A was born slimy and pink the way animals sometimes are and I kept trying to hold him but he slipped out of my hands and bounced down the hall, leaving a trail of mucus. Probably Nolan's book says something about this, but I haven't looked it up. I have, however, learned that babies are born with a greasy white coating called vernix to help them slip out and keep them warm when they get here. More than likely it's just some common strain of guilt, the morality 'flu. Nolan's taken to wearing this white angel-girl nightgown and often waits up for me and what do you say when you walk in the door? How can a guy not feel like a complete tool seeing her there all sleepy-eyed, waiting. I mean, she's My Pregnant Wife. The Mother Of My Child.

Jen was like Nancy. Same deal, different clothes: a cleaner version of hippie. I think they call it vintage. Oh, and she was Asian. I'm finding it harder and harder to stay up late. When you're in your twenties, you don't need much sleep. When you're old, you can get up at 5 AM no problem. Trust me to choose a career in music and have a baby right in the middle: at the time in my life when I want my bed the most. Jen had a music-box voice and I wanted to fall asleep beside her. I had a feeling she would be still, but I never got a chance to find out. Left at 3 AM.

B.B. and the Guys know — "Right on, man," they say, slapping my back — and I hope it's not because they don't like Nolan. I think they like her. Probably, it's just a lifestyle thing, which depresses me because this feels so new to me and it's a cliché to everyone else. Well, probably there are lots of musicians who go home to a wife and babies. Like me, after this is over.

These girls are so soft, all lotion and exfoliation, and this is the part that makes me nervous. One of my hands has nails and the other has calluses and I have no perfect hand to touch someone with. Nolan's are getting softer now that she's not playing ball. She still goes to the gym — mostly to wander along the treadmill — but her hands haven't suffered. One time last week she touched me from behind and it took me a minute to realize it was her. I kind of miss that friction.

Another dream: this one better. Nolan's belly-button popped out and she was all proud to show me, so that night I had a dream that the belly button had turned into a photo right in the skin — I forget what the image was — and it glowed a pure beam that could shoot me across the room like that old cartoon with the bears. The Care Bears. Right. The Care Bear Stare . . . And something about walnuts and it being very important that I find a pumpkin pie. Who the hell knows? I liked that dream because when her stomach lit up I could see the silhouette of Kid A and Nolan's veins around him glowed red and orange like a blown-glass bowl and I imagined he was so warm in there.

~

I have something like sadness. Organic, though. It definitely feels natural. Not right, but natural. Like a vine growing on a brick wall, wood silvering, copper earning its green. So, okay, this is clearly out of my league. This is obviously something to do with hormones, which is worrisome because this synaptical, chemical math isn't my area of expertise. I'm more of an anatomy girl. Gaining weight I understand. Curves of the biceps shrinking back to more motherly arms: this, I get. But hormones, pheremones, pregnancy brain: my knowledge stops at high school science, where they said that physical and chemical changes are two different states.Weird that what's wrong with me can't be X-rayed. Hormones may be fairy dust for all I know. They leave me with no picture: chameleon molecules zipping around my brain. Darren likely has both the scientific and herbal knowledge to explain and fix me, but I don't want that route.

During the day, I keep the radio on because it's supposed to be a comfort. I read that somewhere: the radio, its voices, jingles, promises. Actually, maybe it was supposed to be comforting to puppies recently weaned from their mother. Right, that was it: a radio and a hot water bottle to mimic a companion. My hot water bottle's trying its best on my low-back pain but it still hasn't fooled me into making a human out of that warmth. My back. I was tricked by daytime television, but now I know. This baby is an injury.

The radio asks people to call in and complain. Can do. Well, I could but I don't. The thought of tears on the airwaves. The radio segment is called "Lick me today." For example, Mark from Burnaby wants the people at Robbins Parking to lick him today for giving him a ticket even though there was no dispenser to pay at. Sandra from Coquitlam wants her ex-husband to lick her today for taking the bread maker even though he's on the Atkins diet because he's such a vain prick and doesn't he know that fad went out years ago?

The entire prenatal class can lick me today. Maybe it's because Quinn's not with me to take notes so we can mock their earnestness and matching track outfits in the car on the way home. We're making a ritual out of it. We go to Denny's for the milkshakes and dissect their answers to the questions, imitate their tones and note which women (and men) have gotten fat. Probably we should be making friends, but the urge to feel like superior parents is overwhelming.

The LaMaze Lady is entirely too skinny. Skinny girls shouldn't be allowed to teach courses for pregnant women. Their bodies have no empathy. What we need is some mother of five with a face soft and sweet as whatever pastry I've been craving. What we need is real pastry served at this thing, not Blonde Yoga Woman and her apple slices with ginger-yogurt dip. Ginger for our stomachs, to soothe us. Yogurt for good bacteria, to keep us well. These women are so thoughtful. They can lick me today.

"Today we're going to talk about a concern we have about the pregnancy," says LaMaze Lady. She has the kind of voice you hear on daytime talk shows. Probably, that's where she learned it. "Nolan, why don't you start?"

"Right, okay." I take a breath. I'm a public speaker; this should be no problem. "You mean a concern now or in the future?"

"What about now?" She squats down on her knees showing off a bend I could probably do now with the replacement, but have never tried. Most likely, my stomach will get in the way now. It's always one or the other. "What's been bothering you, say, today?"

Quinn not being here makes me more willing to tell the truth. "Today? Well, okay. Sometimes I just feel sad all the time. For no reason. I don't know if it's hormones or that it's a big change with me retiring or what, but I feel . . . " I shrug. "I'm sad all the time." I don't say that my sadness makes my brain feel like burnt toast and I want to scrape the blackness off. I don't mention all the things I wonder about Quinn.

LaMaze Lady smiles. "Good, I'm glad you brought this up. The pregnancy blues. It's very common."

"The pregnancy blues," I repeat. Maybe that's the riff my inflamed back and my spasmy bladder are playing: The Pregnancy Blues.

"Right. That's what they call them."

"Really? Because, I don't know, that name seems imprecise to me."

"I'm sorry?"

"Well, okay, does the sadness fit into a 12-bar structure? No. Does it have a nice beat and you can dance to it? No. So, why use the term 'blues?' Why not something Latin? Or medical?"

"I'm sure there's a Latin name," tries the LaMaze lady, fumbling for a diagnosis. I suspect women like me weren't covered in her training.

"Because as an art form, blues make you feel good. That's their purpose. It's inherently optimistic music. At the very least it's cathartic."

"Ms. McLeod," the LaMaze Lady says gently.

"Well, what kind of music do you listen to? Do you know what I mean?" Quinn would know what I mean about the blues, if not about the sadness.

"Ms. McLeod, it's just a term. Just a saying about a very common feeling that pregnant women have." And, wait — Ms. McLeod? Between this chick and my mother, I'll be married right off to Quinn. You don't really need the ceremony: only the name.

"Yeah, but the term's wrong. It's inaccurate. At least get your genre right. The feeling's more easy listening, like the 'pregnancy Kenny Gs.' That would be a good name. I feel sappy like that." Snickers from the gold-star crew. Pregnancy is a team sport and I'm not being a very good team player. I'm going to have to bring a lot of organic, home-made granola to atone for this. But if pregnancy's a team sport, where's Quinn? Quinn's benched himself. He can lick me today.

"Nolan," says the LaMaze Lady, gentle as a crooner. "It's okay. We're allowed to get frustrated. We just have to find the appropriate outlet." This probably isn't the time to ask for clarification of who she means by 'we.' It must be this classroom, the too-low tables and pregnant chicks in pigtails. I feel young. Younger than the LaMaze Lady, who is really a LaMaze Girl. I'm too full of tantrums.

"Right," I mutter. "Sorry." Where is Quinn? Maybe it's the swelling: these days I feel like a balloon and he holds the string.

"Andrew and I find that classical music is very helpful to stimulate the fetus," notes one of the Pigtails.

The LaMaze Lady beams. The conversation is back on target. "Music is definitely good for the developing fetus.

How many people here have tried putting the headphones to their belly to expose the baby to music?"

I stare at LaMaze Lady's bony physique as she gestures. I have been skinny and blonde all my life. I have been a skinny, blonde little bitch.

The class ends at eight and Quinn won't be home until at least two. He's playing at some Front Street bar. I've never seen Quinn on stage and should make the effort, but that's not the reason I decide to go. It's live music I want: to be in a place where everyone's tapping their toes to the same tune, where there's the same song in everyone's head.

The place is no one's idea of respectable. The carpet is more like a paste and the throb of the bass must be the only thing that keeps the rats at bay. A few women in halter tops stumble around the dance floor to Jimmy Buffett, which means the band's on a break and my timing's off. I step into the stage light and squint.

For a moment, it's as if I can see auras. This seems natural, another gift of the pregnancy: overactive bladder, overactive imagination, sixth sense, whatever. This girl. Woman, really. Woman trying to be a girl. Hair in pigtails — again! Pigtails! — even though she's got to be in her thirties. I see a crackly red aura around her head and think fire, think danger, think warning. Only when I blink through the smoke do I see it's just the red Christmas lights strung around the bar reflecting her frizzy hair. Even pigtails can't tame that hair.

I shouldn't be here. Every breath is bad for Kid A and I. A buzz off the fumes by the dance floor is certainly possible. I shouldn't be here and yet here I am and I blame Quinn.

Seven months means I'm too big for all my clothes, but panel pants are saggy in the butt. The sweatpants stage of pregnancy. So this girl with her pigtails and short skirt that looks like it's made out of fish scales and a shirt with so many complicated straps I probably couldn't put it on even before I was pregnant. She's laughing and there's static in the sound and a crackly red aura around her head because of the Christmas lights, even though it isn't Christmas. Isn't even near Christmas. Quinn laughs too, and she's sitting on his lap and kisses him. I shouldn't be here. Every breath I take.

I can't think of anything to say so I walk over, give my best job-interview smile and say, "Hi." The woman-girl is unphased. Quinn isn't wearing his wedding ring. This is because Quinn doesn't have a wedding ring.

"Yeah?" asks the girl. She's chewing gum. Kissing my husband — no, he's not my husband — while chewing bubble gum. My grown husband.

"Nolan," says Quinn and the woman-girl clues in and her smile gets all slinky.

"If you're thinking that he's cheating on me because I've gone soft, I want to be clear that I'm not fat," I tell her because lately this seems like something I should explain. My belly bulges: a person could mistake it for laziness or a lack of exercise. I don't want any misunderstandings. This is temporary. Maybe I should get one of those 'Baby on Board' T-shirts. "I'm pregnant. Seven months. And as you know — well, maybe you don't know — but stress isn't good for pregnant women. It can lead to miscarriages or early labour."

"Nolan," says Quinn.

" — and in light of the fact that you're making out with my husband, I'm just wondering how badly you want to kill my baby."

The woman-girl is off my husband's — yes, husband's — lap so quickly. I make her cry and stammer and leave instantly. This is a disappointment. I'm supposed to be the crier. She's not supposed to crumple. All this adrenaline and where's the cat fight?

"Harsh, man," says B.B and that's all I hear because the smoke and the booze fumes and this rage can't be good for Kid A so I leave, feet moving before I even decide to go, and soon I'm out the door with Quinn following behind. If he were a different kind of musician, he would probably call this baby-mama drama.

"Nolan," he says. That's all he knows how to say, apparently: my name.

"You have another set to do," I tell him, all that air down my lungs. "You won't get paid if you leave now."

Quinn blinks. "Can I just — can you listen?"

I shake my head. Hand on the belly for emphasis. "No, I don't think I'm ready to listen right now." This calm: maybe I *am* ready to become a mother.

The girl-woman is sitting on the sidewalk by the bar crying. I feel almost sorry for her: the hunched child's posture that's almost fetal position. Fucking hell, why do I always have to be the good guy?

I walk over to her and imagine myself backlit, beatified by headlights and streetlamps."Look," I say. "I'm sorry I yelled at you. Clearly the problem is him. You're not going to kill my baby. Premature delivery, maybe. Kill, no. I shouldn't have yelled."

I get into the car before either of them can respond. It's surprising how quickly I move now, how well the metal has become part of my body. I've adapted. Healed, even. Quinn looks small out the rear window, watches me leave, then goes back inside.

Quinn:

She knows, she knows, and I have a shower with just water — hot water — wanting no scent but my own. She knows, she'll leave me, she'll take Kid A and run; (I guess she can run now). She knows and I scour the cigarettes, the booze, the girls with their vanilla lotion and even more vanilla sex. When I slide into bed still damp, I expect Nolan to be sleeping or at least pretending. Hiding her puffy eyes or something like that. God knows she's been crying about everything else lately. Instead, she takes my hand. And I mean takes it. Repossesses it.

"How well do you know that girl?" she asks into her pillow.

"Not well." I'm too tired for anything but the truth. I wait for, 'Well enough to stick your tongue down her throat, though,' but it doesn't come.

"Is she your mistress?"

"No. Listen, I was just . . . Things are changing so much and I was — "

"I'm not kicking you out because I hate the thought of you going to her house. I hate that thought. You're staying here." Her eyes remain closed. "Okay? You're staying."

"I wouldn't — ," I try to say, but she tightens the grip until my fingers are numb and throbbing.

"Go to fucking sleep Quinn."

I don't move, don't sleep, my back cramping up and my arm going numb under her grip. Kid A takes nutrients from Nolan and Nolan takes sensation from my arm and we're one big, happy, symbiotic family.

We stay attached like this all through the night, me watching her pretend not to watch me. Neither of us sleeping. She knows, she knows, she'll leave I'm sure but for now it's dark and my fingers are too numb to tell where I end and she begins. This may be some romantic's definition of love, but I don't think so. Just heat and tingling. This should be comfort. I try to sleep, but my mind twists and flips and I want to turn over with it, but she has my hand, has me tight, and I have no idea what fucked up kind of forgiveness this is.

I show up prepared. So far, Darren's been running half of the practices because of the morning sickness or fatigue, but I'm better now. I was up at six a.m. to finish the planning. Clipboard, check. Little magnets and eraseable felt pens for diagrams. Check. Lunch with emphasis on lean proteins and whole grains, check. Notes on drills and systems lectures. Check.

The whole car-ride over, I was eager for the gym, even the smell of it. I've missed the colour-coded lines and simple rules. Two pushes then a dribble. Three seconds in the key. Eight seconds to get over centre. Twenty-four second shot clock. This, I can handle.

Darren and I arrive first and sit in darkness as the lights hum and power up. He hands me a thermos.

"What's this?"

"Nettle leaf tea. Promotes energy, gives you iron and tones the uterine muscles."

I sip. The name 'nettle leaf' is familiar from my pregnancy books and Darren's been researching the pregnancy. "Thanks. I'm sure my uterine muscles will thank you." Even language is too complicated compared to the game, so we lapse into silence.

Mandy arrives first. She's either on the pudgy side or wears clothes too small for her. Maybe a little of both. Darren wants me to give her my old chair, but doesn't understand that it won't fit her. It's built too much for me. Men are like that; they see only the height, not the whole body. The fluorescence turns on slowly, imitates sunrise.

"Hey Mandy," I say.

"How's the baby?" she asks.

"Good, good. Practicing for her career as a soccer player."

"Can I feel it the next time she kicks?"

"Sure thing. Go warm up."

"Why is it that when you're pregnant people only see your belly?" I ask Darren when she leaves.

"Why is it that when you're disabled, people only see your wheelchair? People are stupid. Generally."

I can't give these kids the vision I want them to have. Court sense: eyes that see in patterns. It takes years, I know, but it's been so long since I learned this. It's worse since I can't get into the chair to demonstrate. I rely on the white board but the explanation's too easy without motion. Darren can give some live demonstrations, but he works best with the lower-class players who play his position. He's been out for a very long time.

"Okay, listen," I say. "Why is this play not working? Can anyone tell me?" Dull-eyed silence. They're waiting for the lunch break. "Mandy? Can you tell me?"

She shrugs. "You're the coach."

"I am the coach. Yes, I certainly am. That's why I know. The point is getting you to guys to realize what's going wrong."

"Oh." I've watched her all day. She'll be a role player, like me. Always the Centre. Always the Post. When she learns her role it will be a comfort, like a lighthouse she can climb into and look down on the play. I want to peel off her skin, climb into her eyes and give her that. I want to wear her beginner's skin.

"Okay. It's all about timing. You're working the pick and roll with Sam, right?"

"Right."

"And Nick's working the pick and roll with Paul. And Eliza's there for balance, right? Right. Now, if both Paul and you get in at the same time, why is that bad?"

Mandy blinks. "That's bad?" I have to remind myself of my first year, the defenders rotating around me.

"Okay. I'm here. I'm the defender." I draw it on the board, since I couldn't defend anyone with a belly like this. "You and Paul are both in the key at the top, side by side. Why is that a good thing for me as a defender and a bad thing for me as a coach?" I try to lend her my vision.

"Because you can defend both of us?"

"Right." It feels like a miracle, telepathy. "Right! Exactly. Good. Exactly. It's all about timing. You can't just worry about yourself. You have to look around to make sure you don't take someone else's lane. Keep your head up. Be on alert. If you keep your spacing when they're working the pick and roll, the defenders will be spread out. They'll have to make a decision. And if they leave you, just roll in and shoot."

During the lunch break, I notice Darren over at a hoop with Sam and Nick. He's trying to demonstrate the reverse underhand layup, but the motion eludes him. His fingers forget, his arms, his shoulders. The angle he takes is too narrow and the ball lacks backspin, so it goes directly upwards, hits the rim of the basket and comes down towards his head.

"Okay, just a minute," he says. "There's sometimes a line between knowing how to do something and knowing how to teach it."

When the ball again narrowly avoids concussing him, he reddens and I intervene. It has, of course, been a long time. The teaching was supposed to be my job.

"Darren's right, but let's break this into parts," I say, wishing again I had a chair to demonstrate in. "Let's think of the trajectory of the ball." I guide Sam through the motion: the way the path to the basket must cut a wide swoop, how the spine arcs back long and smooth, the eyes stay up and one hand protects the ball, the other adding the right spin. It's a skill you need so many pieces of your body for and the movement is different depending on what you lack.

"That's not what Darren told us," says Sam.

"Listen to your coach," says Darren.

After the kids leave, Darren spins the ball on his functioning hand, as if to prove he still has a trick. "I never used to do the reverse layup," he says. "Or if I did, not often."

"For some reason, I have it in my head that you were the one who taught me the reverse."

He shakes his head. "Must have been some other handsome and intelligent quad."

After the practice, the children — I shouldn't call them that, they're near adult and Mandy's an alternate for the national team — are quick to leave. Darren pats my thigh. There's been too much standing and I want someone to gut out my spine like a filleted fish and shake it around for me.

"I'm assuming I was like that when I was a girl?"

Darren nods. "Don't shoot the messenger, but . . . yeah, pretty much. Takes time. Court vision isn't easy."

"Did you ever just want to grab me by the head and say, 'Look here. Keep your spacing. Pick and fucking roll?'"

Darren shrugs, rubbing at the callus on the side of his bad hand, where he pushes. "Me teaching you was a bit different. There were — well, you know — there were different factors."

"Indeed."

"Hey, did I tell you that I made you a salve?" He roots through his backpack. "I adapted the formula I use for myself. It's to soothe the skin and prevent stretch marks."

"So it's like lotion?"

He shakes his head. "More like massage oil." He blushes, an expression I've missed. "Not that I'm offering to massage you or — " He runs his hand through his hair. "I just thought that you could do it yourself or . . . your partner . . . what's his name again?" He holds the yogurt container with both hands, as if to make it disappear.

"Quinn." I rub his shoulder. "Thank you. I appreciate it. You've been so — the tea's really helped. Think that stuff will really fix stretch marks?" I raise my shirt so he can see the red and pink streaks on my belly. They already look permanent and I suspect they'll remind as further proof of Kid A's presence. Lately, I've become attracted to the cure-all skin cream commercials that promise to correct wrinkles, brown spots, stretch marks, unsightly blemishes and imperfections. We wreck in such mundane ways. The scars we get aren't very interesting at all. It's only years later that we want to look at them, after they've become opaque and smooth to the touch: a worry stone, a piece of sea glass, something for a lover to finger and wonder about.

"That's quite a tummy. I never thought you of all people would . . . Can I . . . ?"

I nod, take his good hand, and place it where Kid A's been moving. We wait. Sometimes with Kid A it's like being on the ferry, hoping that orcas will breach. My surface is so calm. "Guess she's playing shy," I say. "No, wait, here." It's good to have a touch on me that isn't trying to apologize.

"Holy shit . . . He's really moving . . . Miracle of birth, eh?" he says. "I bet you get that a lot."

"Not so much." His hand stays and I remember how his fingers used to slide across contours that no longer exist on my body.

"Geez," he says, his palm moving in circles. "I'm sorry, I just can't get over . . . "

Sweat forms its own balm between our skin. I imagine him polishing me, all of the marks this baby has left on me oiled and glowing.

~

I've stopped wanting Quinn's breath in me. The very taste of him. He's started smoking again — seems to enjoy it more now that he has to do it outside and it's no longer a creature comfort — and now, only now after thirteen years, do I hate the taste. I give him gum, make him brush his teeth, but the cigarettes remain. He tastes of bars and set lists and my old guitar with a new amp and the girls with the pigtails — or maybe even more girls, women — taking drags of their menthols and breathing into his throat, touching my husband's lungs, leaving a greater mark on his body than I have.

Maybe that's it: he tastes like something more now. Not just cigarettes. There's almost a rancid lipstick taste to him: whale fat and dye, petroleum and glitter, whatever the hell they make makeup out of these days. New nose, weak stomach, brave face. All these reasons not to kiss my mustard-gas husband.

Quinn isn't in my bones, though he's probably in my lungs something deep. Quinn is that slight rasp that keeps my voice from pure when I sing to Kid A in the shower. He's a soft-tissue injury, the black mood of my lungs when I get a cold. He showers until his skin's rough, then borrows my body cream until he smells like a different version of me. My evil twin. The one who's allowed to go to bars and double-fist drinks bought by admirers. I'm embarrassed to bring him to the prenatal class, since I suspect those other pregnant women can smell the transgressions on him. They must bury their noses into the clean flannel of their own men and turn away in disgust.

I'm not that disappointed when Quinn has an early gig on prenatal class night again. Since the pigtailed girl, we've reinvented the word 'silence.' We're loud in other ways: Quinn in the Rock Cave playing songs I know are about forgiveness, though he only mouths the words, me packing loudly, reminding him with every knick-knack I pitch into the box.

We've lost the house. We put it on the market after the bank threatened to evict us. We're moving a few weeks before I'm due to give birth. I let him pick the apartment by himself with Donna, since he disapproved of the choices Darren and I found. I couldn't stand it. Now he wants to talk about It, which either means the move or the infidelity. He wants to sit down and explain. I walk away.

"Take notes," he says as he kisses my cheek on the way out the door. "The important stuff: number of times the phrase 'miracle of childbirth' arises, snacks served, number of times the phrase 'what is your body telling you?' is used, weight gain of participants, male as well as female."

"Without you, I might pay attention and wind up learning something." We're playing at sitcom banter.

It's true, though. Without someone to whisper to, I'm forced to pay attention to the other women in the class. Most of them are my age, except for that teenage girl who brings Cheetos instead of granola and offers them shyly. She's drawn on her sneakers in pen and writes notes on her hands even though the Lamaze lady lectures about the baby's sensitive ecosystem and our constant threat of pollution. Quinn and I have been calling her the "Degrassi High teen pregnancy episode girl" because she's usually alone, her eyes made deer-like by too much mascara and eyeliner. Sometimes there's a skinny man with her who isn't even in the same universe as the word 'father.' He came once or twice, bored and droopy-eyed like he was in high-school math class and smoked and discussed car parts and weed sales on his elaborate cellphone at breaks. He used the word 'fuck' as noun, verb, adjective and general linguistic seasoning and the girl would cringe and say his name and touch his shirt as if to smooth him.

The glossy-haired women are, yes, talking 'miracle of childbirth' again, so I keep a running tally for Quinn. The phrases 'blessing from God,' 'will enrich and complete our lives,' and 'I didn't know how much love I had in my heart until I felt this little thing growing inside of me' are being used. Kleenex and watercolours are being offered. I've piped up once or twice with my own deep and meaningful observations, ("Really? Because I didn't know how much urine I had in my system until I felt this little thing growing inside of me,") which has earned me scowls from the women and little half-chuckles from the men.

"You're funny," noted one of them. "She's kind of funny. Isn't she, sweetheart?" Sweetheart smiled politely.

The LaMaze lady offers up whimsical topics aimed to get us thinking about our bodies. Today's topic: if it were Halloween today, what would you dress up as? (As if birth doesn't have enough science-fiction and movie-set gore). If we like, we can draw a corresponding picture. The women who've bonded — there's talk of a non-alcoholic daiquiri party and some video nights — have decided to go as a fruit basket. They will brag to the wraith-like corporate women and the thin girls in yoga classes, all the skinny little bitches, about how ripe they are. If Quinn were here, he would ask if their men are also going as fruits or if they're already in costume and I would both cringe and laugh.

"I was thinking of going as Courtney Love the year before Kurt's death," I say, and the teen offers the first interested expression I've seen on her.

"Right on," she says, which is the biggest contribution she's made to the discussion so far. "And your baby would be dressed up as Francis Bean!" Blank stares from the Fruit Basket, which is odd since Nirvana was our era, our anthem. We were teens when everyone smelled like teen spirit. This girl wasn't even born yet.

"Quinn's already got the professional musician thing going on," I note with unexpected pride. "He could be Kurt Cobain, though he's a bit high-and-mighty about power chords these days. Artistic integrity and whatnot."

"I met Kurt Cobain once in 1987 when I was working at a Seattle club," says one of the men, the guy in his forties with a second wife who calls himself a 'born again father.'

"You gave him a muffin," says his wife. "Hardly counts as meeting him."

"We talked."

"For, like, a minute."

This isn't something Quinn and I do. We each have our stock tales and don't mind variations, towing the line the other person is spooling out even if we know otherwise. Maybe these count as family secrets; maybe family secrets categorize us as a family.

During break, the girl and I sit outside with the bag of Cheetos between us, eating furtively as if smoking.

"I guess I should've taken the 'teen mother' course they offer at the hospital, but those chicks are a little too hard core for me," she says. "I'm just a poor little knocked-up honours student. Okay, maybe not an honours student, but I'm not a thirteen-year-old pregnant by my twenty-four-year-old drug-dealer boyfriend." She sucks back another Cheeto and smirks. "Eighteen-year-old drug-dealer boyfriend, maybe."

"I think some of these women are hard core. I get the sense their pregnancies were planned right down to the minute. I overheard that Jeanette woman going on about how she and her husband were trying to have a Scorpio child."

The girl shrugs. She's wearing sweat pants that brand her as a member of this year's grad class. "They're fucked up. All their kids are going to be on Ritalin before the age of two. But I guess that's how adults are. You and me are probably the youngest people in the class."

I hold a Cheeto like a cigarette, its obscenely orange coating stains my fingers like Quinn's. "I'm thirty-two."

"You're shitting me."

"I shit you not."

"And your boyfriend? He's hot, man."

"Same, if you're talking biological age. Mental age, that's a different story. Although, between you and me, he's fucking a girl in pigtails, so maybe her youth is rubbing off on him." This is something I haven't told to either my mother or Sophia. When we got here, the air was short-sleeve weather, but now we can see our breath.

The girl nods. She appraises me, fingering the chain around her neck. The skin underneath has reddened from the chill of metal on skin. A car passes and its headlights blot out our prenatal acne. Well, my prenatal acne, hers is probably the normal kind. "That sucks."

"Yeah."

"You going to kick him to the curb? My boyfriend cheated on me and I took him back once I found out he was pregnant, but then he did it again so I figured, screw it. Not like he's going to give two shits about the kid once it's born. Who the hell needs him?"

"I haven't decided," I say. "It really depends on a lot of things, I guess. We haven't done a lot of talking about it, either. But good for you for kicking him out."

The girl shrugs again. "Yeah, well." Her shoulders are thin and her belly is large. We eat Cheetos until the LaMaze lady comes out to summon us back to the primary-colour world. We're going to be talking about decorating on a budget. We will learn how to colour our rooms. Now all I have to figure out is what people to fill them with.

Quinn:

It's this desire to bring her things, real things that smell of cedar or wet paint. It starts with the fence because the realtor says we can get extra on the house if we have one, even a cheap one. We're moving out in a few weeks, but our place hasn't sold yet. The question is whether to bring it down a few thousand, but I say hold out a couple weeks because we've already gotten two offers, even though they fell through. Someone will come. You just need one person to say yes. People like fences, our realtor says. Makes them feel safe. (Also, other peoples' dogs are shitting on our yard). Nolan says yes — well, she nods, waves a hand in my direction — and I go to Home Depot and ask questions. Nothing technical: I know dick-all about building, so I ask the questions a young son would ask a father. What tools can I use? How can I help? What can I do? I pay way too much and leave with good, strong wood and a varnish to treat it and keep it stronger.

My back and arms smolder too quickly — sunburn, muscle burn — so now I work in the early mornings when it's cool. Sometimes, Nolan brings me a cup of cold tea when it starts to heat up: some kind of steeped herbs that smell great but taste bitter. Probably something Darren has sent for her: that fucking guy. I want to sit with her on our porch, especially those mornings after a recent rain. I want to drink her tea, pat her leg, relate the story of each bruise the hammer, the wood, the nails, the mallet give me.

Instead, she stands at the door until a few moments after I see her. Stands there in her white nightgown, holding the tea and leaning her head against the doorframe. She watches my back, but the minute I turn she spooks, leaving the glass mug on the steps. Sometimes her fingerprints are left in the condensation. I fit my hand over them.

Every hour I spend out here is an hour I'm not practicing guitar or handing out resumés. Enough rest, enough rock-star bullshit. After the baby's born, I should get real work, maybe something I can do from home and still rock out at nights. Still, the fence won't take long and I can measure progress by walking around my property, running a hammer across the slats just for the noise. Sometimes people walk their dogs past us. I watch their eyes: Nolan on the porch, pregnant and dressed in white. Me with my shirt off, making myself useful, the office-worker belly disappearing. I want to think the tea is a good sign, her watching me work. At least she can stand the sight of me. To an outsider, this could be calm. Sometimes I pretend I'm an outsider. Lately, it doesn't take that much pretending.

22

TWO DAYS BEFORE I WAS SET to leave for Athens, Darren and I went the wooded area in Queen's Park. The Paralympic media jacket had arrived and despite the heat and the fact that it was three sizes too big, I was wearing it to break it in. It looked like a race car driver's outfit and I wanted the days to speed by, fast forward to the victory lap.

Queen's Park isn't really a forest because wherever you are you can see cars and houses through the trees. Also: children, a playground, tents and barbeques. Not a forest, really but the same confetti of light through trees, same crunch under the shoes like you're doing real damage. That's what I wanted: damage.

"Let's go for a stroll," I said and we started civilized through the rose garden. Darren ambled easily on the cobblestones. The roses were just blooming and the place smelled of manure. A couple was getting married in the gazebo, the wind tearing at the crepe paper bells they'd strung around the trellises. In the hopes of getting in the shot, we walked behind their wedding photographs.

But now the woods, which was hard for Darren to walk through. I knew it would be and this was what I wanted.

So many roots below the surface, sucking patches of mud, stones the foot couldn't see. But Darren came with me because he couldn't say no. Couldn't decline because we were Having Sex and I was young and fit and he knew he should be grateful. Should be.

We didn't speak, so I listened to other people's conversations. *Come here, sweetie, give me your face. It won't sting — just hold still. We'll get licorice when we're done.*

The goats, James. That's why he's — oh, don't cry, Sammy, it's not so bad — they ate his cracker. Yes, baby, didn't they? Those bad old goats. He's very upset.

Did they now? Those buggers. Those little buggers.

The sunlight was spread thin, trying too hard to be everywhere at once: the trees' pitch, the eye of a squirrel, Darren's crutches. The sun was overworked. All that brightness: it couldn't keep up.

Darren's crutch sank too deep into dead needles and he almost went down.

"What?" I said. "Come on."

He shrugged. "I'm fine. Thanks for your concern."

"Well, it's not like this is rugged terrain." I gestured to a girl in a silver lamé halter top and heels clipping by. "She doesn't seem to be having a problem."

Darren shrugged again. He would follow because we were Having Sex. Because he was grateful.

"What did Valerie want?" I asked. "Seems like you were on the phone for hours last night."

"Nothing much. Just to talk."

"Talk about what? You probably see her more now than you did when you were married."

Darren tripped over a root and went down on one knee like he was proposing.

"Fuck," he said and the girl in the silver shirt turned, her ponytail bobbing in disapproval. We were ruining that sparse patch of solitude in the middle of traffic. Darren brushed himself off. "God fucking dammit."

"Hey," I said. "Kids here."

He swatted at pine needles on his knee like they were mosquitoes. "God damn it. Why is it so hard for you to get your head around the idea that I still might like to talk to her once in awhile? We ended because it was time for something new, not because we hate each other's guts. I'm not going to hate her for your sake."

"Seems like you hate her less and less every time you see her. Let's talk about this when we're on level ground. Did you hurt anything?"

Darren shrugged, gave his muddy knee one last slap and began to walk. "Fine. I'm fine."

The trees had torn the light up into manageable chunks. We stepped out of the not-really-a-forest into all the heat that it had been protecting us from. "Are you sure you're okay?" I asked because we were Having Sex, because I was grateful. "And who said I care either way? I was just asking. Just — you know — making conversation. Like people do."

"Pretty pointed conversation. I'm not going to feel bad about talking with Val. You may think you can get me to feel bad about it, but I won't. She hasn't been feeling well lately. You can't just leave people all by themselves."

"How come you broke up in the first place? If you don't hate each other?"

He shrugged. "Irreconcilable differences. We really only had basketball in common. And we were young when we started dating and neither of us had ever lived outside of New West." He shrugged again and peeled a strip of bark off a nearby arbutus tree, staring at the green wound he'd created.

"Has she moved out of New West now?"

Darren shook his head and broke the branch into a smaller piece. The leaves were curled from the heat. "Nah. Lives with her mom. So, yeah, that's the whole painful story. My failed marriage. Now are you convinced that she's not trying to get me back?"

"I wasn't worried," I said. "Maybe I would be if the Paralympics weren't so close. You're driving me, right?"

"Yeah, and I'll bring all the tranquillizers and meditation music I can find." I wasn't sure if he was blushing or sunburned. We needed both shade and level ground, though it was an either/or situation: high road or low road. The skin by Darren's hairline where it was receding was smooth and I imagined all his rough layers sloughed, though I still couldn't picture what he must have looked like at my age. We limped back home, both of us having exceeded our walking quota for the day.

Valerie stayed home for my last practice at the Church of Perpetual Smackdowns: a parting gift. We hadn't played Cage Match since she'd shown up. Maybe it was something they used to play or maybe he was embarrassed that I was now beating him ninety percent of the time. I expected that the teams would even out again, but that wasn't the case. She'd changed my playing style: the new and subtle Big Girl moves. Valerie had lumbered in and raised me to her level.

That night I wanted closed doors, the dusty scent of the rafters and the walls active with mould and condensation. When I shouted, I wanted the sound to have nowhere to go but up: startle the creaking rafters, the roving lamps that followed me like movie cameras. This was impossible. It was August: a heat so dense you could carve your name into it. Such heat wasn't natural in BC. This was weather borrowed from another province, come to visit on some renegade air flow. The women who ran the place told us that every other team who practiced in this gym had taken the month of August off, but our bodies wouldn't siesta. We had disregarded the weather, not knowing when to call it quits.

"Shirts against skins," said Vern. "That's the only way we'll get through. Hell, let's go skins against skins. Boys against girls." The doors were open and the gym smelled of the parking lot, the earthly scent of garbage, rust and the lilac bushes that grew along the church. The blossoms had been tracked across the floor. They swirled by the open door, showing us the pattern of the wind.

"You all ready for Athens?" everyone kept asking me. "You all packed and ready to go?"

"Well, I'm packed," I would say. I'd been packed for a week. The team-issue suitcase was the size of a body bag. With better hip flexion, I could have curled myself inside it. We were getting a whole new bag full of Paralympic clothing when we arrived, so the suitcase was only half full. Every time I looked at it, I felt like I was forgetting something.

"We don't want to talk about Nolan leaving," said Rob. "You're still going to show up when she's gone, aren't you Dare? You can flirt with me all practice if it'll make you feel better."

"Been showing up for twenty years," said Darren.

The heat wouldn't let us get up to a good tempo, though we sweated as if we were working hard. This was good. I was supposed to be taking it easy and the weather was forcing me into it. We took frequent breaks, Darren flicking me with ice water from his waterbottle, the drops evaporating on my boiling-point skin. The glue of the tape he used to bond the three bad fingers together wouldn't hold, diluted by sweat.

From the door, the church ladies watched us, fanning themselves with a newspaper article that had been written about me. "Look," they'd keep saying each time we took a break. "Have you seen this yet? Look, it says 'Proof of What is Possible: Local Girl Overcomes Obstacles.'"

"She's not local," Darren would say. "They got that part wrong. She's from the Island." There'd been a write-up in the Victoria papers that my mother had been carrying in her purse for weeks. Both sides of the straight claimed me as their own.

Everyone else left early, though the temperature was dropping. Darren and I were alone and the room was right for a high heartbeat, a good workout.

"Are you sure?" Darren kept asking. "I don't want to injure you right before the big competition. Aren't you supposed to be tapering?"

My hair was so damp with sweat that it wasn't even blonde anymore. "What? You scared of challenging me?"

Darren tore another strip of tape off with his teeth, trying to get his three fingers to hold. "I take all challengers. Bring it on, Little Big Girl."

"That's Ms. Big Girl to you."

"My ball, Ms. Little Big Girl. You won last time, if memory serves."

The trick in Cage Match — any basketball, really — is to know exactly what you're giving up on D. Darren's crafty: low to the ground and quick with a head fake. All that camber combined with a slip of the torso I didn't realize he could muster and he'd get around, go baseline on me. The trick is to make him earn it. Get on the chair, shoot from outside the paint, pound in for the boards, don't give up an easy basket. In Tony's words, prevent the dispy-fucking-doodle and capitalize when you get in close. Defense sounds simple: figure out what your opponent wants to do and stop it.

When I realized that Darren couldn't shoot left handed — the gimp hand and wrist — it was easy in a way that made me a little regretful that I ever figured it out in the first place. Deny the baseline, keep his bad hand facing the hoop and he won't score. Can't score. Won't ever score. Hasn't, in fact, made a basket in the past five games.

Four to nothing and the tape around Darren's fingers is already yellowing with sweat. Keep the taped hand facing the hoop and own the paint. That's all there is to it. It's silent except for our breathing, the chairs striking against one another and he's frustrated. It feels like cheating. The paint on his frame is chipped along the usual points of contact, the metal scratched past the rust-proof coating, deeper than steel. Not just from me, this damage, not all my doing: Vern with his crash landings, Rob making his beer-gut presence felt, Val. Mostly, though, it's from me. From here. Cage Match.

I need one more basket for the win. I have the ball and he gets up a good head of speed and collides with me, his arms against me in predictable places I'll heal from.

"Come on, Little Big Girl," he says.

We are forehead against forehead, arms linked around the ball, frames tangled. We hold each other against the places we are metal, the places we are warm. His bad hand is slipping and if I wanted, I could hold him aloft, carry him in my arms. But I don't. He wretches it from me, chortling.

"Losing the ball to quads?" he says. "What're you going to do against the Yanks, huh?"

It was wrong to let him have it, to watch as he deeks baseline and scores. He always made me earn it, even when I was young and one time didn't score for a month of Cage Matches. But, then again, he'd retired: wasn't training for anything.

I hit my next shot, sank the foul shot and won.

"I didn't mean it about the ball," Darren said, patting my leg.

"That's okay."

"I'm pretty strong for a quad when I get my good hand around something. You'll learn, young grasshopper."

We went home. It wasn't my home. I was just a scent on the sheets, hair in the drain. That night we had sex, mostly because I was leaving. A month away from home and my body wanted to hoard each sensation. I was getting used to sex. The novelty was wearing off: a good thing, since it felt more like joining.

Maybe the sex was part was a dream. I viewed it as if from above. A white sheet and us under it like shadows puppets. The moonlight did that. We were all negative image, above hot or cold, bloodstream or nerve endings. Maybe it was the heat. The house was fevered, despite the windows being open. There were mosquitoes and the scent of wet grass and I imagined weeds pushing from underneath the floorboards and sprouting like wings, whirlygig seeds falling like plaster on to our damp skin. Darren was angry: I remember that. Maybe it wasn't anger, maybe it was. He could hardly look at me. The windows let the outdoors in. They made us homeless. We lived in a sheet pinned to his shoulder blades by sweat and it was enough.

After, I remember standing on the balcony naked. This couldn't have happened, since there was no balcony. It must have been an open window I stood in front of: my Rapunzel, Rapunzel hair unbraided by wind, nipples high like the noses of animals reading the air. Come in, Nolan, someone might see you, Darren was saying, whispering it because the windows were open, our voices amplified by night air. It felt like a balcony: so far down to go and the air healing all the traces he had left on me.

We were pale, despite the season of good weather. I'd been indoors training; fluorescence is not a sun. Darren had no excuse, though he was worried about the summer's hardships and skin cancers. We were pale, sitting on the living-room couch, the leather reminding me that it had once been someone else's skin. Darren was naked, too: this was rare. The brace wasn't on either and it made his worse leg seem wispy: smoke trailing upwards, Darren some conjured genie. His biceps shone despite freckles. He had a good shape: muscles bunched against his chest like they were protecting him, a long reach, longer than he deserved given his frame.

The kitten was sleeping on my knees: requisite 'pussy' jokes had been made. Probably, I'd made them. Darren hated that word. It made him blush and stammer.

"You shouldn't be nervous about all this," he said.

"I don't think I can help it."

Darren had his arm on the back of the couch, half around me. "Hey, you're stronger than me now. Those German women don't stand a chance."

"It's not the body I'm worried about."

The house smelled impossibly of blackberries and rainwater, the path that led me through Mystic Vale into Cadboro Bay, down to the house I grew up in.

"Does Tony do mental training with you?"

"Yeah, relaxation exercises. Inner mental room and all that. I don't think my brain's built for it, though. I never quite get there."

"Close your eyes," he said and maybe this is why I'm now unsure if any of this ever happened. Maybe I'd been dreaming all along. "There's a trick to it. They always tell you to imagine a room, but it's hard to just invent one on the spot."

"Right," I said.

"Shh . . . Are your eyes closed? To build a room, you have to start with the walls." I imagined the walls, erected them in my untamed mind. "Now, a floor and ceiling, so nothing can escape . . . So you can go in there and scream and no one can hear you." I tried to imagine something cathedral-like with rafters like the Church of Perpetual Smackdowns, but my mind kept generating the room I was in. To this day, it still does. Even when I'm halfway across the world, I imagine myself in Darren's living room. "Now, whatever else you need. A chair, a fire, whatever." Darren changed the architecture of my brain, building a little cage in the middle of all that psychobabble wilderness. His voice was like the dark wood of rafters, the double meaning of the word timbre.

It wasn't like dreaming. It was a different kind of fantasy. I sat in the room and imagined playing well, visualizing it over and over.

"I don't know," said Darren after I'd opened my eyes and found my body again. "It works for me. I still do it sometimes, even though I'm not playing. I guess I should have taught you this sooner. It needs to be routine." He had a half erection, a sign that he hadn't forgotten his body during these mind games.

The kitten twitched on my knees, her paws kneading my bare skin, leaving a bramble of scratches there. She was running in dreams. No one had shown her how to build walls. The living room was nothing but routine: a place I visited over and over. The curtains fanned the moonlight and Darren drew me down on to the couch beside him like a submersion. The couch had a tanned smell — I swear I could feel its pores — and I went down into all that skin: mine and his and the couch's. I laid my head on his hot chest and dreamed Cadboro Bay, dreamed Greecian water, which I'd heard was a shade of blue I hadn't seen yet.

I spent my last night before Athens in my own bed, lying on top of the sheet naked, too hot and nervous to sleep. I'd called Darren twice the night before to make sure that he'd set his alarm clock.

"If you're going to keep phoning me, you might as well come over," he'd said.

"With all my pacing you won't sleep."

"I won't anyways if you keep phoning me."

The wind stroked the slats on my venetian blinds. "Okay, okay, this is the last time. I promise."

Around 2 AM it cooled and I was able to fall into an odd sleep where I dreamed I was in Darren's house, then my parent's house in Victoria, back and forth. I awoke at 5:30, disappointed to not be in either place but alone, the clunking of the fridge still startling me even though I'd lived here for nearly a year. Outside, it was bright and quiet and cool. For once, there was no one on the street and this lulled me.

Darren was supposed to pick me up at nine. At 8:45, the phone rang.

"Hello?" I was expecting my mother with her last-minute well-wishes.

"It's Darren."

"It's nine. We have to go."

"Valerie's in the hospital."

"Shit. That's too bad."

"She called and asked me to come. She might have to have surgery right away. I'm sorry to jam out on you."

"Darren."

"I'm sorry, but I said I'd — "

"This is the worst thing that could possibly happen. I'm going to miss my flight. I'm going to miss Athens."

"Do you know how long it takes to load a plane full of gimps? On Air Canada?"

"And I'm sure you would know this because you've been to so many Paralympics."

"Hey now. Easy there. You don't have to be an elite athlete to know what Air Canada's like."

"I have to go. Okay, I have to find another ride right away." I tried for calm: failed. "Okay, I have to go now."

I phoned Sammy on her cellphone, which was the only phone she had. Just as well, she always said. Between her girlfriend, her job and her social life, she said she couldn't remember what her couch looked like. She had no home base.

"My ride just cancelled out on me. I have all my stuff: a taxi will take forever. Are you in the area? Or anywhere nearby?"

"Hey, hey, calm down Big Girl," she said. In the background, I could hear street noise: a car trunk slamming, everything locked-down and ready. "Be right there. You live on 6th street, right?"

"Are you sure? I'm sorry to be a pain in the ass."

"An extra fifteen minutes won't matter, Nole," she said. "We have room and it'll be a total C.F. when we get to the airport anyways. You won't even believe it until you see it. Team Canada jackets as far as the eye can see and customer-service people freaking right out."

She picked me up in her long, white car wearing movie-star sunglasses.

"My driving glasses," she said. "We'll put on The Ramones and they'll get us there on time. My boy Joey won't steer us wrong. Driving music. Never fails."

Her girlfriend was with her: a skinny woman with a head scarf and long earrings that kept getting caught in it. The girlfriend was babysitting the car. Someone had drawn a pair of breasts on the wheelchair symbol on her disabled parking pass.

The Ramones blessed us: traffic was charmed. We nodded our heads to the music. We were both wearing our mandatory traveling jackets open to let in the last of the hometown air.

"Did it take you long to pack?" asked Sammy.

"Nah."

At a stop light, she tapped her fingers on the knob of her hand controls. "How excited are you?"

"Very," I said.

"So Darren was supposed to pick you up?"

"Yeah."

"Okay. Hey, did I tell you I had a going-away party? It was madness. There must have been over a hundred people there."

Sammy was right: total C.F. The team uniforms let us budge in time behind some quad rugby players. After I got my ticket and my luggage was sent off, I leaned over the railing stared at all the people in the arrivals area below. People looking for their loved ones. People waiting with roses. People checking the schedule screen every few minutes. And the hugging: couples joining so briefly, moving arm and arm, fantasizing they were one person.

~

Darren:

During a game, small people will feel the effect of gravity. All that crossing of paths and then you're drawn to someone, find your push rim up against theirs, your wheel in theirs. Just when you think you're safely across, you go metal on metal. It's not like love or anything, just science. When you're small as a moon or an asteroid, you will be drawn in by planets.

So, yes. Planet Valerie. Gravity. I hurt Nolan and physics was to blame.

I arrived at the Royal Columbian knowing only that Valerie's new knee had become infected. How can steel do that, I wondered, but it turned out to be the bones around it, the blood. She was in the emergency room because they'd run out of places to stash people. I was born in that hospital. My mother often told stories of hot blankets after delivery and the starched pleats in the nurse's skirts: so nice, so clean, she would say.

Val said that she called me because she didn't want her mother to worry. Her mother would, of course, find out pretty soon because Val lived with her for Christ's sake. When I pulled back the curtains, Val was staring at the ceiling: pupils eclipsing the hazel in her irises, lips fever-chapped. The mint green curtains attempted to form a room. The bed, faux-wood table and chair tried to back them up, but failed. This was like a pen.

"Darren," she said and in her voice I heard morphine. The same tone as when she woke up from the replacement three years ago. See? I wanted to tell her. Sometimes replacements don't work. There are some things you can't replace. Meaning me, meaning her, meaning eleven years.

"How you feeling?" I asked her, morphine-voiced too so she wouldn't startle.

"They've got me on an IV," she said and struggled to sit up. "I'm apparently stable."

"You? Stable? First time for everything." I wondered if it was okay to tease this way.

"That's what they say. And surgery."

I jangled the healing magnets in my pocket and imagined them charming the steel from her body with their pull. I brought them because I hoped this would be a minor thing. Pick her up, take her home, put her to bed with a glass of juice. I'm good at that. Minor improvements.

The hospital gown tugged over her Big Girl arms. She noticed me watching and went shy.

"I expected the muscles to go away," she said. She'd retired but the arms remained. She gave up her girlish figure for the sport and her arms were payment, receipt, reward. The daub of blood on her fever-split lip looked brighter because of the room's lack of colour. The fine hairs at her temple were damp.

I watched her: the gown, the blankets, her shape underneath. When I sat in the chair by the bedside, she reached for my good hand. It wasn't not nostalgia: didn't spark the first teenage touch or the time she threw the only MVP trophy I ever won at me and it broke into its plastic shards or the King Motor Inn wedding-night bed or the last year when she'd cringe if I'd touch her. It wasn't nostalgia, just gravity. Maybe precognition. Holding her hand was like coming home to a solid room: oak furniture so heavy it had warped the floor to its weight, the attic so full we could never move because of the immense task of cleaning it out.

None of this negated what happened with Nolan. That was something. But Nolan would be a different girl every time you looked at her. She would return from Athens headstrong and crowing: some sort of hardware around her neck. Nolan would get the Big Girl arms. Might even chop off her hair and dye it blue for all I know.

"It's only been three years," said Valerie. "They may have to replace it again. You need to take notes."

"I will."

"I guess my mother will have to find out."

"Don't worry. I'll take care of it." And I did: phoned her mother, the place she volunteered at, her friend Kat, armed myself with flowers and murder mysteries, took time off work, made a list.

"I can't believe it," she said and crushed the styrofoam cup in her hand as if to prove her strength. "Only three years. And two of those playing ball."

"Hey, cheer up Valley Girl." The nickname came from ten years before and I carried it carefully down from my mind, giving it to her like a photo album.

"Valley Girl," she said. "I remember that."

The curtains swelled; a nurse passed by with a cart of needles; I kissed my sometimes-wife in the middle of all those temporary rooms.

23

I ALWAYS NEED A BASKETBALL REASON to go to Darren's house. The closed curtains and unkempt lawn don't encourage drop-in guests, so I make an appointment days in advance: to drop off the kids' fitness testing, to talk defensive systems, to fill out forms.

Darren and I sit at the table and drink tea. Every time I've been in the house, we've gone to this kitchen. I haven't been upstairs. Darren's house is a constant and I don't want to see any lacy pillows on the bed or makeup in the bathroom. The kitchen is the same. The living room is the same. It looks nearly exactly as it has in the inner mental room I've been imagining for twenty years. Darren reads me the ingredients of the tea. He crushed the herbs himself and wants me to know that his sources are pure, his intentions good.

"Raspberry leaf, oat straw, chamomile, clover . . . I think if you have a girl, you should name her Clover," he says. Darren has his own scent of herbs. I can smell what's in his bloodstream.

"Or Basil for a boy."

"Or Lavender."

"Rosehips. Rosehips Taylor . . . Or Rosehips McLeod. Either way, sounds like a porn star name."

Darren runs his hand through his hair, but it doesn't rise like it used to. Grey hair is a different texture. It's not just the colour that's gone. "Have you decided on names?"

"We haven't talked about it. We've been so busy . . . the move and all. Quinn's still a bit . . . in denial."

"He better get out of denial quick. You're eight months pregnant."

"He will." Darren's not wearing his brace and his feet are bare. They must be smooth from having gone so long without touching the ground. With his bad hand, he squeezes a sponge ball. No matter how little physical activity he gets, he maintains this one exercise.

"He will," I say.

"How's Quinn . . . I mean, how's he handling this?" He pauses. "No, forget it. I shouldn't ask. It's not my place." He shifts in his chair, tapping his fingers on the sideguards.

Valerie will be home soon, though I still haven't run into her. She's working at a thrift shop and I've been resisting the urge to shop for baby clothes there. Just to see.

"We've been . . . " There must be a root in here that makes me tell the truth, loosening my tongue while it calms my lower-back pain. "Actually, well. There was this girl. And he was kissing her. And we haven't been very good since then, I guess you could say." The pattern on the table is the same as thirteen years ago: Arborite stars that will probably last as long as real ones.

"He's cheating on you?"

"I wouldn't call it that. He just kissed her. It's just because of the stress of not having a job and the baby coming and . . . all . . . that."

Darren watches me in a way that makes me feel teenaged. I focus on his pale feet, the way his toes curl against the steel bar. "Nolan," he says. "Oh, honey."

"I don't know. I'm sure it'll be fine once the baby arrives. It's really a one-time thing. This book I'm reading — it says that prenatal infidelity is quite common. It even has a name. Prenatal infidelity. People have studied it. And I haven't exactly made the situation better."

"You sure it's a one-time thing?" The fingers are still and I don't want to look at him.

"I don't want to think about that. What else can I do? A baby's coming."

"That's not what I asked." He taps the side of his mug with his good hand in the silence that follows. "Okay," he finally says. "Okay, what about this? I'm sorry. What about this? Let's go to the computer and look up baby names on the internet. That's the only advice I feel like I'm in a position to give."

Darren:

Taina *is Native American for returning moon.*

Elysia *means blessed home.*

Jenski *is Old English for coming home.*

She's keeping her list secret, but we laugh over the definite 'no's.

"Dolores," says Nolan, "It means Lady of Sorrows. I wonder if there's a kid's name that means Lady of Perpetual Smackdowns."

"That was the best gym I've ever been in. You should name your kid Cage Match. You could call him C.M. for short."

"I think I still have a few bruises from Cage Match," she says and smiles. "Dolores, Lola, they all mean sorrow. Why would you name your kid after sadness? Isn't that asking for trouble? Might as well name the little tyke 'bad case of colic'"

Atara is Hebrew for blessed.

Gwyneth is Welsh for blessed.

"Too bad Philyra is such a weird-sounding name," she says. "It means 'to love music.' This kid better love music in a household such as ours. In a family such as ours."

Ours. She doesn't mention Quinn directly. His name translates into 'five,' practically meaningless. My wheelchair is higher than her chair so she rests her head on my shoulder. At first I was startled: her breath against my collar bone, my chest hairs prickling. Now that I'm greying, we have nearly the same colour hair.

"This is hard," she says. "There are so many names. And so much to consider. Meanings, how it's going to fit with the kid's personality, middle names . . . I still don't know whose last name she's going to have. Or he. Whatever it ends up being."

"You seem to be gravitating towards girl's names," I say. "Sometimes you can figure out the sex of the baby just based on that."

Kaiya is Japanese for forgiveness.

Hamlet means home if you disregard the name's other baggage.

I can't figure out whether she's picking names based on her wishes for the baby or her wishes for herself. We do a search based on meanings. It's easy to figure out what the parents' biggest prayer is, whoever it's for.

"Amanda . . . worthy of love. Jaimie . . . I love. Shirina . . . love song . . . look at all these," she says. "136 different names meaning 'love.'"

"Understandable, I guess."

"That might be an idea: name the kid after 'love.' Remind damn Quinn how we got into this mess in the first place."

~

Quinn arrived home from his gig yesterday with boxes and newspaper and has left the reminder of our impending move in every room in the house.

When the phone rings, I have to search under old newspapers to find it.

"Hey mom," I say. "How's it going?" She's never gotten used to the fact that I have call display and I hear her startle, a brief stage fright in the monologue she's about to deliver. The kitchen looks exactly as it used to, except for the 'Discard Box' that Quinn has placed on the table. In it, he's put the wellness pills that Darren's been buying for me. I want to take them with us to the apartment, but Quinn is insistent that they're going to harm Kid A. We've had the "but they're natural/ but so's fox glove/ but they're good for me/ but that's what they said about thalidomide," argument twice today.

"Fine, dear. Just fine. Now, tell me something, honey. Does Quinn smoke marijuana?"

I can hear Quinn playing a farewell dirge in his practice space. Our new apartment is too small for closed doors. After the baby's born, he'll move his music equipment to B.B.'s place and look for a day job.

"I'm sorry?"

"Does he smoke marijuana?"

"Huh?"

"You know, weed . . . pot . . . ganja . . . whatever you call it."

"What's bringing this on?" I ask. I don't actually know. He used to, but I've always been drug tested. When we first moved in together, he'd go outside with his friends to do it. It wasn't a secret, but he kept it from my bloodstream.

"Well, marijuana is part of all that rock-and-roll shit, isn't it? And now that Quinn's a musician, I'm concerned that he might be, you know, getting high."

I pick up one of the bottles and read the label, which is decorated with a cheerful vine and a woman dancing. I imagine the little flecks inside the capsule sprouting into vines, strengthening the mortar in my old-brick insides.

"I haven't smelled anything on him."

"Did he used to get high? When you guys were kids?"

I sigh. The empty house feels colder. I want to boil something, to fill the room with enough steam to blot out the windows, shrink everything back to size with the scent of common herbs and stewed tomatoes. "I don't know. Maybe once or twice."

There's a pause and again I hear my mother's fingertips on the wood table: a Love Supreme, a Love Supreme. "You know, your father smoked marijuana once or twice." Another pause. A Love Supreme. "And, okay, I might have had the odd toke — is that a word people still use . . . 'toke'? — Well, just once or twice, really. Maybe three times."

"I've seen your college photos. You guys were straight out of a Woodstock documentary."

"We weren't druggies or anything. Don't think we were druggies. It was just one of those — "

"I don't think that, mom."

"Because I've often wondered if those kind of pollutants might have something to do with your difficulties. You know, passed down through the genes."

"I'm pretty sure that casual pot smoking in college doesn't give your kids a weak growth plate."

"It's been linked to schizophrenia. And something else too. I forget. But if smoking can give babies a low birth weight, think of what marijuana can do."

"It's also been linked to the destruction of civilization." I shake the bottle of pills for the noise. The hippy woman underneath the vine appears to be dancing. "Mom, don't worry."

Soon, this kitchen will be free of our pollutants. Maybe the walls need bleaching and the countertops need dusting, but after five years we haven't left a mark on the structure. Not like me: the hip replacement's drugs and metals are like an oil slick in my soft tissue, the child in me a beached bird after a spill. Quinn and I wanted to become clean before the pregnancy, but my ecosystem didn't even get a chance to recover from its latest disaster.

"That bad growth plate came from somewhere," she says. Her nails are still firm thanks to calcium supplements. She paints them partly because she loves the fumes. She's post-menopausal so she can inhale whatever the hell she wants.

"Just some genetic mutation. That's how we evolve. Maybe I'm a higher species."

"Fuck the Darwinism," says my mother with surprising vehemence. "Just tell Quinn that if he's smoking marijuana, he should quit. Is he still smoking? He's still smoking, isn't he?"

"Playing in bars must be really tempting. It's hard to tell. He comes home smelling of it."

"Just tell him that if an iota of soot gets on my little grandchild's lungs once it's out of the womb, I'll kill him. Tell him that. Or, actually, use the word 'castrate.' Don't say kill. Tell him I'll cut his balls off. When are you moving?"

"A week."

"I'm coming down. You need to rest."

"Mom."

"I'm coming down. No arguing."

My talk hadn't gone well. I couldn't fit in my chair so I just stood at the sidelines and tried to describe what it feels like to score. Not that it mattered. All the children were interested in was the belly. There's no coat big enough to hide in and besides, the last thing I want to look like is a bloated old veteran bragging about her prime. Still, my stomach feels like a birth mark, a scar, a second head I've grown. It's all the children ask about during question period. Is it a boy or a girl? When will the baby be born? What will you name it? Will you name it after me? I was expecting one of them to ask where babies come from, but luck was with me.

I walk (waddle) in the door wanting nothing but a cup of Darren's tea. Instead, I find a letter on the table from Quinn. It's a bad sign that whatever he needs to tell me has to be spelled out in complete sentences.

In his letter, he stresses the impermanence of it. This isn't leaving, he says, though it looks suspiciously like it.

Is he here? No. Did he take his toothbrush and only dress suit? Yes. He says he needs to think things through, find a way to apologize, make amends, make ends meet. He thinks the space will be good for us, though the fact that we're moving into a 600-square-foot apartment suggests our life is moving in the opposite direction. My moods are draining him, my unwillingness to discuss What Happened. He isn't leaving. He promises that. He says it over and over. He loves Kid A. I extrapolate and decide that since I'm on the other end of the umbilical cord, I must be included.

There are no tears. This is a surprising and welcome thing. Maybe it's because I've wasted them all on the newspaper headlines, the little boy across the street whose parents make him wear one of those harnesses that look like collars, the grocery store clerk asking me if I needed help with my bags; (Do I look that weak? A year ago, I could bench 185). Crying over this mess is impossible. Tears aren't enough. I'd need a whole new bodily function: something akin to sweating.

Instead, I go to bed. I pull the eiderdown comforter up around my chin, loving the dusty smell that I'll soon have to clean out of it, and curl my arms around my belly. We fall asleep like that — Kid A and I — pretending we're united by choice.

"Where's that Quinn?" asks my mother. Her scarves have finally become practical, taming her hair and catching the dust. She's come with running shoes and boxes stolen from the dumpster outside Starbucks. "We need a strong back for all the lifting."

"I'm not sure. Sophia will be here in a few days, though, and she said she'll be happy to help us get settled." I've done just enough packing that the house no longer looks like ours.

"When'd he go out?" She opens the linen closet. "I'll hold it up, you yell out keep or toss. Sit down. You're severely pregnant. Jesus, look at you. I don't want you going into labour here."

"Four days ago," I say, obeying. She's holding up a tablecloth that Quinn's mother gave us. "Toss that one."

"And I'm assuming he's not on a North American tour." She hands me a stack of dishtowels. "Sort and fold. You don't need your hands to talk. So, tell me. Do I need to murder him or just slap him upside the head?"

"I'm not sure . . . Well, okay, he cheated on me — well, that's a strong word, I caught him kissing this groupie chick — and then we didn't talk about it because I wanted to pretend it didn't happen until Kid A's born and everything goes back to normal and then he left but says he'll be back." I fold the towels. "I think he'll be back."

My mother sets down her stack of linens and stands behind me, running her fingers through my hair. When I was a child she loved to twist it around her fingers, though no amount of effort could coax even the slightest curl. "You think any day with a newborn is going to be 'normal'? Oh, sweetie. What are they teaching you in that class anyways?"

"Not much. Diaper changing, breathing exercises, listening to our feelings. There's not exactly a class on what to do when your husband cheats on you."

"He's not your husband and kissing another woman isn't exactly cheating." I look into our bare kitchen. Since arriving, she's emptied our cabinets with alarming speed, tossing out knicknacks according to her own judgment. I'd only packed away everything on the countertops, hoping to trick myself into thinking we were ready to move. We haven't been here long enough that the wallpaper has faded around our pictures. "I guess I shouldn't mention that a wedding comes in handy at times like this."

"No, you shouldn't."

I move to stand up, my hair slipping out from between her fingers. "Sit down, Nolan. For crying out loud. You're eight-months pregnant. Here's some newspaper, here are your dishes; you know what to do."

I wrap the dishes like gifts, padding them for the journey in articles bragging about someone else's tragedies. "No, I don't know what to do. This whole thing with Quinn . . . "

My mother sits down at the kitchen table with two handfuls of my silverware in her fists. She lays them in front of her and shines each with a dishcloth. My mother aims for a fresh start, the traces and stains from happier mealtimes wiped off. "Okay, okay. Darling daughter of mine." I wrap the dishes, she cleans the silverware; we are preoccupied with the mundane process of going away and never coming back. "Let's review the facts. You are in a relationship with a man who is unsure of whether or not he wants to be a daddy or a rock star. Mother Nature makes the decision for him. You're unemployed, he's unemployed, your parents can only bail you out so much, and he's scared shitless. As he should be. As you should be. You're lucky the only thing he did was kiss some groupie. It's not like he fell in love and headed for the border."

"How do I know he just kissed her? Or that there weren't others?"

"Point is that you're having a baby in a month. He says he wants to stay. You obviously want him to stay, since who the hell wants to raise a child alone? Where's he living? I'll go bring him back for you." Each fork and knife gleams, all the tiny weapons lined up. My mother places them in a box and tapes it up. Our kitchen is bare and I'm not sure it's refreshing.

"I don't need you to — "

"No, really, dear. You're pregnant, I'm spry. I'll just go over there, knock on the door and tell him all is forgiven and you can talk about it once he gets home." She pats my hand. "No heavy lifting while I'm gone. I'll tell him we need a hand in moving. Even if he's not planning on staying, he can lug his crap into the new place."

"I'll go," I say. "Just give me a minute." I don't mean it. We continue packing until the house is empty. We eat take-out on the last remaining couch, with the windows open to let out the scent of the pregnant-woman-friendly cleaning products.

The next day, the movers come with their ponytails and big arms and little booties over the shoes to protect the carpets that aren't ours anymore. I leave my mother to supervise and drive to B.B.'s place. On the way over, I decide that Quinn left the house, not me. It was too hard to walk away that last time — the death row shuffle down the path flanked with grass we should have cut more often, looking back at the house we should have painted a year or two ago — so he chose to slink out with a note on the table and no one looking. Pretend he'd left out of anger. The furniture was still in the house, the silverware in the drawer: he could fantasize that he was coming back. The explanation suits me. I take his absence and pin it to empty walls.

My mother will be the one to leave the house for the last time. With or without Quinn, I will return to the new apartment and set up shop. Last night, my mother rolled up her sleeves and washed the walls until eczema followed the path soap made down her arms. I walked through the rooms with a vacuum cleaner. When it was done, I swung the cord like a censer and willed our ghosts away. Maybe I should have left something for the new owners — a photo of us, a lock of hair — so they'll know what needs to be exorcized.

Quinn's left the building, the first to walk away. He left the house, not me. I just happened to be in it at the time. This is a trick Darren might have used: blame the walls. Quinn will never see the rooms empty. My mother and I were the ones who did that,washing the ceiling as plaster and dust were released like confetti. We had to vacuum again because of everything we'd released.

This is the gift my mother gives to us: washes the walls, sweeps the floor, uses caustic chemicals to make our place shine. The movers are lifting boxes. Right now, they're loading the last of our stuff, leaving dolly tracks over the vacuum's prints. I will shrug out of the rooms like a dress. Okay, I will say to Quinn when I see him, it's finished, we've moved. Oh, baby, don't worry. We've taken care of it. It's finally over.

We'll move on to bigger and better things and I'll drag him with me. The plans we must make are supposed to be exciting. A new baby! A new house! Quinn wants second chances and here they are: a blank slate human being — disregard the nature versus nurture argument — new walls that smell of pine cleaner. Someone else washed them for us: this must be a wish for the future, a good luck greeting.

Quinn has left the house — Quinn has left the building, ladies and gentlemen! — and I will pick him up and drive him to the new place. We'll stand in the stripped home before my mother arrives. The rooms will be too small, but I'll make him dance with me anyways.

Quinn's staying at B.B.'s house. When I ring the doorbell, B.B. opens the door just enough to stick his head out and gives me the once-over for weapons or divorce papers.

"Hi," I say. "I'm looking for Quinn."

He stares at my belly. I was never one of those women who get their breasts stared at; I'm not used this. "Do you want me to give him a message?"

"No." I strike a pregnant woman sympathy pose: left hand on the belly, right hand on the oh-my-aching back. "I'd like to see him."

B.B. shrugs, sighs. "Come on in. He's in the shower."

I expected B.B. to live in some kind of rock-out space like the apartment Quinn used to have when we first started dating: the one that was so messy that the occupants would wake up in the morning and stand in the hurricane-zone of their living room waiting for a pair of clean underwear to appear. The kind that makes teenage boys grateful for their mothers.

Instead, B.B.'s house is immaculate right down to the vacuum prints on the carpet. It's all adult, tasteful furniture except for the futon in the corner partitioned off by wall-hangings. B.B. appears well-equipped to handle run-away husbands. He's like some kind of underground fucking railway.

"I can see why Quinn likes it here," I say. "Your house is way tidier than ours. We're moving." Emphasis on the word 'ours.'

B.B. gestures to the couch. Quinn's Gibson rests against it. Either he's given back the Gretsch or he didn't want the reminder of me. I pick it up and try to press it against The Belly. It disappears in my new blind spot, so I play a few riffs by pure muscle memory.

When I look up, B.B.'s gone. I crane my neck to see the strings and play "House of the Rising Sun." My fingers are shaking, making the notes waver with unintended butterfly vibrato. Who's B.B. King now, huh?

"Nolan," says Quinn. He stands in front of me, hair and skin damp, button-up shirt open. He's lost weight even in four days, which means he's been worrying: a good sign. I can almost read his bones. I love the shower scent of him.

Okay, it was just a kiss. Just one kiss. Some silly woman he could never love. And he was scared, wasn't he? And things were changing pretty quickly, weren't they? He just kissed her. She sat on his lap. That wouldn't even be a PG-13 rating in a movie.

"Hey," I say. My attempt at casual comes out thin, like an electric guitar without an amp.

"Hey," he says.

"So, anyways, Sophia's coming to visit and I just wondered when you're coming back because if you're gone she'll know something's up and when I tell her she'll convince me to dump you and, I don't know, raise Kid

A in a nudist commune on organic vegetables and goat's milk. You know Sophia."

Quinn blinks. He sits down beside me on the couch. B.B. remains, as if waiting for me to lull Quinn into complacency then attack.

"Okay, wait a minute. You haven't told Sophia? She's, like, your best friend."

"Yeah, but I knew what she'd say and my mom says — "

"You told your mom?" He looks around the room. "Where's the lynch mob?"

"She was on your side. Long story. Anyhow, let's go. We can talk about this when we get home."

"You don't have to do this, Quinn," says B.B. He stands posed by the couch like one of those life-sized cutouts of rock stars they use to promote videos: hand on hip, feet apart. "You can stay here as long as you like."

"S'cool, man," says Quinn, which either means 'stop trying to fuck up my ticket home' or 'thanks for the offer. I will stay here forever in your den of minimalism and blues rock.'

"Because the way I see it, you still need to explore your options — " B.B. talks like those videos they show teenagers about conflict resolution, the ones that never resolve anything.

"And the way I see it, you need to stay the hell out of this," I say. I'm not doing this pregnant-woman thing very well at all. I'm supposed to be rosy-cheeked and dress in pastels and say, "Oh, you *guys,*" like that chick in the diaper-rash cream commercial. I forget how I'm supposed to act. But isn't that a side-effect of pregnancy? Forgetting?

B.B. does the patient, motherly expression that I haven't quite mastered yet. "This is what I'm talking about," he says. I ball my fists and look around the room to distract myself from his pink, smirking face. The room's free of the clutter that comes with a life that's full of people. The only brightness is Quinn's open sleeping bag with clothes strewn on top of it.

Quinn is silent. He stands in front of me with his shirt undone like Napoleon daring his troops to shoot him. How is it that I can remember events from 19th century history but can't recall what the pigtail groupie girl's face looked like?

"Okay, listen," I say. "Here's the deal. I hate the fact that you kissed the pigtail woman but I can understand that this has been a pretty rough year and we were just kids when we started dating and maybe you missed out on the whole 'groupie fucking' thing. In return for my forgiveness, you come home right after gigs for the next while so I don't go crazy worrying and then Kid A is born and neither of us will have the energy to cheat on anyone. Does that sound like a plan?" It has to sound like a plan. It has to be our plan.

Quinn nods. He looks stunned, but willing to follow. He holds his hands out for me, which is a good thing because I wasn't sure how else I was going to get up from the couch. See? We still work. He had to say yes. We'll talk about it later. The pigtail girl, his music career: everything. Right after the baby's born and my pregnancy hormones settle down. He had to say yes. I give his life direction and he sets me upright when my fat ass has gotten stuck somewhere.

Sophia counts one, two, three to know whether or not the date wants to kiss her. This is the theory, anyhow. If they make eye contact for more than two seconds, no matter what he says he wants you. Get up to ten seconds and you'll either fuck on the spot or kill each other, that's for sure. That's what the book says.

"What about shy guys?" I ask.

Sophia shrugs and her earrings sway. She has the best earrings. These ones are small squares of stained glass, a deep and holy red that might have come from a censer. "Fuck the shy guys," she says. "They can just get over it. Besides, it's useless anyhow. I'm internet dating. The rules just fly out the fucking window." She looks down at my belly. "Sorry baby. Darn window." Since arriving, Sophia has been talking as much to Kid A as to me. She read something about that too.

She arrived yesterday. We met at a restaurant for drinks — orange juice with 7-Up for me, red wine for her — and her expression was a watermark for how I've changed. ("Jesus H. Christ, look at you," she said when she saw me, though I'd done my best with a black maternity dress and a necklace that pointed down like an arrow to divert attention to the new breasts. "Would you look at you? Jesus H. Christ. Who are you and what have you done with my skinny best friend?") Years of body consciousness and I'm tired of it. My belly's bigger, my back is sore, but beyond that I haven't looked at myself too hard. Our new place is still without mirrors. We sit in the kitchen, our old furniture mismatched against the new walls.

"Internet dating? Sure that's safe?"

Sophia shrugs again. "We'll see, won't we?" She dangles a cigarette holder between her fingers, owns a cigarette case with a scorpion on it. She wears colours that don't go with red hair, but she makes them fit. Sophia reinvents the colour wheel for her own purposes. I wonder what the single men think of her in Saint John's.

"I don't want you murdered," I say.

"Yeah, well I don't want to go the next twenty years without getting laid. So, whatever. We'll see." She shrugs again. "How's The Daddy to Be?"

"Fine," I tell her. "Not looking for work as hard as I'd like, but what can you do?"

"How's he handling this whole baby thing?"

"Oh fine. I don't know. Fine, I'm sure."

"I can't believe that you have an ass now. And tits! You're like a whole new person. I can't tell you how much I'm gloating over the fact that you finally grew an ass."

"I aim to please." I want to direct her eyes upwards. Sophia plans to stay for the birth. She says she's known me longer than Quinn has, which gives her the right.

"We need to get you a baby shower. You need presents."

"I don't know enough people for a baby shower."

"What about those girls from your team?"

I shrug. Sophia is also coming to help us move in, though we've been spending most of the time around the kitchen table, drinking tea and complaining. We have very little in common anymore, but there's always something to complain about. I pick the small hurts: back pain, money troubles.

Sophia holds a pencil as if it's a cigarette. She doesn't even want to smell like cigarettes around me, so she chews on the end of a pencil and pretends. She will be Kid A's godmother. "Now, Nolita," she says, peering at me as if through a smoke ring. "There's this matter of Darren."

"What about him?"

"Didn't we get rid of him a few decades ago? I seem to recall heartbreak and suffering."

"I needed a manager for the Canada Games team."

"Right. And of all the people who've ever played wheelchair basketball in the whole history of the world, it just had to be him, right?" She taps the pencil on the side of the table. Her earrings find new light sources in the kitchen, ones that won't settle on my skin. I'm the pregnant one, but she glows.

"He's good at the job so far. Don't be a bitch about this."

"He must be, what, 150 years old by now. And we all know how well he does with the teenage crowd. Great credentials: he broke your heart — actually, more than your heart if we want to be honest — and he's got a thing for little girls."

"Sleeping with one nineteen-year-old doesn't make him a pedophile. He's been great so far. Really great. Running the practices when I'm sick, planning lessons, teaching systems."

"Yeah, starting with the reproductive system." She exhales against the pencil in her mouth, then reaches over to touch my belly again. "Nolita, Nolita, Nolita."

Naked in the bedroom, the baby in me like a blood-borne virus. The shower was too much: all steam and scent and the realization I can't see my feet anymore. Just when I'd finally been able to touch them. The apartment is cool and I lie damp on the bed, steaming.

"What's the matter?" mutters Quinn, who's recently showered off the effects of a hard night with a tough crowd and is dressed in briefs and socks. They were filling in for the weekly karaoke night usually led by a guy dressed like Elvis. Everyone wanted to sing along and hated the amps for obscuring their voices. The tightly crafted licks were lost on them. The night devolved into Abba covers brought down to a drunk man's vocal range. ('Fucking cover band bullshit,' Quinn summarized last night when he slid into bed and I've filled in the details.) "You better dry off, Nole. You'll catch your death of cold."

He's practicing these old wives tale maxims. It's the only parenting practice he's done. It's the only time he's allowed himself to age. He flicks on the light and I watch him. Quinn's gained muscle: the long, angry walks, loading and unloading the gear, filling his own protein needs out of concern for mine. His legs are taut. He stands to look for a towel. From the back, his narrow waist makes him look almost feminine. It's a waist I used to have. When he turns around, just a hint of sympathy belly.

"You still nauseous?" he asks as he towels off my collar bone. "Isn't this supposed to stop soon?"

A dark line has appeared on my belly. It splits me in half: before and after, left brain and right brain, pre and post. I don't know what has broken in me to make this line. Quinn traces it down to my pubic hair with one guitar-player fingernail. I want him to go lower. Once, I burst a blood vessel in my hand and for years after the pattern of the injury would reappear whenever my hands became flushed, like how breathing on a mirror will steam up old fingerprints. This line must make sense, though I don't understand the biology. The disappearing act of my skin. Quinn touches the line, tries to read between it.

"Hey," I say.

"Hey," he says and smells so clean and shower fresh and touches my damp hair. The guitar playing hasn't bulked him, but he's changed all the same. The veins in his hands are thick, his palms are pink, rich with nerve endings and good circulation. My veins have increased — forty to fifty percent more blood, says the book — but I feel like I'm sloshing around in it.

"I'm just tired." I try to remember how I used to turn him on: what I used to say. "You could wake me up, you know."

Quinn stares at the line and I want him to follow the blatant map of my veins while it still exists. "Gotta meet the guys soon," he says.

"Just a few minutes," I say and imagine those pink palms as ginger for my brain and body. There must be some part of me left under this belly.

"Well, you do have great tits now," he notes and lies down beside me as gently as he did when I was in pain.

I find some familiar crook on his torso, a place I used to rest. "What do you think about giving the baby Taylor as a middle name?"

"Would work as a first name, don't you think? For a girl or boy?"

"Taylor McLeod. I don't know if I like Taylor as a first name. It doesn't really mean anything, except that it's my last name. It's either a job or my last name."

He pulls the covers up around me. "Ah, so we want meaning as well? You didn't say that."

"Or at least a story behind it."

"Let's just spell Kid A some crazy way. Lots of Ys. It'll be very chic and save us a lot of time. K-y-d - a - i."

"Right. If anyone asks, we'll say it means peace and love."

"And bravery and courage and forgiveness and strength and perfection."

I laugh and the sudden movement makes Kid A hiccup. "Ah, Quinn," I say. "You make me laugh."

"Ah, Nolan," he says.

Then I kiss him. I kiss his skin and love the way it tastes before the clothes and cologne, before his first cigarette of the day, before he smells like his new life.

Quinn:

Her wet hair soaks a halo on to the pillow, but there's no virgin girl hidden in her body anymore. The teenaged hips and Lolita belly: gone. Nolan is a new girl each month. She has a whole new body. Each month a new body, like a brand new person. My wife shapeshifts into the three remaining women I should have had. I lie down and feel the drafts of this new apartment and know how it must feel on her skin, so I pull up the covers. Her breasts defy my hands. Her breasts defy everything. Who knows where her ribs have gone? Who knows what happened to all those bones I used to know?

The new rooms are too small for pacing: good because they force me into sunshine, bad because there is no urge to rearrange. I know what I have to work with. It's not enough. At least there is this: my parents have given us two month's rent both as a baby shower gift and an acknowledgement that there will be no wedding.

Nothing is fixed here. It all needs to be unpacked. I have empathy with Kid A, how she must feel in my narrow hips, uterine walls with only so much give. There are compromises. The rooms are small but I always know what Quinn's up to. The place is its own baby monitor; at least we won't need one of those.

The apartment is a Russian doll: layers of other people's odours and decorating tastes, our unpacked boxes inside. If I set up the tea kettle first, Quinn will sulk about my attachment to Darren and his medicine. If I set up the cradle — my mother's second-hand find — I'll be thinking too far ahead.

Dr. Taylor:

"Hey, uh, Nolan," I say.

"Hey Dad," she says and her voice sounds like she needs to cough, the result of the baby's pressing and shifting up higher, ruining her ability to get one good breath. These are the facts I know. The side effects.

"How's it going?" I ask.

"Good," she says. She always says. Even with the baby and the unemployment and what have you, she always says. "How're you?"

It's always been this way: hey, how're you? Fine. How're you? Fine. How's work? Pretty good.

"Not so hot actually," I say. For once I say. She pauses, the expected response — "that's good. Good to hear it." — lodged in her and she can't even cough. "Your mom actually," I say. "On the way to the ferry, got into a bit of a car accident. Well, more than a bit, really. A lot more than a bit."

There is a pause. I should have veered more often. But it's hard with such a quiet daughter if you're not one to pry. There are no obvious questions to ask that cannot be answered with fine, good, pretty good. Work is fine. Basketball is fine. Was always fine. No need for conversation. What do you say to such a daughter? A ferry ride away with her sport and boyfriend and all that. Pale and thin—all these secrets.

"Oh," says Nolan. "Oh my God. Is she okay?"

"You should come over. She's under. Can you come right away? She's at Vic General. I can't turn my cellphone on, but you can ask at the desk and I'm sure they'll tell you."

"We'll take the — what time is it? — The one o'clock. We could probably catch the one."

"You should fly. She's pretty rough. Can you fly? Just drive out to the airport and get the first one." What do you say to a daughter — thirty-three years old, still needing her mom to pack up her cutlery, scrub down the walls, wash the floor, get her boyfriend to take her back.

"Oh," she says in a voice I can't read. "I mean, can I fly being so far along? Doesn't it — cause labour or something?" Shouldn't she know? Aren't there books she could have read? Linda had been reading 'What to Expect When You're Expecting."

"It's not a long flight. Even if you go into labour — They'll let you. Just explain it, Nolan. They'll let you. Just tell them what's happening."

"We'll be right there," she says in a voice that may be a question. There was never time for diversions. That was the problem. "We'll fly," she decides. "We'll be right there. She's okay, isn't she? I mean, she'll be okay, won't she?"

What do you say to that? To those questions I can't possibly answer? I don't even know what they're bloody doing in there, just saw a glimpse of her bleeding and collared into a neck brace as they pushed past me and no doctor's come out yet. Who knows what surgery? The head or the heart or the shoulder? The neck or the ribs or the legs or the spine?

On the drive to the airport, I comfort myself with the notion that women my mother's age don't get seriously injured in car accidents. No one dies in car accidents but drunk teenagers on prom night. She's entirely outside the age bracket for this kind of drama. Women her age fall down stairs or have heart attacks during aqua fit. So surely this is a "broken rib and exciting story to tell the coffee group" kind of injury. At worst she'll lose a limb. The thought it weird: my mother as a gimp. My mother with a prosthesis becoming disabled just as I'm restored to able bodied. The passing on of a baton. We will fly there just in case. We will fly and she will be fine.

24

MEMORIES THE LENGTH OF CAMERA FLASHES: sun and wind, the famous Greek light diffused through smog, though it still made me squint for days, a bus ride past the ocean where I napped in brief submersions. We staged at a camp outside of Athens with puppies running wild, Kenyans bowed together by the water trough, singing and slapping their soapy track outfits against the taps, a man with an instrument I couldn't name: like a guitar but with more sobbing behind the strings.

Then the Olympic Village and police escorts up to the gates and metal detectors. A city with no cars, an accreditation pass the only key. There was a McDonald's right in the cafeteria and I watched the entire Chinese contingent arrive en masse and head there: red track suits and Big Macs. The apartments were so white: probably we were supposed to think 'fresh start,' though the Olympics had been there before us. After we were gone, they would be sold to low-income families. Maybe they would consider it lucky.

I have postcard memories from the photogenic blue sky. They'd installed an elevator up the Parthenon and we creaked along the side of ancient rock. The sight of bolts in the strata was impossible and falling seemed the only way down: sacrifice us to the gods. Which gods, I wasn't sure. My father would have known. Once at the top, we saw factories rubbing against arches Plato may have lectured under and I wasn't sure what time it was, what year, what millennium.

At the Canadian Team flag-raising ceremony, a handsome quad rugby player sang "O Canada" and it was like a garden party: white lights in the trees, all of us in polo shirts and a waiter circulating cocktails. The men's team was reading a book called *How to Make Someone Fall in Love with you in 90 Minutes or Less* and I wondered if it was too late to try it on Darren. The Greeks didn't use shower curtains, so water sprayed all over the bathroom. That was a good way to conserve water. There was no easy drain, so you knew exactly what you were wasting.

The opening ceremony: everyone dressed the same and the weird power of that. Women in body suits danced under a massive, lit tree, but we marched in halfway through and missed what story they were trying to tell. I remember that: marching. Everyone waving flags. I was crying and the lights blurred and the people blurred. Sammy grabbed my hand once we were ushered to our seats and said, "Your first Paralympics. I envy you, kiddo."

The first game. The lights were direct and I cast no shadow. My jersey had never been worn. The wheelchair was new.

The first game was against Mexico. We entered to a tape-recorded horn section on a red carpet, though its colour was soon changed by tire tracks.

On the bench, my heart was fast as if I was already in the game. It preceded me, my body more prepared than I was. I went in. I don't remember the act of it, only having an opponent fall forward, her sweat against my jersey and I realized I was in. The first shot sunk smooth as water and I hadn't realized I was shooting. The first shot sunk and the girls on the sidelines cheered and swung their towels around their heads in celebration, a gesture I'd never seen them do before. I got five points that game. Seven minutes of playing time, five points. It's one of the few scores I remember.

The Paralympics, my first Paralympics and time stopped. We were surrounded by high gates and I forgot Darren. I didn't worry. I didn't call. There was no time. To calm me, I scammed a volunteer's guitar and sat on the balcony playing old blues and the quad rugby players below clapped and sang along. *Oh, they call it stormy Monday,* I sang, *but Tuesday's just as bad.* But nothing was bad and there was so such thing as Monday. From when the first game started to the final, I didn't take any pictures. I wasn't thinking of what people back home would want to see.

To find out by email was the worst. So clean. His grammar was perfect and somehow this was another blow. I wanted tears, body language, breakup sex. Instead: a short email received in a foreign land the day before the Final. Darren was going back to Valerie. He had to think of the future and the past, couldn't simply live in the present like people my age were allowed to do. So that was it: baby's first breakup.

This was how it was supposed to happen with girls my age: the first snap and curl of a heartstring. Now I could get on with the real business of dating. Whatever Darren was, he wasn't dating. He was a different animal: who knows? Darren was something done behind closed doors, lacked the right ritual. Almost like masturbating, if I thought hard enough about it.

I wanted real dating: movie theatres, live shows, worrying what to wear, an arm around the shoulder, a hand under my shirt in a dark theatre. That's what people were supposed to do at nineteen, but after Darren all of that felt like regression. Maybe you can never go back, I thought; maybe Darren had changed my taste and I would always fall in love with men like this: aged like wine or scotch or steak, like something I couldn't afford.

Maybe, I figured, people don't even date anymore and that only ever happened in Archie comics. It seemed clear that I would never date. None of the teenage formality and sweetness. The men I love would always be a little embarrassed by the fact that they like being with me. They would not walk arm in arm, would not cut class to see me.

I was far away with women who were much older, wondering how nineteen-year-olds in my country are supposed to fall in love. So that was it: a wrong ending. I didn't cry but the Polish girl on the computer next to me patted my arm and smiled.

There was no one to tell. The final was the next day and I had to make my mind deep and clear. I couldn't. I slept in images, woke to the prehistoric moon and slept to honeycombs of light and shadows, none of my dreams related to basketball. I woke with smoggy eyes and people mistook my silence for concentration.

The gold medal game against the US. Everything had gone as planned. The right teams had been defeated by both sides. Darren was gone and it was a gift. I tried to believe that he had miscalculated the time difference, but he was a bright man.

The American girls lined up in front of us. They were just girls, more my age. They had fat ponytails and Southern tans and I tried to hate them but I didn't. They didn't matter. Darren was gone and basketball was ten people trying to put a ball of inflated rubber into a hoop.

Tony played me and to this day I have no idea why. He needed the height, but we had two fairly tall 4.5s on the team. I remember only that anger united my limbs. I imagined them crackling red and black like wires; maybe this is what they meant by being 'on fire.' My skin was lit like magnesium, my body so tall that no room could hold me. Anger silenced my hurts and we won.

I remember that game — that it existed — but I don't remember winning. As Tony hugged me and they hoisted the team captain up to cut down the net, I felt nothing but parched. They played "O Canada" and when someone put a gold medal around my neck, I used it as an excuse to cry.

~

The Paralympics would have been an easy place to fall in love. The apartments had already been rented to another family and I had a set day of departure. It was exactly the place for a temporary love affair: no laundry, groceries, or school work, just competing and that done now. Everyone's country was sewn on their clothing, everyone's name on their accreditation card. I'd been dumped, but inside the gates none of that mattered. It was so easy to pretend that there was no 'back home." Here, I didn't even have a name.

Hey, Canada! That was how people greeted me. Hey, Miss Canada! You are what sport? Hey, Canada! What is the mistake in your body? The Egyptian sitting-volleyball team serenaded me on the bus, I was asked out by a single-amp Maori powerlifter. A Kenyan blind runner wanted my T-shirt, a Polish trackie wanted in my pants. I was ready for the full Paralympic experience: Little Miss International Relations. Hey, you, Canada!

So the final game and the email and the two canceling each other out until I was nothing: no name, just a country. The last night, there was a party hosted by the Canadian contingent. I'd vowed to live in the moment — Sammy's favourite line — and that particular moment was sponsored by Molson Canadian. That party was an easy place to fall in love: Bosnia-Hertzogovians on the guitar, an Aussie couple going at it so hard the guy fell backwards out of his chair and had to be helped up, Germans singing songs about slaughtering pigs, French tolerating the Canadian edition of their language. All countries united under free Canadian beer. Oh, Canada. Hey, Canada!

There were many men, so many different body types, but I picked a Brazilian guy who didn't speak any English. He brought his friend to translate and the three of us got so drunk that everyone forgot their own language anyhow. When I asked if he was going to Beijing for the next Olympics, the two boys giggled and eventually confessed that 'Beijing' means kiss in Portuguese. Better not to talk about the future.

Eventually, the two of us wandered off. I forget his name now. Maybe I never knew it. I liked him for his eyes, which were not like Darren's, and his skin tone, which was not like Darren's, and the cool, pale stump of his missing leg, also not like Darren's. The Brazilian was so neatly divided; he had either everything or nothing. His only pains were phantom.

I remember sitting against a tree. Maybe this didn't really happen. In the village, the trees were newly planted, though they already looked ancient and stunted. No, it was a huge tree and the roots were raised like it was about to be pulled right out. There was red dirt. Red dirt for sure. I know that because it didn't wash off until I was home and in the bath water it looked like old blood. So a tree, red dirt, the Brazilian man and I kissed him, wanting to taste Brazil again on his tongue, but the alcohol had burned the native bacteria from everyone's mouths. Probably we would have tasted the same anyways after three weeks of McDonald's and cafeteria food.

I probably told him everything: Darren, Valerie, my first breakup. Likely, he listened to me like a piece of music. He did pat my leg. I remember that. He was wearing a shirt that he traded with someone from the Japanese contingent and he wanted my Team Canada track pants so I took them off and in the heat I didn't feel naked and thought I might never feel naked again. Maybe Darren had taken that too: my sense of modesty. He gave me his pants, even though one of the legs had been cut at the knee and pinned up, and drew a line across my leg with his finger, either showing me where his amputation was or suggesting that I could make them into a pair of shorts. He drew a line across my thigh, I kissed him again, poured the last of my vodka into the parched ground and watched it absorb, willing the tree to die, and the Brazilian man kissed me and I said obrigata, obrigata, obrigata for everything.

I woke up in someone else's pants in my own temporary bed, the sun too bright through the hand I'd flung over my eyes. Sammy and Sue were peering over me.

"Think we should wake her up?" asked Sammy.

"It's noon. We leave at five."

"I'm awake, you jerks," I muttered.

"We're jerks? I put you to bed at 3 AM and we're the jerks?" Sammy laughed and turned on the light. I winced.

"Who was the guy?" asked Sue.

"The Brazilian guy? Oh, I don't know."

"What's Darren going to think about that?"

I wouldn't have minded them believing that I'd cheated on Darren and that the end of our relationship could have been chalked up to a rookie mistake. Let them think I'd outgrown him.

"Whatever he thinks, he can tell it to Valerie. We're not really . . . well, you know. He kind of . . . .went."

In the silence that followed, I could hear the Village being closed down: trucks backing up outside to load the gear, cleaning staff going through our castoffs, girls in other rooms packing.

Sue touched my hair as if I was sick and they left me to sleep.

It was strange how the contents of the room fit back into my bag. All the good-luck messages from family and friends back home, all the new clothes and pins. We'd decorated the apartment like a home, but now the walls were blank again. The flight was that night and I wore my first bad hangover like a souvenir. I didn't think 30,000 feet up would be a good place not to feel well, but I took a few Gravol and someone had blessed me with a bulkhead seat so I leaned against the cool window and tucked the blankets up around my head. I pretended to nap but instead cried silently with my face hidden in the blankets and everyone thought I was just sick and had brought it upon myself.

After a thirteen-hour flight, we landed in Vancouver: my parched skin soothed by British Columbian rain. The taxi driver dropped me off at the Sky Train and I took another taxi home. There was no time to fall asleep because I had to find my own way.

Sophia came to my house ready for a ritual.

"Time to mourn," she said cheerfully, holding a tub of ice cream and a box of matches.

I was in my pajamas though it was late afternoon, my first gold medal already in a box in the closet. "There's nothing to mourn. It was just a stupid thing. He wasn't my boyfriend."

"Boyfriend, OldManFriend, whatever. He still went away and we should get drunk."

"No drinking." I was still stunned and jet lagged, unsure of how old I was, what continent I was on. "But bring on the ice cream."

"That's my girl."

We opened the windows. It was September, one of the last weeks we could still do that. People were burning leaves nearby and I imagined the odour smoking out the mould and self-pity that had been accumulating for the past week. We ate ice cream out of the tub with two spoons, like we'd seen in movies.

"I think you should burn stuff," said Sophia. "People do that, don't they? To get closure? I think we need some fire."

"I'm not allowed candles in this apartment."

There was almost nothing of him in the apartment anyways, so Voodoo would be impossible. We gathered up the condoms I'd bought in case he ever visited, a few photos from team trips and his Christmas card and put them in a Kleenex box. I'd buried countless pet hamsters in Kleenex boxes, so it felt appropriate. The card said, "Peace. Love. Joy." on it in sparkly letters and he had drawn an asterisk in red pen, then written, "Please note that all peace, love and joy will be suspended during the upcoming Cage Match season when I defend my title." At the time, I'd taken it as a confession of love, since love had to exist before it could be suspended.

"Don't you think that's funny?" I asked Sophia, showing her the card.

"In the box it goes. Ooh, hey, we should burn this at a graveyard or something. Nothing says 'closure' like the presence of dead people."

We settled for the parking lot of the Church of Perpetual Smackdowns. The main doors were open and someone was singing in an earthly baritone.

"I think that's the janitor," I said. He was singing that one about the bullfrog.

"Think he takes requests?" asked Sophia. "Maybe he could hum 'Taps' while we torch the stuff."

"He didn't die. He just left me."

"Close enough," said Sophia. We took the lid off the garbage can and peered at the programs from the church service inside. It was dusk, dark enough that I couldn't really see Darren's face in the photos but could make out way he tilted his head towards me. I tossed the condoms in one by one.

"Get mad," said Sophia. "Say something ritual-like."

"This is for going back to your ex-wife," I said and dropped in a condom. "This is for not wanting me to meet your friends. Think we should burn these? They'll probably stink."

Sophia considered this. "Nah, good point. Take them out. Save them for your next boyfriend and use them out of spite."

"Eww, they've been in the garbage." I picked them out of the can. Though the refuse inside was mostly paper, the can smelled of pee and rust. I wanted the scent of the church: wondered what lemon polish smelled like as it burned.

"They're wrapped."

"But now I'll think of them as garbage condoms."

"Moving on. Keep going. Do the photos."

"This is for not trusting me to take my Baby Pills. And for not wanting me to leave a toothbrush at your place," I said and ripped the picture up before tossing it in.

"Good," said Sophia. "I can feel it working. That old black magic."

"Joy across the world," sang the janitor. *"Love your boys and girls."*

We tossed in the photos and the Christmas card: scant kindling.

"And this is for leaving me right before the biggest game of my life and don't give me bullshit about the time difference because you did it on purpose, little dick."

"Hear that, Darren? Little dick." Sophia stood over the barrel like a priestess. She held the match. "Yeah, that's right. Okay, Darren . . . whatever your last name is . . . for crimes against humanity and a lack of tact, good taste, decency, and fashion sense — especially fashion sense — you are sentenced to be forgotten by the lovely and talented Nolan Taylor. We hereby recognize that she can do much better and will now send your earthly remains up to heaven and out of Nolan's life forever." She paused. "Uh, amen."

"Amen," I said. We stood before the altar we'd cobbled together. Sophia lit a match, which smelled of struck metal, wheelchairs clashing in Cage Match. All of our useless rituals: I imagined them burning. The mementos smoldered, but didn't burn, and the wind came up with its scent of cars and wooded areas and thwarted every match we tried. The photos wouldn't rise.

"Ah well," said Sophia. "But you get the point, right? Forgetting?"

But still, there was Quinn. I planned to devolve with Quinn, start acting my age. He was frivolous. It could never last. Quinn seemed like my best option. He seemed like a good thing at the time.

I phoned him when I got home that night.

"I'm sorry for being a bitch and not making out with you on your birthday," I said. "Mostly for being a bitch, though."

"It was still a good birthday," he said. "There was much cheer in the form of a French-Canadian exchange student."

"Oh."

"How was Athens? Congratulations, by the way."

"Yeah, thanks. You want to go for coffee . . . or something?"

"Does 'something' involve forgiveness sex?"

"Will you settle for a latte?"

He sat with me on the steps of the university. It was September: cool, but the light was mood-enhanced by trees. The glow was not quite sunset. I was thinking of Darren and Valerie setting up house again. All of her dishes coming back, the good china. He'll wash, she'll dry. Quinn didn't notice where my mind was. He was happy to talk to some prof who gave him a shitty mark.

"Cold yet?" he asked, slipping an arm around me. He offered me his sweater. He was trying hard and this delighted me. I put my head against his shoulder, though I had to slouch to do it, and inhaled the boy smell of him. The absence of Old Spice was a good, good thing.

When he kissed me, I wondered if I was finally something official. Someone's girlfriend. A girl again. Darren was really just dress up. The relationship was too big, like a child trying to walk in her mother's high heels. Quinn kissed me in back-to-school light. He kissed with entirely too much tongue.

Quinn is frivolous, I thought. He can't possibly last, will not last. Even as I kissed him, it felt like a memory. Darren was a relationship: who knows what to call it? I felt as if I'd divorced him. Quinn's just dating, I told myself. Maybe he'll take me to sock hop or to meet his parents. Quinn's summer lovin' and the livin's easy. He's willing to be seen in public with me — to kiss in front of all these people wandering to their next class — and this is enough.

But, God, when I sat back against those steps into a September warmth laced with the coming winter. God, when he looked at me, said nothing, touched my cheek. One kiss and the silence was already good with him.

25

THE PLANE RISES AND THE AIR PRESSURE IN THE CABIN changes the texture of my face. Below, Vancouver turns into a grid-work with a gleaming stream of traffic through it like spawning salmon. From up here, it looks like a law of nature, as if there was a biologically determined reason for where everyone's going so fast. During a high school science class, I once saw a video where a shot of traffic taken from an airplane merged with a cross-section of blood through veins. So, okay, traffic is veins. And the city is what? I think as I fly over New Westminster. (I see the bridge, the water). Is it flesh or bone? The city: would it be an organ? And then I can't see the ground anymore — cloud cover — and lose any sense of comparison. The tendency is to lapse into third person at a time like this: she can't see; she can't understand. My little ecosystem and maybe I'm a planet, a God, omniscient.

We fly over disorientating water and I open my novel. I can't focus on reading, so I stare at the contrast of letters on the page. Black and white. Black and white.

The pregnancy has made me more forgetful than omniscient and now I can't even remember what the book's about or who the characters are. I flip the pages, then put it down, though there's no longer anywhere on my lap to hold the book. Instead I fold my hands over my belly like some sort of floatation device. Quinn laces his fingers with mine and says, "Hey, it'll be okay. It'll be okay, you know," and I look out the window, wishing for ultrasound eyes that could see through this cloud cover to the hospital and my mother. Quinn turns back to his book and I remember some English class we took together, how the teacher said that before the invention of the airplane, no one could conceive of omniscient narration. People needed flight to find the third-person perspective of God.

Quinn:

I see Nolan's calculations. Sixty minutes too late. She's replaying the past few hours: that SUV going eighty in the fast lane, the plane landing ten minutes late, the bloody island that's not a car ride away. Her mother's already in surgery.

"Under the knife or just in that little holding area?" Nolan asks. "You know, that place with the curtains that they put you before they're ready."

"She's under, Ms. Taylor," says the nurse. "And she was unconscious when she got here. We'll get you updates when we can."

Nolan paces, refusing coffee but accepting the nurses' cookies and orange juice, what they give to patients on the verge of swooning. Nolan won't swoon. Her feet are planted apart, belly and new hips around her like an inner tube. She makes a circuit out of the mix-matched chairs and couches, around a man pretending to sleep curled in a brown love seat, past the doors to the O.R. and back.

"Nole," I say, but no, she completes her figure eight, has a cookie, sits, flips through a magazine, completes another figure eight. Her father watches her. He's silent under a thick moustache and eyebrows. I wish they would huddle together, even to the exclusion of me. Maybe I should go over to him, give him God knows what kind of man-to-man pep talk. Keep your chin up, dad. Night's always darkest before the dawn. She's a real trooper. She'll pull through. Is that what people say? He's not technically my father-in-law. Instead, I sit down beside him and offer him a coffee. He stares ahead.

"Hey," says Nolan. "We could pop up to the maternity ward and do that little tour. Impress the hell out of those prenatal class assholes."

Her father frowns at the word, as if this is the one place where the body should be sacred, no derogatory words for it.

It's bad when the doctor comes out too soon. I know from Nolan's surgery that they send the nurse when things are fine. Her dad knows it too. The doctor should be in there mending, saying things like 'stat' and '5 ccs of morphine, nurse.' He shouldn't be out here, his skull cap with tropical fish and palm trees on it in hand. There's residue of the antiseptic wash on his forearms that didn't rinse off. Her father knows. Probably knew already or else why would he have asked her to fly? He must know this hospital inside out.

Nolan doesn't swoon when they tell her. She just sits down, staring straight ahead. Both of them: almost catatonic. This is a family that turtles.

So I do what I can: details. The doctor explains that sometimes the vein becomes attached to the wall of the chest so that when you open it up . . . He breaks his pencil in half to demonstrate. You don't know until you're in there, he says. There was damage from the crash and we had to go in. She was bleeding internally. The ribs had all cracked. Maybe the vein burst during the crash, maybe when we went in there — difficult to say. Common in patients with previous heart surgeries, but very rare in a situation like this. Young-ish woman. No previous heart problems. I write that down on the back of a bank receipt, planning to look it up on the internet. Her dad will understand, but who knows if he's even listening? When she's ready, later, I can give her the comfort of specific terms, of science.

"I'm sorry," says the doctor and he sounds it. He scrunches the skull cap into his hands, looking young and ashamed.

"I want to see her," Nolan announces and stands.

"Ms. Taylor," says the doctor, "I can't imagine that you would want to see the body in this state."

"Nolan," says her father.

Ten minutes dead and she's already 'the body.' Medicine has a short memory. I touch Nolan's shoulder, "Nole," I say, but she flinches.

"I want to see her," Nolan repeats and the doctor nods.

"Give us a few minutes to prepare her," he says and shakes my hand after Nolan shrugs him off.

When they pull back the sheet, Nolan's father becomes a chameleon, his face the same shade as his wife's, which is the same as the sanitized linens. They haven't bothered to sew her up, just placed a towel over the area, which Nolan has removed. The place where her heart should be is packed in white gauze turning pink.

Nolan picks up her mother's grey hand, taking a pulse she can't possibly expect to be there. Then she moves each waxy finger, trying to find a rhythm. I think this little piggy went to market, this little piggy stayed home. This little piggy had roast beef. This little piggy had none. This little piggy went wee wee wee wee wee all the way home.

But, no, it's got to be some other melody. Some private joke. I wish I knew that song. I wish I could play it for her.

A Love Supreme. A Love Supreme.

~

Dr. Taylor:

The fact of the matter is. The fact of the matter. As Nolan called it: my dad voice. The fact is. When she wanted to do something. When she wouldn't see. The fact of the matter is.

The facts of the matter:

My child, an injury, a limp, a replacement.

My wife, a car accident, the coronary sinus rupturing when the rib cage was broken.

Me thinking concussion, few broken ribs, paraplegic at worst. Give her enough coagulants to stop the bleeding, go in and stitch her up. Cauterize. Who thinks growth plate? Who thinks heart?

Nolan's trying to reanimate her hands; Quinn should give us a moment as a family, though I suppose this baby means he's in to stay. Linda's been using a shimmery body lotion and it's garish now that the blood has left her. Her fingernails, too: purple. What good is it to have memorized each of her muscles, to know the names of even the littlest vein in her eye? Heart's the wrong word for the organ, anyhow. It needs a long and guttural sound, a word that comes wet off the back of the throat. And Nolan — the capital femoral epiphasis, osteoarthritis of the acetabulum and the sacroiliac joint, avascular necrosis of the femoral head — the fact of the matter is that even at eleven she was so long and blonde and lovely that I mistook her for an adult and thought she'd stopped growing.

Twenty-seven hours until the funeral and I can't stop cleaning. My hands are eager for tasks, anticipating the years without her. In the living room, I kneel down between the off-coloured trails that decades of traffic have ground in: going down slow as if adjusting to the shock of cold water. Think: camping trip, her Chinese brocade robe amidst foliage calling me to the shore. Think: physiotherapy pools as she read murder mysteries, hair wilting in the chlorine humidity.

My belly won't allow me to see the area directly beneath me. This body with its new blind spots. Until labour, I can only look upwards.

I shouldn't be near fumes, so I'll settle for soap and water, baking soda for stains, opening all the window to take the scent out, though I know it won't help. This place smells like someone else's life and will remain so, despite my best intentions.

My father emerges from their bedroom as I'm dusting the TV. He holds her World's Best Mother mug, touching the edge of the lipstick stain while being careful not to smudge it, and watches me like I'm a thief. He holds her mug and the mug holds the scent of her sour-coffee morning breath.

"Nolan," he says. "I appreciate — but — it's too soon. Don't go changing — " His tone is too close to pleading.

I stop and brush the dust off my stomach. "I'm supposed to do this," I say. "I read it in a book."

He's likely thinking: a book on the grief process? This room contains enough of her skin and hair to resurrect her a hundred times over, no need for ghosts.

I look down at the cloth, the grey furry smear on it that is my mother, maybe my father, maybe me. My father stares at it as well, probably thinking that this is the only product of their combined DNA that makes sense.

"It's hormonal," I try to explain. "I read it somewhere. There's a word for it."

"Nesting," he says. Taps the mug. World's Best Mother, it says, an adult's rendition of a child's stick-drawing beneath the words. "I know."

"Right," I say. Still, he stares at me as if puzzled. My mother was his translator.

What position on the court does our little girl play again, honey?

Post, sweetie. The Centre.

Why does she like that long-haired kid?

That's just the way she is.

What do we call her? Is handicapped a word they use these days?

How will I ever talk to him now? What can I possibly say?

My father gives me one last wary stare, then heads back to the bedroom. I'm a wolf in whale's clothing stealing his memories.

I keep cleaning until it's terrible archeology. In the kitchen junk drawer, I have to stop after each item I pull out. Each object is a wound. Remember that deck of cards? That Christmas ornament? Remember that time? With those batteries and how we put dead ones in thinking they were fresh and took the damn radio back to the store to get a new one and they laughed at us? Instead, I shut the drawers, stuff the knick-knacks into odd cupboards then scour the surfaces. It's no good: the sun has done its own cleaning, bleached the linoleum around where that vase of artificial flowers and ornamental teapot were kept.

The task is so big. I brew my mother's tea and sit down at that old oak table, her toast crumbs still in the knot holes on the surface. The window's open and the salt air smells like distance. On afternoons when I was sick, my mother used to wrap me in the afghan on the couch and sit me at this table. She'd let me wear some of her lipstick and we'd pretend to be old fashioned ladies in shawls watching the sea and waiting for our famous and handsome husbands to return from the sea. Who knows where they went or why?

The full-length mirror is the same one from when I was a child, warped now. In it, I waver fat, thin, fat. No, more like fat to fatter and back again. No wonder my mother was constantly on a diet, never sure of what she looked like. But, no, this mirror gives hope. My body stretches in it as if I could reshape myself like so much clay. There's a circular patch worn thinner in the carpet. My mother twirled here, feeling the weight of faux pearls against her chest, the loop swishing against her cleavage. Here, she tested how well her scarves could fly.

The scarves hang on a rack beside the mirror. I choose one in green silk and drape it around my neck, wishing I knew what knot to use. When I was young, I would sit on her bed and watch her dress. She told me once how to tie them right: some type of sailor's knot. The kind you would use to anchor a boat to the harbour or batten down the hatches. Scarves want the air; you have to work hard to affix them to your body.

The scarf smells of her perfume and I want to remember the half-twirl she did when the outfit was finished: all the fashion rules followed. These are facts I should write down: no white shoes after Labour Day, blue and green should never be seen without a colour in between. I want to remember that half twirl, but the silk is light and grainy: ash against my skin. The scarf lifts from me in the slight breeze and all I can think of is box they gave me at the crematorium and how it was warm, still warm, but not from the heat of her body. This is what I've reduced her to.

Quinn stands in the doorway, holding a sandwich and a glass of milk.

"I found organic milk, so you don't have to worry," he says and offers it to me. "Better drink up. My grandma used to say that each bubble in the milk was a dollar you'd get."

I take the milk for something cold and weighty to hang on to.

"Come on," he says. "You and Kid A need the nutrients, I need the money. I was going to make you a peanut butter sandwich, but then I remembered that pregnant women aren't supposed to have nuts, so I made ham."

I sip the milk, hoping it will make him leave. "Thanks, Quinn."

He puts the plate on the bed and stands behind me. I want to slow dance in this room with him, but my stomach gets in the way. This is the only way we can sway together.

"I was thinking we could move in here for a little while," I say. "That apartment is awful . . . It really is . . . We could get jobs and dad could maybe use some company. It'd be good to be near him. Haven't asked him yet, though."

"You mean right away? Have Kid A here and everything?"

"Something like that. I know it would be hard with the band."

"It would be hard with the band," he says. "But at a time like this." I wonder if he's talking about the pregnancy. Birth plus death. They should cancel each other out and I should feel better.

"Or I could stay and you could live on the mainland," I say. "Just for a while."

Quinn's fingers tense around my belly. "I don't think either one of us should use the word 'leaving' for a while."

I nod and lean against him. The scarf is the only item of my mother's clothing that would fit me.

"At a time like this," says Quinn and trails his sentence off into my collarbone. His hands under my belly brace me, but I want more than to be propped up. Let him twirl me. Let us make her outfits right for dancing again.

~

Quinn comes home late. He's taken my father out to see some blues, like we need more blues, like now's the time for some father-son bonding. I suspect the outing was less about bonding and more so that both of them could get away from me. Though he swears he's not smoking, Quinn smells like mundane poison. I want him to shower until his skin throbs and I can feel his good, good heartbeat everywhere on his body.

We go to sleep in my old bed, which smells more of mould than of me. It's a single bed and Quinn's squashed against the wall, trying to spoon because it's the only way we can hold me anymore. There's no easy spot for his arm to rest. It doesn't fit. We don't fit.

I swear he's been smoking Winston Milds. My senses have sharpened as my body softened. Quinn's veiny guitar-player hands only reach half-way across my belly. Before, he was a perfect fit: rubbing my hip bone like a good luck charm, his fingers in my pubic hair. Now I just want him to keep his hands to himself. It's ridiculous, in a way. Me, baby-swollen in my childhood bed with its preteen pattern of roses and rainbows, planning the details of a funeral. Past, meet present. Present, meet future. Sex! Death! Birth! Grieving! These are big questions. Quinn should be glad that he can't see my front because my eyes flash them around. Look! Here comes adulthood! Here comes responsibility! He sleeps, his head resting against my shoulder. He would rather close his eyes. Would rather play guitar.

I slide out of his embrace. He doesn't have a good hold on me anymore. Hell, I don't have a good hold on me anymore, never sure exactly what space I take up. I dress without looking down: a summer dress and no bra or underwear on. Undergarments don't fit and haven't for weeks.

It's 3 AM and thirty-seven kilometers to the ferry terminal, a straight line once I'm out of the city: farms on either side, the sleepy smell of damp trees and earth now that all the cars are gone. I sing along to the radio: only minor-chord songs because you've got to have a sad reason to be up at this hour. Halfway to the terminal, I switch it off and put in one of Quinn's Ramones CDs because, what the hell, I'm wearing a thin dress with no underwear and going to meet a man who's not my husband at 3 AM.

The ferries don't run at this hour. Right. There are no ferries at three AM and this is strangely a surprise. I'd hoped for a straight and easy line. Sometimes, I forget what it means to be on an island.

Outside, I can smell the contribution the sea is making to the air. As I get closer to the ocean: the sustaining tang of seaweed; small, dying creatures. Quinn would be horrified. How much great literature ends with tragic women walking into the water with stones in the pockets? This setting — the sea beating its brains out against the rocks, the rusted car parts and drums — calls for some kind of hysteria. Madness, at least. Maybe some swooning, fainting, beating of breasts or gnashing of teeth. But I feel neither Victorian nor energetic enough for such dramatics. Besides, I'm without an audience. The sand is cold as I wait out morning sitting on a rock wishing I could swim to the mainland. Inside me, Kid A walks on water.

~

Darren's slumped on the couch, wheelchair rocking in the slight breeze, maybe from a slope in the floor. He stares at the TV like it should be on, but only the stereo is playing. *I oughta know,* it says. *I oughta know. I oughta know about lonely girls.* Lucinda Williams and the smell of ginger. How can this place not be medicine?

He's dozing, maybe dazed, turns to see me and squints from the backlighting. I must be bleary with natural light. *Heavy blankets,* says the stereo. *Heavy blankets. Heavy blankets cover lonely girls.* He must have known I was coming. Why else this song? How can this place not be magic?

Magic or medicine. One of the two. Magic, all flighty and plumed, heartbeat so fast you can't hear it, wings so fast you can't see them. Medicine, good old western medicine. The knee bone's connected to the leg bone. The vein's connected to the chest cavity, severing upon — .

"Nolan, hey, what're you doing here?" he asks, looking ashamed at being caught in this posture. He sits up straight and picks at the bleach stains on his sweatpants as if they might come off. *Sparkly rhinestones,* says the stereo. *Sparkly rhinestones. Sparkly rhinestones shine on lonely girls.*

"I'm moving," I say.

"Oh yeah?" When he reaches for his chair, the pushrims reflect patterns up the grotto walls: medallions of spangly dust. I want to make this place big with light. Pull down the curtains.

"We're moving. I mean, Quinn and I. To the Island. The house I grew up in, I mean. Because my dad can't really."

He transfers into his chair and wheels to the doorway. I wonder if he's blocking my entrance. "Nole, I'm sorry about your ma." Ma: his Little House on the Prairie vocabulary. "She was a great woman."

"You only met her once."

"I've met you. You're a great woman."

All this Hallmark bullshit. "I guess I'm going to have a garage sale and give clothes to Good Will."

"I found this pregnant woman tea at the store. Come on. Val's visiting her mother. Come on in. Jesus, look at you." Still, this need to be secret, though there's nothing to hide.

I sit at the table, blowing on the tea. "Are you sure this organic stuff is good?" I ask him. "It's not regulated."

"It's all natural," he says.

"So's foxglove." Still, I raise it to my lips.

"I checked it out. It's good for you and the little one." My new name: Nol-and-the-little-one. Nole-and-the-baby. Nole-and. Nole-and. "Trust me."

"I don't recall that worked out too well for me last time around."

When I turn around again, he's standing, hand holding the counter. A tremor of disuse runs through his legs. He takes a few coltish steps towards me, puts his hands on my shoulders part to support me, part for support.

"You must be tense," he says, his hands kneading the muscle knots, needing to do something to make me feel better.

"My lower back," I say. "That's the trouble spot. From the injury."

"Mm," he says, fingers spreading like warmth and warmth spreading further than his reach. "How'd that happen again, anyways?"

"Oh," I say, shrugging into his fingertips. "It was a long time ago."

Darren:

She keeps talking about opening the curtains, says these dark rooms make her squint, so I let her. Go ahead, I say, and when she does the house doesn't feel like mine. The place is huge. It doesn't fit anymore. All the tricks light can play.

"This can't be natural," she says, gesturing to her stomach. "My back hurts. My skin itches. How can this be natural? How can we be meant to do this?"

"Sit," I tell her and motion to the floor in front of me. She does and I sit behind her, letting my fingers find those knots. I can still read them like a fucking Boy Scout. She leans forward, bringing her hair over her head as if to dry it in this sudden sun that she's brought in with her. I touch the birch trunk of her spine. Her shape has changed but the spine's the same. If I could decipher her smell, I would say her skin is to Dove soap as wine is to grapes. No, maybe that's not right. Why do equations never work when you want them to?

"Hello in there, Kid A," she says against her stomach. "Nearly done cookin'?" The fine hairs at the base of her neck seem made of pure light. "Quinn and I call the baby Kid A. It's from an album."

"Ah."

"Radiohead."

"Ah."

"Remember that time you pulled me over at practice and I fell and my back hit your caster?"

I didn't, but now it's all memory: the soft heat of her skin and the contrast of bones. Her hair against my face as she fell.

"Yeah," I say.

"And I fell right on my spine?" she says and guides my fingers to the spot. I want to think of all the places Nolan's hands have guided me to before: her glowing in that church gym, spine intersecting collar bones: a cross. But I can't. Just her head striking my knees and me not feeling bad. Not even feeling bad about not feeling bad. Thinking she deserved it for leaning back too far into the personal space bubble I'm allowed by IWBF rules. To be fair, she initiated the contact . . . but of course it was a technical foul, even though it was a practice and there aren't supposed to be fouls.

But I was going to say, before truth broke in with all her matter of fact about the ice storm.

"Can you feel it?" I ask him.

This should be done around the front for baby kicks. Instead, the pulse of the worn point. I can feel his fingers down my spine sparking the memory of first touch and the years in between. This joint is an old, buried ruin where magic was once performed.

His hands continue over the lats, the skin, the whole strata.

"I don't know," he says. I feel his breath flutter against my hair.

I slip the dress up over my head, forgetting — no, not really forgetting — that I'm wearing nothing underneath. I want him to feel it. If I could let him touch my bones I would.

Pretend that the back is a map, I want to tell him. The shoulder blades are mountains, the slope of spine a good and vital river. Pretend that the back is a map: each scar a crossroad, each freckle a hamlet. Never mind the front with its showy breasts.

Forget the nipples darkening, rounder. The contrast of them against the white skin like stained glass windows in a cathedral. And, my God, the belly, the dome of it looking like man-made architecture, too smooth to be an accident. Forget the front.

Pretend that the back is a map and pretend that a map is an optimistic attempt to write a story. Like you could know everything, shrink the inches of terrain into something you can spread on a dashboard. I reach behind, take his hands and navigate them to the hurt. There's no bruise, no scar, no X marks the spot.

"From behind you don't really look pregnant," he says, speaking it against the pod of my spine and something akin to breath jolting down me. Kid A jams a heel high against my ribs. Darren's hands massage my back, across my shoulder blades. Mid-stroke, one hand reaches around to cup my breast. It's too gentle and I want to tell him, but his fingers startle at the realization that there's too much breast to fit neatly in his palm. I cannot be held.

From behind, my boundaries must be easily defined. I turn around and there's that bulk that refuses to be named as one substance: part fat, part water, part child.

"I didn't realize I did that," he says, touching my lower back almost reverently: not exactly an apology.

I oughta know, says the stereo, *I oughta know. I oughta know about lonely girls.* The song's been on repeat the whole time. It can't be my theme song. It can't be for me. What do I know about lonely girls? What do I know about their heavy blankets, sparkly rhinestones, sweet sad songs? I was Dare'n'olan and now I'm Nole'an'Quinn. Now I'm Nole'an'the'baby. For nearly as long as I can remember, I've been in some fucked-up kind of love.

"I need to call Quinn," I say.

Darren:

She's naked and then she stands. It takes long moments, even more awkward than before the hip replacement. She stands and walks through this new sunlight to pick up the phone. The stretch marks on her belly are like weave of her skin is coming loose and maybe I could pull and she would step out of this roundness into thirteen years before. All this sunlight and I want her back in a time when she and I were behind closed doors.

Before Valerie returned, Darren and I were always on opposite teams. He checked me, I checked him, and we neutralized each other. Our game was somehow different, always one-on-one even though it was supposed to be a team sport. People left us alone to grind our pushrims against each other. But Valerie had changed that and after coming back from Athens, I didn't want to be against him. Everyone on The Handicaps congratulated me, but he hung back, tied his shoelaces twice, and tightened his strap three times, as if rushing over this ritual had caused the decline in his skill.

Along with some photos and small gifts, I'd brought the gold medal. The weight of it was cool in my damp palm. It calmed me, reminded me of the healing magnet, hummed with the energy of the final match.

"Hey Nole," said Darren, trying to smile at me without making eye contact. "Hey, I have a question for you. Does your apartment allow pets? Because I'm looking for a good home for the kitten and I thought — "

"Wow, you're just giving everyone away, aren't you?" I said, wheeling away. "You should have a garage sale."

"Listen, hey. Nolan. I was thinking we could go for coffee after practice, just to — "

"I'm here to play basketball."

Everyone else knew and their smiles stopped at their mouths. Rob and Erika fussed over the photos I'd brought. Look at those columns. Are they really that old? How beautiful. The colours. That temple. Look at all those people! Cheering for wheelchair basketball? Finally, half an hour after practice was supposed to start, Darren said, "Well, guys, should we get going? Rob, you pick the teams."

And so Rob, unthinking, pitted Darren against me again. I was determined to be calm. If I'd learned anything from being with Darren, it was the value of a secret. So I wore the memory of the email like a hip injury. Invisible disability.

"Yeah, let's go," I said. Darren had on a white shirt so I changed my reversible, drawing out the moment where I stood in only a sports bra. I stretched my arms high above my head, letting Darren see the muscle tone and tan lines, all these lines of me like a court for a game he wouldn't get to play anymore. I was strong. I worked. My torso was proof that I'd improved.

"Guess we'll give the world champion the ball," said Darren and we started. The email and his refusal to make eye contact pressed against my chest round and cold as a medal, canceling out the buzz of the gold.

My mind and body were united, as if I was pure electricity, freed from skin. The Paralympics had taught me the value of anger. I enforced my will on the game, hitting every shot I took. Darren tried to check me legally at first, adding polite, distant praise to the "Nice shot"s of everyone around him. Then, he started fouling me. We rotated around each other like stuck gears. One by one, our teammates stopped playing and let us go. I don't remember when this happened, only looking up from his chair, his hands, his torso, the smell of his sweat to realize that they were gone, clustered in a knot on the sidelines pretending to sip from their water bottles.

This was Cage Match. No, this wasn't Cage Match. In Cage Match, the fouls didn't mean anything. It was exactly what it seemed to be, had no subtext, no code to crack. People like sports because they don't mean anything. Cage Match was safe.

Darren and I ground against each other. I tried not to look at him, tried to make myself focus on his chair and hands: the bare essentials of what I needed to defend him. To defend myself from him. On offence, it was as if he wasn't even there. I moved through him easily: scored and scored and scored.

"You can't be in the key that long," said Darren. "Three seconds."

"That's crap," I said, and ground around him into the key counting aloud. "One steamboat. Two steamboats." I shot. The ball dropped through the net smooth as water. "Three steamboats. There. Three steamboats." Three steamboats, and I could see them. Three steamboats chugging away down the Fraser, gathering the river up against their sterns. Three steamboats, a churn of foam behind. Three steamboats leaving.

"Whatever. If you need to break the rules to win."

I was winning four to zero — since we realized that we were playing one on one we'd started keeping score — and needed only one more shot to win the game.

I squared up, cocked the ball to shoot, and felt his hands hook into my collarbones. He was behind me and below me and he pulled me back, over the fifth wheel, over all the safe guards that were supposed to prevent me from getting hurt. He pulled me back like a Southern Baptist priest baptizing a new convert in a river. That's what I thought when I was falling: those women crying in white dresses, bending down towards the current, the outline of their bodies under the wet fabric, faces streaming and blessed.

But this wasn't a blessing. I went down hard, felt the front caster strike against my spine in a way that wasn't water. It was rock against rock, the first fire, and it ignited across my back and down my legs and then I laid there. On the ground, for the first time that night, I was forced to see all of Darren. Darren, who was raising his hand to an imaginary ref.

"I guess that was my foul," he said.

I wished the ref were real and this wasn't just a scrimmage, that there was a numbered jersey on his chest and some official would blow the whistle and say, "Technical foul. Intent to injure. Number fifteen." Not Darren. Number fifteen. Not real life. Just a game. I would get a foul shot with no line up and everyone would have to stand outside the three-point line as I shot. I wanted that: to be outside of everyone's reach making my peace with the foul by two swishes through the hoop. I wanted that: everyone behind the three-point line, its shape a setting sun arcing between the sidelines, the out-of-bounds line a long, long horizon.

Instead, just Darren, who shrugged off the fact that I was still lying there and headed for his water bottle. I couldn't move.

"Nole," asked Erika, squatting on her knees over me. "Are you okay?"

"I don't think so," I said. There'd been an electric jolt down my back and legs — hard to explain the feeling — but now there was pain, so much I couldn't think of standing or walking. I lay inside the key, thought one steamboat, two steamboats, three steamboats. I was supposed to be the Post, muscle my way in, shoot, leave after the job's done.

"Do you want me to call an ambulance?" she asked.

"She's fine," said Darren, as if I wasn't in the room. "She's fine. Give her a minute. Just wait a minute, okay?" His voice crackled like an old Victrola record player, an old, old song I'd heard before.

"I'm sure it's just muscular," I said. "But I still can't move." I tried to remember what my mother had taught me about broken bones. Can you wiggle your toes? I could wiggle my toes. Nothing was broken. I still couldn't move. I could wiggle my toes.

"I'm going to call an ambulance," said Erika. "She can't get up. Okay, this practice is over. Rob, go home. Wayne, Max, Vern, go home. Darren, get the fuck out of here. No, really now. Everyone go home."

And he did. Darren left. Darren left and Erika stayed and I lay on the ground still strapped to the chair in case I'd broken my back. The paramedics came and poked my feet with needles and I was so glad to be able to feel it. I wasn't paralyzed. Erika stayed, telling me stories about work and her new boyfriend. I was taken to the hospital and a CT scan revealed that I'd fractured my spine at L5. An injury waiting to happen, said the doctor, since my lack of hip flexion meant this spot took a lot of pressure. I looked at the ghost photos of my X-rays, the spinal facets looking like little wings.

"Guess you're off for awhile," said Erika. I'd been given muscle relaxants to slacken every taut fibre that had pulled around the injury. They were keeping me over night for observation.

"Aren't you supposed to come to wheelchair ball because of a broken spine?" I asked her. "Isn't this working backwards?"

But it wasn't a career-ending injury. I healed in six weeks, though it never stopped hurting. Darren didn't show up with flowers or candy or apologies or explanations even though that night in the hospital I woke up every time someone used crutches to walk down the hall expecting him. I healed, but was left with reduced joint space on L5, the lowest joint right below the sacrum. Arthritis developed. I get cortisone injections, but beyond that there's nothing anyone can do. People can say what they want about broken hearts, the spine's the only body part that modern medicine can't mend.

"Quinn's coming," she says and hangs up the phone.

"Are you going back to the Island?"

She reaches for her dress, but can't bend enough. I pick it up and wish I was tall and stable enough to dress her. Valerie could come home at any minute, but that's not why I want to ease the clothing over her head. Just something gentle to do to her skin. Enough gestures like that, you'll never have to apologize.

What would Valerie think about Nolan naked in our living room, the blinds open for once. And me, in some state of arousal that's for sure, but yet not. Not thinking of sex, anyhow. What would it be like: Valerie naked in this room. Her grey hair would be great in this light.

"Well," Nolan says, and stands in front of me.

The curtains are open and Darren stands with one hand on the sofa. The light here is grey, the colour of a body recently cooled. I'd rather think in this way, of bodies not of ashes, my mother through my fingertips. But yes, this grey light. This ambivalent light. Clouds on the verge of either sun or rain. I feel as if Kid A is taking all the air in my veins for her own purposes. Maybe she's practicing breathing. The room tilts; I hold the couch to steady myself. This is as close to the recurring dream as I'm ever going to get.

She wavers and I reach out to steady her.

"I'm okay," she says but touches my hip right above my brace and now who's steadying whom? That little spark you get with some people: we can still generate minor electricity. Or maybe that's only me feeling it.

"Sure?" I ask and the baby kicks as if to warn me off. Sweet little act of violence.

"I guess you felt that." For a moment I'm unsure if she meant the spark or the baby's kick. Maybe one was responding to the other.

"Yeah."

"Some party trick, eh?"

I run my finger along the dark line that bisects her stomach. Us in the gym, the first time, her little breath and fingers down from my navel, following the trail and maybe that act is scarred into her skin — scarlet letter, albatross — though it should be on mine.

"Yeah," I say.

"Yeah," she says.

"So, yeah," I say, but we stay still. Her belly hides even her pubic hair. She's too pregnant and I'm too old for sex, which is the only goodbye we know.

"Want to hear something funny?" she asks.

"Sure."

"I'm going into labour. Did you hear me talking to Quinn? I mistook this kind of back pain — it's not the kind you gave me — I think it's labour."

"Why's that funny?"

She shrugs. "This baby has an excellent sense of comedic timing. You're going to have to drive."

Darren drives, but there's no time for the long road. No scenery to distract me, either. I've lived here for too long, driven the nervous route down the hill to the hospital too many times. Darren drives and the colours outside break apart, the whole spectrum unravelling. Concrete and grass and neon lights and headlights on wet asphalt and sky. It's raining and we drive on.

"Are you okay?" he keeps asking. The pain is wise and clean, different from the dirty throb of the hip and back. It knows that short clenches hurt more because you're reminded of the rest in between. I think of nothing but fuck, fuck, fuck, fuck, fuck, fuck, fuck, fuck: not quite the mantra the Lamaze Lady would pick, but it works.

"Drive," I say.

"Do you want the radio on or off? Or a CD?"

"You got the 'Chariots of Fire' soundtrack?"

We go down the Queens Avenue hill. Darren used to say that the road had been washed away by a storm, aiming to scare me. I would pretend we were driving off the edge of the world and imagined us aloft, startled into flight.

In the back seat of the car parked next to us, someone has left their false teeth. Braced against the side huffing my way through a contraction, I'm forced to stare at the dentures with a bit of what appears to be apple skin stuck between two teeth. My breath flares and retreats against the glass but the dentures remain, half open against the brown fabric beside a magazine on boating.

"In the movies, pregnant women get wheelchairs," says Darren, returning with the parking payment ticket. "Want me to get you a chair? I'll push you."

I laugh. The sound is its own spasm and my body reacts in kind.

"What?" he asks.

The contraction passes and my sense of humour returns. "Can you imagine the scene? That would be like the blind leading the blind. The quad leading the knocked-up. You couldn't see over me. I bet I'm like pushing a sack of wet cement."

"Yes, very funny, we're a sight for sore eyes. Can you get a move on, then? I don't want this baby coming in the bloody parking lot."

The nurse at the admissions desk must be the same one who checked me in for my hip replacement, unless the position calls for highlighted hair and over-plucked eyebrows.

"And are you the father?" she asks Darren. He pauses, shrugs, looks at me.

"He's a friend," I say. "The father will be coming." Boyfriend, partner, whatever: finally I have a name endorsed by biology. Quinn is the father. The father is coming.

"I don't mind staying," says Darren. "I'll just phone Valerie."

"At her mother's?" I ask. An orderly brings up a wheelchair, an old E & J.

"And here you thought your sports career was over," says Darren. "Don't say I wasn't right about the wheelchair."

"I'd like to push myself," I tell the orderly as he tries to wheel me down the hall.

"Sorry ma'am. People squish their fingers in the brakes. You see the brakes there? That's why we don't allow it. Nothing hurts more than a barked thumb."

"Except for maybe childbirth," says Darren and winks at me. He's here and I'm grateful.

"I'll walk," I say, hunched by another contraction. I stand. Let gravity do its good work.

The doctor is called. I want to phone Quinn again but he has no cell, so I close my eyes and will him to hurry. Quinn is the father, I think. The father is coming.

Darren sits by the bed and rubs ice chips along my lips. He's washed his hands, but his fingers still taste of push rim metal: some element I'm maybe lacking. The nurses are chatty; they whisper encouragement and make Darren wait outside the curtain during examinations.

"He doesn't really have to leave," I say. "He's not the father, but he's seen it all before."

Darren jolts. This is the first time we've mentioned that particular aspect of the past, but I have my legs in stirrups and the urge is to lay everything bare. "I'll wait outside," he says.

"The situation's not that complicated," I tell the nurse. "My husband's coming. Darren's an ex-turned-friend. Not a Jerry Springer thing."

"Right," she says. "Okay."

I watch the monitor, which appears to be tracking the seismic activity in my body. Maybe I will split open along the weak lines. It seems likely.

Quinn:

When I woke up in the morning to find her gone, it was like relief. Like when someone's been lying on your arm and she moves away and the blood prickles back into your fingertips. Like when she's sleeping with her head on your chest in the summer and she tosses back to her own side of the bed, your mutual sweat cooling in a breeze you didn't realize was there, a balm the exact shape of her skull.

Six months away from the office and I've grown unused to suits. I've gained much-needed bulk in the shoulders and thinned in the waist and the fabric shows the places I don't fit anymore.

When I woke up, the window was open and it smelled like the medicine that Darren guy's been giving Nolan. Wasn't until I felt that scent on my lungs that I could see the appeal. Maybe not the appeal of Darren himself — the gimped-up hand and old man's belly — but the herbs made sense. I wasn't angry, wasn't sick with worry over where she's gone. Her mother's dead and everything is to scale. This is her brand of coping.

She will return.

The funeral is today.

I will wear my suit.

This, too, shall pass.

It's Zen and the art of parenthood, though there's no one to raise except maybe myself. Harder, though, to explain it to her father.

"Grief," he said, and shook his head. "And pregnancy hormones." I could tell he'd had a terrible night. He's sleeping on the couch with the dog's blanket, since that's the only linen that doesn't smell of his wife.

We could use a woman's touch. Nolan hired a caterer for the reception and they show up with their perky hats and clean, clean aprons to set everything up. They have the efficiency and hygiene of nurses. The service will be at the funeral home and then there'll be a drive back home and a walk to the sea — I imagine a parade — and her husband will give her to the water, like something out a myth. Mermaids, sirens, Caddysaurus and now my mother-in-law, the stuff of legends. I'm not sure if we're allowed to put her ashes in Caddy Bay, but who's going to stop us?

Problem is, we don't know how to set up the food on the table so it looks sophisticated. People will be coming by to receive finger food and cheap wine in exchange for their condolences. This is a ritual my mother-in-law would have approved of: such decorum. My father-in-law finds a Christmas centrepiece that Nolan's cleaning turned up, so we use that. The angel fits, hope people will mistake baby Jesus for Kid A. I wanted to put a picture of Nolan's mother to make it more relevant, but he said no. Winced and said no. I left it at that, showered and put on my suit.

"We'll be a bunch of good-looking dudes," says my father-in-law. If he can't manage calm, he'll try for hip.

"Hep cats indeed," I say and clap him on the shoulder.

My father-in-law winces again when the phone rings and my heart gives a nicotine jolt. Maybe I have been worried about Nolan. If we end up living here, I'll buy a new phone. The ring-tone bloody screams. "Hello?" I say.

"Quinn?"

"Nole," I say it mostly to alert her father she's okay. "Where are you?"

"In labour." It feels like a destination: Nolan's body renovating itself into a little room that grew so big she became hard to hold. We'd been joking about that. The Nolan Taylor Apartment Complex: if you think the womb's small, you've never been apartment hunting.

"How 'in labour?'"

"I believe they call this active labour. Getting a little too active for my tastes. It started on the ferry and I just ignored it, since now isn't really a good time. Guess I don't get to make decisions like that."

"Jesus. Where are you geography wise?"

"New West. Going to the RCH. Can you just get here?"

"Do you want me to call Sophia?"

"I want you to get here."

"How much time do we have? The funeral's this afternoon."

"I don't know. I've never done this. I don't know. I want you here."

Nolan has taken our car and it's a long, expensive way to New Westminster. One of the caterers drives me to the airport, talking about rhubarb tarts at caffeinated speed in an attempt to calm me. I get on the next flight out. Apparently, there's a procedure for men rushing to see the birth of the first born. The women at the counter are efficient as angels as they print off a ticket and walk me to the gate. I chalk the blessing up to my mother-in-law.

The credit card is maxed from the flight, the bank machine nearly empty. I will Nolan to wait and try to assemble a God-figure to pray to, coming up with a Santa Claus in a white robe and that angel lady from the cream cheese commercials. My mother-in-law is up there somewhere too, pacing. She taps her fingers and it turns into rain.

I wish I could run to Nolan. It would be better than this plastic seat and nothing to occupy my hands. The Airporter Bus will have to do. At least my mother-in-law could have tried for a free limo.

"My wife's in labour in New Westminster and I'm afraid I'm going to miss it but I'm nearly broke," I tell the bus driver. "Is there anything you can do?" Might as well have asked, 'I cheated on my pregnant wife and now her mother died, is there anything you can do?' He shrugs, chewing gum.

"This is the milk run. Takes, oh, I don't know. Three hours sometimes. This the first baby?"

"Yeah."

The bus driver nods, considering this. He has a wedding band on a chain around his neck: probably his fingers grew out of it. "First babies take awhile. You probably got time. I'll take you there. No charge for the new papa."

"Thank you so much."

"The baby's a boy, you name it after me. My name's Dave. The world has a constant need for Daves. You remember that."

"Right," I say. "Dave."

"I'm joking," he slaps me on the back. "Just a little joke. Ease up, new pappa. You name that little baby whatever you want, you hear me?"

Quinn comes or he doesn't. Darren stays or he doesn't. When I ask later, both will say that they were there. Quinn claims he arrived with two hours to go and breathed with me, having learnt the technique from the prenatal class and the timing from music. Darren says he stayed and there was one man on either side. He offered his bad hand to do my worst damage on and I squeezed like a son of a bitch.

The birth was without drugs, mostly because I was glad that someone finally gave me a choice in the matter. My clearest memory: the doctor saying C-section, me saying no, the head crowning, the decision made for us. If they'd let me, I might have undergone the hip replacement without drugs. I would've passed out — pain the most natural anaesthetic — and there wouldn't be any traces leaching into my womb. The painkillers I took as a child were later shown to cause heart attacks. Same thing with the anti-inflammatories that helped me through the first years on the national team: heart damage. There are worse things than pain and most of them have to do with either my heart or Kid A.

When I imagined birth, I thought of the baby slipping through me like a ball through a hoop: my body a net that keeps nothing. It's not like that. It defies metaphor. The birth is pure sensation, as if all the pain I'd ever had in my life had stayed with me and waited to be called upon. After it's over, someone will likely say I screamed. I don't remember sound. Only a bloodrush silence like being underwater. I don't think of Quinn and this is good. Nor do I think of Darren. Anyone could be beyond that bed. Anyone could be stroking my hand. In that hot slip, my daughter names herself. She slides out, is caught and pressed to my chest still attached by that tough, slick cord multi-hued against the white hospital gown. We stay like this, self-sufficient, mouths moving but silent.

There are so many ways to detach. Someone — Quinn? — cuts the cord, the child's fingers reaching past me to the light or to block the light. Still, the room won't settle and this is wrong. I'd been focusing on her eyes — all those songs about blue eyes — so much that I'd forgotten my own bones. Which are not still. Which are not quiet, despite the hot blankets. The doctors' hands are pale with latex, coats lifting as they take her from me. The hip, it seems. Just as I'd gotten used to the easy steel walk, the ball and socket. My daughter wails her pure, pure lungs out. The soft spot, the growth plates: she will gain new bones. She flails her temporary legs, all of her unfused.

People are saying I'm going to be fine. Quinn is crying, unsure of who to cry over, and Darren is by the isolette, stroking her fingers and not looking as they stitch me up.

"It's okay, Nole," says Quinn, here with me though his eyes are on our daughter. "You're going to be fine. They've just got to go in there." But I am fine, self-contained. For the first time since the replacement, I am the only thing attached to me.

NOTE:

THE FIELD OF ORTHOPAEDIC MEDICINE IS changing rapidly and it is difficult to predict what innovations may occur over the next few years. New surgical methods and prosthetic technologies are shortening recovery times and stem-cell research could even eliminate the need for joint replacements all together. It is therefore entirely possible that the medical details in this book will be outdated shortly after publication. I have done my best to use the most current medical research.

When choosing between medical verisimilitude and the needs of the story, however, literary concerns won out. This applies both to information on hip replacements and on the disabilities of various characters. I hope that any inaccuracies are not large enough to hamper the enjoyment of the story.

Lines from "Birches" are from *Mountain Interval* by Robert Frost (New York: H. Holt & Co., 1916) .